THE CALL
OF EARTH

THE CALL
OF EARTH

HOMECOMING
VOLUME 2

ORSON SCOTT CARD

A Tom Doherty Associates Book
New York

THE CALL OF EARTH

This book is printed on acid-free paper.

Maps by Ellisa Mitchell

A Tor Book
Published by Tom Doherty Associates, Inc.
175 Fifth Avenue
New York, N.Y. 10010

Tor® is a registered trademark of Tom Doherty Associates, Inc.

ISBN   0-312-93037-2

First trade edition: January 1993

Printed in the United States of America

0 9 8 7 6 5 4 3 2 1

To
Dave Dollahite
Teacher and dreamer
Husband and father
Friend and fellow citizen

ACKNOWLEDGMENTS

I owe thanks to many for easing my way through the writing of this book. Clark and Kathy Kidd provided me with a refuge during the last week of the writing of this novel; half of it came forth under their roof, and with their good company.

A writer's life can so easily slip into undisciplined sloth; my body has long reflected the physical indolence of a mentally exhausting career. This book owes much to the fact that during the writing of it I woke my body up again: I owe thanks to Clark Kidd and Scott Allen for sweating with me as I tortured a new bicycle into submission on the roads and bikepaths of northern Virginia and on the streets and strands of North Myrtle Beach.

Several readers helped me reconcile this book with its predecessor, reading scraps of manuscript as they emerged from my printer, most notably Kathy Kidd and Russell Card. My editor on this series is Beth Meacham; my publisher is Tom Doherty; it is no accident that I have done the best work of my life so far for them. And my agent, Barbara Bova, has been a constant help and wise counselor during a turbulent time.

This novel was supposed to be easy, but it turned out not

to be. Moozh complicated everything, and yet made it all worth doing. During the long struggle to make Moozh and the rest of the story fit together, I imagine that I was barely tolerable to live with, but still my wife, Kristine, and our children, Geoffrey, Emily, and Charlie Ben, were willing to keep me around; it is the joy of my life to find them always around me when I surface from immersion in my work. And, as always, Kristine has been my first and best editor and audience, reading my work with a sharp and trustworthy eye, then telling me what I have written so I can keep or alter it as need be.

CONTENTS

Major
Streets
of Basilica

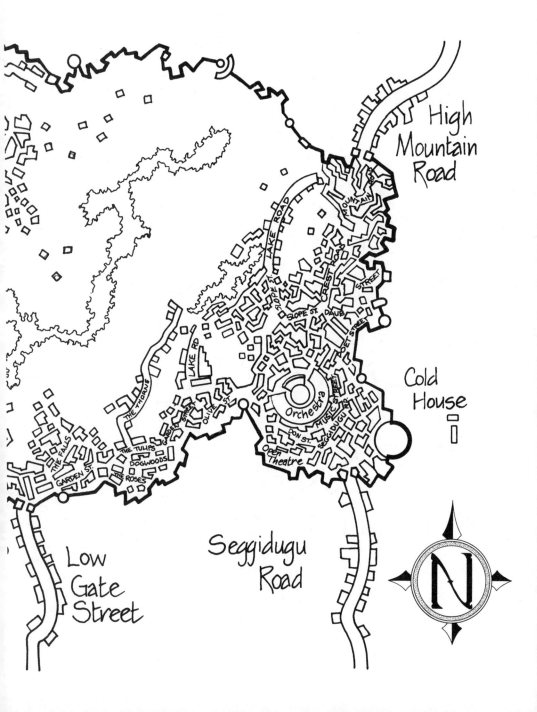

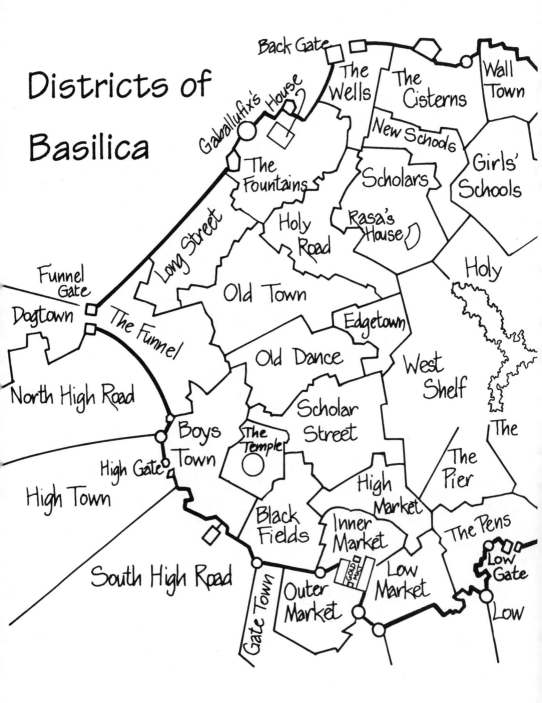

Districts of Basilica

Back Gate

The Wells

The Cisterns

Wall Town

Gaballufix's House

New Schools

Girls' Schools

The Fountains

Scholars

Rasa's House

Holy Road

Holy

Long Street

Old Town

Edgetown

West Shelf

Funnel Gate

Dogtown

The Funnel

Old Dance

The

North High Road

Scholar Street

Boys Town

The Temple

High Gate

The Pier

High Town

Black Fields

High Market

The Pens

South High Road

Inner Market

Low Gate

Gate Town

Outer Market

GOLD MKT

Low Market

Low

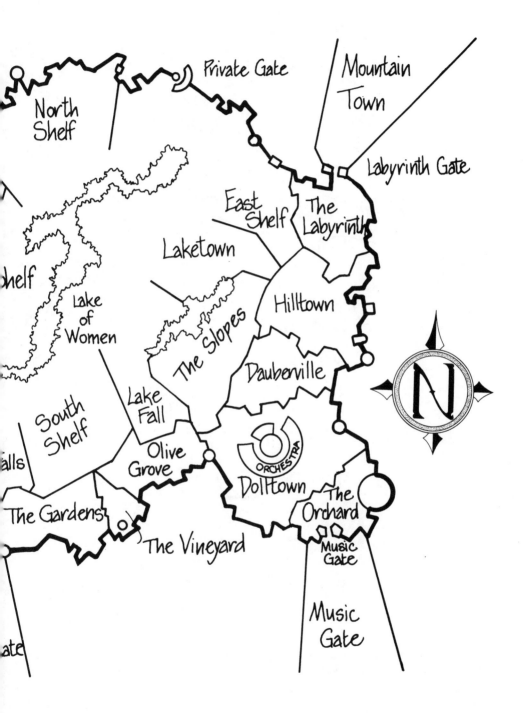

Environs of Basilica

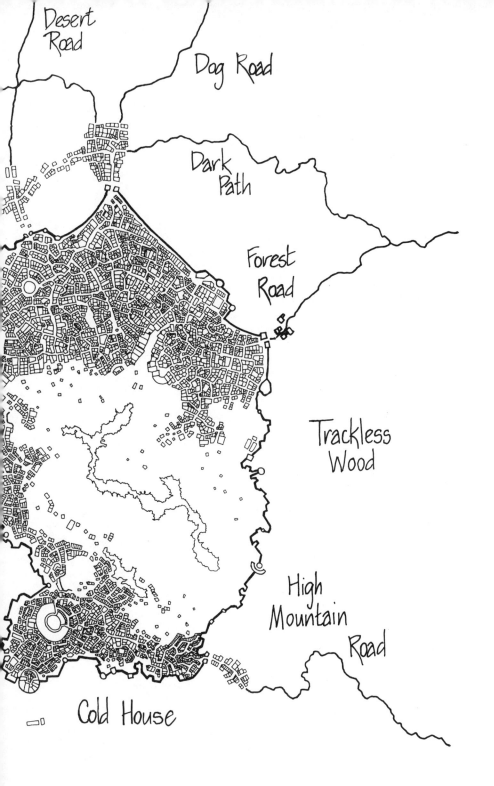

Desert
Road

Dog Road

Dark
Path

Forest
Road

Trackless
Wood

High
Mountain
Road

Cold House

NOTES ON PARENTAGE

Because of the marriage customs in the city of Basilica, family relationships can be somewhat complex. Perhaps these parentage charts can help keep things straight. Women's names are in italics.

WETCHIK'S FAMILY

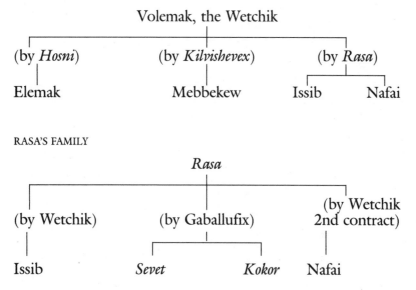

Volemak, the Wetchik

(by *Hosni*)   (by *Kilvishevex*)   (by *Rasa*)

Elemak   Mebbekew   Issib   Nafai

RASA'S FAMILY

Rasa

(by Wetchik)   (by Gaballufix)   (by Wetchik 2nd contract)

Issib   *Sevet*   *Kokor*   Nafai

RASA'S NIECES

(her prize students, "adopted" into a permanent relationship of sponsorship)

Shedemei   *Dol*   *Eiadh*   *Hushidh* and *Luet* (sisters)

HOSNI'S FAMILY

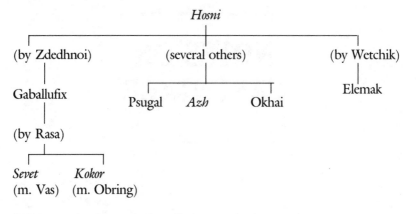

NICKNAMES

Most names have diminutive or familiar forms. Thus Gaballufix's near kin, close friends, current mate, and former mates could call him Gab. Other nicknames are listed here. (Again, because these names are so unfamiliar, names of female characters are set off in italics):

Dhelembuvex—Dhel
Dol—Dolya
Drotik—Dorya
Eiadh—Edhya
Elemak—Elya
Hosni—Hosya
Hushidh—Shuya
Issib—Issya
Kokor—Kyoka
Luet—Lutya
Mebbekew—Meb
Nafai—Nyef
Rasa—(no diminutive)
Rashgallivak—Rash
Roptat—Rop
Sevet—Sevya
Shedemei—Shedya
Smelost—Smelya
Volemak—Volya
Wetchik—(no diminutive;
    Volemak's family title)
Zdorab—Zodya

NOTES ON NAMES

For the purpose of reading this story, it hardly matters whether the reader pronounces the names of the characters correctly. But for those who might be interested, here is some information concerning the pronunciation of names.

The rules of vowel formation in the language of Basilica require that in most words, at least one vowel be pronounced with a leading *y* sound. With names, it can be almost any vowel, and it can legitimately be changed at the speaker's preference. Thus the name Gaballufix could be pronounced *Gyah*-BAH-loo-fix or Gah-BAH-*lyoo*-fix; it happens that Gaballufix himself preferred to pronounce it Gah-BYAH-loo-fix, and of course most people followed that usage.

Dhelembuvex
  [thel-EM-byoo-vex]
Dol [DYOHL]
Drotik [DROHT-yik]
Eiadh [A-yahth]
Elemak [El-yeh-mahk]
Hosni [HYOZ-nee]

Hushidh [HYOO-sheeth]
Issib [IS-yib]
Kokor [KYOH-kor]
Luet [LYOO-et]
Mebbekew
  [MEB-bek-kyoo]
Nafai [NYAH-fie]

Rasa [RAHZ-yah]
Rashgallivak
    [rahsh-GYAH-lih-vahk]
Roptat [ROPE-taht]
Sevet [SEV-yet]
Shedemei [SHYED-eh-may]

Smelost [SMYE-lost]
Truzhnisha
    [troozh-NYEE-shah]
Volemak [VOHL-yeh-mak]
Wetchik [WET-chyick]
Zdorab [ZDOR-yab]

PROLOGUE

The master computer of the planet Harmony was not designed to interfere so directly in human affairs. It was deeply disturbed by the fact that it had just provoked young Nafai to murder Gaballufix. But how could the master computer return to Earth without the Index? And how could Nafai have got the Index without killing Gaballufix? There was no other way.

Or was there? I am old, said the master computer to itself. Forty million years old, a machine designed to last for nowhere near this long. How can I be sure that my judgment is right? And yet I caused a man to die for my judgment, and young Nafai is suffering the pangs of guilt because of what I urged him to do. All of this in order to carry the Index back to Zvezdakroog, so I could return to Earth.

If only I could speak to the Keeper of Earth. If only the Keeper could tell me what to do now. Then I could act with confidence. Then I would not have to doubt my every action, to wonder if everything I do might not be the product of my own decay.

The master computer needed so badly to speak to the Keeper; yet it could not speak to the Keeper except by returning to Earth. It was so frustratingly circular. The master computer could not act wisely without the help of the Keeper; it had to act wisely in order to get to the Keeper.

What now? What now? I need wisdom, and yet who can guide me? I have vastly more knowledge than any human can hope to master, and yet I have no minds but human minds to counsel me.

Was it possible that human minds might be enough? No computer could ever be so brilliantly dysorganized as the human brain. Humans made the most astonishing decisions based on mere fragments of data, because their brain recombined them in strange and truthful ways. It was possible, surely, that some useful wisdom might be extracted from them.

Then again, maybe not. But it was worth trying, wasn't it?

The master computer reached out through its satellites and sent images into the minds of those humans most receptive to its transmissions. These images from the master computer began to move through their memories, forcing their minds to deal with them, to fit them together, to make sense of them. To make from them the strange and powerful stories they called dreams. Perhaps in the next few days, the next few weeks, their dreams would bring to the surface some connection or understanding that the master computer could use to help it decide how to bring the best of them out of the planet Harmony and take home to Earth.

All these years I have taught and guided, shaped and protected them. Now, in the end of my life, are they ready to teach and guide, shape and protect *me?* So unlikely. So unlikely. I will surely be forced to decide it all myself. And when I do, I will surely do it wrong. Perhaps I should not act at all. Perhaps I should not act at all. I should not act. Will not. Must.

Wait.

Wait.

Again, wait. . . .

ONE

BETRAYAL

THE DREAM OF THE GENERAL

General Vozmuzhalnoy Vozmozhno awoke from his dream, sweating, moaning. He opened his eyes, reached out with his hand, clutching. A hand caught his own, held it.

A man's hand. It was General Plodorodnuy. His most trusted lieutenant. His dearest friend. His inmost heart.

"You were dreaming, Moozh." It was the nickname that only Plod dared to use to his face.

"Yes, I was." Vozmuzhalnoy—Moozh—shuddered at the memory. "Such a dream."

"Was it portentous?"

"Horrifying, anyway."

"Tell me. I have a way with dreams."

"Yes, I know, like you have a way with women. When you're through with them, they say whatever you want them to say!"

Plod laughed, but then he waited. Moozh did not know why he was reluctant to tell *this* dream to Plod. He had told him so many others. "All right, then, here is my dream. I saw a man standing in a clearing, and all around him, terrible flying creatures—not birds, they had fur, but much larger than bats—they kept circling, swooping down, touching him. He stood there and did nothing. And when at last they all had touched him, they flew away, except one, who perched on his shoulder."

"Ah," said Plod.

"I'm not finished. Immediately there came giant rats, swarming out of burrows in the Earth. At least a meter long—half as tall as the man. And again, they kept coming until all of them had touched him—"

"With what? Their teeth? Their paws?"

"And their noses. *Touched* him, that's all I knew. Don't distract me."

"Forgive me."

"When they'd all touched him, they went away."

"Except one."

"Yes. It clung to his leg. You see the pattern."

"What came next?"

Moozh shuddered. It had been the most terrible thing of all, and yet now as the words came to his lips, he couldn't understand why. "People."

"People? Coming to touch him?"

"To . . . to kiss him. His hands, his feet. To *worship* him. Thousands of them. Only they didn't kiss just the man. They kissed the—flying thing, too. And the giant rat clinging to his leg. Kissed them all."

"Ah," said Plod. He looked worried.

"So? What is it? What does it portend?"

"Obviously the man you saw is the Imperator."

Sometimes Plod's interpretations sounded like truth, but this time Moozh's heart rebelled at the idea of linking the Imperator with the man in the dream. "Why is that obvious? He looked nothing like the Imperator."

"Because all of nature and humankind worshipped him, of course."

Moozh shrugged. This was not one of Plod's most subtle interpretations. And he had never heard of animals loving the Imperator, who fancied himself a great hunter. Of course, he only hunted in one of his parks, where all the animals had been tamed to lose their fear of men, and all the predators trained to act ferocious but never strike. The Imperator got to act his part in a great show of the contest between man and beast, but he was never in danger as the animal innocently exposed itself to his quick dart, his straight javelin, his merciless blade. If this was worship, if this was nature, then yes, one could say that all of nature and humankind worshipped the Imperator. . . .

Plod, of course, knew nothing of Moozh's thoughts in this vein; if one was so unfortunate as to have caustic thoughts about the Imperator, one took care not to burden one's friends with the knowledge of them.

So Plod continued in his interpretation of Moozh's dream. "What does it portend, this worship of the Imperator? Nothing in itself. But the fact that it *revolted* you, the face that you recoiled in horror—"

"They were kissing a rat, Plod! They were kissing that disgusting flying creature . . ."

But Plod said nothing as his voice trailed off. Said nothing, and watched him.

"I am *not* horrified at the thought of people worshipping the Imperator. I have knelt at the Invisible Throne myself, and felt the awe of his presence. It wasn't horrible, it was . . . ennobling."

"So you say," said Plod. "But dreams don't lie. Perhaps you need to purge yourself of some evil in your heart."

"Look, *you're* the one who said my dream was about the Imperator. Why couldn't the man have been—I don't know— the ruler of Basilica."

"Because the miserable city of Basilica is ruled by women."

"Not Basilica, then. Still, I think the dream was about . . ."

"About what?"

"How should *I* know? I *will* purge myself, just in case you're right. I'm not an interpreter of dreams." That would mean wasting several hours today at the tent of the intercessor. It was so tedious, but it was also politically necessary to spend a certain amount of time there every month, or reports of one's impiety soon made their way back to Gollod, where the Imperator decided from time to time who was worthy of command and who was worthy of debasement or death. Moozh was about due for a visit to the intercessor's tabernacle anyway, but he hated it the way a boy hates a bath. "Leave me alone, Plod. You've made me very unhappy."

Plod knelt before him and held Moozh's right hand between his own. "Ah, forgive me."

Moozh forgave him at once, of course, because they were friends. Later that morning he went out and killed the headmen of a dozen Khlami villages. All the villagers immediately swore their eternal love and devotion to the Imperator, and when General Vozmuzhalnoy Vozmozhno went that evening to purge himself in the holy tabernacle, the intercessor forgave him right readily, for he had much increased the honor and majesty of the Imperator that day.

IN BASILICA, AND NOT IN A DREAM

They came to hear Kokor sing, came from all over the city of Basilica, and she loved to see how their faces brightened when—finally—she came out onto the stage and the musicians began gently plucking their strings or letting breath pass through their instruments in the soft undercurrent of sound that was always her accompaniment. Kokor will sing to us at last, their faces said. She liked that expression on their faces better than any other she ever saw, better even than the look of a man being overwhelmed with lust in the last moments before satisfaction. For she well knew that a man cared little who gave him the pleasures of love, while the audience cared very much that it was Kokor who stood before them on the stage and opened her mouth in the high, soaring notes of her unbelievably sweet lyric voice that floated over the music like petals on a stream.

Or at least that was how she wanted it to be. How she imagined it to be, until she actually walked onstage and saw them looking at her. The audience tonight was mostly men. Men with their eyes going up and down her body. I should refuse to sing in the comedies, she told herself again. I should insist on being taken as seriously as they take my beloved sister Sevet with her mannishly low, froggishly mannered voice. Oh, they look at *her* with faces of aesthetic ecstasy. Audiences of men and women together. *They* don't look *her* body up and down to see how it moves under the fabric. Of course, that could be partly because her body is so overfleshed that it isn't really a pleasure to watch, it moves so much like gravel under her costume, poor thing. Of *course* they close their eyes and listen to her voice—it's so much better than *watching* her.

What a lie. What a liar I am, even when I'm talking only to myself!

I mustn't be so impatient. It's only a matter of time. Sevet is older—I'm still barely eighteen. *She* had to do the comedies, too, for a time, till she was known.

Kokor remembered her sister talking in those early days— more than two years ago, when Sevet was almost seventeen— about constantly having to dampen the ardor of her admirers, who had a penchant for entering her dressing room quite primed for immediate love, until she had to hire a bodyguard to discourage the more passionate ones. "It's all about sex," said Sevet then. "The songs, the shows, they're all about sex, and that's all the audience dreams of. Just be careful you don't make them dream too well—or too specifically!"

Good advice? Hardly. The more they dream of you, the greater the cash value of your name on the handbills advertising the play. Until finally, if you're lucky, if you're *good* enough, the handbill doesn't have to say the name of a show at all. Only *your* name, and the place, and the day, and the time . . . and when you show up they're all there, hundreds of them, and when the music starts they don't look at you like the last hope of a starving man, they look at you like the highest dream of an elevated soul.

Kokor strode to her place on the stage—and there *was* applause when she entered. She turned to the audience and let out a thrilling high note.

"What was that?" demanded Gulya, the actor who played the old lecher. "Are you screaming already? I haven't even touched you yet."

The audience laughed—but not enough. This play was in trouble. This play had had its weaknesses from the start, she well knew, but with a mere smattering of laughter like that, it was doomed. So in a few more days she'd have to start rehearsing all over again. Another show. Another set of stupid lyrics and stupid melodies to memorize.

Sevet got to decide her own songs. Songwriters came to her and begged her to sing what they had composed. *Sevet* didn't have to misuse her voice just to make people laugh.

"I wasn't screaming," Kokor sang.

"You're screaming now," sang Gulya as he sidled close and started to fondle her. His gravelly bass was always good for a laugh when he used it like that, and the audience was with him. Maybe they could pull this show out of the mud after all.

"But now you're *touching me!*" And her voice rose to its highest pitch and hung there in the air—

Like a bird, like a bird soaring, if only they were listening for beauty.

Gulya made a terrible face and withdrew his hand from her breast. Immediately she dropped her note two octaves. She got the laugh. The best laugh of the scene so far. But she knew that half the audience was laughing because Gulya did such a fine comic turn when he removed his hand from her bosom. He was a master, he really was. Sad that his sort of clowning had fallen a bit out of fashion lately. He was only getting better as he got older, and yet the audience was slipping away. Looking for the more bitter, nasty comedy of the young physical satirists. The brutal, violent comedy that always gave at least the illusion of hurting somebody.

The scene went on. The laughs came. The scene ended. Applause. Kokor scurried off the stage in relief—and disappointment. No one in the audience was chanting her name; no one had even shouted it once like a catcall. How long would she have to wait?

"Too pretty," said Tumannu, the stagekeeper, her face sour. "That note's supposed to sound like you're reaching sexual climax. Not like a bird."

"Yes yes," said Kokor, "I'm so sorry." She always agreed with everybody and then did what she wanted. This comedy wasn't worth doing if she couldn't show her voice to best advantage at least now and then. And it got the laugh when she did it her way, didn't it? So nobody could very well say that her way was *wrong*. Tumannu just wanted her to be obedient, and Kokor didn't intend to be obedient. Obedience was for children and husbands and household pets.

"Not like a bird," said Tumannu again.

"How about like a bird reaching sexual climax?" asked Gulya, who had come offstage right after her.

Kokor giggled, and even Tumannu smiled her tight sour little smile.

"There's someone waiting for you, Kyoka," said Tumannu.

It was a man. But not an aficionado of her work, or he'd have been out front, watching her perform. She had seen him before. Ah, yes—he showed up now and then when Mother's permanent husband, Wetchik, came to visit. He was Wetchik's chief servant, wasn't he? Manager of the exotic flower business when Wetchik was away on caravan. What was his name?

"I am Rashgallivak," he said. He looked very grave.

"Oh?" she said.

"I am deeply sorry to inform you that your father has met with brutal violence."

What an extraordinary thing to tell her. She could hardly make sense of it for a moment. "Someone has injured him?"

"Fatally, madam."

"Oh," she said. There was meaning to this, and she would find it. "Oh, then that would mean that he's . . . dead?"

"Accosted on the street and murdered in cold blood," said Rashgallivak.

It wasn't even a surprise, really, when you thought about it. Father had been making such a bully of himself lately, putting all those masked soldiers on the streets. Terrifying everybody. But Father was so strong and intense that it was hard to imagine anything actually thwarting him for long. Certainly not *permanently*. "There's no hope of . . . recovery?"

Gulya had been standing near enough that now he easily inserted himself into the conversation. "It seems to be a normal case of death, madam, which means the prognosis isn't good." He giggled.

Rashgallivak gave him quite a vicious shove and sent him staggering. "That wasn't funny," he said.

"They're letting critics backstage now?" said Gulya. "*During* the performance?"

"Go away, Gulya," said Kokor. It had been a mistake to sleep with the old man. Ever since then he had thought he had some claim to intimacy with her.

"Naturally it would be best if you came with me," said Rashgallivak.

"But no," said Kokor. "No, that wouldn't be best." Who was *he*? He wasn't any kin to her at all, not that she knew of. She would have to go to Mother. Did Mother know yet? "Does Mother . . ."

"Naturally I told her first, and she told me where to find *you*. This is a very dangerous time, and I promised her that I would protect you."

Kokor knew he was lying, of course. Why should she need this stranger to protect her? From what? Men always got this way, though, insisting that a woman who hadn't a fear in the world needed watching out for. *Ownership,* that's what men always meant when they spoke of protection. If she wanted a man to own her, she *had* a husband, such as he was. She hardly needed this old pizdook to look out for her.

"Where's Sevet?"

"She hasn't been found yet. I must insist that you come with me."

Now Tumannu had to get into the scene. "She's going nowhere. She has three more scenes, including the climax."

Rashgallivak turned on her, and now there was some hint of majesty about him, instead of mere vague befuddlement. "Her father has been killed," he said. "And you suppose she will stay to finish a *play?*" Or had the majesty been there all along, and she simply hadn't noticed it until now?

"Sevet ought to know about Father," said Kokor.

"She'll be told as soon as we can find her."

Who is *we?* Never mind, thought Kokor. *I* know where

to find her. I know all her rendezvous, where she takes her lovers to avoid giving affront to her poor husband Vas. Sevet and Vas, like Kokor and Obring, had a flexible marriage, but Vas seemed less comfortable with it than Obring was. Some men were so . . . territorial. Probably it was because Vas was a scientist, not an artist at all. Obring, on the other hand, understood the artistic life. He would never dream of holding Kokor to the letter of their marriage contract. He sometimes joked quite cheerfully about the men she was seeing.

Though, of course, Kokor would never actually insult Obring by mentioning them herself. If he heard a rumor about a lover, that was one thing. When he mentioned it, she would simply toss her head and say, "You silly. You're the only man I love."

And in an odd sort of way it was true. Obring was such a dear, even if he had no acting talent at all. He always brought her presents and told her the most wonderful gossip. No wonder she had stayed married to him through two renewals already—people often remarked on how faithful she was, to still be married to her first husband for a third year, when she was young and beautiful and could marry anyone. True, marrying him in the first place was simply to please his mother, old Dhel, who had served as her auntie and who was Mother's dearest friend. But she had grown to like Obring, genuinely *like* him. Being married to him was very comfortable and sweet. As long as she could sleep with whomever she liked.

It would be fun to find Sevet and walk in on her and see whom she was sleeping with tonight. Kokor hadn't pounced on her that way in years. Find her with some naked, sweating man, tell her that Father was dead, and then watch that poor man's face as he gradually realized that he was all done with love for the night!

"*I'll* tell Sevet," said Kokor.

"You'll come with *me*," insisted Rashgallivak.

"You'll stay and finish the show," said Tumannu.

"The show is nothing but a . . . an *otsoss*," said Kokor, using the crudest term she could think of.

Tumannu gasped and Rashgallivak reddened and Gulya chuckled his little low chuckle. "Now *that's* an idea," he said.

Kokor patted Tumannu on the arm. "It's all right," she said. "I'm fired."

"Yes, you are!" cried Tumannu. "And if you leave here tonight your career is *finished!*"

Rashgallivak sneered at her. "With her share of her father's inheritance she'll buy your little stage and your mother, too."

Tumannu looked defiant. "Oh, really? Who was her father, *Gaballufix?*"

Rashgallivak looked genuinely surprised. "Didn't you know?"

Clearly Tumannu had *not* known. Kokor pondered this for a moment and realized it meant that she must not ever have mentioned it to Tumannu. And that meant that Kokor had not traded on her father's name and prestige, which meant that she had got this part on her own. How wonderful!

"I knew she was the great Sevet's *sister,*" said Tumannu. "Why else do you think I hired her? But I never dreamed they had the same *father.*"

For a moment Kokor felt a flash of rage, hot as a furnace. But she contained it instantly, controlled it perfectly. It would never do to let such a flame burn freely. No telling what she would do or say if she ever let herself go at such a time as this.

"I must find Sevet," said Kokor.

"No," said Rashgallivak. He might have intended to say more, but at that moment he laid a hand on Kokor's arm to restrain her, and so of course she brought her knee sharply up into his groin, as all the comedy actresses were taught to do when an unwelcome admirer became too importunate. It was a reflex. She really hadn't even meant to do it. Nor had she meant to do it with such *force.* He wasn't a very heavy man, and it rather lifted him off the ground.

"I must find Sevet," Kokor said, by way of explanation.

He probably didn't hear her. He was groaning too loudly as he lay there on the wooden floor backstage.

"Where's the understudy?" Tumannu was saying. "Not even three minutes' warning, the poor little bizdoon."

"Does it hurt?" Gulya was asking Rashgallivak. "I mean, what *is* pain, when you really think about it?"

Kokor wandered off into the darkness, heading for Dauberville. Her thigh throbbed, just above the knee, where she had pushed it so forcefully into Rashgallivak's crotch. She'd probably end up with a bruise there, and then she'd have to use an opaque sheen on her legs. Such a bother.

Father's dead. I must be the one to tell Sevet. Please don't let anyone else find her first. And *murdered*. People will talk about this for years. I will look rather fine in the white of mourning. Poor Sevet—her skin always looks red as a beet when she wears white. But she won't dare stop wearing mourning until *I* do. I may mourn for poor Papa for years and years and years.

Kokor laughed and laughed to herself as she walked along.

And then she realized she wasn't laughing at all, she was crying. Why am I crying? she wondered. Because Father is dead. That must be it, that must be what all this commotion is about. Father, poor Father. I must have loved him, because I'm crying now without having decided to, without anybody even watching. Who ever would have guessed that I loved him?

"Wake up." It was an urgent whisper. "Aunt Rasa wants us. Wake up!"

Luet could not understand why Hushidh was saying this. "I wasn't even asleep," she mumbled.

"Oh, you were sleeping, all right," said her sister Hushidh. "You were snoring."

Luet sat up. "Honking like a goose, I'm sure."

"Braying like a donkey," said Hushidh, "but my love for you turns it into music."

"That's why I do it," said Luet. "To give you music in the

night." She reached for her housedress, pulled it over her head.

"Aunt Rasa wants us," Hushidh urged. "Come quickly." She glided out of the room, moving in a kind of dance, her gown floating behind her. In shoes or sandals Hushidh always clumped along, but barefoot she moved like a woman in a dream, like a bit of cottonwood fluff in a breeze.

Luet followed her sister out into the hall, still buttoning the front of her housedress. What could it be, that Rasa would want to speak to her and Hushidh? With all the troubles that had come lately, Luet feared the worst. Was it possible that Rasa's son Nafai had not escaped from the city after all? Only yesterday, Luet had led him along forbidden paths, down into the lake that only women could see. For the Oversoul had told her that Nafai must see it, must float on it like a woman, like a waterseer–like Luet herself. So she took him there, and he was not slain for his blasphemy. She led him out the Private Gate then, and through the Trackless Wood. She had thought he was safe. But of course he was not safe. Because Nafai wouldn't simply have gone back out into the desert, back to his father's tent—not without the thing that his father had sent him to get.

Aunt Rasa was waiting in her room, but she was not alone. There was a soldier with her. Not one of Gaballufix's men—his mercenaries, his thugs, pretending to be Palwas-hantu militia. No, this soldier was one of the city guards, a gatekeeper.

She could hardly notice him, though, beyond recognizing his insignia, because Rasa herself looked so . . . no, not frightened, really. It was no emotion Luet had ever seen in her before. Her eyes wide and glazed with tears, her face not firmly set, but slack, exhausted, as if things were happening in her heart that her face could not express.

"Gaballufix is dead," said Rasa.

That explained much. Gaballufix was the enemy in recent months, his paid tolchoks terrorizing people on the streets, and then his soldiers, masked and anonymous, terrifying people even more as they ostensibly made the streets of

Basilica "safe" for its citizens. Yet, enemy though he was, Gaballufix had also been Rasa's husband, the father of her two daughters, Sevet and Kokor. There had been love there once, and the bonds of family are not easily broken, not for a serious woman like Rasa. Luet was no raveler like her sister Hushidh, but she knew that Rasa was still bound to Gaballufix, even though she detested all his recent actions.

"I grieve for his widow," said Luet, "but I rejoice for the city."

Hushidh, though, gazed with a calculating eye on the soldier. "This man didn't bring you *that* news, I think."

"No," said Rasa. "No, I learned of Gaballufix's death from Rashgallivak. It seems Rashgallivak was appointed . . . the new Wetchik."

Luet knew that this was a devastating blow. It meant that Rasa's husband, Volemak, who *had* been the Wetchik, now had no property, no rights, no standing in the Palwashantu clan at all. And Rashgallivak, who had been his trusted steward, now stood in his place. Was there no honor in the world? "When did Rashgallivak ascend to this honor?"

"Before Gaballufix died—Gab appointed him, of course, and I'm sure he loved doing it. So there's a kind of justice in the fact that Rash has now taken leadership of the Palwashantu clan, taking Gab's place as well. So yes, you're right, Rash is rising rather quickly in the world. While others fall. Roptat is also dead tonight."

"No," whispered Hushidh.

Roptat had been the leader of the pro-Gorayni party, the group trying to keep the city of Basilica out of the coming war between the Gorayni and Potokgavan. With him gone, what chance was there of peace?

"Yes, both dead tonight," said Rasa. "The leaders of both the parties that have torn our city apart. But here is the worst of it. The rumor is that my son Nafai is the slayer of them both."

"Not true," said Luet. "Not possible."

"So I thought," said Rasa. "I didn't wake you for the rumor."

Now Luet understood fully the turmoil in Aunt Rasa's

face. Nafai was Aunt Rasa's pride, a brilliant young man. And more—for Luet knew well that Nafai also was close to the Oversoul. What happened to him was not just important to those who loved him, it was also important to the city, perhaps to the world. "This soldier has word of Nafai, then?"

Rasa nodded at the soldier, who had sat in silence until now.

"My name is Smelost," he said, rising to his feet to speak to them. "I was tending the gate. I saw two men approach. One of them pressed his thumb on the screen and the computer of Basilica knew him to be Zdorab, the treasurer of Gaballufix's house."

"And the other?" asked Hushidh.

"Masked, but dressed in Gaballufix's manner, and Zdorab called him Gaballufix and tried to persuade me not to make him press his thumb on the screen. But I had to make him do it, because Roptat was murdered, and we were trying to prevent the killer from escaping. We'd been told that Lady Rasa's youngest son, Nafai, was the murderer. It was Gaballufix who had reported this."

"So did you make Gaballufix put his thumb on the screen?" said Luet.

"He leaned close to me and spoke in my ear, and said, 'And what if the one who made this false accusation was the murderer himself?' Well, that's what some of us already thought—that Gaballufix was accusing Nafai of killing Roptat to cover up his own guilt. And then this soldier— the one that Zdorab was calling Gaballufix—put his thumb on the screen and the name the computer displayed for me was Nafai."

"What did you do?" Luet demanded.

"I violated my oath and my orders. I erased his name immediately and let him pass. I believed him . . . that he was innocent. Of killing Roptat. But his passage from the city was recorded, and the fact that I let him go, knowing who he was. I thought nothing of it—the original complaint came from Gaballufix, and here was Gaballufix's own treasurer with the boy. I thought Gaballufix couldn't protest if his man was along. The worst that would happen is that I'd lose my post."

"You would have let him go anyway," said Hushidh. "Even if Gaballufix's man hadn't been with him."

Smelost looked at her for a moment, then gave a little half-smile. "I was a follower of Roptat. It's a joke to think Wetchik's son might have killed him."

"Nafai's only fourteen," said Luet. "It's a joke to think he'd kill anybody."

"Not so," said Smelost. "Because word came to us that Gaballufix's body had been found. Beheaded. And his clothing missing. What should I think, except that Nafai got Gaballufix's clothing from his corpse? That Nafai and Zdorab almost certainly killed him? Nafai's big for fourteen, if that's his age. A man in size. He could have done it. Zdorab—not likely." Smelost chuckled wryly. "It hardly matters now that I'll lose my post for this. What I fear is that I'll be hanged as an accomplice to a murder, for letting him go. So I came here."

"To the widow of the murdered man?" asked Luet.

"To the mother of the supposed murderer," said Hushidh, correcting her. "This man loves Basilica."

"I do," said the soldier, "and I'm glad that you know it. I didn't do my duty, but I did what I thought was right."

"I need advice," said Rasa, looking from Luet to Hushidh and back again. "This man, Smelost, has come to me for protection, because he saved my son. And in the meantime, my son is named a murderer and I believe now that he might be guilty indeed. I'm no waterseer. I'm no raveler. What is right and just? What does the Oversoul want? You must tell me. You must counsel with me!"

"The Oversoul has told me nothing," said Luet. "I know only what you told me here, tonight."

"And as for raveling," said Hushidh, "I see only that this man loves Basilica, and that you yourself are tangled in a web of love that puts you at cross-purposes with yourself. Your daughters' father is dead, and you love them—and him, too, you love even *him*. Yet you believe Nafai killed him, and you love your son even more. You also honor this soldier, and are bound to him by a debt of honor. Most of all you love Basilica. Yet you don't know what you must do for the good of your city."

"I knew my dilemma, Shuya. It was the path out of it that I didn't know."

"I must flee the city," said Smelost. "I thought you might protect me. I knew of you as Nafai's mother, but I'd forgotten that you were Gaballufix's widow."

"Not his widow," said Rasa. "I let our contract lapse years ago. He has married a dozen times since then, I imagine. My husband now is Wetchik. Or rather the man who used to be Wetchik, and now is a landless fugitive whose son may be a murderer." She smiled bitterly. "I can do nothing about that, but I *can* protect *you,* and so I will."

"No you can't," said Hushidh. "You're too close to the center of all these mysteries, Aunt Rasa. The council of Basilica will always listen to you, but they won't protect a soldier who has violated his duty, solely on your word. It will simply make you both look all the guiltier."

"This is the raveler speaking?" asked Rasa.

"It's your student speaking," said Hushidh, "telling you what you would know yourself, if you weren't so confused."

A tear spilled out of Rasa's eye and slipped down her cheek. "What will happen?" said Rasa. "What will happen to my city now?"

Luet had never heard her so afraid, so uncertain. Rasa was a great teacher, a woman of wisdom and honor; to be one of her nieces, one of the students specially chosen to dwell within her household—it was the proudest thing that could happen to a young woman of Basilica, or so Luet had always believed. Yet here she saw Rasa afraid and uncertain. She had not thought such a thing was possible.

"Wetchik—my Volemak—he said the Oversoul was guiding him," said Rasa, spitting out the words with bitterness. "What sort of guide is this? Did the Oversoul tell him to send my boys back to the city, where they were almost killed? Did the Oversoul turn my son into a murderer and a fugitive? What is the Oversoul doing? Most likely it isn't the Oversoul at all. Gaballufix was right—my beloved

Volemak has lost his mind, and our sons are being swallowed up in his madness."

Luet had heard enough of this. "Shame on you," she said.

"Hush, Lutya!" cried Hushidh.

"*Shame* on you, Aunt Rasa," Luet insisted. "Just because it looks frightening and confusing to you doesn't mean that the Oversoul doesn't understand it. I *know* that the Oversoul is guiding Wetchik, and Nafai too. All this will somehow turn to the good of Basilica."

"That's where you're wrong," said Rasa. "The Oversoul has no special love for Basilica. She watches over the whole world. What if the whole world will somehow benefit if Basilica is ruined? If my boys are killed? To the Oversoul, little cities and little people are nothing—she weaves a grand design."

"Then we must bow to her," said Luet.

"Bow to whomever you want," said Rasa. "I'm not bowing to the Oversoul if she's going to turn my boys into killers and my city into dust. If that's what the Oversoul is planning, then the Oversoul and I are enemies, do you understand me?"

"Lower your voice, Aunt Rasa," said Hushidh. "You'll waken the little ones."

Rasa fell silent for a moment, then muttered: "I've said what I have to say."

"You are not the Oversoul's enemy," said Luet. "Please, wait awhile. Let me try to find the Oversoul's will in this. That's what you brought me here to do, isn't it? To tell you what the Oversoul is planning?"

"Yes," said Rasa.

"I don't command the Oversoul," said Luet. "But I'll ask her. Wait here, and I'll—"

"No," said Rasa. "There's no time for you to go down to the waters."

"Not to the waters," said Luet. "To my room. To sleep. To dream. To listen for the voice, to watch for vision. If it comes."

"Then hurry," said Rasa. "We have only an hour or so

before I have to do something—more and more people will come here, and I'll have to *act.*"

"I don't command the Oversoul," Luet said again. "And the Oversoul sets her own schedule. She does not follow yours."

Kokor went to Sevet's favorite hideaway, where she took her lovers to keep them from Vas's knowledge, and Sevet wasn't there. "She doesn't come here anymore," said Iliva, Sevet's friend. "Nor any of the other places in Dauberville. Maybe she's being faithful!" Then Iliva laughed and bade her good night.

So Kokor wouldn't be able to pounce after all. It was so disappointing.

Why had Sevet found a new hiding place? Had her husband Vas gone in search of her? He was far too dignified for that! Yet the fact remained that Sevet had abandoned her old places, even though Iliva and Sevet's other friends would gladly have continued to shelter her.

It could only mean one thing. Sevet had found a new lover, a real liaison, not just a quick encounter, and he was someone so important in the city that they had to find new hiding places for their love, for if it became known the scandal would surely reach Vas's ears.

How delicious, thought Kokor. She tried to imagine who it could be, which of the most famous men of the city might have won Sevet's heart. Of course it would be a married man; unless he was married to a woman of Basilica, no man had a right to spend even a single night in the city. So when Kokor finally discovered Sevet's secret, the scandal would be marvelous indeed, for there'd be an injured weeping wife to make Sevet seem all the more sluttish.

And I *will* tell it, thought Kokor. Because she hid this liaison from me and didn't tell me, I have no obligation to keep her secret for her. She didn't trust me, and so why should I be trustworthy?

Kokor wouldn't tell it *herself,* of course. But she knew many a satirist in the Open Theatre who would love to know of this, so he could be the first to dart sweet Sevet and her lover in a play. And the price she charged him for the story wouldn't be high—only the chance to play Sevet when he darted her. That would put a quick end to Tumannu's threat to blackball her.

I'll get to imitate Sevet's voice, thought Kokor, and make fun of her singing as I do. No one can sound as much like her as I can. No one knows all the flaws in her voice as I do. She will regret having hidden her secret from me! And yet I'll be masked when I dart her, and I'll deny it all, deny everything, even if Mother herself asks me to swear by the Oversoul, I'll deny it. Sevet isn't the only one who knows how to keep a secret.

It was late, only a few hours before dawn, but the last comedies wouldn't be over for another hour. If she hurried back to the theatre, she could probably even go back onstage and be there for the finale, at least. But she couldn't bring herself to play the scene she'd have to play with Tumannu—begging forgiveness, vowing never to walk away from a play again, weeping. It would be too demeaning. No daughter of Gaballufix should have to grovel before a mere stage manager!

Only now that he's dead, what will it matter if I'm his daughter or not? The thought filled her with dismay. She wondered if that man Rash had been right, if Father would leave her enough money to be very rich and buy her own theatre. That would be nice, wouldn't it? That would solve everything. Of course, Sevet would have just as much money and would probably buy her own theatre, too, just because she would have to overshadow Kokor as usual and steal any chance of glory, but Kokor would simply show herself to be the better promoter and drive Sevet's miserable imitative theatre into the dust, and, when it failed, *all* Sevet's inheritance would be lost, while Kokor would be the leading figure in Basilican theatre, and the day would come when Sevet would come to Kokor and beg her to put her in the starring role in one of her plays, and Kokor would embrace her sister and weep and say, "Oh, my darling sister, I'd love nothing better than to put on your little play, but I have a responsibility to my backers, my sweet, and I can't very well risk their money on a show starring a singer who is clearly *past her prime.*"

Oh, it was a delicious dream! Never mind that Sevet was only a single year older—to Kokor that made all the difference. Sevet might be ahead *now,* but someday soon youth would be more valuable than age to them, and then it would be Kokor who had the advantage. Youth and beauty—Kokor would always have more of both than Sevet. And she was every bit as talented as Sevet, too.

Now she was home, the little place that she and Obring rented in Hill Town. It was modest, but decorated in exquisite taste. That much, at least, she had learned from her Aunt Dhelembuvex—Obring's mother—that it's better to have a small setting perfectly finished than a large setting badly done. "A woman must present herself as the blossom of perfection," Auntie Dhel always said. Kokor herself had written it much better, in an aphorism she had published back when she was only fifteen, before she married Obring and left Mother's house:

A perfect bud
of subtle color
and delicate scent
is more welcome than a showy bloom,
which shouts for attention but has nothing to show
that can't be seen in the first glance,
or smelled in the first whiff.

Kokor had been proudest of the way the lines about the perfect bud were short and simple phrases, while the lines about the showy bloom were long and awkward. But to her disappointment no noted melodist had made an aria of her aphorism, and the young ones who came to her with their tunes were all talentless pretenders who had no idea how to make a song that would suit a voice like Kokor's. She didn't even sleep with any of them, except the one whose face was so shy and sweet. Ah, he was a tiger in the darkness, wasn't he! She had kept him for three days, but he *would* insist on singing his tunes to her, and so she sent him on his way.

What was his name?

She was on the verge of remembering who he was as she entered the house and heard a strange hooting sound from the back room. Like the baboons who lived across Little Lake, their pant-hoots as they babbled to each other in their nothing language. "Oh. Hoo. Oo-oo. Hoooo."

Only it wasn't baboons, was it? And the sound came from the bedroom, up the winding stair, moonlight from the roof window lighting the way as Kokor rushed upward, running the stairs on tiptoe, silently, for she knew that she would find her husband Obring with some whore of his *in Kokor's bed,* and that was unspeakable, a breach of all decency, hadn't he any consideration for her at all? She never brought *her* lovers home, did she? She never let them sweat on *his* sheets, did she? Fair was fair, and it would be a glorious scene of injured pride when she thrust the little tartlet out of the house *without her clothes!* so she'd have to go home naked and then Kokor would see how Obring apologized to her and how he'd make it up to her, all his vows and apologies and whimpering but there was no doubt about it now, she would *not* renew him when their contract came up and then he'd find out what happens to a man who throws his faithlessness in Kokor's face.

In her moonlit bedroom, Kokor found Obring engaged in exactly the activity she had expected. She couldn't see his face, or the face of the woman for whom he was providing vigorous companionship, but she didn't need daylight or a magnifying glass to know what it all meant.

"Disgusting," she said.

It worked just as she had hoped. They obviously had not heard her coming up the stair, and the sound of her voice froze Obring. For a moment he held his post. Then he turned his head, looking quite foolish as he gazed mournfully over his shoulder at her. "Kyoka," he said. "You're home early."

"I should have known," said the woman on the bed. Her face was still hidden behind Obring's naked back, but Kokor knew the voice at once. "Your show is so bad they closed it in mid-performance."

Kokor hardly noticed the insult, hardly noticed the fact that there wasn't a trace of embarrassment in Sevet's tone. All she could think of was, That's why she had to find a new hiding place, not because her lover was somebody famous, but to keep the truth from *me*.

"Hundreds of your followers every night would be glad for a yibattsa with you," Kokor whispered. "But you had to have my husband."

"Oh, don't take this personally," said Sevet, sitting up on her elbows. Sevet's breasts sagged off to the sides. Kokor loved seeing that, how her breasts sagged, how at nineteen Sevet was definitely older and *thicker* than Kokor. Yet Obring had wanted *that* body, had used that body on the very bed where he had slept beside Kokor's perfect body so many nights. How could he even be aroused by a body like that, after seeing Kokor after her bath so many mornings.

"You weren't using him, and he's very sweet," said Sevet. "If you'd ever bothered to satisfy him he wouldn't have looked at *me*."

"I'm sorry," Obring murmured. "I didn't mean to."

That was so outrageous, like a little child, that Kokor could not contain her rage. And yet she did contain it. She held it in, like a tornado in a bottle. "This was an accident?" whispered Kokor. "You stumbled, you tripped and fell, your clothes tore off and you just happened to bounce on top of my sister?"

"I mean—I kept wanting to break this off, all these months . . ."

"Months," whispered Kokor.

"Don't say any more, puppy," said Sevet. "You're just making it worse."

"You call him 'puppy'?" asked Kokor. It was the word they had used when they first reached womanhood, to describe the teenage boys who panted after them.

"He was so eager," said Sevet, sliding out from under Obring. "I couldn't help calling him that, and he likes the name."

Obring turned and sat miserably on the bed. He made no

attempt to cover himself; it was obvious he had lost all interest in love for the evening.

"Don't worry about it, Obring," Sevet said. She stood beside the bed, bending over to pick up her clothing from the floor. "She'll still renew you. This is *one* story she won't be eager to have people tell about her, and so she'll renew you as long as you want, just to keep you from telling."

Kokor saw how Sevet's belly pooched out, how her breasts swung when she bent over. And yet *she* had taken Kokor's husband. After everything else, she had to have even *that*. It could not be borne.

"Sing for me," whispered Kokor.

"What?" asked Sevet, turning to face her, holding her gown in front of her.

"Sing me a song, you davalka, with that pretty voice of yours."

Sevet stared into Kokor's eyes and the look of bored amusement left her face. "I'm not going to sing right now, you little fool," she said.

"Not for me," said Kokor. "For Father."

"What *about* Father?" Sevet's face twisted into an expression of mock sympathy. "Oh, is little Kyoka going to tell on me?" Then she sneered. "He'll laugh. Then he'll take Obring drinking with him!"

"A *dirge* for Father," said Kokor.

"A dirge?" Sevet looked confused now. Worried.

"While you were here, boffing your sister's husband, somebody was busy killing Father. If you were human, you'd care. Even baboons grieve for their dead."

"I didn't know," said Sevet. "How could I know?"

"I looked for you," said Kokor. "To tell you. But you weren't in any of the places I knew. I left my play, I *lost my job* to search for you and tell you, and this is where you were and what you were doing."

"You're such a liar," said Sevet. "Why should I believe this?"

"I never did it with Vas," said Kokor. "Even when he begged me."

"He never asked you," said Sevet. "I don't believe your lies."

"He told me that just once he'd like to have a woman who was truly beautiful. A woman whose body was young and lithe and sweet. But I refused, because you were my sister."

"You're lying. He never asked."

"Maybe I'm lying. But he *did* ask."

"Not *Vas*," said Sevet.

"Vas, with the large mole on the inside of his thigh," said Kokor. "I refused him because you were my sister."

"You're lying about Father, too."

"Dead in his own blood. Murdered on the street. This is not a good night for our loving family. Father dead. Me betrayed. And you—"

"Stay away from me."

"Sing for him," said Kokor.

"At the funeral, *if* you're not lying."

"Sing *now*," said Kokor.

"Little *hen*, little *duck*, I'll never sing at *your* command."

Accusing her of cackling and quacking instead of singing, that was an old taunt between them, that was nothing. It was the contempt in Sevet's voice, the loathing that got inside her. It filled her, it overfilled her, it was more than she could contain. Not for another moment could she hold in the tempest that tore at her.

"That's right!" cried Kokor. "At my command, you'll *never* sing!" And like a cat she lashed out, but it wasn't a claw, it was a fist. Sevet threw up her hands to protect her face. But Kokor had no desire to mark her sister's face. It wasn't her face she hated. No, her fist connected right where she aimed, under Sevet's chin, on her throat, where the larynx lay hidden under the ample flesh, where the voice was made.

Sevet didn't make a sound, even though the force of the blow knocked her backward. She fell, clutching at her throat; she writhed on the floor, gagging, hacking. Obring cried out and leapt to her, knelt over her. "Sevet!" he cried. "Sevet, are you all right?"

But Sevet's only answer was to gurgle and spit, then to choke and cough. On blood. Her own blood. Kokor could see it on Sevet's hands, on Obring's thighs where he cradled her head on his lap as he knelt there. Glimmering black in the moonlight, blood from Sevet's throat. How does it taste in your mouth, Sevet? How does it feel on your flesh, Obring? Her blood, like the gift of a virgin, my gift to both of you.

Sevet was making an awful strangling sound. "Water," said Obring. "A glass of water, Kyoka—to wash her mouth out. She's bleeding, can't you see that? What have you done to her!"

Kyoka stepped to the sink—her own sink—and took a cup—her own cup—and brought it, filled with water, to Obring, who took it from her hand and tried to pour some of it into Sevet's mouth. But Sevet choked on it and spat the water out, gasping for breath, strangling on the blood that flowed inside her throat.

"A doctor!" cried Obring. "Cry out for a doctor—Bustiya next door is a doctor, she'll come."

"Help," murmured Kokor. "Come quickly. Help." She spoke so softly she almost couldn't hear the sound herself.

Obring rose up from the floor and looked at her in rage. "Don't touch her," he said. "I'll fetch the physician myself." He strode boldly from the room. Such strength in him now. Naked as a mythic god, as the pictures of the Gorayni Imperator—the image of masculinity—that was Obring as he went forth into the night to find a doctor who might save his lady.

Kokor watched as Sevet's fingers scratched on the floor, tore at the skin around her neck, as if she wanted to open up a breathing hole there. Sevet's eyes were bugging out, and blood drooled from her mouth onto the floor.

"You had everything else," said Kokor. "Everything else. But you couldn't even leave me *him*."

Sevet gurgled. Her eyes stared at Kokor in agony and terror.

"You won't die," said Kokor. "I'm not a murderer. I'm not a *betrayer*."

But then it occurred to her that Sevet just *might* die. With so much blood in her throat, she might drown in it. And then Kokor would be held responsible for this. "Nobody can blame me," said Kokor. "Father died tonight, and I came home and found you with my husband, and then you taunted me—no one will blame me. I'm only eighteen, I'm only a *girl*. And it was an accident anyway. I meant to claw out your eyes but I missed, that's all."

Sevet gagged. She vomited on the floor. It smelled awful. This was making such a mess—everything would be stained, and the smell would never, never go. And they *would* blame Kokor for it, if Sevet died. That would be Sevet's revenge, that the stain of this would never go away. Sevet's way of getting even, to die and have Kokor called a murderer forever.

Well, I'll show you, thought Kokor. I won't let you die. In fact, I'll *save your life*.

So it was that when Obring returned with the doctor they found Kokor kneeling over Sevet, breathing into her mouth. Obring pulled her aside to let the doctor get to Sevet. And as Bustiya pushed the tube down into Sevet's throat, as Sevet's face became a silent rictus of agony, Obring smelled the blood and vomit and saw how Kokor's face and gown were stained with both. He whispered to her as he held her there, "You do love her. You couldn't let her die."

She clung to him then, weeping.

"I can't sleep," Luet said miserably. "How can I dream if I can't sleep?"

"Never mind," Rasa said. "I know what we have to do. I don't need the Oversoul to tell us. Smelost has to leave Basilica, because Hushidh is right, I can't protect him now."

"I won't leave," said Smelost. "I've decided. This is my city, and I'll face the consequences of what I've done."

"Do you love Basilica?" said Rasa. "Then don't give Gaballufix's people somebody they can pin all the blame on. Don't give them a chance to put you on trial and use it as an excuse to take command of the guards so that his masked soldiers are the *only* authority in the city."

Smelost glared at her a moment, then nodded. "I see," he said. "For the sake of Basilica, then I'll go."

"Where?" asked Hushidh. "Where can you send him?"

"To the Gorayni, of course," said Rasa. "I'll give you provisions and money enough to make it north to the Gorayni. And a letter, explaining how you saved the man who—the man who killed Gaballufix. They'll know what that means—they must have spies who told them that Gab was trying to get Basilica to make an alliance with Potokgavan. Maybe Roptat was in contact with them."

"Never!" cried Smelost. "Roptat was no traitor!"

"No, of course he wasn't," said Rasa soothingly. "The point is that Gab was their enemy, and that makes you their friend. It's the least they can do, to take you in."

"How long will I have to stay away?" asked Smelost. "There's a woman that I love here. I have a son."

"Not long," said Rasa. "With Gab gone, the tumult will soon die down. He was the cause of it, and now we'll have peace again. May the Oversoul forgive me for saying so, but if Nafai killed him then maybe he did a good thing, for Basilica at least."

There was a loud knocking at the door.

"Already!" said Rasa.

"They can't know I'm here," said Smelost.

"Shuya, take him to the kitchen and provision him. I'll stall them at the door as long as I can. Luet, help your sister."

But it wasn't Palwashantu soldiers at the door, or city guards, or any kind of authority at all. Instead it was Vas, Sevet's husband.

"I'm sorry to disturb you at this hour."

"Me and my whole house," said Rasa. "I already know that Sevet's father is dead, but I know you meant well in coming to—"

"He's dead?" said Vas. "Gaballufix? Then maybe that explains . . . No, it explains nothing." He looked frightened and angry. Rasa had never seen him like this.

"What's wrong, then?" Rasa asked. "If you didn't know Gab was dead, why are you here?"

"One of Kokor's neighbors came to fetch me. It's Sevet. She's been struck in the throat—she almost died. A very bad injury. I thought you'd want to come with me."

"You *left* her? To come to me?"

"I wasn't with her," said Vas. "She's at Kokor's house."

"Why would Sevya be there?" One of the servants was already helping Rasa put on a cloak, so she could go outside. "Kokor had a play tonight, didn't she? A new play."

"Sevya was with Obring," said Vas. He led her out onto the portico; the servant closed the door behind them. "That's why Kyoka hit her."

"Kyoka hit her in the—*Kyoka* did it?"

"She found them together. That's how the neighbor told the story, anyway. Obring went and fetched the doctor stark naked, and Sevya was naked when they got back. Kyoka was breathing into her mouth, to save her. They have a tube in her throat and she's breathing, she won't die. That's all the neighbor knew to tell me."

"That Sevet is alive," said Rasa bitterly, "and who was naked."

"Her throat," said Vas. "It might have been kinder for Kokor simply to kill her, if this costs Sevet her voice."

"Poor Sevya," said Rasa. There were soldiers marching in the streets, but Rasa paid them no attention, and—perhaps because Vas and Rasa seemed to intent and urgent—the soldiers made no effort to stop them. "To lose her father and her voice in the same night."

"We've all lost something tonight, eh?" said Vas bitterly.

"This isn't about *you*," said Rasa. "I think Sevet really loves you, in her way."

"I know—they hate each other so much they'll do anything to hurt each other. But I thought it was getting better."

"Maybe now it will," said Rasa. "It can't get worse."

"Kyoka tried it, too," said Vas. "I sent her away both times. Why couldn't Obring have had the brains to say no to Sevet, too?"

"He has the brains," said Rasa. "He lacks the strength."

At Kokor's house, the scene was very touching. Someone had cleaned up: The bed was no longer rumpled with love; now it was smooth except where Sevet lay, demure in one of Kokor's most modest nightgowns. Obring, too, had managed to become clothed, and now he knelt in the corner, comforting a weeping Kokor. The doctor greeted Rasa at the door of the room.

"I've drained the blood out of the lungs," the physician said. "She's in no danger of dying, but the breathing tube must remain for now. A throat specialist will be here soon. Perhaps the damage will heal without scarring. Her career may not be over."

Rasa sat on the bed beside her daughter, and took Sevya's hand. The smell of vomit still lingered, even though the floor was wet from scrubbing. "Well, Sevya," whispered Rasa, "did you win or lose this round?"

A tear squeezed out between Sevet's eyelids.

On the other side of the room, Vas stood over Obring and Kokor. He was flushed with—what, anger? Or was his face merely red from the exertion of their walk?

"Obring," said Vas, "you miserable little bastard. Only a fool pees in his brother's soup."

Obring looked up at him, his face drawn, and then he looked back down at his wife, who wept all the harder. Rasa knew Kokor well enough to know what while her weeping was sincere, it was being played for the most possible sympathy. Rasa had almost none to give her. She was well aware how little her daughters had cared for the exclusivity clause in their marriage contracts, and she had no sympathy for faithless people who felt injured upon discovering that their mates were faithless, too.

It was Sevet who was suffering, not Kokor. Rasa could not be distracted from Sevet's need, just because Kokor was so noisy and Sevet was silent.

"I'm with you, my dear daughter," said Rasa. "It's not the end of the world. You're alive, and your husband loves you. Let that be your music for a while."

Sevet clung to her hand, her breath shallow, panting.

Rasa turned to the doctor. "Has she been told about her father?"

"She knows," Obring said. "Kyoka told us."

"Thank the Oversoul we have but one funeral to attend," said Rasa.

"Kyoka saved her sister's life," said Obring. "She gave her breath."

No, *I* gave her breath, thought Rasa. Gave her breath, but alas, I could not give her decency, or sense. I couldn't keep her out of her sister's sheets, or away from her sister's husband. But I did give her breath, and perhaps now this pain will teach her something. Compassion, perhaps. Or at least some self-restraint. Something to make good come out of this. Something to make her become *my* daughter, and not Gaballufix's, as they both have been till now.

Let this all turn to good, Rasa silently prayed. But then she wondered to whom she was praying. To the Oversoul, whose meddling had started so many other problems? I'll get no help from *her*, thought Rasa. I'm on my own now, to try to steer my family and my city through the terrible days to come. I have no power or authority over either of them, except whatever power comes from love and wisdom. I have the love. If only I could be sure I also had the wisdom.

TWO

OPPORTUNITY

THE DREAM OF THE WATERSEER

Luet had never tried to have an emergency dream before, and so it had never occurred to her that she couldn't just go to sleep and dream because she wished it. Quite the contrary—the sense of urgency was no doubt what had kept her awake and made it impossible for her to dream. She was furious and ashamed that she hadn't been able to learn anything from the Oversoul before Aunt Rasa had to make a decision about what to do with that soldier, Smelost. What made it worse was that, even though the Oversoul had told her nothing, she was certain that sending Smelost to the Gorayni was a mistake. It seemed too simple, to think that because Gaballufix had been an enemy of the Gorayni, the Gorayni would automatically welcome Gaballufix's enemy and give him sanctuary.

Luet had wanted to speak up and tell her, "Aunt Rasa, the Gorayni aren't necessarily our friends." She might even have said so, but Rasa had rushed out of the house with Vas and there was nothing to do but watch as Smelost gathered up the food and supplies the servants brought for him and then slipped out the back way.

Why couldn't Rasa have thought just a moment more?

Wouldn't it have been better to send Smelost out into the desert to join Wetchik? But he wasn't the Wetchik anymore, was he? He was nothing but Volemak, the man who *had* been Wetchik until Gaballufix stripped him of the title— when?—only yesterday. Nothing but Volemak—yet Luet knew that Volemak, of all the great men of Basilica, was the only one who was part of the Oversoul's plans.

The Oversoul had begun all these problems by giving Volemak his vision of Basilica on fire. She had warned him that an alliance with Potokgavan would lead to the destruction of Basilica. She hadn't promised that Basilica could trust the Gorayni to be *friends*. And from what Luet knew of the Gorayni—the Wetheads, as they were called, from the way they oiled their hair—it was a bad idea to send Smelost to ask for refuge. It would give the wrong impression to the Gorayni. It would lead them to think that their allies were not safe in Basilica. Might that not entice them to do exactly what everyone wanted to keep them from doing—invade and conquer the city?

No, it was a mistake to send Smelost. But since Luet didn't reach this conclusion as a waterseer, but rather reached it through her own reasoning, no one would listen to her. She was a child, except when the Oversoul was in her, and so she only had respect when she was not herself. It made her angry, but what could she do about it, except hope that she was wrong about Smelost and the Gorayni, and then wait impatiently until she turned fully into a woman?

What worried her perhaps even more was that it was unlike Rasa to reach such a faulty conclusion. Rasa seemed to be acting out of fear, acting without thinking. And if Rasa's judgment was clouded, then what could Luet count on?

I want to talk to someone, she thought. Not her sister Hushidh—dear Shuya was very wise and kind and would listen to her, but she simply didn't care about anything outside Basilica. That was the problem with her being a raveler. Hushidh lived in the constant awareness of all the connections and relationships among the people around her. That web-sense was naturally the most important thing in her life, as she watched people connect and detach from each other, forming communities and dissolving them. And underlying all was Shuya's powerful awareness of the fabric of Basilica itself. She loved the city—but she knew it so well, focused so closely on it that she simply had no idea of how Basilica related to the world outside. Such relationships were too large and impersonal.

Luet had even tried to discuss this with her, but Hushidh fell asleep almost at once. Luet couldn't blame her. After all, it was nearly dawn, and they had missed hours of sleep in the middle of the night. Luet herself should be asleep.

If only I could talk with Nafai or Issib. Nafai especially—*he* can talk with the Oversoul when he's awake. He may not get the visions that I get, he may not see with the depth and clarity of a waterseer, but he can get *answers*. Practical, simple answers. And he doesn't have to be able to fall asleep to get them. If only he were here. Yet the Oversoul sent him and his father and all his brothers away into the desert. That's where Smelost should have gone, definitely. To Nafai. If only anyone knew where he was.

At last, at long last Luet's frenzied thoughts jumbled into the chaotic mentation of sleep, and from her fitful sleep a dream came, a dream that she would remember, for it came from outside herself and had meaning beyond the random firings of her brain during sleep.

"Wake up," said Hushidh.

"I *am* awake," said Luet.

"You've answered me that twice already, Lutya, and each time you stay asleep. It's morning, and things are even worse than we thought."

"If you said that every time I woke up," said Luet, "then no wonder I went back to sleep."

"You've slept long enough," said Hushidh, and then proceeded to tell her all about what happened at Kokor's house the night before.

Luet could hardly grasp that such things could actually happen—not to anyone connected with Rasa's house. Yet it wasn't just rumor. "That's why Vas took Aunt Rasa with him," said Luet.

"You have such a bright mind in the morning."

Her thoughts were coming so sluggishly that it took Luet a moment to realize that Hushidh was being ironic. "I was dreaming," she said, to explain her stupidity.

But Hushidh wasn't interested in her dream. "For poor Aunt Rasa the nightmare starts when she wakes up."

Luet tried to think of a bright spot. "At least she has the comfort of knowing Kokor and Sevet were auntied out to Dhelembuvex—it won't reflect on her house—"

"Won't reflect . . . ! They're her *daughters,* Lutya. And Auntie Dhel was over here with them all the time as they were growing up. This has nothing to do with how they were raised. This is what it means to be the daughters of Gaballufix. How deliciously ironic, that the very night he dies, one of his daughters strikes the other dumb with a blow to the throat."

"Sweet kindness flows with every word from your lips, Shuya."

Hushidh glared at her. "You've never loved Aunt Rasa's daughters, either, so don't get pure with me."

The truth was that Luet had no great interest in Rasa's daughters. She had been too young to care, when they last were in Rasa's house. But Hushidh, being older, had clear memories of what it was like to have them in the house all the time, with Kokor actually attending classes, and both of them surrounded by suitors. Hushidh liked to joke that the pheromone count couldn't have been higher in a brothel, but Hushidh's loathing for Kokor and Sevet had nothing to do with their attractiveness to men. It had to do with their vicious jealousy of any girl who had actually earned Rasa's love and respect. Hushidh was no rival to them, and yet they had both persecuted her mercilessly, taunting her whenever the teachers couldn't hear, until she became virtually a ghost in Rasa's house, hiding until the moment of class and rushing away afterward, avoiding meals, shunning all the parties and frolics, until Kokor and Sevet finally married at a mercifully young age—fourteen and fifteen, respectively—and moved out. Sevet was already a noted singer even then, and her practicing—and Kokor's—had filled the house like birdsong. But neither she nor Kokor had brought any true music to Rasa's house. Rather the music returned when they finally left. And Hushidh remained quiet and shy around everyone except Luet. So of course Hushidh cared more when Rasa's daughters played out some bitter tragedy. Luet only cared because it would make Aunt Rasa sad.

"Shuya, all this is only scandal. What's being said about that soldier? And about Gaballufix's death?"

Hushidh looked down in her lap. She knew that Luet was, in effect, rebuking her for having given false priority to trivial matters; but she accepted the rebuke, and did not defend herself. "They're saying that Smelost was Nafai's co-conspirator all along. Rashgallivak is demanding that the council investigate who helped Smelost escape from the city, even though he wasn't under a warrant or anything when he left. Rasa is trying to get the city guard put under the control of the Palwashantu. It's very ugly."

"What if Aunt Rasa is arrested as Smelost's accomplice?" said Luet.

"Accomplice in what?" said Hushidh. Now she was Hushidh the Raveler, discussing the city of Basilica, not Shuya the schoolgirl, telling an ugly story about her tormentors. Luet welcomed the change, even if it meant Hushidh's acting so openly astonished at Luet's lack of insight. "How insane do you think people actually are? Rashgallivak can try to whip them up, but he's no Gaballufix—he doesn't have the personal magnetism to get people to follow him for long. Aunt Rasa will hold her own against him on the council, and then some."

"Yes, I suppose so," said Luet. "But Gaballufix had so many soldiers, and now they're all Rashgallivak's. . . ."

"Rash isn't well-connected," said Hushidh. "People have always liked him and respected him, but only as a steward—as Wetchik's steward, particularly—and they aren't likely to give him the full honor of the Wetchik right away, let alone the kind of respect that Gaballufix was given as head of the Palwashantu. He doesn't have half the power he imagines he has—but he has enough to cause trouble, and it's very disturbing."

Luet was fully awake at last, and crawled off the foot of her bed. She remembered that there was something she must tell. "I dreamed," she said.

"So you said." Then Hushidh realized what she meant. "Oh. A little late, wouldn't you say?"

"Not about Smelost. About something—very strange. And yet it felt more important than any of what's going on around us."

"A true dream?" asked Hushidh.

"I'm never *sure,* but I think so. I remember it so clearly, it must come from the Oversoul."

"Then tell me as we go to breakfast. It's nearly noon, but Aunt Rasa told the cook to indulge us since we were up half the night."

Luet pulled a gown over her head, slipped sandals on her feet, and followed Hushidh down the stairs to the kitchen. "I dreamed of angels, flying."

"Angels! And what is that supposed to mean, except that you're superstitious in your sleep?"

"They didn't look like the pictures in the children's books, if that's what you mean. No, they were more like large and graceful birds. Bats, really, since they had fur. But with very intelligent and expressive faces, and somehow in the dream I knew they were angels."

"The Oversoul has no need of angels. The Oversoul speaks directly to the mind of every woman."

"And man, only hardly anybody listens anymore, just as you're not listening to *me,* Shuya. Should I tell you the dream or just eat bread and honey and cream and figure that the Oversoul has nothing to say that might interest you?"

"Don't be nasty with *me,* Luet. You may be this wonderful waterseer to everybody else, but you're just my stupid little sister when you get snippy like this."

The cook glared at them. "I try to keep a kitchen full of light and *harmony,*" she said.

Abashed, they took the hot bread she offered them and

sat at the table, where a pitcher of cream and a jar of honey already waited. Hushidh, as always, broke her bread into a bowl and poured the cream and honey on it; Luet, as always, slathered the honey on the bread and ate it separately, drinking the plain cream from her bowl. They both pretended to detest the way the other ate her food. "Dry as dust," whispered Hushidh. "Soggy and slimy," answered Luet. Then they both laughed aloud.

"Much better," said the cook. "You should both know better than to quarrel."

With her mouth full, Hushidh said, "The dream."

"Angels," said Luet.

"Flying, yes. Hairy ones, like fat bats. I heard you the first time."

"Not fat."

"Bats, anyway."

"Graceful," said Luet. "Soaring, that's how they were. And then I was one of them, flying and flying. It was so beautiful and peaceful. And then I saw the river, and I flew down to it and there on the riverbank I took the clay and made a statue out of it."

"Angels playing in the mud?"

"No stranger than bats making statues," Luet retorted. "And there's milk slobbering down your chin."

"Well, there's honey on the tip of your nose."

"Well, there's a big ugly growth on the front of your head—oh, no, that's your—"

"My face, I know. Finish the dream."

"I made the clay soft by putting it in my mouth, so that when I—as an angel, you understand—when I made the statue it contained something of me in it. I think that's very significant."

"Oh, *quite* symbolic, yes." Hushidh's tone was playful, but Luet knew she was listening carefully.

"And the statues weren't of people or angels or anything else. There were faces on them sometimes, but they weren't portraits or even *things*. The statues just took the shape that we needed them to take. No two of them were alike, yet I knew that at this moment, the statue I was making was the only possible statue I could make. Does that make sense?"

"It's a dream, it doesn't have to."

"But if it's a *true* dream, then it *must* make sense."

"Eventually, anyway," said Hushidh. Then she lifted another gloppy spoonful of bread and milk to her mouth.

"When we were done," said Luet, "we took them to a high rock and put them in the sun to dry, and then we flew around and around, and everyone looked at each other's statues. Then the angels flew off and now I wasn't with them anymore, I wasn't an angel, I was just there, watching the rocks where the statues stood, and the sun went down and in the dark—"

"You could see in the dark?"

"I could in my *dream*," said Luet. "Anyway, in the nighttime these giant rats came, and each one took one of the statues and carried it down, into holes in the ground, all the way to deep warrens and burrows, and each rat that had stolen a statue gave it to another rat and then together they gnawed at it, wet it down with their spit and rubbed it all over themselves. Covered themselves with the clay. I was so angry, Hushidh. These beautiful statues, and they wrecked them, turned them back into mud and rubbed it—even into their private parts, *everywhere*."

"Lovers of beauty," said Hushidh.

"I'm serious. It broke my heart."

"So what does it mean?" asked Hushidh. "Who do the angels represent, and who are the rats?"

"I don't know. Usually the meaning is obvious, when the Oversoul sends a dream."

"So maybe it was just a dream."

"I don't think so. It was so different and so clear, and I remember it so forcefully. Shuya, I think it's perhaps the most important dream I've ever had."

"Too bad nobody can understand it. Maybe it's one of those prophecies that everybody understands after it's all over and it's too late to do anything about it."

"Maybe Aunt Rasa can interpret it."

Hushidh made a skeptical face. "She's not at her best at the moment."

Secretly Luet was relieved that she wasn't the only one to notice that Rasa wasn't making the best decisions of her life right now. "So maybe I *won't* tell her, then."

Suddenly Hushidh smiled her tight little smile that showed she was really pleased with herself. "You want to hear a wild guess?" she said.

Luet nodded, then began taking huge bites of her long-ignored bread as she listened.

"The angels are the women of Basilica," said Hushidh. "All these millennia here in this city, we've shaped a society that is delicate and fine, and we've made it out of a part of ourselves, the way the bats in your dream made their statues out of spit. And now we've put our works to dry, and in the darkness our enemies are going to come and steal what we've made. But they're so stupid they don't even understand that they're statues. They look at them and all they see are blobs of dried mud. So they wet it down and wallow in it and they're so *proud* because they've got all the works of Basilica, but in fact they have *nothing* of Basilica at all."

"That's very good," said Luet, in awe.

"I think so, too," said Hushidh.

"So who are our enemies?"

"It's simple," said Hushidh. "Men are."

"No, that's *too* simple," said Luet. "Even though this is a city of women, the men who enter Basilica contribute as much as the women do to the works of beauty we make. They're part of the community, even if they can't own land or stay inside the walls without being married to a woman."

"I was sure it meant men the moment you said they were giant rats."

The cook chortled over the stew she was making for dinner.

"Someone else," insisted Luet. "Maybe Potokgavan."

"Maybe just Gaballufix's men," said Hushidh. "The tolchoks, and then his soldiers in those horrible masks."

"Or maybe something yet to come," said Luet. And then,

in despair. "Or maybe nothing to do with Basilica at all. Who can tell? But that was my dream."

"It doesn't exactly tell us where we should have sent Smelost."

Luet shrugged. "Maybe the Oversoul thought we had brains enough to figure that out on our own."

"Was she right?" asked Hushidh.

"I doubt it," said Luet. "Sending him to the Gorayni was a mistake."

"I wouldn't know," said Hushidh. "Eating your bread dry—now *that's* a mistake."

"Not for those of us who have teeth," said Luet. "We don't have to sog our bread to make it edible."

Which led to a mock argument that got silly and loud enough that the cook threw them out of the kitchen, which was fine because they were finished with breakfast anyway. It felt good, for just a few minutes, to play together like children. For they knew that, for good or ill, they would both be involved in the events that were swirling in and near Basilica. Not that they wanted to be involved, really. But their gifts made them important to the city, and so they would do their best to serve.

Luet dutifully went to the city council and told her dream, which was carefully recorded and handed over to the wise women to be studied for meanings and portents. Luet told them how Hushidh had interpreted it, and they thanked her kindly and as much as told her that having dreams was fine—any idiot child could do *that*—but it took a real expert to figure out what they meant.

IN KHLAM, AND NOT IN A DREAM

It was a hot dry storm from the northwest, which meant it came across the desert, not a breath of moisture in it, just sand and grit and, so they said, the ground-up bones of men and animals that had got caught in the storm a thousand kilometers away, the dust of their flesh, and, if you listened closely, the howling of their souls as the wind bore them on and on, never letting go of them, either to heaven or to hell. The mountains blocked the worst of the storm, but still the tents of Moozh's army shuddered and staggered, the flaps of the tents snapped, the banners danced crazily, and now and then one of them would whip away from the ground and tumble, pole and all, along a dirty trampled avenue between the tents, some poor soldier often trying to chase it down.

Moozh's large tent also shuddered in the wind, despite its blessing from the Imperator. Of course the blessing was completely efficacious . . . but Moozh also made sure the stakes were pounded in hard and deep. He sat at the table by candlelight, gazing wistfully at the map spread out before him. It showed all the lands along the western shores of the Earthbound Sea. In the north, the lands of the Gorayni were outlined in red, the lands of the Imperator, who was of course the incarnation of God on Earth and therefore entitled to rule over all mankind, etc. etc. In his mind's eye Moozh traced the unmarked boundaries of nations that were at least as old as the Gorayni, and some of them much older, with proud histories—nations that now did not exist, that could not even be remembered, because to speak their names was treason, and to reach out and trace their old boundary on this map would be death.

But Moozh did not have to trace the boundary. He knew the borders of his homeland of Pravo Gollossa, the land of the Sotchitsiya, his own tribe. They had come across the desert from the north a thousand years before the Gorayni, but once they had been of the same stock, with the same language. But in the lush well-watered valleys of the Skrezhet Mountains the Sotchitsiya had settled down, had ceased both wandering and war, and become a nation of free men. They learned from the people around them. Not the Ploshudu or the Khlami or the Izmennikoy, for they were tough mountain people with no culture but hunger and muscle and a will to live despite all. Rather the Sotchitsiya, the people of Pravo Gollossa, had learned from the traders who came to them from Seggidugu, from Ulye, from the Cities of the Plain. And above all the caravanners from Basilica, with their strange songs and seeds, images in glass and cunning tools, impossible fabrics that changed colors with the hours of the day, and their poems and stories that taught the Sotchitsiya how wise and refined men and women spoke and thought and dreamed and lived.

That was the glory of Pravo Gollossa, for it was from these caravanners that they learned of the idea of a council, with decisions made by the vote of councilors who had themselves been chosen by the voice of the citizens. But it was also from these Basilican caravanners that they learned of a city ruled by women, where men could not even own land . . . and yet the city did not collapse from the incompetence of women to rule, and the men did not rebel and conquer the city, and women were able not only to vote but also to divorce their husbands at the end of every year and marry someone else if they chose. The constant pressure of those ideas wore down the Sotchitsiya and turned the once-strong warriors and rulers of the tribe into woman-hearted fools, so that in Moozh's great grandfather's day they gave the vote to women, and elected women to rule over them.

That was when the Gorayni came, for they knew that the Sotchitsiya had at last become women in their hearts, and so were no longer worthy to be free. The Gorayni brought their great army to the border, and the women of the council—as many males as females, but all women nonetheless—voted not to fight, but rather to accept Gorayni overlordship if the Gorayni would allow them to rule themselves in all but military matters. It was an unspeakable surrender, the final castration of the Sotchitsiya, their humiliation before all the world, and Moozh's own great-grandfather was the delegate who worked out the terms of their surrender with the Gorayni.

For fifty years the agreement stood—the Sotchitsiya governed themselves. But gradually the Gorayni military began to declare more and more of Sotchitsiya affairs to be military matters, until finally the council was nothing but a bunch of frightened old men and women who had to petition the Imperator for permission to pee. Only then did any of the Sotchitsiya remember their manhood. They threw out the women who ruled them and declared themselves to be a tribe again, desert wanderers again, and swore to fight the Gorayni to the last man. It took three days for the Gorayni to defeat these brave but untrained rebels on the battlefield, and another year to hunt them down and kill them all in the mountains. After that there was no pretense that the Sotchitsiya had any rights at all. It was forbidden to speak the Sotchitsiya dialect; children who were heard speaking it had the privilege of watching their parents' tongues cut off, one centimeter for each offense. Only a few of the Sotchitsiya remembered their own language anymore, most of them old and many of them tongueless.

But Moozh knew. Moozh had the Sotchitsiya language in his heart. Even though he was the most successful, the most dangerous of the Imperator's generals, in his heart he knew his true language was Sotchitsiya, not Gorayni. And even though his many victories in battle had brought the great coastal nations of Uslavat and Ulye under the Imperator's dominion, even though his clever strategy had brought the thorny mountain kingdoms of Plosh and Khlam to obedience without a single pitched battle, Moozh's secret was that he loathed the Imperator and defied him in his heart.

For Moozh knew that the Imperator truly *was* God in the flesh, for better than most, Moozh could feel the power of God trying to control him. He had felt it first in his youth, when he sought a place in the Gorayni army. God didn't speak to him when he learned to be a strong soldier, his arms and thighs heavy with muscle, able a drive a battleaxe through the spine of his enemy and cleave him in half. But when Moozh imagined himself as an officer, as a general, leading armies, then came that heavy stupid feeling that made him want to forget such dreams. Moozh understood— God knew his hatred of the Imperator, and so was determined that one like Moozh would never have power beyond the strength of his arms.

But Moozh refused to capitulate. Whenever he sensed that God was making him forget an idea, he clung to it—he wrote it down and memorized it, he made a poem of it in the Sotchitsiya language so he could never forget. And thus, bit by bit, he built up in his heart his own rules of warfare, guided every step of the way by God, for whatever God tried to prevent him from thinking, that was what he knew that he must think of, deeply and well.

This secret defiance of God was what brought Moozh out of the ranks and made him a captain when his regiment was in danger of being overrun by the pirates of Revis. All the other officers had been killed, yet when Moozh thought of taking command and leading the few men near him in a counterattack against the flank of the uncontrolled, victorious Reviti, he felt that dullness of mind that always told him that God did not want him to pursue the idea. So he shouted down the voice of God and led his men in a foolhardy charge, which so terrified the pirates that they broke and ran, and the rest of the Gorayni took heart and followed Moozh in hot pursuit of them until they caught them on the riverbank and killed them all and burned their ships. They had brought Moozh for a triumph of the city of Gollod itself, where the Imperator had rubbed the camel-milk butter into his hair and declared him a hero of the Gorayni. But in his heart, Moozh knew that God had no doubt planned to have some loyal son of the Gorayni achieve the victory. Well, too bad for the Imperator—if the incarnation of God didn't understand that he had just oiled the hair of his enemy, then so much the worse for him.

Step by step Moozh had risen in command, until now he was at the head of a vast army. Most of his men were quartered in Ulye now, it was true, for the Imperator had commanded that they delay the attack against Nakavalnu until calm weather a month from now, when the chariots could be used to good advantage. Here in Khlam he had only a regiment, but that was all that was needed. Step by step he would lead the Gorayni onward, taking nation after nation along the coast until all the cities had fallen. Then he would face the armies of Potokgavan.

And then what? Some days Moozh thought that he would take his vengeance by orchestrating a complete and utter defeat for the armies of the Gorayni. He would gather all their military might into one place and then contrive to have them all slaughtered, himself among them. Then, with the Gorayni broken and Potokgavan having their will throughout the plain—then the Sotchitsiya would rise up and claim their freedom.

On other days, though, Moozh imagined that he would destroy the army of Potokgavan, so that along the entire western coast of the Earthbound Sea there was no rival to contest the supremacy of the Gorayni. Then he would stand before the Imperator, and when the Imperator reached out to smear the camelmilk butter on his hair, Moozh would slice off his his head with a buck knife, then take the camelhump cap and put it on his own head, and declare that the empire that had been won by a Sotchitsiya would now be ruled by the Sotchitsiya. *He* would be Imperator, and instead of being the incarnation of God he would be the enemy of God, and the Sotchitsiya would be known as the greatest of men, and no longer as a nation of women.

These were his thoughts as he studied the map, while the storm flung sand at his tent and tried to tear it out of the ground.

Suddenly he came alert. The sound had changed. It wasn't just the wind; someone was scratching at his tent. Who would be so stupid as to walk about in this weather? He felt a sudden stab of fear—could it be the assassin sent by the Imperator, to prevent him from the treachery that God surely knew was in his heart?

But when he untied the flap and opened it, no assassin came in with a flurry of sand and hot wind. Instead it was Plod, his dear friend and comrade in arms, and another man, a stranger, in military garb that Moozh did not recognize.

Plod himself fastened the tent closed again—it would have been improper for Moozh to do it, with a junior officer present who could do it for him. So Moozh had a few moments to study the stranger. He was no soldier, not really—his breastplate was sturdy, his blade sharp, his clothing was fine, and he bore himself like a man. But his skin was soft-looking and his muscles lacked the hardness of a man who has wielded a sword in battle. He was the kind of soldier who stood guard at a palace or a toll road, bullying the common people but never having to face a charging horde of enemies, never having to run behind a chariot, hacking to death any who escaped the blades that whirred on the hubs of the chariot wheels.

"What portal do you guard?" asked Moozh.

The man looked startled, and he glanced back at Plod.

Plod only laughed. "No one told him anything, poor man. Did you think you could face General Vozmuzhalnoy Vozmozhno and keep anything secret from his eyes?"

"My name is Smelost," said the soft soldier, "and I bring a letter from Lady Rasa of Basilica."

He spoke the name as though Moozh should have heard of it. That's how these city people were, thinking that fame in their city must mean fame all over the world.

Moozh reached out and took the letter from him. Of course it was not written in the block alphabet of Gorayni—which they had stolen from the Sotchitsiya centuries ago. Instead it was the flowery vertical cursive of Basilica. But Moozh was an educated man. He could read it easily.

"It seems this man is our friend, dear Plod," said Moozh. "His life isn't safe in Basilica because he helped an assassin escape—but the assassin was *also* our friend, since he killed a man named Gaballufix who was in favor of Basilica forming an alliance with Potokgavan and leading the Cities of the Plain in war against us."

"Ah," said Plod.

"To think we never guessed how many dear and tender friends we had in Basilica," said Moozh.

Plod laughed.

Smelost looked more than a little ill at ease.

"Sit down," said Moozh. "You're among friends. No harm will come to you now. Find him some ale to drink, will you, Plod? He may be a common soldier, but he brings us a letter from a fine lady who has nothing but love and concern for the Imperator."

Plod unhooked a flagon from the back tentpole and gave it to Smelost, who looked at it in puzzlement.

Moozh laughed and took the flagon out of Smelost's hands and showed him how to rest it on his arm, tip it up, and let the stream of ale fall into his mouth. "No fine glasses for us in this army, my friend. You're not among the ladies of Basilica now."

"I knew that I was not," said Smelost.

"This letter is so cryptic, my friend," said Moozh. "Surely you can tell us more."

"Not much, I fear," said Smelost, swallowing a mouthful of ale. It was far sweeter than beer, and Moozh could see that he didn't like it much. Well, that hardly mattered, as long as Smelost got enough of the drug concealed in it that he'd speak freely. "I left before anything had come clear." He was lying, of course, thinking that he ought not to say more than Lady Rasa had said.

But soon Smelost overcame his reticence and told Moozh far more than he ever meant to. But Moozh was careful to pretend that he already knew most of it, so that Smelost would not feel he had betrayed any secrets when he thought back on the conversation and how much he had told.

There was obviously much confusion in Basilica at the moment, but the parts of the picture that mattered to Moozh were very clear. Two parties, one for alliance with Potokgavan, one against it, had been struggling for control of the city. Now the leaders of both parties were dead, killed on the same night, possibly by the same assassin, but, in Smelost's opinion, probably not. Accusations of murder were flying wildly; a weak man now controlled one group of hired soldiers who would now wander the streets uncontrolled, while the official city guard was under suspicion because this man, Smelost, had let the suspected assassin sneak out of the city two nights ago.

"What should we expect of a city of women?" said Moozh, when the story was done. "Of course there's confusion. Women are always confused when the violence begins."

Smelost looked at him warily. That was the sweet thing

about the drug that Plod had given him—the victim was quite capable of believing that he was still being clever and deceptive, even as he poured out his heart on every subject. Moozh, of course, had immunized himself to the effects of the drug years ago, which was why he had no qualms about taking a mouthful of ale from the same flagon. He was also sure that Plod had no idea that Moozh was immune, and more than once he had suspected that Plod had given him some of the drug, whereupon Moozh always made a point of sharing a few harmless but indiscreet-sounding revelations— usually just his personal opinion of a few other officers. Never anything incriminating. Just enough to let Plod think the drug had worked its will on him.

"Oh, you know what I mean," said Moozh. "Nothing against the women, but they can't help their own biology, can they? It's the way they are—when the violence begins, they must rush to a male to find protection, or they're lost, wouldn't you say?"

Smelost smiled wanly. "You don't know the women of Basilica, then."

"Oh, but I do," said Moozh. "I know *all* women, and the women I don't know, Plod knows—isn't that right, Plod?"

"Oh, yes," said Plod, smiling.

Smelost glowered a little but said nothing.

"The women of Basilica are frightened right now, aren't they? Frightened and acting hastily. They don't like these soldiers running the streets. They fear what will happen if no strong man is there to control them—but they fear just as much what will happen if a strong man *does* come. Who knows how things will turn out, once the violence starts? There's blood on the street of Basilica. A man's head has drunk the dust of the street through both halves of his neck, as we say in Gollod. There's fear in every womanly heart in Basilica, yes, there is, and you know it."

Smelost shrugged. "Of course they're afraid. Who wouldn't be?"

"A *man* wouldn't be," said Moozh. "A *man* would smell the opportunity. A man would say, When others are afraid then anyone who speaks boldly has a chance to lead.

Anyone who makes decisions, anyone who *acts* can become the focus of authority, the hope of the desperate, the strength of the weak, the soul of the spiritless. A *man* would *act*."

"Act," Smelost echoed.

"Act *boldly*," said Plod.

"And yet . . . you have come to us with a letter from a *woman* pleading for protection." Moozh smiled and shrugged.

Smelost immediately tried to defend himself. "Was I supposed to stand trial for having done what I knew was right?"

"Of course not. What—to be tried by women?" Moozh looked at Plod and laughed; Plod took the cue and joined in. "For acting as a man must act, boldly, with courage— no, you shouldn't stand trial for *that*."

"So I came here," said Smelost.

"For protection. So *you* could be safe, while your city is in fear."

Smelost rose to his feet. "I didn't come here to be insulted."

In an instant Plod's blade was poised at Smelost's throat. "When the General of the Imperator is seated, all men sit or they are treated as assassins."

Smelost gingerly lowered himself back into his chair.

"Forgive my dearest friend Plod," said Moozh. "I know you meant no harm. After all, you came to *us* to be *safe,* not to start a war!" Moozh laughed, staring in Smelost's eyes all the time, until Smelost also forced himself to laugh.

Smelost clearly hated it, to be forced to laugh at himself for seeking protection instead of acting like a man.

"But perhaps I've misunderstood you," said Moozh. "Perhaps you didn't come, as this letter says, just for yourself. Perhaps you have a plan in mind, some way that you can help your city, some strategem whereby you can ease the fears of the women of Basilica and keep them safe from the chaos that threatens them."

"I have no plan," said Smelost.

"Ah," said Moozh. "Or perhaps you don't yet trust us enough to tell it to us." Moozh looked sad. "I understand.

We're strangers, and this is your city at stake, a city that you love more than life itself. Besides, what you would need to ask of us is far greater than a common soldier would ordinarily dare to ask a general of the Gorayni. So I will not press you now. Go—Plod will show you to a tent where you can drink and sleep, and when this storm dies down you can bathe and eat, and by then perhaps you'll feel confident enough of me to tell me what you want us to do, to save your beautiful and beloved city from anarchy."

As soon as Moozh finished talking, he gave a subtle hand signal and then leaned his elbow on the arm of his chair, pretending to be a bit saddened by Smelost's reluctance to help. Plod caught the hand signal, of course, and immediately rushed Smelost out of the tent and back out into the storm.

As soon as they were outside, Moozh leapt to his feet and stood hunched over the table, studying the map. Basilica—so far to the south, but in the highest part of the mountains, right up against the desert, so that it would be possible to get there from here through the mountains. In two days, if he took only a few hundred men and pressed them hard. Two days, and he could easily be in possession of the greatest city of the Western Shore, the city whose caravanners have made their language the trading argot of every city and nation from Potokgavan to Gorayni. Never mind that Basilica had no meaningful army. What mattered was how it would seem to the Cities of the Plain—and to Potokgavan. *They* would not know how few and weak the Gorayni army would be. They would know only that the great General Vozmuzhalnoy Vozmozhno had stolen a march, conquered a city of legend and mystery, and now, instead of being a hundred and fifty kilometers north, beyond Seggidugu, now he loomed over them, could watch their every move from the towers of Basilica.

It would be a devastating blow. Knowing that Vozmuzhalnoy Vozmozhno would watch their fleet arrive and have plenty of time to bring his men down from Basilica and slaughter their army as it tried to land, Potokgavan would not dare to send an expeditionary force to the Cities of the Plain.

And as for the cities themselves, they would surrender one by one, and soon Seggidugu would find itself surrounded, with no hope of succor from Potokgavan. They would make peace on any terms they could get. There probably wouldn't even be a battle—complete victory, at no cost, all because Basilica was in chaos and this soldier had come to tell Vozmuzhalnoy Vozmozhno of his glorious opportunity.

The tent flap reopened, and Plod came back in. "The storm is dying down," he said.

"Very good," said Moozh.

"What was all that about?" said Plod.

"What?"

"That nonsense you were saying to that Basilican soldier."

Moozh could not imagine what Plod was talking about. Basilican soldier? He had never seen a Basilican soldier in his life.

But Plod glanced at one of the chairs, and now Moozh vaguely remembered that not long ago *someone* had sat in that chair. Someone . . . a Basilican solider? That would be important—how could he have forgotten?

I didn't forget, thought Moozh. I didn't forget. God has spoken, God has tried to make me stupid, but I refuse. I will not be forced into obedience.

"How do *you* assess the situation?" he asked. It would never do to let Plod think that Moozh was actually confused or forgetful.

"Basilica is far away," said Plod. "We can give this man sanctuary or kill him or send him back, it hardly matters. What is Basilica to us?"

Poor fool, thought Moozh. That's why you're merely the dear friend of the general, and not the general yourself, though I know you long to be. Moozh knew what Basilica was. It was the city of women whose influence had castrated his ancestors and cost them their freedom and their honor. It was also the great citadel poised above the Cities of the Plain. If Moozh could possess it, he wouldn't have to fight a single battle—his enemies would collapse before him. Was this the plan that he had had before, the one that God was trying to make him forget?

"Write this down," said Moozh.

Plod opened his computer and began to press the keys to record Moozh's words.

"Whoever is master of Basilica is master of the Cities of the Plain."

"But Moozh, Basilica has never exercised hegemony over those cities."

"Because it's a city of women," said Moozh. "If it were ruled by a man with an army, that would be a different story."

"We could never get there to take it," said Plod. "All of Seggidugu lies between us and Basilica."

Moozh looked at the map and another part of his plan came back to his mind. "A desert march."

"During the month of western storms!" cried Plod. "The men would refuse to obey!"

"In the mountains there's shelter. There are plenty of mountain roads."

"Not for an army," said Plod.

"Not for a *large* army," said Moozh, making up the plan as he went along.

"You could never hold Basilica against Potokgavan with the size army you could bring," said Plod.

Moozh studied the map for a moment longer. "But Potokgavan will never come, not if we already hold Basilica. *They* won't know how large an army we have, but they *will* know that we can see the whole coastline from there. Where would they dare to bring their fleet, knowing we could see them from far off and greet them at the shore, to cut them apart as they land?"

Plod finished typing, then studied the map himself. "There's merit in that," he said.

Why is there merit in it? Moozh asked silently. I haven't the faintest idea why I have this plan, except that a Basilican soldier apparently came here. What did he tell me? Why does this plan have merit?

"And with the present chaos in Basilica, you could probably take the city."

Chaos in Basilica. Good. So I wasn't wrong—the Basilican soldier apparently let me know of an opportunity.

"Yes," said Plod. "We have the perfect excuse for doing it, too. We aren't coming to invade, but rather to save the people of Basilica from the mercenary soldiers who are wandering their streets."

Mercenary soldiers? The idea was absurd—why would Basilica have mercenary soldiers running loose? Had there been a war? God had never made Moozh so forgetful that he couldn't remember a whole war!

"And the immediate provocation—the murders. The blood was already flowing—we had to come, to stop the bloodshed. Yes, that will be plenty of justification for it. No one can criticize us for attacking the city of women, if we come to save them from blood in the streets."

So that's my plan, thought Moozh. A very good one it is. Even God can't stop me from carrying it out. "Write it up, Plod, and have my aides draw up detailed orders for a thousand men to march in four columns through the mountains. Only three days' worth of supplies—the men can carry it on their backs."

"Three days!" said Plod. "And what if something goes wrong?"

"Knowing they have but three days' worth of food, dear Plod, the men will march very fast indeed, and they will allow nothing to delay them."

"What if the situation has changed at Basilica, when we arrive? What if we meet stout resistance? The walls of Basilica are high and thick, and chariots are useless in that terrain."

"Then it's a good thing we'll bring no chariots, isn't it? Except perhaps one, for my triumphal entry into the city—in the name of the Imperator, of course."

"Still, they might resist, and we'll arrive with scarcely any food to spare. We can't exactly besiege them!"

"We'll have no need to besiege them. We have only to ask them to open the gates, and the gates will open."

"Why?"

"Because I say so," said Moozh. "When have I been wrong before?"

Plod shook his head. "Never, my dear friend and beloved general. But by the time we get the Imperator's permission to go there, the chaos in the streets of Basilica may well have been settled, and it will take a much larger army than a thousand men to force the issue."

Moozh looked at him in surprise. "Why would we wait for the Imperator's permission?"

"Because the Imperator forbade you to make any attack until the stormy season is over."

"On the contrary," said Moozh. "The Imperator forbade me to attack Nakavalnu and Izmennik. I am not attacking them. I'm passing them by on their left flank, and marching as swift as horses through the mountains to Basilica, where again I will not attack anybody, but will rather enter the city of Basilica to restore order in the name of the Imperator. None of this violates any order of the Imperator."

Plod's face darkened. "You are interpreting the words of the Imperator, my general, and that is something only the intercessor has the right to do."

"Every soldier and every officer must interpret the orders he is given. I was sent to these southlands in order to conquer the entire western shore of the Earthbound Sea— that was the command the Imperator gave to me, and to me alone. If I failed to seize this great opportunity that God has given me"—ha!—"then I would be disobedient indeed."

"My dear friend, noblest general of the Gorayni, I beg you not to attempt this. The intercessor will not see it as obedience but as insubordination."

"Then the intercessor is no true servant of the Imperator."

Plod immediately bowed his head. "I see that I have spoken too boldly."

Moozh knew at once that this meant Plod intended to tell the intercessor everything and try to stop him. When Plod meant to obey, he did not put on this great pretense of obedience.

"Give me your computer," said Moozh. "I will write the orders myself."

"Don't shame me," said Plod in dismay. "I must write them, or I have failed in my duty to you."

"You will sit with me here," said Moozh, "and watch as I write the orders."

Plod flung himself to his knees on the carpets. "Moozh, my friend, I'd rather you kill me than shame me like this."

"I knew that you didn't intend to obey me," said Moozh. "Don't lie and say you did."

"I meant to delay," said Plod. "I meant to give you time to reconsider. Hoping that you'd realize the grave danger of opposing the Imperator, especially so soon after you dreamed a dream that was contemptuous of his holy person."

It took a moment for Moozh to remember what Plod was referring to; then his rage turned cold and hard indeed. "Who would know of that dream, except myself and my friend?"

"Your friend loved you enough to tell the dream to the intercessor," said Plod, "lest your soul be in danger of destruction without your knowing it."

"Then my friend must love me indeed," said Moozh.

"I do," said Plod. "With all my heart. I love you more than any man or woman on this Earth, excepting God alone, and his holy incarnation."

Moozh regarded his dearest friend with icy calm. "Use your computer, my friend, and call the intercessor to my tent. Have him stop on the way and bring the Basilican soldier with him."

"I'll go and get them," said Plod.

"Call them by computer."

"But what if the intercessor isn't using his computer right now?"

"Then we'll wait until he does." Moozh smiled. "But he *will* be using it, won't he?"

"Perhaps," said Plod. "How would I know?"

"Call them. I want the intercessor to hear my interrogation of the Basilican soldier. Then he'll know that we must go now, and not wait for word from the Imperator."

Plod nodded. "Very wise, my friend. I should have known that you wouldn't flout the will of the Imperator. The intercessor will listen to you, and *he'll* decide."

"We'll decide *together*," said Moozh.

"Of course." He pressed the keys; Moozh made no effort to watch him, but he could see the words in the air over the computer well enough to know that Plod was sending a quick, straightforward request to the intercessor.

"Alone," said Moozh. "If we decide not to act, I want no rumors to spread about Basilica."

"I already asked him to come alone," said Plod.

They waited, talking all the time of other things. Of campaigns in years past. Of officers who had served with them. Of women they had known.

"Have you ever *loved* a woman?" asked Moozh.

"I have a wife," said Plod.

"And you love her?"

Plod thought a moment. "When I'm with her. She's the mother of my sons."

"I have no sons," said Moozh. "No children at all, that I know of. No woman who has pleased me for more than a night."

"None?" asked Plod.

Moozh flushed with embarrassment, realizing what Plod was remembering. "I never loved *her*," he said. "I took her—as an act of piety."

"Once is an act of piety," said Plod, chuckling. "Two months one year, and then another month three years later—that's more than piety, that's *sainthood*."

"She was nothing to me," said Moozh. "I took her only for the sake of God." And it was true, though not in the way Plod understood it. The woman had appeared as if out of nowhere, dirty and naked, and called Moozh by name. Everyone knew such women were from God. But Moozh knew that when he thought of taking her, God sent him that stupor that meant it was *not* God's will for Moozh to proceed. So Moozh proceeded anyway, and kept the woman—bathed her, and clothed her, and treated her as tenderly as a wife. All the while he felt God's anger boiling at the back of his mind, and he laughed at God. He kept the woman with him until she disappeared, as suddenly as she had come, leaving all her fine clothing behind, taking nothing, not even food, not even water.

"So that wasn't love," said Plod. "God honors you for your sacrifice, then, I'm sure!" Plod laughed again, and for good fellowship Moozh also joined in.

They were still laughing when there came a scratching at the tent, and Plod leapt to open it. The intercessor came in first, which was his duty—and an expression of his faith in God, since the intercessor always left himself available to be stabbed in the back, if God did not protect him. Then a stranger came in. Moozh had no memory of ever having seen the man before. By his garb he was a soldier of a fine city; by his body he was a soft soldier, a gate guard rather than a fighting man; by his familiar nod, Moozh knew that this must be the Basilican soldier, and he must indeed have spoken with him, and left the conversation on friendly terms.

The intercessor sat first, and then Moozh; only then could the others take their places.

"Let me see your blade," Moozh said to the Basilican soldier. "I want to see what kind of steel you have in Basilica."

Warily the Basilican arose from his seat, watching Plod all the while. Vaguely Moozh remembered Plod with a blade at the Basilican's throat; no wonder the man was wary now! With two fingers the man drew his short sword from its sheath, and handed it, hilt first, to Moozh.

It was a city sword, for close work, not a great hewing sword for the battlefield. Moozh tested the blade against the skin of his own arm, cutting only slightly, but enough to draw a line of blood. The man winced to see it. Soft. Soft.

"I've thought about what you said, sir," the Basilican said.

Ah. So I gave him something to think about.

"And I can see that my city needs your help. But who am I to ask for it, or even to know what help would be right or sufficient? I'm only a gate guard; it's only the sheerest chance that I got caught up in these great affairs."

"You love your city, don't you?" asked Moozh, for now he knew what he must have told the man. "I *am* sharp enough even on my bad days, Moozh thought with some satisfaction. Sharp enough to lay God-proof plans.

"Yes, I do." Tears had suddenly come to the man's eyes. "Forgive me, but someone else asked me that, just before I left Basilica. Now I know by this omen that you are a true servant of the Oversoul, and I can trust you."

Moozh gazed steadily into the man's eyes, to show him that trust was appropriate indeed.

"Come to Basilica, sir. Come with an army. Restore order in the streets, and drive out the mercenaries. Then the women of Basilica will have no more fear."

Moozh nodded wisely. "An eloquent and noble request, which in my heart I long to fulfil. But I am a servant of the Imperator, and you must explain the situation in your city to the intercessor here, who is the eyes and ears and heart of the Imperator in our camp." As he spoke, Moozh rose to his feet, facing the intercessor, and bowed. Behind him he could hear Plod and the Basilican soldier also standing and bowing.

Surely Plod is clever enough to know what I plan to do, thought Moozh with a thrill of fear. Surely his knife is even now out of its sheath, to be buried in my back. Surely he knows that if he does not do this, the Basilican blade I hold in my hands will snake out and take his head clean off his shoulders as I rise.

But Plod was not that clever, and so in a moment his blood gouted and spattered across the tent as his body collapsed, his head flopping about on the end of the half-severed spine.

Moozh's blow had been so quick, so smooth, that neither the Basilican nor the intercessor quite understood how Plod came to be so abruptly dead. That gave Moozh plenty of time to drive the Basilican blade upward under the intercessor's ribs, finding his heart before the intercessor could speak a word or even raise himself from his chair.

Then Moozh turned to the trembling Basilican.

"What is your name, soldier?"

"Smelost, sir. As I told you. I've lied about nothing, sir."

"I know you haven't. Neither have I. These men were determined to stop me from coming to the aid of your city. That's why I brought them here together. If you wanted me to help you, I had to kill them first."

"Whatever you say, sir."

"No, not whatever I say. Only the truth, Smelost. These men were both spies set to watch every move I made, to hear every word I spoke, and judge my loyalty to the Imperator constantly. This one"—he pointed at Plod—"interpreted a dream I had as a sign of disloyalty, and told the intercessor. It would only have been a matter of time before they reported me and I lost my command, and then who would have come to save Basilica?"

"But how will you explain their deaths?" asked Smelost.

Moozh said nothing.

Smelost waited. Then he looked again at the bodies. "I see," he said. "The blade that killed them was mine."

"How much do you love your city?" asked Moozh.

"With all my heart."

"More than life?" asked Moozh.

Gravely Smelost nodded. There was fear in his eyes, but he did not tremble.

"If my soldiers think I killed Plod and the intercessor, they will tear me to pieces. But if they think—no, if they *know* that *you* did it, and I killed you for it—then they will follow me in righteous indignation. I'll tell them that you were one of the mercenaries. I will besmirch your name. I will say you were a traitor to Basilica, trying to prevent me from going to the city's aid. But because they believe those lies about you, they will follow me there and we will save your city."

Smelost smiled. "It seems that my fate is to be thought a worse traitor the better I serve my city."

"It is a terrible day when a man must choose between

being thought loyal, and being loyal in fact, but that day has come to you."

"Tell me what to do."

Moozh almost wept with admiration for the courage and honor of the man, as he explained the simple play they would put on. If I did not serve a higher cause, thought Moozh, I would be too ashamed to deceive a man of such honor as yourself. But for the sake of Pravo Gollossa I will do any terrible thing.

A moment later, in a lull in the windstorm, Moozh and Smelost both began to bellow, and Moozh let out a high scream that witnesses would later swear was the death cry of the intercessor. Then, as soldiers stumbled out of their tents, they saw Smelost, already bleeding from a wound in his thigh, lurch from the general's tent, carrying a short sword dripping with blood. "For Gaballufix! Death to the Imperator!"

The name of Gaballufix meant nothing to the Gorayni soldiers, though soon enough it would be rich with meaning. What they cared about was the latter part of Smelost's shout—death to the Imperator. No one could say such a thing in a Gorayni camp without being flayed alive.

Before anyone could reach him, though, the general himself staggered from the tent, bleeding from his arm and holding his head where he must have been struck a blow. The general—the great Vozmuzhalnoy Vozmozhno, called Moozh whenever they thought he could not hear—held a battle-ax in his left arm—his left, not his right!—and struck downward into the base of the assassin's neck, cleaving him to the heart. He should not have done it; everyone knew he should have let the man be taken and tortured to punish him. But then, to their horror, the general sank to his knees—the general with ice in his veins instead of blood—he sank to his knees and wept bitterly, crying out from the depths of his soul, "Plodorodnuy, my friend, my heart, my life! Ah, Plod! Ah, Plod, God should have taken me and left you!"

It was a grief both glorious and terrible to behold, and without speaking a word openly about it, the soldiers who heard his keening resolved to tell no one of his blasphemous suggestion that perhaps God might have ordered the world improperly. When they entered the tent they understood perfectly why Moozh had forgotten himself and killed the assassin with his own hand, for how could any mortal man see his dearest friend and the intercessor both so cruelly murdered, and still contain his rage?

Soon the story spread through the camp that Moozh was taking a thousand fierce soldiers with him on a forced march through the mountains, to take the city Basilica and destroy the party of Gaballufix, a group of men so daring and treacherous that they had dared to send an assassin against the general of the Gorayni. Too bad for them that God so dearly loved the Gorayni that he would not permit their Moozh to be slain by treachery. Instead God had caused Moozh's heart to be filled with righteous wrath, and Basilica would soon know what it meant to have God and the Gorayni as their overlords.

THREE

PROTECTION

THE DREAM OF THE ELDEST SON

The camels had all gathered under the shade of the large palm fronds that Wetchik and his sons had woven into a roof between a group of four large trees near the stream. Elemak envied them—the shade was good there, the stream was cool, and they could catch the breeze, so the air was never as stuffy as it was inside the tents. He was done with his work for the morning, and now there was nothing useful to do during the heat of the day. Let Father and Nafai and Issib drip their sweat all over each other as they huddled around the Index of the Oversoul in Father's tent. What did the Oversoul know? It was just a computer—Nafai himself said that, in his adolescent fanatic piety—so why should Elemak bother with a conversation with a machine? It had a vast library of information . . . so what? Elemak was done with school.

So he sat in the hot shade of the southern cliff, knowing that he would have at most an hour of rest before the sun rose high enough that the shade would disappear, and he would have to move. That didn't really bother Elemak—in fact, on his caravans he had counted on that to awaken him, so that he didn't sleep overlong during the day when they rested at oases. What made him so angry that he felt it like a pain in his stomach all the time was the fact that it was all so useless. They were not traveling, they were merely waiting here in the desert—and for what? For nothing. The Oversoul said that Basilica would be destroyed, that the world of Harmony was going to collapse in war and terror. It was laughably unlikely that any such thing would happen. The world had gone forty million years without being devastated by war. Now, for the first time, two great empires were on the verge of collision, and the Oversoul was treating it as if it were some cosmic event.

I could have understood leaving Basilica, he told himself, if we had taken our fortune with us and gone to another city and started over. What was vital in the plant trade was the knowledge inside Father's and my heads, not the buildings or the hired workers. We could have been rich. Instead we're here in the desert, we lost our entire fortune to my half-brother Gaballufix, and now Nafai has murdered *him* and we can never go back to Basilica again, or if we did, we'd be poor so why bother?

Except that even poverty in Basilica would be better than this meaningless waiting out here in the desert, in this miserable little valley that barely supported the troop of baboons downstream of them. Even now he could hear them barking and hooting. Beasts that couldn't decide whether to be men or dogs. That's exactly what we are now, only we didn't even have the sense to bring mates with us when we left, so we can't even form a reasonable tribe.

Despite the arrhythmic noises of the baboons and the occasional snorting of the camels, Elemak soon slept. He woke moments later, or so it felt; he could feel the burning heat of the sun on his clothing, so he assumed that the sun had wakened him. But no, it was something else; there was a shadow moving near him. With his eyes closed he thought of where his knife was and remembered how the ground was near him. Then, with a sudden rush of movement, he was on his feet, his long knife in his hand, squinting in the bright sunlight to see where his enemy was.

"It's only me!" squeaked Zdorab.

Elemak put away his knife in disgust. "You don't come up silently when a man is asleep in the desert. You can get yourself killed that way. I assumed you were a robber."

"But I wasn't all that quiet," said Zdorab reasonably. "In fact, you were noisy yourself. Dreaming, I expect."

That bothered Elemak, that he had not slept silently. But now that Zdorab mentioned it, he remembered that he *had* dreamed, and he remembered the dream with remarkable clarity. In fact he had never had such a clear dream, not that he remembered, anyway, and it made him think. "What was I saying?" asked Elemak.

"I don't know," said Zdorab. "It was more of a mumble. I came up here because your father asked to see you. I wouldn't have disturbed you otherwise."

It was true. Zdorab was the consummate servant, invisible most of the time, but always ready to help—even when he was completely incompetent, which was usually the case here in the desert, where the skills of a treasurer were quite useless. "Thanks," said Elemak. "I'll come in a minute."

Zdorab waited for just a moment—that hesitation that all good servants acquired sooner or later, that single moment in which the master could think of something else to tell before they left. Then he was gone, shambling clumsily down the shale slope and then across the dry stony soil to Wetchik's tent.

Elemak pulled up his desert robe and peed out in the open, where the sun would evaporate his urine in moments, before too many flies could gather. Then he headed for the stream, took a drink in his cupped hand, splashed water into his face and over his head, and only then made his way to where Father and all the others were waiting.

"Well," said Elemak as he entered. "Have you learned everything the Oversoul has to teach you?"

Nafai glared at him with his typical look of disapproval. Someday Elemak knew he'd have to give Nafai the beating of his life, just to teach him not to get that expression on his face, at least not toward Elemak. He had tried to give him that beating once before, and he had learned that *next* time he'd have to do it away from Issib's chair, so the Oversoul couldn't take control of it and interfere. But for now there was nothing to be gained by letting Nafai's snottiness get under his skin; so Elemak pretended not to notice.

"We need to start hunting for meat," said Father.

Elemak immediately let his eyes half close as he thought of what that meant. They had brought enough supplies for eight or nine months—for a year, if they were careful. Yet Father was talking about needing to hunt. That could only mean that he didn't expect to get anywhere civilized within a year.

"How about shopping for groceries in the Outer Market," said Meb.

Elemak agreed wholeheartedly, but said nothing as Father lectured Meb on the impossibility of returning to Basilica any time soon. He waited until the little scene had played itself out. Poor Meb—when would he learn that it's better to remain silent except to say what will accomplish your purpose?

Only when silence had returned did Elemak speak up. "We can hunt," he said. "This is fairly lush country, for desert, and I think we could probably bring in something once a week—for a few months."

"Can you do it?" asked Father.

"Not alone," said Elemak. "If Meb and I hunt every day, we'll find something once a week."

"Nafai too," said Father.

"No!" moaned Mebbekew. "He'll just get in the way."

"I'll teach him," said Elemak. "For that matter, I don't imagine Meb will be worth anything more than Nafai at first. But you have to tell them both—when we're hunting, my word is law."

"Of course," said Father. "They'll do exactly what you tell them, and nothing more."

"I'll take each of them every other day," said Elemak. "That way I won't have to put up with their arguing with each other."

Mebbekew glared at him with loathing—so subtle, Meb, no wonder you were such a successful actor—but Nafai only looked at the carpet on the floor of the tent. What was he thinking? No doubt conniving to find some way to turn this to his advantage.

Sure enough, Nafai lifted up his head and spoke solemnly to Elemak. "Elya, I'm sorry I've given you cause to think that's what I'd do, if you took Meb and me at once. If having us both come at once would be more efficient, I can promise I'll not say a word of argument, either to you or Meb."

Just like the little sneak, to make himself look so pious and cooperative, when Elemak knew that he would be snotty and argumentative the whole way, no matter what he promised now. But Elemak said nothing, as Father quietly praised Nafai's attitude, then told him that Elya's decision would stand. They would go hunting with Elya one at a time. "You'll learn better one on one, I assure you," said Father.

At times like this Elemak almost believed that Father saw through Nafai's righteous act. But it wasn't so; in a moment Father would go off talking about what the Oversoul wanted, and then he and Nafai would be as thick as thieves.

Thinking of thieves made Elemak remember how Zdorab had wakened him a few moments ago; and thinking of waking up reminded him of his vivid dream. And it occurred to him that it might be amusing to play Nafai's game, and pretend that his dream was some vision from the Oversoul. "I was sleeping by the rocks," said Elemak into the silence, "and I dreamed a dream."

Immediately all eyes were on him, waiting. Elemak sized them up under heavy-lidded eyes; he saw the immediate joy on his father's face, and was almost ashamed of the sham he was going to play—but the consternation on Nafai's face and the utter horror on Meb's made it well worth doing. "I dreamed a dream," he said, "in which I saw all of us coming out of a large house."

"Whose house was it?" asked Nafai.

"Hush and let him tell the dream," said Father.

"A kind of house I've never seen before. And we didn't come out alone—the six of us, all six of us, each came out with a woman. And there were two other men, each with a woman as well. And many children. All of us had children."

There was silence for a long moment.

"Is that all?" asked Nafai.

Elemak said nothing, and the silence resumed.

"Elya," said Issib. "Did *I* have a wife?"

"In my dream," said Elemak, "you had a wife."

"Did you see her face?" asked Issib. "Did you know who she was?"

Now Elemak felt truly ashamed of himself, for he could see that Issib believed that this was a true vision, and for the first time in his life it occurred to him that poor Issib, palsied as he was, nevertheless yearned for a woman as any other man might yearn, and yet had no hope of finding one who would want him. In Basilica, where women had their pick of men, it would be one piss-poor specimen of womanhood who would choose a cripple like Issib for a mate. Even if he ever managed to have sex, it would be because some jaded female was curious about him— especially with his floats, that might interest some of the more adventurous ones. But to mate with him, to bear him children, to give him father's rights, no, that wouldn't happen, and Issib knew it. Which meant that by telling this dream, Elemak wasn't just manipulating Father, he was also setting Issib up for cruel disappointment. Elemak felt like shit.

"I didn't see her face," said Elemak. "It probably didn't mean anything. It was just a dream."

"It meant something," said Father.

"It means Elemak is ridiculing us," said Nafai. "He's making fun of us for having visions from the Oversoul."

"Don't call me a liar," said Elemak softly. "If I say I dreamed, I dreamed. Whether it means anything, I can't say. But I saw what I saw. Isn't that what Father said? Isn't that what *you* said? I saw what I saw."

"It meant something," said Father again. "Now an odd message I received through the Index makes perfect sense."

Oh no, thought Elemak. What have I done?

"I have thought for some time that we couldn't accomplish the Oversoul's purpose without wives. And yet where could we possibly find women who would join us here?"

Where could you find *men* who would join you here, for that matter, Father, except that you trapped your own sons into coming with you?

"But when I asked the Oversoul, the answer I got was to wait. That's all, just wait, which made no sense to me. Would wives sprout from the rocks? Would we mate with baboons?"

Elemak couldn't resist a jab. "Meb already has, from time to time."

Meb simpered.

"And now Elemak has dreamed," Father said. "I think that is what the Oversoul wanted me to wait for—Elemak's dream. For the answer to come to my eldest son, to my heir. So, Elya, you must think, you must remember—did you recognize *any* of the women in your dream?"

Father was taking this way too seriously, tying it with Elemak's status as his eldest. Elemak had been a fool to start this whole vision business today, he could see that now; how could he have forgotten that Father was willing to ruin everybody's lives for the sake of a vision? "No," said Elemak, to silence him, though it wasn't true.

"Think," said Father. "I know that you recognized at least one."

Elemak looked at him, startled. Had the old man started reading his mind now? "If the Oversoul has told you more about my dream than I know myself, then *you* tell us who they are," said Elemak.

"I know you recognized one because you said her name. If you think hard enough, you'll remember."

Elemak glanced at Zdorab, who was looking at the carpet. So, thought Elemak. When Zdorab said that he understood nothing of what I said in my sleep, it wasn't quite true. "What name?" asked Elemak.

"Eiadh," said Nafai. "Am I right?"

Elemak said nothing, but he hated Nafai for saying the name of the woman Elemak had been courting before Father dragged them out into the desert.

"It's all right," said Father. "I understand perfectly. You didn't want to tell us her name for fear that we would think that your dream was just an erotic wish for the woman you loved, and not a true dream."

Since that was exactly what Elemak thought his dream actually was, he couldn't argue with Wetchik's conclusion.

"But think, my sons. Would the Oversoul require you to choose strangers as your mates? You dreamed of Eiadh because the Oversoul intends her to be your mate," said Father. "And it makes sense, doesn't it? For you saw *me* with a mate as well, didn't you?"

"Yes," said Elemak, remembering. The dream was still *so* vivid in his mind that he could call it back, not just as a vague memory, but clearly. "Yes, and children. Young ones."

"There is only one woman I would take as my mate," said Father. "Rasa."

"She'd never leave Basilica," said Issib. "If you think she would, you don't know Mother."

"Ah," said Father. "But *I* would never have left Basilica, either, except that the Oversoul led me. Nor would Elemak and Mebbekew, except that the Oversoul brought them."

"Nor I," said Zdorab.

"Could the woman you saw in your dream, the woman who was *my* mate . . . she was Rasa, wasn't she?" asked Father.

Of course it was Rasa, but that didn't prove anything. Rasa had been Father's wife, year after year, so of course it was Rasa who would show up as his woman in Elemak's dreams. It would take no vision from the Oversoul for *that*. "Perhaps," said Elemak.

"And did you recognize any of the other women? For instance, the two other men who were strangers—could their mates have been Rasa's daughters?"

"I don't know your wife's daughters all that well," said Elemak. How far would this game have to go before he could have done with it?

"Don't be absurd," said Father. "They're your nieces, aren't they? Gaballufix's daughters."

"And one of them is famous," chimed in Meb. "Sevet, the singer—you've seen her."

"Yes," said Elemak. "The wives of the two strangers were Rasa's daughters." Of course he knew them, and their husbands, too, Vas and Obring.

"There, you see?" said Father. "The Oversoul has given you a true vision. The women you saw are all connected with Rasa. Her daughters, and Eiadh, one of the nieces of her household. I'm sure the others are all of her household, too. So this isn't some impossible dream that came to you because you had a hunger for venery, my son. This came from the Oversoul, because the Oversoul knows that to accomplish our purpose we must have wives who will bear us children. All of us."

"Well," said Elemak, "if it's really a vision, then *I'm* happy enough for the Oversoul to give me Eiadh. But I think there's a better chance of finding a falcon in a frog's mouth than of anyone *but* the Oversoul ever persuading Eiadh to come out into the desert to marry a penniless, homeless man like me, with no hope of wealth."

"You forget that the Oversoul has promised us a land of unspeakable richness," said Father.

"And you forget that we haven't found it yet," said Elemak. "We're not likely to find it, either, squatting in the desert like this."

"The Oversoul has shown us what we must do," said Father. "And as Nafai said to me before you left to seek the Index—if the Oversoul requires us to do something, he'll open a way for us to do it."

"Great idea," said Mebbekew. "Whom will Nafai kill to get us some women?"

"That's enough," said Father.

"Come on," said Mebbekew. "How else would Nafai ever get a wife, except by killing some drunk passed out on the street and stealing his blind, crippled daughter."

To Elemak's surprise, Nafai said nothing to Mebbekew's gibes. Instead, the boy got up and left the tent. So, thought Elemak. Nafai isn't entirely a child. Or else he was ashamed to have us see him cry.

"Meb," said Issib softly, "Nafai brought the Index, and you didn't."

"Oh, come on," said Mebbekew. "Can't anybody take a joke around here?"

"It isn't a joke to Nafai," said Issib. "Killing Gaballufix is the most terrible thing he ever did, and he thinks about it all the time."

"You were out of line to throw it up to him," said Father. "Don't do it again."

"What am I supposed to do," Mebbekew insisted, "pretend that Nafai got the Index by saying Pity Please?"

It was time for Elemak to get Mebbekew back in line—no one else could do it, and it needed to be done. "What you're supposed to do is shut up," said Elemak softly.

Meb looked at him defiantly. It was all an act, though, Elemak knew. All he had to do was meet Meb's gaze and hold it, and Meb would back down. It didn't take long, either.

"Elemak," said Father, "you must go back, you and your brothers."

"Don't put this on *me*," said Elemak. "If anyone can persuade Rasa, it's *you*."

"On the contrary," said Wetchik. "She knows me, she knows I love her, she loves me too—and that didn't bring her with me before. Do you think I didn't suggest it? No, if anyone persuades her it will be the Oversoul. All you have to do is go and suggest it to her, wait for the Oversoul to help her understand that she must come, and then provide safe escort for her and her daughters and the young women of her household who come with her."

"Oh, fine," said Elemak. He could wait a long cold time for the Oversoul to persuade anybody but Father to do something as idiotic as leaving Basilica for the desert. But at least he'd be waiting in Basilica, even if he had to do it in hiding. "Should I have her bring along a servant for Zdorab, too?"

Father's face went icy. "Zdorab isn't a servant now," he said. "He's a free man, and the equal of any man here. A woman of Rasa's household would do for him as well as for any of you, and as for that, a serving girl in Rasa's house would also do for any of you. Don't you understand that we're no longer in Basilica, that the society we form now will have no room for snobbery and bigotry, for castes and classes? We will be one people, all equals, with all our children equal in the eyes of the Oversoul."

In the eyes of the Oversoul, perhaps, but not in my eyes, thought Elemak. I'm the eldest son, and my firstborn son will be my heir as I am *your* heir, Father. Even if you gave up the lands and holdings that should have been my inheritance, I will still inherit your authority, and no matter where we end up settling, *I* will rule, or no one will. I may say nothing of this now, because I know when to speak and when not to speak. But be sure of this, Father. When you die, I will have your place—and anyone who tries to deprive me of it will follow you quickly into the grave.

Elemak looked at Issib and Meb, and knew that neither would resist him when that day came. But Nafai would cause trouble, bless his dear little heart. And Nafai knows it, thought Elemak. He knows that someday it will come down to him and me. For someday Father will try to pass his authority on to this miserable little toady of a boy, all because Nafai is so thick with the Oversoul. Well, Nafai, I've had a vision from the Oversoul, too—or at least Father thinks I have, which amounts to the same thing.

"Leave in the morning," Father said. "Come back with the women who will share the inheritance the Oversoul has prepared for us in another land. Come back with the mothers of my grandchildren."

"Mebbekew and I," said Elemak. "No others."

"Issib will stay home because his chair and his floats make him too conspicuous, and he increases your chances of being caught by our enemies there," said Father. "And Zdorab will stay."

Because you don't quite trust him yet, thought Elemak, no matter how much you claim that he's our equal and a free man.

"But Nafai goes with you."

"No," said Elemak. "He's even more dangerous to us than Issib. They're bound to have figured out that he killed Gaballufix—the city computer got his name on the way out of town, and the guards saw him wearing Gaballufix's clothing. And he had Zdorab with him, to clinch the connection between him and Gab's death. Bringing Nafai is like asking to have him killed."

"He goes with you," said Father.

"Why, when he only increases our danger?" demanded Elemak.

"Yes, *make* him say it, Elya," said Mebbekew. "Father doesn't want to insult you, but *I* don't mind. He wants Nafai there because, as someone recently pointed out, Nafai got the Index and none of the rest of us did. He wants Nafai there because he doesn't trust us not to just find some woman to take us in and stay in Basilica and never come back to this paradise by the sea. He wants Nafai there because he thinks Nafai will make us be good."

"Not at all," said Issib. "Father wants him to learn strength and wisdom by associating with his older brothers."

No one was ever sure whether Issib was being ironic or not. Nobody believed that this was Father's true purpose, but nobody—least of all Father—cared to deny it openly, either.

In the silence, the words that still rang in Elemak's ears were the last ones he himself had said: Bringing Nafai is like asking to have him killed.

"All right, Father," said Elemak. "Nafai can come with me."

IN BASILICA, AND NOT IN A DREAM

Kokor could not understand why *she* should be in seclusion. For Sevet it made sense—she was recuperating from her unfortunate accident. Her voice wasn't back yet; she was no doubt embarrassed to appear in public. But Kokor was in perfect health, and for her to have to hide out at Mother's house made it look as if she were ashamed to come out in public. If she had deliberately injured Sevet, then perhaps such isolation might be necessary. But since it was simply an unfortunate accident, the result of a psychological disturbance due to Father's death and the discovery of Sevet's and Obring's adultery, why, no one could blame Kokor. In fact, it would do her good to be seen in public. It would surely speed her recovery.

At least she should be able to go home to her own house, and not have to stay with Mother, as if she were a little girl or a mental incompetent who needed a guardian. Where was Obring? If he ever intended to make things up with her, he could begin by coming and getting her out of Mother's unbearably staid environment. There was nothing interesting going on here. Just endless classes in subjects that hadn't interested Kokor even when she was failing them years ago. Kokor was a woman of substance now. Father's inheritance probably would enable her to buy a house and keep her own establishment. And here she was living with mother.

Not that she saw that much of Mother. Rasa was constantly in meetings with councilors and other influential women of the city, who were making virtual pilgrimages to see her and talk to her. Some of the meetings seemed to be somewhat tense; Rasa began to gather the idea that some people, at least, were blaming Rasa for everything. As if Mother would try to kill Father! But they remembered that it was Rasa's current husband, Wetchik, who had his inflammatory vision about Basilica in flames, and then her former husband, Gaballufix, who put tolchoks and then mercenary soldiers on the streets of the city. And now the word was that her youngest son, Nafai, was the killer of both Roptat and Gaballufix.

Well, even if all that was true, what did that have to do with Mother? Women can't very well control their husbands—didn't Kokor have proof of that herself? And as for Nafai killing Father—well, even if he did it, *Mother* wasn't there, and she certainly didn't *ask* the boy to do it. They might as well blame Mother for what happened to Sevet, when anyone could see it was Sevet's own fault. Besides, wasn't Father's death his own fault, really? All those soldiers—you don't bring soldiers into Basilica and expect not to have violence, do you? Men never understood these things. They could turn things loose, but they were always surprised when they couldn't tame them again at will.

Like Obring, poor fool. Didn't he know that it wasn't a clever thing to come between sisters? He was really more to blame for Sevet's injury than Kokor was.

And why doesn't anybody have any sympathy for *my* injury? The deep psychological harm that has come to me because of seeing Obring and my own sister like that! No one cares that *I'm* suffering, too, and that maybe I need to go out at night as *therapy*.

Kokor sat painting her face, practicing looks that might project well in her next play. For there would certainly be a next play *now*, once she got out of Mother's house. Tumannu's little attempt to blacklist her would certainly fail—there wasn't a comedy house in Dolltown that would refuse an actress whose name was on the lips of everyone in Basilica. The house would sell out every night just from curiosity seekers—and when they saw her perform and heard her sing, they'd be back again and again. Not that she would ever dream of deliberately hurting someone in order to advance her career; but since it had happened, why not make use of it? Tumannu herself would probably be in line to beg Kokor to take the lead in a comedy.

She had drawn a little pout on her mouth that looked quite fetching. She tried it out from several angles and liked the shape of it. It was too light, though. She'd have to redden it or no one would see it past the first row.

"If you make it any rounder it'll look as though somebody made a hole under your nose with a drill."

Kokor turned slowly to face the intruder who stood in her doorway. An obnoxious little thirteen-year-old girl. The younger sister of that nasty bastard girl Hushidh. Mother had taken them both in as infants, out of pure charity, and when Mother made Hushidh one of her nieces the girl obviously thought she should then be taken as seriously as if she were one of the nieces of high birth who would amount to something in Basilica. She and Sevet had had such fun cutting Hushidh down to size, back when they were still students here. And now the little sister, equally a bastard, just as ugly and just as uppity, dared to stand in the doorway of the bedroom of a *daughter* of the house, of a highborn woman of Basilica, and ridicule the appearance of one of the famous beauties of the city.

But it would be beneath Kokor to go to the effort of putting this child in her place as she so deserved. Enough to make her go away. "Girl, there is a door. It was closed. Please restore it to its previous condition, with yourself on the other side."

The child didn't move.

"Girl, if you were sent with a message, deliver it and vanish."

"Are you speaking to me?" asked the child.

"Do you see another girl here?"

"I am a niece in this house," said the child. "Only servants are addressed as 'girl.' I therefore assumed that since you are rumored to be a lady who would know correct forms of address, you must have been speaking to some invisible servant on the balcony."

Kokor rose to her feet. "I've had enough of you. I had enough before you came in here."

"What are you going to do?" asked the child. "Strike me in the throat? Or is that a sport you keep within your family?"

Kokor felt an unbearable rage rise within her. "Don't tempt me!" she cried. Then she controlled herself, penned in the anger. This girl was not worth it. If she wanted correct address, she would have it. "What's your business here, my dear young daughter-of-a-holy-whore?"

The girl did not seem abashed, not for a moment. "So you *do* know who I am," she said. "My name is Luet. My friends call me Lutya. You may call me Young Mistress."

"Why are you here and when will you leave?" demanded Kokor. "Have I come to my mother's house to be tormented by bastard children with no manners?"

"Have no fear of that," said Luet. "For as I hear it, you will not be in this house another hour."

"What are you talking about? What have you heard?"

"I came here as an act of kindness, to let you know that Rashgallivak is here with six of his soldiers to take you under the protection of the Palwashantu."

"Rashgallivak! That little pizdook! I showed him his place when he last tried to pull this stunt, and I'll do it again."

"He wants to take Sevet, too. He says that you're both in serious danger and you need protection."

"Danger? In Mother's house? I only need protection from obnoxious ugly little girls."

"You are so gracious, Mistress Kokor," said Luet. "I will never forget how you answered my thoughtfulness in bringing you this news." She turned and left the room.

What did the girl expect? If she had come in with dignity instead of with an insult, Kokor would have treated her better. A child of such low background could hardly be expected to understand how to behave, however, so Kokor would try not to hold it against her.

Mother was being so bossy lately that she might even think that sending her and Sevet to Rashgallivak would be a good idea. Kokor would have to take steps herself to ensure that nothing of the kind occurred.

She wiped off the pout and replaced it with daypaint, then chose a particularly fragile-looking housedress and put it on with the tiniest hint of disarray, so that it would seem that she was simply on her way to the kitchen when she was surprised to discover that Rashgallivak was here to try to kidnap her.

The plan was spoiled, though, by the fact that when she stepped into the hall, there was Sevet, leaning on the arm of that wretched Hushidh girl, Luet's older sister. How could Sevet—even with her injury—abase herself by leaning on a girl that she had once treated with such despite? Had she no shame? And yet her presence in the hall made it impossible for Kokor to ignore her. She would have to be solicitous. She would have to hover near her. Fortunately, since Sevet was already leaning on Hushidh, Kokor wouldn't have to offer *that* service. It would completely spoil her freedom of action, to have Sevet leaning on her.

"How are you, poor Sevet?" asked Kokor. "I've wept myself hoarse over what happened. We're so bad to each other sometimes, Sevet. Why do we do it?"

Sevet merely looked at the floor a meter ahead of her.

"Oh, I can understand why you're not speaking to me. You'll never forgive me for the accident. But I've forgiven *you* for what *you* did, and *that* was no accident, *that* was on purpose. Still, one can hardly expect you to feel forgiving yet, you're in such pain, you poor thing. Why are you even up? I can handle this thing with Rashgallivak. I jammed his balls into his spleen the other night, and I'll be glad to do it again."

At that Sevet actually smiled a little. Just a trace of a smile. Or perhaps she only winced as she started jolting down the stairs.

Mother hadn't even brought Rashgallivak into one of the sitting rooms. He was standing with his soldiers right at the door, which was still open. Mother turned and glanced at her daughters and Hushidh as they came down the hall from the stairs to the entryway.

"You can see that they are well," Mother said to Rashgallivak. "They are safe and in good hands here. In fact, no men have come here at all, except you and these superfluous soldiers."

"I'm not worried about what *has* happened," said Rashgallivak. "I'm concerned about what *might* happen, and I will not leave here without Gaballufix's daughters. They are under the protection of the Palwashantu."

"You are welcome to keep your soldiers out in the street," said Mother, "to prevent any tolchoks or marauders or assassins from entering our house, but you will not take my daughters. A mother's claim is superior to the claim of a clan of men."

While Mother and Rash continued arguing, Kokor leaned toward Sevet and, forgetting that her sister could not speak, asked her, "Why does Rashgallivak want us in the first place?"

Because Sevet couldn't answer, Hushidh did. "Aunt Rasa is at the center of resistance to Palwashantu rule in Basilica. He thinks if he has the two of you as hostages, she will behave."

"Then he doesn't know Mother," said Kokor.

"Rashgallivak is a weak man," whispered Hushidh. "And he's stupid at politics. If he were as smart as your father, he would have known that he could not get possession of the two of you without violence, and that violence would be against his best interests. Therefore he would never have made the request. But if for some reason he *did* decide to take you, he would have acted far more boldly. The two of you would already be in the grasp of two soldiers each, with the other two holding your mother at bay."

Hushidh was no fool, after all. That had never occurred to Kokor, that Hushidh might have some attribute worthy of respect. Her idea of Father was exactly true—yet Kokor herself would never have been able to express it so clearly.

Of course, Father would also have had some kind of right to try to take her and Sevet. Not a *legal* right, of course, not in the city of women, but people might have understood it if he tried. What claim did Rashgallivak have? "The Oversoul must have driven Rash mad, even to try this," whispered Kokor.

"He's afraid," said Hushidh. "People do strange things when they're afraid. Your mother already has."

Like keeping me in seclusion, thought Kokor.

Then she realized that if she had been at home with Obring, Rash would have had no trouble getting to her. Obring would have tried to fight with the soldiers, they would have knocked him down in an instant, and Kokor would have been carried off. So Mother *was* right to keep her in seclusion. Imagine that. "You mustn't criticize Mother," said Kokor. "She's doing very well, I think."

In the meantime, the argument between Rasa and Rash had continued, though now they were both repeating old arguments, and not always in new words. Hushidh had brought them to the very threshold of the foyer, so that they were as far as they could be from the soldiers and still be in the room. Till now Kokor had stayed with her and Sevet. Seeing the soldiers standing there, horribly identical in their holographic masks, took away her determination to show Rashgallivak what was what. He had seemed much smaller and weaker in the darkness backstage at the theatre. The soldiers made him much more menacing, and Kokor found herself admiring Mother's courage in facing them down like this. In fact, she wondered if Mother was not being just the tiniest bit foolish. For instance, why had she called Kokor and Sevet down here to be in plain sight, within easy reach of these soldiers? Why hadn't she kept them hidden away upstairs? Or warned them to sneak away into the woods? Perhaps this was what Hushidh meant about Mother already doing strange things because of fear.

Yet Mother didn't seem afraid.

"I think perhaps we should leave now," Kokor whispered to Hushidh.

"Not so," said Hushidh. "You must stay."

"Why?"

"Because if you tried to leave, it would alarm Rashgallivak and probably cause him to act. He would order the soldiers to detain you and all would be lost."

"He'll do that eventually anyway," whispered Kokor.

"Ah, but will he wait long enough?"

"Long enough for what?"

"Think," said Hushidh.

Kokor thought. What would mere delay profit them?

Unless someone was coming to help. But who could possibly stand against the soldiers of the Palwashantu?

"The city guard!" cried Kokor, delighted to have thought of it.

Could she help it if her words fell into a chance silence in the argument between Mother and Rash?

"What?" cried Rashgallivak. "What did you say?" He whirled and looked out the door. "There's no one there," he said. Then he looked at Rasa. "But they *are* coming, aren't they? That's what this is all about—delaying me until you can get the guard to come and stop me. Well, the delay is over. Take them!"

At once the soldiers strode toward the women in the hallway, and Kokor screamed.

"Run, you little fools!" cried Mother.

But Kokor could not run, because one of the soldiers already had her by the arm and another pair of soldiers had Sevet, too, and that bastard Hushidh wasn't doing *one thing* to help them.

"Do something, you little bitch!" cried Kokor. "Don't let them do this to us!"

Hushidh looked her in the eye for a moment as the soldiers dragged her toward the door. Then she seemed to make a decision.

"Stop, Rashgallivak!" cried Hushidh. "Stop this instant."

Rash only laughed. It chilled Kokor to the bone, his laugh. It was the laugh of a man who knew he had won. This pathetic man who had been the steward in the house of Wetchik only a few days ago now laughed in delight at the power his soldiers gave him.

"Order them to stop!" cried Hushidh. "Or you will never be able to order them to do anything again!"

"No, Hushidh!" cried Mother.

What in the world did Mother think that Hushidh could do *now?* Kokor could see Sevet in the grasp of the soldiers, their blank faces so terrifying, so inhuman. It was wrong, for her sister to be in their grasp. Wrong for these hands to be gripping Kokor's arms and dragging her away. "Do it, Hushidh!" Kokor cried. Whatever it is Mother thinks you can do, do it.

To anyone but Hushidh, the scene was simple—Rash and two of his soldiers blocking anyone from interfering, as the other four soldiers were dragging Kokor and Sevet through the wide front door of Rasa's house. Aunt Rasa herself was shouting ineffectually—"It's *you* who's injuring Sevet! You'll be expelled from the city! Kidnapper!"— and other women and girls of the house were gathering, huddling in the hallway, listening, watching.

To Hushidh the Raveler, however, the scene was very different. For she could see not only the people, but also the webs that bound them together. To Hushidh, the frightened girls and women were not individuals or even little clumps—all of them were tightly bound to Rasa, so that instead of being helplessly alone as others would see her, Hushidh knew that she spoke from the strength of dozens of women, that their fear fed her fear, their anger her anger, and when she cried out in the majesty of her wrath, she was far larger than one mere woman. Hushidh even saw the powerful webs connecting Rasa to the rest of the city, great ropy threads like arteries and veins, pumping the lifeblood of Rasa's identity. When she cried out against Rashgallivak, it was the fury of the whole city of women in her voice.

Yet Hushidh could also see that Rasa, though she was surrounded by this vast web, also felt herself to be quite alone, as if the web came right up to her but didn't quite connect, or touched her only slightly. That was what Rash's exercise of raw power was doing to Rasa—making her feel as if her strength and power in the city amounted to nothing after all, for she could not resist the power of these soldiers.

At the same time, there was another web of influence—Rashgallivak's. And this one Hushidh knew was actually contemptible and weak. Where Rasa's links with her household were strong and real, her power in the city almost tangible to Hushidh, Rashgallivak had very little respect from his soldiers. He was able to command them only because he paid them, and then only because they rather liked what he was commanding them to do. Rashgallivak, compared to Rasa, was almost isolated. As for his men, their connections to each other were much stronger than their connections to *him*. And even then, they were nothing like the bonds among the women.

Most men were like this, Hushidh knew—relatively unconnected, unbound, alone. But these men were particularly untrusting and ungiving, and so the bonds that held them to each other were fragile indeed. It was not love at all, really, but rather a yearning for the honor and respect of the other men that held them. Pride, then. And at this moment they were proud of their strength as they dragged these women out of the house, proud to defy one of the great woman of Basilica; they looked so grand in each other's eyes. Indeed, all their connection with each other at this moment was tied up with the respect they felt they were earning by their actions.

So fragile. Hushidh had only to reach out and she could easily snap the bonds between these men. She could leave Rashgallivak hopelessly alone. And even though Rasa was demanding that she *not* do it, at this moment Hushidh felt much more deeply her connection to Sevet and Kokor, for these girls had been her tormentors, her enemies, and now she had the chance to be their savior, to set them free, and they would *know she had done it*. It would undo one of the deepest injuries in her heart; what was Rasa's command compared to that need?

Hushidh knew exactly why she was acting even as she acted—so well did she understand herself, for as a raveler she could see even her own connections with the world around her—yet she acted anyway, because that was who she was at this moment, the powerful savior who had the power to undo these powerful men.

So she spoke, and undid them. It wasn't the words she said; this was no magical incantation that would disconnect the bonds that held them to each other. It was her tone of contempt, her face, her body, that gave her words the power to strike at the heart of each of the soldiers and make them believe that they were utterly alone, that other men would have only contempt for what they were doing. "Where is your honor in dragging this injured woman away from her mother," she said. "Baboons in the wild have more manhood than you, for mothers can trust their infants with the males of the tribe."

Poor Rash. He heard the words, and thought that he could counter Hushidh by arguing with her. He didn't realize that, with these men caught up in the story Hushidh was weaving around them, every word he said would drive these men farther away from him, for he sounded weaker and more cowardly with every sound he made. "You shut up, woman! These men are soldiers who do their duty—"

"A coward's duty. Look what this so-called man has led you to do. He's made you into filthy rodents, stealing bright and shining beauty and dragging it off to his hole where he will cover you with shit and call it glory."

First one, then another of the men let go of Kokor and Sevet. Sevet immediately sank to her knees, weeping silently. Kokor, for her part, put on a very convincing show of disgust and loathing, shuddering as she tried in vain to brush away the very memory of the soldiers' touch on her arms.

"See how you have disgusted the beautiful ones," said Hushidh. "That's what Rashgallivak has made of you. Slugs and worms, because you follow him. Where can you go to become men again? How can you find a way to be clean? There must be somewhere you can hide from your shame. Slither off and find it, little slugs; burrow deep and see if you can hide your humiliation! Do you think those masks make you look strong and powerful? They only mark you as servants of this contemptible gnat of a man. Servants of *nothing*."

One of the soldiers pulled off the cloak that created the holographic image that till now had hidden his face. He was an ordinary, rather dirty-looking man, unshaven, somewhat stupid, and very much afraid—his eyes were wide and filled with tears.

"There he is," Hushidh said. "That's what Rashgallivak has made of you."

"Put your mask back on!" cried Rashgallivak. "I order you to take these women back to Gaballufix's house."

"Listen to him," said Hushidh. *"He's* no Gaballufix. Why are you following *him?"*

That was the last push. Most of the other soldiers also swept off their masks, leaving the holo-cloaks on the porch of Rasa's house as they shambled off, running from the scene of their humiliation.

Rash stood alone in the middle of the doorway. Now the whole scene had changed. It didn't take a raveler to see that

Rasa had all the power and majesty now, and Rash was helpless, weak, alone. He looked down at the cloaks at his feet.

"That's right," said Hushidh. "Hide your face. No one wants to see that face again, least of all you."

And he did it, he bent over and swept up one of the cloaks and pulled it across his shoulder; his body heat and magnetism activated the cloaks, which were still powered on, and suddenly he was no longer Rashgallivak, but rather the same uniform image of false masculinity that all the soldiers of Gaballufix had worn. Then he turned and ran away, just like his men, with that same defeated rounding of the shoulders. No baboon beaten by a rival could have shown more abjectness than Rash's body showed as he ran away.

Hushidh felt the web of awe that was forming around her; it made her tingle, knowing that she had the adulation of the girls and women of the house—and above all, the honor of Sevet and Kokor. Kokor, vain Kokor, who now looked at her with an expression stupid with awe. And Sevet, cruel in her mockery for so many years, now looking at her through eyes streaked with tears, her hands reaching out toward Hushidh like a supplicant, her lips struggling to say Thank you, thank you, thank you.

"What have you done," whispered Rasa.

Hushidh could hardly understand the question. What she had done was obvious. "I've broken Rashgallivak's power," she said. "He's no more threat to you."

"Foolish, foolish girl," said Rasa. "There are thousands of these villains in Basilica. Thousands of them, and now the one man who could control them, however weak he was, that man is broken and undone. By nightfall these soldiers will all be out of control, and who will stop them?"

All of Hushidh's sense of accomplishment slipped away at once. She knew that Rasa was right. No matter how clearly Hushidh saw in the present moment, she hadn't looked ahead to anticipate the larger consequences of her act. These men would no longer be bound by their hunger for honor, for it would no longer be seen as honorable to serve Rashgallivak. What would they do, then? They would be unbound in the city, soldiers starving to prove their strength and power, and no force could channel them to some useful purpose. Hushidh remembered the holos she had seen of apes displaying, shaking branches, charging each other, slapping at whoever was weak, whoever was near. Men on the rampage would be far, far more dangerous.

"Bring my daughters inside," Rasa said to the others. "Then all of you work to shutter the windows behind their bars. Tighten down the house. As if a tempest were coming. For it is."

Rasa then stepped onto the porch between her daughters.

"Where are you going, Mama!" wailed Kokor. "Don't leave us!"

"I must warn the women of the city. The monster is loose in the streets tonight. The Guard will be powerless to control them. They must secure what can be secured, and then hide from the fires that will burn here tonight in the darkness."

Moozh's troops were exhausted, but when, late in the afternoon, they crested a pass and saw smoke in the distance, it put new vigor into their steps. They knew as well as Moozh did that a city on fire is a city that is not about to defend itself. Besides, they knew that they had accomplished something remarkable, to cover such a distance on foot. And even though there were only a thousand of them, they knew that if they achieved a victory, their names would live forever, if not individually, then as a part of Moozh's Thousand. They could almost hear their grandchildren already asking them, Was it true you marched from Khlam to Basilica in two days, and took the city that night without resting, and without a man of you killed?

Of course, that last part of the story wasn't yet a foregone conclusion. Who knew what the condition inside Basilica really was. What if the soldiers of Gaballufix had already consolidated their position inside the city, and now were prepared to defend it? The Gorayni soldiers well knew they had barely food for another meal; if they didn't take the city tonight, in darkness, they would have to break their fast in the morning and take the city by daylight—or flee ignominiously down into the Cities of the Plain, where their enemies could see how few they really were, and cut them to pieces long before they could make it back north. So yes, victory was possible—but it was also essential, and it had to be now.

So why were they so confident, when desperation would have been more understandable? Because they were *Moozh's* Thousand, and Moozh had never lost. There was no better general in the history of the Gorayni. He was careful of his men; he defeated his enemies, not by expending his men in bloody assaults, but through maneuver and deft blows, isolating the enemy, cutting off supplies, dividing the enemy's forces, and so disorienting the opposing generals that they began taking foolish chances just to get the battle *over* with and stop the endless, terrifying ballet. His soldiers called it "Dancing with Moozh," the quick marches; they knew that by wearing out their feet, Moozh was saving their yatsas. Oh, yes, they loved him—he made them victors without sending too many of them home as a small sack of ashes.

There were even whispers in the ranks that their beloved Moozh was the *real* incarnation of God, and even though usually none would say it aloud—at least not where an intercessor could hear them—on this march, with no intercessor along, the whispers became a good deal more frequent. That fat-assed fellow back in Gollod was no incarnation of God, in a world that included a *real* man like Vozmuzhalnoy Vozmozhno!

A kilometer away from Basilica, they could hear some of the sounds coming out of the city—screams, mostly, carried by the wind, which was blowing smoke toward them now. The order came through the ranks: Cut down branches, a dozen or more per man, so we can light enough smoky bonfires to make the enemy think we are a hundred thousand. They hacked and tore at the trees near the road, and then followed Moozh down a winding trail from the mountains into the desert. Moonlight was a treacherous guide, especially burdened as they were with boughs, but there were few injuries though many fell, and in the darkness they fanned out across the desert, separating widely from each other, leaving vast empty spaces between the groups of men. There they built their piles of branches, and at the blare of a trumpet—who in the city could hear it?—they lit all the fires. Then, leaving one man at each bonfire to add boughs to keep the flames alive, the rest of the army gathered behind Moozh and marched, this time in four columns abreast, as if they were the bold advance guard for a huge army, up a wide flat road toward a gap in the high walls of the city.

Even before they reached the walls, they found themselves in the middle of a veritable city. There were men running and shouting there—many of them clearly oversatisfied with wine—but when they saw Moozh's army marching through their street, they fell silent and backed away into the shadows. If any of the Gorayni had lacked confidence before, they gained it now, for it was clear that the men of Basilica had no fight in them. What boldness they had was nothing but the bravado of drink.

As they drew near to the gate, they heard the clang of metal on metal that suggested a pitched battle. Cresting a rise they saw a battle in progress, between men clad in the same uniform as the assassin that Moozh had killed, and other men who were terrifyingly identical—not just their clothing, but even their faces were all the same!

Word passed down the columns: The men in the uniform of the Basilican guard will probably be our allies; our true enemies are the ones in masks. But slay no one until Moozh gives the order.

They reached the flat, clear area before the gate, and quickly split into two ranks left, two ranks right, until a semicircle formed surrounding the gate. In the middle of the semicircle stood Moozh himself.

"Gorayni, draw your weapons!" He bawled out the command—clearly he meant to be heard as much by the men fighting at the gate as by his own army, which normally would have received the command as a whisper down the ranks.

The fighting at the gate slackened. The men in the uniforms of the Basilican guard—few of them indeed to be making such a brave stand—saw the Gorayni troops and despaired. They fell back against the wall, uncertain which enemy to fight, but certain of this: That they would not live out the hour.

In the middle of the gate, their enemies withdrawn, the soldiers of identical faces also stood, uncertain of what to do next.

"We are the Gorayni. We have come to help Basilica, not to conquer her!" Cried Moozh. "Look out in the desert and see the army we could bring to bear against the gates of your city!"

Moozh had chosen his gate well—from here all the Basilicans, guard and Palwashantu mercenaries alike, could see the bonfires, at least a hundred of them, stretching far across the desert.

"Yet only these five hundred have I brought to the gate!" Of course he lied about the number of men he had; his men smiled inwardly to know that for once he was only four hundred off, instead of forty thousand, which was the more usual lie. "We are here to ask if the City of Women, the City of Peace, might use our services to help quell a domestic disturbance. We will enter, serve the city at your pleasure, and leave when our task is accomplished. Thus do I speak in the name of General Vozmuzhalnoy Vozmozhno!" There was no reason to let them know that the most fearsome general on the western shores of the Earthbound Sea was standing before their gates with his sword sheathed and only nine hundred men to back him up. Let them think the general himself was out with the tens of thousands of troops tenting around the great bonfires in the desert!

"Sir," cried one of the guard. "You see how it is with us! We are the guard of the city, but how can we find out the will of our council, when we are fighting for our lives against these mad criminals!"

"*We* are the masters of Basilica now!" shouted one of the identical Palwashantu mercenaries. "No more taking the orders of women! No more being forced to stay outside the city that is ours by right! We rule this city now in the name of Gaballufix!"

"Gaballufix is dead!" shouted the officer of the guard. "And you are ruled by no man!"

"In the name of Gaballufix this city is ours!" And with that the mercenaries brandished their weapons and shouted.

"Men of Gaballufix!" cried Moozh. "We have heard the name of your fallen leader!"

The mercenaries cheered again.

"We know how to honor Gaballufix!" Moozh shouted. "Come out to us, and stand with us, and we will give you the city you deserve!"

With a cheer the mercenaries poured out from the gate toward the Gorayni. The Basilican guard shrank back against the walls, their weapons ready. Some few started slinking away to the left or the right, hoping to escape, but to their honor most of the guard remained in their places, prepared to end their lives doing their duty. Moozh's Thousand took note of this; they would treat the guard with respect, should a reckoning come between them.

As for the mercenaries, those closest to the Gorayni came with their guard down, prepared to embrace these new-comers as their brothers. But they found that swords and pikes and bows were pointed at them, and confusion spread from the rim to the center of the mob.

Moozh still stood where he had stood all along, only now he was surrounded by mercenaries, cut off from his own men. He seemed to show no alarm at all, though it made his men more than a little nervous. To their consternation, he began to push his way through the mob, not *toward* his men, but away from them and toward the gate. The mercenaries seemed content with this—it was a sign that he meant to lead them.

Moozh strode out into the open area in the middle of the gate, his back to the mercenaries. "Ah, Basilica," he said—

loudly, but not in the voice of command. "How often I have dreamed of standing in your gate and seeing your beauty with my own eyes!" Then he turned to face the officer of the guard, who stood at the post of the gate, his weapon drawn. Moozh spoke softly to him. "Would Basilica regard it as a great service, my friend, if these hundreds of ugly twins were to die on this ground at this hour?"

"I think so, yes," said the officer, confused once again, but also glad with new hope.

Moozh turned back to face the mob—and his men behind them. "Every man who loves the name of Gaballufix, raise your sword high!"

Most of the mob—all but the wariest of them—raised their weapons. No sooner had they raised their arms, however, than Moozh drew his sword from its sheath.

That was the signal. Three hundred arrows were loosed at once, and every man at the periphery of the mob—their arms conveniently raised so that every arrow struck them in the body—fell, most of them pierced many times. Then, with a thunderous shout, the Gorayni fell on the remaining mercenaries and in only two or three minutes the carnage was over. The Gorayni immediately formed themselves into ranks again, standing before the bodies of their fallen enemies.

Moozh turned to the officer of the guard. "What is your name, sir?"

"Captain Bitanke, sir."

"Captain Bitanke, I ask again: Would Basilica welcome our intervention to help restore order in these beautiful streets? I have here a letter from the Lady Rasa; is her name known to you?"

"Yes it is, sir," said Bitanke.

"She wrote to me, asking for succor for her city. I came, and now respectfully ask your permission to bring these men within your gates, to serve as auxiliary troops in your effort to control the violence in your streets."

Bitanke bowed and then unlocked the guard booth in the gate and stepped inside. Moozh could see that he was typing into a computer. After a few moments he stepped back into the open. "Sir, I have told them what you did here. The situation of our city is desperate, and since you come in the name of the Lady Rasa, and you have proven your will to defeat our enemies, the city council and the guard invite you to enter. Temporarily you are placed under my immediate command, if you will accept one of my low rank, until a more orderly system can be arranged."

"Sir, it is not your rank but your courage and honor that make me salute you, and for that reason I will accept your leadership," said Moozh. "May I suggest that we deploy my men in companies of six, and authorize them to deal with any men they find who are behaving in a disorderly fashion. We will in all cases respect those who wear your uniform; any other men we find who have weapons drawn or who offer violence to us or to any woman of the city, we will slay on the spot and hang up on public display to quell any notion of further resistance by others!"

"I don't know about the hanging, sir," said Bitanke.

"Very well, we have our orders!" Ignoring Bitanke's hesitation, Moozh turned to his soldiers. "Men of the Gorayni, by sixes!"

Immediately the ranks shifted and suddenly there were a hundred and fifty squads of six men each.

"Harm no woman!" cried Moozh. "And whomever you see in that loathsome mask, hang him up, mask and all, until no man dares wear it by night or day!"

"Sir, I think . . ."

But Moozh had already waved his arm, and his soldiers now entered the city at a trot. Bitanke came closer to Moozh, to remonstrate perhaps, but Moozh greeted him with an embrace that stifled conversation. "Please, my friend—I know your men are exhausted, but couldn't they be usefully employed? For instance, I think this village outside the gate could profit from a little cleaning out. And as for you and me, we should make our way to those who are in authority, so I can receive the orders of the city council."

Whatever misgivings Captain Bitanke might have had were swept away by Moozh's embrace and his smile.

Bitanke gave his orders, and his men spread out through Dogtown. Then Moozh followed him into the city. "While my men are restoring order, we must see about putting out some fires," said Moozh. "Can you call others of the city guard with your computer?"

"Yes, sir."

"It's not my place to tell you your business, but if your men can protect the firefighters, perhaps we can keep Basilica from burning down before dawn."

"Do you think the rest of your men might be able to come and help?"

Moozh laughed. "Oh, General Vozmuzhalnoy Vozmozhno would never allow that. If such a force came to your gates, someone in Basilica might fear that we meant to conquer the town. We are here to extend you our protection, not to rule over you, my friend! So we bring no more men than these five hundred."

"The Oversoul must have sent you, sir," said Captain Bitanke.

"You have only to thank the Lady Rasa," said Moozh. "Her and a brave man of your number named, I believe, Smelost."

"Smelost," whispered Bitanke. "He was a dear friend of mine."

"Then I am glad to tell you that he was received with honor by General Vozmuzhalnoy Vozmozhno, who lost no time in acting on his information and coming to the aid of your city."

"You came in good time," said Bitanke. "It began like this last night, and spread through the day, and I feared that tomorrow morning would find the city in ashes and all the good women of Basilica in despair or worse."

"I'm always glad to be a messenger of hope," said Moozh.

By now they were walking along a street with houses and shops on either side. Yet there was no one moving, and lights shone from many upper windows. The only sign that the rioting had been here was the broken glass in the street, the shattered windows of the shops, and the bodies of dead mercenaries, still wearing their holographic masks, dangling like beeves from upper-story balconies. Bitanke looked at them in faint dismay as they walked along the street.

"How long will those masks remain active?" asked Moozh.

"Until the—bodies cool, I imagine. I've heard that body heat and magnetism are the triggers."

"Ah," said Moozh.

"May I ask—what they are—how your men were able to hang them? I see no ropes and there are no—apparatuses for hanging men in the streets."

"I'm not sure," said Moozh. "Let's take the cloak off one of them and see."

Gingerly Bitanke reached up and tugged on the cloak of the nearest dangling corpse. When it came away, the holograph faded instantly and it was easy to see that the body had been pinned to the wall by a heavy knife through its neck. "His own knife, do you think?" asked Moozh.

"I think so," said Bitanke.

"Not a very secure job," said Moozh, pushing at the body a bit. "I daresay if we have any wind tonight most of these will be down by morning. We'll want to clean them up as quickly as possible, or we'll have quite a problem with the dogs."

"Yes sir," said Bitanke.

"Never seen a dead body?" asked Moozh. "You look a little ill."

"Oh, I've seen dead bodies, sir," said Bitanke. "I've just never heard of . . . treating them this way . . . I wish your men wouldn't . . ."

"Nonsense. These dangling bodies are like reinforcements. Any rioters that my soldiers happen to overlook—there are bound to be some using the toilet, don't you think?—they'll come out, see how quiet things are, notice the bodies, and most of the fight will go right out of them."

Bitanke chuckled a little. "I imagine so."

"You see?" said Moozh. "It's a way of letting these boys make up for a bit of the mischief they've caused, by policing the streets for us all night. Correct me if I'm wrong,

Captain Bitanke, but no one is going to shed many tears, for them, right?"

Within the hour Moozh was meeting with the city council. In the meantime, the hundred soldiers who had been tending the bonfires were moving into position at every gate of the city, standing alongside the guard in those few cases where they were at the gate. There was no quarrel between them; no soldier of the Gorayni came to blows with any of the city guard.

Moozh's meeting with the city council was peaceful, and they concluded a firm agreement that Moozh would have full access to all the boroughs of the city—even those that normally were restricted to women only, since that was where the worst of the fires were burning and the marauders had been most out of control—but that after two and a half days, Moozh would withdraw his men to quarters outside the city, where they would be amply supplied and rewarded from the treasury of the city. It was a wonderful alliance, full of many compliments and much heartfelt gratitude.

Few in Basilica would realize it for several days, but by the time Moozh left the meeting his conquest of the city was complete.

Nafai said as little as possible to Elya and Meb as they set out on their journey back to Basilica. His silence did not make them any more cheerful toward him, but it meant that he didn't have to quarrel with them, or do some verbal dance to avoid quarreling. He could keep his own thoughts.

He could talk to the Oversoul.

As if it mattered what he said to the old computer. For a few days he had fancied that he and the Oversoul were working together. The Oversoul had shown him its memory of Earth, had explained its purpose in the world, to try to keep the planet Harmony from repeating the miserable, self-destructive history of Earth. Nafai had agreed to serve that purpose. Nafai had stood over a drunken man in the street—his enemy—and it never would have come to his own mind to kill the man as he lay there, helpless. But the Oversoul had told him to do it and Nafai had complied. Not because Gaballufix was a murderer himself who deserved to die. Why, then? Because Nafai believed the Oversoul, agreed with the Oversoul that by killing this one man, he could help preserve the whole world.

And, having done the crime, having put blood on his own hands for the sake of the Oversoul's cause, where was the Oversoul now? Nafai had imagined that there was now a special relationship between the Oversoul and himself. Hadn't there been that moment when the Index first spoke to him and Father and Issib? Father and Issib had only partly understood the Oversoul's message—they grasped the idea that the Oversoul meant to lead them on a long journey to a wonderful place where Issib could use his floats again and not be confined to his chair. But only Nafai had understood that the place the Oversoul meant to take them was not on the planet Harmony—that the Oversoul meant to take them back to Earth. After forty million years, home to Earth.

Since then, though, the Index had been nothing but a guide to a vast memory bank. Father and Issib studied, and Nafai with them, but all the time Nafai kept waiting for some word—to all of them, or perhaps to him alone. Perhaps some special private message, some word of encouragement. Something to fulfill the promise made that time when the Oversoul, speaking through Issib's chair, had said that it had chosen Nafai to lead his brothers.

Am I chosen, Oversoul? Why can't I see the results of your favor, then? I have made myself a murderer for you, and yet your vision of our wives came to Elemak. And what did he see? That you had chosen Eiadh for *him!* What has your favor brought me, then? Now you speak to Elemak, who plotted with Gaballufix, who tried to kill me; now you give *him* the woman that *I* have so long desired—why did *he* receive that dream, and not me? I have been humiliated now in front of all of them. I will have to eat dust, I will have to submit to Elya's orders and serve at his pleasure, I will have to watch Elya take that sweet and beautiful girl who has so long inhabited *my* dreams. Why do you hate me, Oversoul? What have I done, except to serve you and obey you?

The camels clambered with lazy strength up a slope, and Elemak led them along the edge of a precipice. Nafai looked out over the landscape and saw the savage knife-edged rocks and crags, with only here and there a bit of grey-green desert foliage. The Oversoul promised me life, promised me greatness and glory and joy, and here I am, in this desert, following my brothers, who plotted with Father's enemy and, wittingly or not, set Father up to be killed. I helped the Oversoul to save Father's life, and now here I am.

Yes, here you are.

It took a moment to realize that this was the voice of the Oversoul, for it spoke in Nafai's mind as if it were his own thought. But he knew, from his few experiences, that this thought was coming from outside himself, if only because it seemed to answer him.

In turn, he answered the Oversoul—and not with any particular respect. Oh, here *you* are, he said silently, sarcastically. Noticed me again? Hope I wasn't a bother.

I bother a great deal for you.

Like choosing Eiadh for my brother instead of me.

Eiadh is not for you.

Thanks for your help, said Nafai silently. Thanks for dealing me such a miserable hand in this game with my brothers.

I'm not doing too badly for you, Nafai.

Maybe I don't give you the same high marks you give yourself. I killed a man for you.

And every moment of this journey, I am saving your life.

The thought startled Nafai. Inadvertently he sat up straighter, looked around him.

Every moment of this journey, I am turning their thoughts away from their decision to kill you.

Fear and hatred, both at once, clawed their way down Nafai's throat and deep into his belly. He could feel them churning there, like small animals dwelling inside him.

It's good that you've been silent, said the Oversoul. It's

good that you haven't provoked them, or even reminded them that you're along with them on this journey. For my influence in their minds, while strong, is not irresistible. If their anger flowed hotly against you, how would I stop them? I don't have Issib's chair to act through now.

Nafai was filled with fear, with a longing to go back to Father's tent. At the same time, he was hurt and angry at his brothers. Why do they still hate me? How have I harmed them?

Foolish boy. Only a moment ago you were longing for me to reward you for your loyalty to me by giving you power over your brothers. Do you think they don't see your ambition? Every time I speak to you, they hate you more. Every time your father's face is filled with delight at your quick mind, at your goodness of heart, they hate you more. And when they see that you desire to have the privileges of the eldest son . . .

I don't! cried Nafai silently. I don't want to displace Elemak . . . I want him to love me, I want him to be a *true* older brother to me, and not this monster who wants me dead.

Yes, you want him to love you . . . *and* you want him to respect you . . . *and* you want to take his place. Do you think you are immune to the primate instincts within you? You are born to be an alpha male in a tribe of clever beasts, and so is he. But he is ruled by that hunger, while you, Nafai, can't you be civilized, can't you suppress the animal part of yourself, and work to help me achieve a far higher purpose than determining who will be the leading male in a troop of erect baboons?

Nafai felt as if he had been stripped naked in front of his enemies. If I am no better than Elemak, no better than any of the troop of baboons downstream from Father's tent, then why did you choose me?

Because you *are* better, and because you *want* to be better still.

Help me, then. Help me curb my own dark desires. And while you're at it, help Elemak, too. I remember him when he was younger. Playful, loving, kind. He's more than an ambitious animal, I know he is, even if he's forgotten it himself.

I know it, answered the Oversoul. Why do you think I gave that dream to Elemak? So he might have a chance to waken to my voice. He has much of the same sensitivity *you* have. But he has long chosen to hate me, to thwart my purposes if he can. So my voice has been nothing to him. This time, though, I could tell him something he wanted to hear. My purpose coincided with his own. What do you think your life would be worth, if I had shown *you* who his wife should be? Do you think he would have taken Eiadh at *your* hand?

I wouldn't have given him Eiadh.

So. You would have ignored me. You would have rebelled against me. You tell yourself that you killed Gaballufix only because you serve me and my noble purpose . . . but then you are willing to rebel against me and thwart my purpose, because you want a woman who would ruin your life.

You don't know that. You may be a very clever computer, Oversoul, but you can't tell the future.

I know her, as I know you, from the inside. And if you ever know her, you will understand that she could never be your wife.

Are you saying she's bad at heart?

I'm saying she lives in a world whose center of gravity is herself. She has no purpose higher than her own desires. But you, Nafai, will never be content unless your life is accomplishing something that will change the world. I am giving you that, if you have the patience to trust me until it comes to you. I will also give you a wife who will share the same dreams, who will help you instead of distracting you.

Who *is* my wife, then?

The face of Luet came into his mind.

Nafai shuddered. Luet. She had helped him escape, and saved his life at great risk to herself. She had taken him down to the lake of women and brought him through rituals that only women were allowed by law to receive. For bringing him there she might have been killed, right along with him; instead she faced down the women and persuaded them that the Oversoul had commanded it. He had floated with her in the mists at the boundary between the hot and cold waters of the lake, and she had brought him through Trackless Wood, beyond the private gate in the wall of Basilica that, until now, only women had known about.

And earlier, Luet had come in the middle of the night to Father's house far outside the city—had come at some risk to herself—solely to warn that Father's enemies planned to murder him. She had precipitated their departure into the wilderness.

Nafai owed her much. And he liked her, she was a good person, simple and sweet. So why couldn't he think of her as a wife? Why did he recoil at the thought?

Because she is the waterseer.

The waterseer—that's why he didn't want to marry her. Because she had been having visions from the Oversoul for far longer than he; because she had strength and wisdom that he couldn't even hope to have. Because she was better than Nafai in every way he could think of. Because if they became partners in this journey back to Earth, she would hear the voice of the Oversoul better than he; she would know the way when he knew nothing at all. When all was silent for him, she would hear music; when he was blind, she would have light. I can't bear it, to be tied to a woman who will have no reason to respect me, because whatever I do, she has done it first, she can do it better.

So . . . you didn't want a wife, after all. You wanted a worshipper.

This realization made him flush with self-contempt. Is that who I am? A boy who is so weak that he can't imagine loving a woman who is strong?

The faces of Rasa and Wetchik, his mother and father, came into his mind. Mother was a strong woman—perhaps the strongest in Basilica, though she had never tried to use her prestige and influence to win power for herself. Did it weaken Father because Mother was at least—at *least*—his equal? Perhaps that was why they had not renewed their marriage after Issib's birth. Perhaps that was why Mother had married Gaballufix for a few years, because Father had not been able to swallow his pride enough to remain happily married to a woman who was so powerful and wise.

And yet she returned to Father, and Father returned to her. Nafai was the child she bore to seal their re-marriage. And ever since then, they had renewed each other every year, not even questioning their commitment to each other. What had changed? Nothing—Mother did not have to diminish herself to be part of Father's life, and he did not have to dominate her in order to be part of *her* life. Nor did domination flow the other way; the Wetchik had always been his own man, and Rasa had never felt a need to rule over him.

In Nafai's mind, the faces of his father and mother flowed together and became one face. For a moment he recognized it as Father; then, without it changing at all, the face became clearly Mother's face.

I understand, he said silently. They are one person. What does it matter which of them happens to be the voice, whose hands happen to act? One is not above the other. They are together, and so there is no question of rivalry between them.

Can I find such a partnership with Luet? Can I bear it, to have her hear the Oversoul when I cannot? I seethed even now when it was Elya who dreamed a true dream; can I listen to Luet's dreams, and not be envious?

And what about *her?* Will she accept *me?*

Almost at once he was ashamed of the last question. She already *had* accepted him. She had brought him down to the lake of women. She had given him all that she was and all that she had, without hesitation, as far as he could tell. He was the one who was jealous and afraid. She was the one with courage and generosity.

The question is not, Can I bear to live as one with her. The question is, Am I worthy to be partnered with such a one as that?

He felt a trembling warmth suffuse through him, as if he were filled with light. Yes, said the Oversoul inside his mind. Yes, that is the question. That is the question. That is the question.

And then the trance of his communion with the Oversoul ended, and Nafai suddenly became aware of his surroundings again. Nothing had changed—Meb and Elya still led the way, the camels plodding along. Sweat still dripped on Nafai's body; the camel still lurched and rolled under him; the dry air of the desert still burned with every breath he drew into his body.

Keep me alive, said Nafai. Keep me alive long enough for me to conquer the animal in myself. Long enough for me to learn to partner myself with a woman who is better and stronger than me. Long enough for me to reconcile myself with my brothers. Long enough to be as good a man as my father, and as good as my mother, too.

If I can, I will. Like a voice in his head, that promise.

And if *I* can, I'll make it soon. I'll become worthy soon.

FOUR

WIVES

THE DREAM OF THE GENETICIST

Shedemei awoke from her dream, and wanted to tell someone, but there was no one there beside her. No one, and yet she had to tell the dream. It was too powerful and real; it had to be spoken, for fear that if she didn't say what she had seen, it would slip away from her memory the way most dreams slipped away. It was the first time she wished that she had a husband. Someone who would have to listen to her dream, even if all he did then was grunt and roll over and go back to sleep. It would relieve her so, to tell the dream aloud.

But where would a husband have slept, anyway, in the clutter of her rooms? There was barely room for her cot. The rest of the place was given over to her research. The lab tables, the basins and beakers, the dishes and tubes, the sinks and the freezers. And, above all, the great dryboxes lining the walls, filled with desiccated seeds and embryos, so she could keep samples of every stage of her research into redundancy as a natural mechanism for creating and controlling genetic drift.

Though she was only twenty-six years old, she already had a worldwide reputation among scientists in her field. It was the only kind of fame that mattered to her. Unlike so many of the other brilliant women who had grown up in Rasa's house, Shedemei had never been interested in a career that would win her fame in Basilica. She knew from childhood on that Basilica was not the center of the universe, that fame here was no better than fame in any other place—soon to be forgotten. Humanity had been forty million years on this world of Harmony, more than forty thousand times longer than all of recorded human history on the ancient home planet of Earth. If there was any lesson to be learned, it was that a singer or actress, a politician or soldier, all would be forgotten soon enough. Songs and plays were usually forgotten in a lifetime; borders and constitutions were redrawn within a thousand years at most. But science! Knowledge! If that was what you wrought, it might be remembered forever. That it was you who discovered something, *that* might be forgotten . . . but the thing you learned, it would be remembered, it would have echoes and reverberations down all the years to come. The plants you created, the animals you enhanced, *they* would endure, if you wrought well enough. Hadn't the plant trader Wetchik, dear Rasa's favorite husband, carried Shedemei's Dryflower plant throughout all the lands on the edges of the desert? As long as Dryflower bloomed, as long as its rich and heavy perfume could make a whole house in the desert smell like a jungle garden, Shedemei's works would be alive in the world. As long as scientists all over the world received copies of her reports from the Oversoul, she had the only fame that mattered.

So this was her husband: the works of her own hands. Her creations were a husband that would never betray her, the way Rasa's poor little daughter Kokor had been betrayed. Her research was a husband that would never rampage through the city, raping and looting, beating and burning, the way the men of the Palwashantu had done, until the Gorayni brought order. Her research would never cause any woman to cower in her rooms, all lights off, a pulse in her hands though she doubted she would even know how to use it against an intruder. No one had come, though twice the shouting seemed almost to be in her street. But she would have fought to protect her seeds and embryos. Would have fought and, if she could figure out how to do it, would have killed to protect her life's work.

Yet now this dream had come. A disturbing dream. A powerful dream. And she could not rest until she had told the dream to someone.

To Rasa. Who was there that she could tell, besides Aunt Rasa?

So Shedemei arose, made a half-hearted effort to straighten her hair from sleep, and headed out into the street. She did not think to change her clothing, though she had slept in it; she often slept in her clothing, and only thought to change what she wore on those occasions when she thought to bathe.

There were a good number of people in the street. It had not been so for many days; the fear and distrust that Gaballufix had brought upon the city had kept many indoors. Thus it was almost a relief to see the turbulent flow of pedestrians rushing hither and thither. Almost a pleasure to jostle with them. The dead bodies of the mercenaries no longer hung from the second stories of the buildings, no longer slumped in the streets. They had been hauled away and buried with more or less ceremony in the men's cemeteries outside the city. Only the occasional sight of a pair of men in the uniform of the Basilican guards reminded Shedemei that the city was still under military rule. And the council was set to vote today on how to repay the Gorayni soldiers, send them on their way, and put the city guard back at gate duty. No more soldiers on the streets, then, except when answering an emergency call. All would be well. All would be as before.

A proof of the restoration of peace was the fact that on the porch of Rasa's house were two classes of young girls, listening to teachers and occasionally asking questions. Shedemei paused for just a moment as she so often did, to hear the lessons and remember her own time, so long ago, as a pupil on this very porch, or in the classrooms and gardens within Rasa's house. There were many girls of aristocratic parentage here, but Rasa's was not a house for snobs. The curriculum was rigorous, and there was always room for many girls of ordinary family, or of no family at all. Shedemei's parents had been farmers, not even citizens; only her mother's distant cousinship with a Basilican servant woman had allowed Shedemei to enter the city in the first place. And yet Rasa had taken her in, solely because of an interview when Shedemei was seven. Shedemei couldn't even read at the time, because neither of her parents could read . . . but her mother had ambitions for her, and, thanks to Rasa, Shedemei had been able to fulfil them all. Her mother had lived to see Shedemei in her own rooms, and with her first money from the keen-eyed roach-killing shrew she had developed, Shedemei was able to buy her parents' farm from their landlord, so that they spent their last few years of life as freeholders instead of tenants.

All because Aunt Rasa would take in a poor, illiterate seven-year-old girl because she liked the way the girl's mind worked when she conversed with her. For this alone, Rasa would deserve to be one of the great women of Basilica. And this was why, instead of teaching classes in the higher schools, the only teaching Shedemei did was here in Rasa's house, where twice a year she taught a class of Aunt Rasa's most prized science students. Indeed, officially Shedemei was still a resident here in Rasa's house—she even had a bedroom here, though she hadn't used it since the last time she taught, and always half expected to find it occupied by someone else. It never was, though, no matter how consistently Shedemei slept on the cot in her rooms. Rasa always kept a place for her.

Inside the house, Shedemei soon learned that Rasa's very greatness meant that it would not be possible to see her till later in the day. Though Rasa was not at present a member of the city council, she had been asked to attend this morning's meeting. Shedemei had not expected this. It made her feel lost. For the dream still burned within her, and had to be spoken aloud.

"Perhaps," said the girl who had noticed her and spoken to her, "perhaps there's something I could help you with."

"I don't think so," said Shedemei, smiling kindly. "It was foolishness anyway."

"Foolishness is my specialty," the girl said. "I know you. You're *Shedemei*." She said the name with such reverence that Shedemei was quite embarrassed.

"I am. Forgive me for not remembering your name. I've seen you here many times before, though."

"I'm Luet," said the girl.

"Ah," said Shedemei. The name brought associations with it. "The waterseer," she said. "The Lady of the Lake."

The girl was clearly flattered that Shedemei knew who she was. But what woman in Basilica had not heard of her? "Not yet," said Luet. "Perhaps not ever. I'm only thirteen."

"No, I imagine you have years yet to wait. And it isn't automatic, is it?"

"It all depends," said Luet, "on the quality of my dreams."

Shedemei laughed. "And isn't that true of all of us?"

"I suppose," said Luet, smiling.

Shedemei turned to go. And then realized again whom she was talking with. "Waterseer," she said. "You must have some idea of the meanings of dreams."

Luet shook her head. "For dream interpretation you have to pay the truthmongers in the Inner Market."

"No," said Shedemei. "I don't mean that kind of dream. Or that kind of meaning. It was very strange. I never remember my dreams. But this time it felt . . . very compelling. Perhaps even . . . perhaps the kind of dream that I imagine one like *you* would have."

Luet cocked her head and looked at her. "If your dream might come from the Oversoul, Shedemei, then I need to hear it. But not here."

Shedemei followed the younger girl—half my age, she realized—into the back of the house and up a flight of stairs that Shedemei barely knew existed, for this region of the house was used for storage of old artifacts and furniture and classroom materials. They went up two more flights, into the attic space under a roof, where it was hot and dark.

"My dream was not so secret that we needed to come *here* to tell it," said Shedemei.

"You don't understand," said Luet. "There's someone else who must hear, if the dream is truly from the Oversoul." With that, Luet removed a grating from the gable wall and stooped through it, out into the bright air.

Shedemei, half blinded by the sunlight, could not see at first that there was a flat porch-like roof directly under the opening in the wall. She thought that Luet had stepped into nothingness and floated on the air. Then her eyes adjusted and, by squinting, she could see what Luet was walking on. She followed.

This flat area was invisible from the street, or from anywhere else, for that matter. A half dozen different sloping roofs came together here, and a large drainage hole in the center of the flat area made it clear why this place existed. In a heavy rain, it could fill up with roof runoff as much as four feet deep, until the drain could carry the water away. It was more of a pool than a porch.

It was also a perfect hiding place, since not even the residents of Rasa's house had any notion that this place existed—except, obviously, Luet and whoever was hiding here.

Her eyes adjusted further. In the shade of a portable awning sat an older girl who looked enough like Luet that Shedemei was not surprised to hear her introduced as Hushidh the Raveler, Luet's older sister. And across a low table from Hushidh sat a young man of large stature, but still too young to shave.

"Don't you know me, Shedemei?" said the boy.

"I think so," she said.

"I was much shorter when last you lived in Mother's house," he said.

"Nafai," she said. "I heard you had gone to the desert."

"Gone and come again too often, I fear," said Nafai. "I never thought to see a day when Gorayni soldiers would be keeping the gate of Basilica."

"Not for long," said Shedemei.

"I've never heard of the Gorayni giving up a city, once they had captured it," said Nafai.

"But they didn't capture Basilica," said Shedemei. "They only stepped in and protected us in a time of trouble."

"There are ashes from dozens and dozens of bonfires out on the desert," said Nafai, "and yet no sign of any encampment there. The story I hear is that the Gorayni leader pretended to have a huge army, led by General Moozh the Monster, when in fact he had only a thousand men."

"He explained it as a necessary ruse in order to psychologically overwhelm the Palwashantu mercenaries who were running wild."

"Or psychologically overwhelm the city guard?" said Nafai. "Never mind. Luet has brought you here. Do you know why?"

Luet interrupted at once. "No, Nafai. She's not part of that. She came on her own, to tell Mother a dream. Then she thought of telling me, and I wanted both of you to hear, in case it comes from the Oversoul."

"Why *him?*" asked Shedemei.

"The Oversoul speaks to him, as much as to me," Luet said. "He forced her to speak to him, and now they are friends."

"A man *forced* the Oversoul to speak to him?" asked Shedemei. "When did such things start happening in the world?"

"Only recently," said Luet, smiling. "There are stranger things on heaven and earth than are dreamt of in your philosophy, Shedemei."

Shedemei smiled back, but couldn't remember where the quotation came from, or why it should be amusing at this time.

"Your dream," said Luet's sister Hushidh.

"Now I feel silly," said Shedemei. "I've made too much of it, to tell it to such a large audience."

Luet shook her head. "And yet you walked all the way here from—where do you live? The Cisterns?"

"The Wells, but not far from the Cisterns district."

"You come all that way to tell Aunt Rasa," said Luet. "I think this dream may be more important to you than even *you* understand. So tell us the dream, please."

Glancing again at Nafai, Shedemei found she couldn't bring herself to speak.

"Please," said Nafai. "I won't mock your dream, or tell anyone else. I want to hear it only for whatever truth might be in it."

Shedemei laughed nervously. "I just . . . I'm not comfortable speaking in front of a man. It's nothing against you. Aunt Rasa's son, of course I trust you, I just . . ."

"He's *not* a man," said Luet. "Not *really.*"

"Thanks," murmured Nafai.

"He doesn't deal with women as men usually do. And not many days ago, the Oversoul commanded me to take him down to the lake. He sailed it, he floated it right along with me. The Oversoul commanded it, and he was not slain."

Shedemei looked at him in new awe. "Is this the time when all the prophecies come together?"

"Tell us your dream," said Hushidh softly.

"I dreamt—this will sound so silly!—I dreamt of myself tending a garden in the clouds. Not just the plants and animals I'm working with, but every plant and animal I'd ever heard of. Only it wasn't a large garden, just a small one. Yet they all fit within it, and all were alive and growing. I floated along in the clouds—forever, it seemed. Through the longest night in the world, a thousand-year night. And then suddenly it was daylight again, and I could look down off the edge of the cloud and see a new land, a green and beautiful land, and I said to myself—in the dream, you understand—This world has no need of my garden after all. So I left the garden and stepped off the cloud—"

"A dream of falling," said Luet.

"I didn't fall," said Shedemei. "I just stepped out and there I was, on the ground. And as I wandered through the forests and meadows, I realized that in fact many of the plants from my garden *were* needed, after all. So I reached up my hand, and the plants I needed *rained* down on me as seeds. I planted them, and they grew before my eyes. And then I realized that many of my animals were also needed. This was a world that had lost its birds. There were no birds at all, and few reptiles, and none of the beasts of burden or the domesticated meat animals. And yet there were billions of insects for the birds and reptiles to eat, and pastures and meadows to feed the ruminants. So again I lifted my hands toward the clouds, and down from the clouds rained the embryos of the animals I needed, and I watered them and they grew quickly, large and strong. The birds took flight, the cattle and sheep wandered off to the brooks and meadows, and the snakes and lizards all slithered and scampered away. And I heard the words as if someone else had spoken them in my ears, 'No one has ever had such a garden as yours, Shedemei, my daughter.' But it wasn't my mother's or father's voice. And I wasn't sure whether the voice was speaking of my garden in the clouds, or this new world where I was restoring the flora and fauna lost so many years before."

That was the dream, all she could remember of it.

At first they said nothing. Then Luet spoke. "I wonder how you knew that the plants and animals you called down to you from the clouds were flora and fauna that had once lived in that place, but had been lost."

"I don't know," said Shedemei. "But that's how I felt it to be. How I *knew* it to be. These plants and animals were not being introduced, they were being restored."

"And you couldn't tell whether the voice was male or female," said Hushidh.

"The question didn't come up. The voice made me think of my parents, until I realized it wasn't either of them. But I didn't think to notice whether the voice was actually female or male. I can't think which it was even now."

Luet and Hushidh and Nafai began to confer with each other, but they spoke loudly enough for Shedemei to hear—they were not excluding her at all. "Her dream has a voyage in it," said Nafai. "That's consistent with what I was told—and the flora and fauna were being restored. That says Earth to me, and no other place."

"It points that way," said Luet.

"But the clouds," said Hushidh. "What of that? Clouds go from continent to continent, perhaps, but never from planet to planet."

"Even dreams from the Oversoul don't come ready made," said Nafai. "The truth flows into our minds, but then our brain draws on our own mental library to find images with which to express those ideas. A great voyage through the air. Elemak saw it as a strange kind of house; Shedemei sees it as a cloud; I heard it as the voice of the Oversoul, saying we must go to Earth."

"Earth," said Shedemei.

"Father didn't hear it, nor Issib either," said Nafai. "But I'm as sure of it as I am that I'm alive and sitting here. The Oversoul plans to go to Earth."

"That makes sense with your dream, Shedemei," said Luet. "Humankind left the Earth forty million years ago. The deep winter that settled over the Earth may have killed off most species of reptiles and all the birds. Only the fish and the amphibians, and a few small warm-blooded animals would have survived."

"But it's been forty million years since then," said Shedemei. "Earth must have recovered long ago. There should have been ample time for new speciation."

"How long was the Earth encased in ice?" asked Nafai. "How slowly did the ice recede? Where have the landmasses moved in the millions of years since then?"

"I see," said Shedemei. "It's possible."

"But that magic trick," said Hushidh. "Raising her hands and the seeds and embryos coming down, and then watering the *embryos* to make them grow."

"Well, actually, that part made sense to me right off," said Shedemei. "The way we store our samples in the kind of research I do is to dry-crystallize the seeds and embryos. It essentially locks all their body processes into exactly the moment in which the crystallization took place. We store them bone dry, and then when it's time to restore them, we just add distilled water and the crystals decrystallize in a very rapid but non-explosive chain reaction. The whole organism, because it's so small, can be restored to full functions again within a fraction of a second. Of course, with the embryos we have to be able to put them immediately in a liquid growing solution and hook them up to artificial yolks or placentas, so we can't restore very many at a time."

"In order to carry with you enough samples to restore a significant amount of the flora and fauna most likely to have been killed off on Earth, how much equipment would it take?" asked Nafai.

"How much? A lot—a huge amount. A caravan."

"But what if you had to choose the most significant ones—the most useful birds, the most important animals, the plants we most need for food and shelter."

"Then any size would do," said Shedemei. "You just prioritize—if you have only one camel to carry it, then that's how many you take—two drycases per camel. Plus a camel to carry each set of restoration equipment and materials."

"So it could be done," said Nafai triumphantly.

"You believe the Oversoul will send you to Earth?" asked Shedemei.

"We believe it's the most important thing going on right now in the entire world of Harmony," said Nafai.

"My dream?"

"Your dream is part of it," said Luet. "So is mine, I think." She told Shedemei her dream of angels and diggers.

"It sounds plausible enough as a symbol of a world where new-life forms have evolved," said Shedemei. "What you're forgetting is that if your dream comes from the Oversoul, it can't possibly be literally true."

"Why not?" asked Luet. She seemed a little offended.

"Because how would the Oversoul know what's happening on Earth? How would it see a true picture of any species there? The Earth is a thousand lightyears away. There has never been an electromagnetic signal tight and true enough to carry significant transmissions that distance. If the Oversoul gave you that dream, she's only making it up."

"Maybe she's guessing," said Hushidh.

"Maybe he's only guessing about the need for Shedemei's seeds and embryos," said Nafai. "But we must still do what the dream commands. Shedemei must collect these seeds and embryos, and prepare to take them to Earth with us."

Shedemei looked at them in bafflement. "I came to tell

Aunt Rasa a dream, not abandon my career on a mad impossible journey. How do you think you're going to Earth? By cloud?"

"The Oversoul has said we're going," said Nafai. "When the time comes, the Oversoul will tell us how."

"That's absurd," said Shedemei. "I'm a scientist. I know the Oversoul exists because our submissions are often transmitted to computers in faraway cities, something that can be done in no other way. But I've always assumed that the Oversoul was nothing more than a computer controlling an array of communications satellites."

Nafai looked at Luet and Hushidh in consternation. "Issib and I struggled to figure that out," he said, "and Shedemei knew it all along."

"You never asked me," said Shedemei.

"We would never have *spoken* to you," said Nafai. "After all, you're *Shedemei.*"

"Just another teacher in your mother's house," said Shedemei.

"Yes, like the sun is just another star in the sky," said Nafai.

Shedemei laughed and shook her head. It had never occurred to her that the young ones would hold her in such awe. She enjoyed knowing it—it felt good to think that someone admired her—but it also made her feel faintly shy and exposed. She had to live up to this image that they had of her, and she was nothing more than a hardworking woman who had been disturbed by a dream.

"Shedemei," said Hushidh, "whether it seems possible or not, the Oversoul is asking us to prepare for this voyage. We would never have dreamed of asking *you,* but the Oversoul has brought you to us."

"Coincidence brought me to you."

"Coincidence is just the word we use when we have not yet discovered the cause," said Luet. "It's an illusion of the human mind, a way of saying, 'I don't know why this happened this way, and I have no intention of finding out.'"

"That was in another context," said Shedemei.

"You had the dream," said Nafai. "You knew it mattered. It made you want to tell Mother. We were here when you arrived, and she was not. But we, too, were brought together by the Oversoul. Don't you see that you have been invited?"

Shedemei shook her head. "My work is here, not on some insane journey whose destination is a thousand lightyears away."

"Your work?" said Hushidh. "What is the value of your work, compared to the task of restoring lost species to Earth? Your work has been notable already, but to be the gardener for a planet . . ."

"*If* it's true," said Shedemei.

"Well," said Nafai, "we've all faced that same dilemma. *If* it's true. None of us can decide that for you, so when you make up your mind, let us know."

Shedemei nodded, but privately she knew that she would do everything within her power to avoid seeing these people again. It was too strange. They made too much of her dream. They demanded too much sacrifice of her.

"She has decided not to help us," said Luet.

"Nothing of the kind!" said Shedemei. But in her heart she wondered, guiltily, How did she know?

"Even if you decide not to go with us," said Nafai, "will you do this much? Will you gather a fair sampling of seeds and embryos—perhaps two camels' load? And the equipment we'll need to restore them? And train some of us in how to do the work?"

"Gladly," said Shedemei. "I should be able to find time over the next several months."

"We don't have *months,*" said Nafai. "We have hours. Or, perhaps, days."

"Don't make me laugh, then," said Shedemei. "What kind of garden am I supposed to assemble in hours?"

"Aren't there bio-libraries here in Basilica?" asked Hushidh.

"Well, yes—that's where I get my starting samples."

"Then couldn't you draw from them, and get most of what you'd need?"

"For two camels' load, I suppose I could get *all* of it. But the equipment to restore them, especially the animal embryos—the only equipment I have is my own set, and it would take months to build more."

"If you come with us," said Luet, "then you could bring your own. And if you don't come with us, you'll have the months to build more."

"You're asking me to give up my own equipment?"

"For the Oversoul," said Luet.

"So *you* believe."

"For Aunt Rasa's son," said Hushidh.

Of course the raveler would know how to break into my heart, thought Shedemei. "If Aunt Rasa asks me to do it for you," said Shedemei, "then I'll do it."

Nafai got a glint in his eye. "What if Mother asked you to go with us?"

"She never would," said Shedemei.

"What if Aunt Rasa was going herself?" asked Luet.

"She never will," said Shedemei.

"That's what Mother herself says," said Nafai, "but we'll see."

"Which of you will learn to use the equipment?" asked Shedemei.

"Hushidh and I," said Luet quickly.

"Then come this afternoon so I can teach you."

"You'll give us the equipment?" asked Hushidh.

Was she delighted, or merely surprised?

"I'll consider it," said Shedemei. "And teaching you how to operate it will cost nothing but time."

With that, Shedemei got up from the carpet and stepped out from under the awning. She looked for the grating through which she had come, but Luet must have replaced it, and she couldn't remember where she needed to go.

She didn't need to say anything, however, for Luet must have noticed her confusion instantly, and now the girl was leading her to the place. The grating hadn't been replaced, it had simply been out of sight behind the roofline. "I know the way from here," said Shedemei. "You needn't come with me."

"Shedemei," said Luet. "I dreamed of *you* once. Not many days ago."

"Oh?"

"I know you'll doubt me, and think I'm saying this only

to try to persuade you to come, but it's not a coincidence. I was in the woods, and it was night, and I was afraid. I saw several women. Aunt Rasa, and Hushidh; Eiadh and Dol. And you. I saw you."

"I wasn't there," said Shedemei. "I never go into the woods."

"I know—I told you, it was a dream, though I was awake."

"I mean what I said, Luet. I *never* go into the woods. I never go down to the lake. I'm sure what you do is very important and fine, but it's not part of my life. It's no part of my life."

"Then perhaps," said Luet, "you should change your life."

To that Shedemei had nothing civil to say, so she stepped through the opening in the wall. Behind her she could hear the murmuring sound of their conversation resuming, but she couldn't make out any of the words. Not that she wanted to. This was outrageous, to ask her to do what they were asking her to do.

And yet it had felt so wonderful, in her dream, to reach up and bring down life from the clouds. Why hadn't she just left in that way—as a beautiful dream? Why had she told these children? Why couldn't she just forget what they had said, instead of having these thoughts that now whirled in her mind.

To return to Earth. Home to Earth.

What did that mean? In forty million years, human beings had been content on Harmony. Why now should Earth be calling to her? It was madness, contagious madness in these troubled times.

Still, instead of going home she went to the bio-library, and spent several hours poring over the catalogue, making up a plausible order for two camels' load of crystalized seeds and embryos that might restore the most useful plants and animals to an Earth that lost them long, long ago.

IN THE CITY COUNCIL, AND NOT IN A DREAM

Rasa had spent her life filled with confidence. There was nothing that could happen, she knew, that she could not handle with a combination of wit, kindness, and determination. People could always be persuaded, or if they could not, then they could be ignored and in time they would fade away. This philosophy had brought her to a point where her household was one of the most respected schools in Basilica, despite the fact that it was so new; it had also made her personally influential in every part of the city's life, though she had never held any office. She was consulted on most major decisions of the city council; she served on the governing boards of many of the arts councils; and, above all, she was privately consulted by the women—and, yes, even the men—who made most of the important decisions concerning Basilica's government and business. She was wooed by many men, but stayed happily married to the one man she had ever known who was neither threatened by nor covetous of her power. She had created a perfect role for herself within the city, and loved to live the part.

What had never occurred to her was how fragile it all was. The fabric of her life had been woven on the loom of Basilica, and now that Basilica was breaking apart, her life was fraying, snagging, tearing apart. Her former husband, Gaballufix, had begun the process, back while they were still married, when he attempted to get her to try to change the laws forbidding men to own property in the city. When she realized what his purpose in marrying her had been, she let the contract lapse and remarried Wetchik—permanently, as far as she was concerned. But Gaballufix hadn't given up, building support among the lowest sort of men in the villages outside the walls of the city. Then he brought them in as tolchoks, terrifying the women of the city, and then as mercenary soldiers in those hideous masks, supposedly to protect the city from the tolchoks—but as far as Rasa could tell, the mercenaries *were* the tolchoks in fancy holographic uniforms.

But Gaballufix might have been containable, if the Oversoul hadn't begun to act so strangely. She actually spoke to a man—and not just any man, but Wetchik himself. The problems this caused Rasa were incalculable. Not only was her former husband attacking the ancient laws of the city of women, but now her present husband was telling everyone who would listen that Basilica was going to be destroyed. Her dear friend Dhel remarked to her at the time—only a few weeks ago—that people were surprised that Rasa hadn't also been married to Roptat, the leader of the pro-Gorayni party. "Perhaps you ought to check your bed for some kind of madness-inducing parasite, my dear," said Dhel. She was joking, of course, but it was a painful joke.

Painful, but nothing compared to these past few days. Everything was falling apart. Gaballufix stole Wetchik's fortune and tried to kill his sons—including both of Rasa's own sons. Then the Oversoul commanded Luet to lead Nafai—of all people, *Nafai,* a mere child—down to the forbidden lake, where he floated on the water like a woman—like a waterseer. That same night, no doubt still wet from the lake of peace, Nafai had killed Gab. In one sense it was fair enough, for Gaballufix had tried to kill *him.* But to Rasa it was the most terrible thing she could imagine, her own son murdering her former husband.

Yet even that was only the beginning. For on that same night, she had found out exactly how monstrous her two daughters were. Sevya, sleeping with Kokor's husband— and Kokor then lashing out and nearly killing her. Civilization didn't even reach into my own home. My son a murderer, one daughter an adulterer and the other a murderer in her heart. Only Issib was still civilized. Issib the cripple, she thought bitterly. Perhaps that's what civilization is composed of—cripples who have banded together to try to control the strong. Wasn't that what Gaballufix said once? "In a time of peace, Rasa, you women can afford to surround yourselves with eunuchs. But when the enemy comes from outside, the eunuchs won't save you. You'll wish for real men, then, dangerous men, powerful men— and where will they be, since you've driven them all away?"

Rashgallivak—he was one of the foolish weaklings, wasn't he? One of the "eunuchs," in the sense that Gaballufix meant. He hadn't the strength to control the animals that Gaballufix had brought under harness. And then

Hushidh cut loose that harness and the city began to burn. In my own house it happened! Why, again, am I the focal point?

The last insult was the coming of General Moozh, for Rasa knew now that it was he—it could be no one else. So audacious—to march to the city with only a thousand men, coming at a time when no enemy could be resisted, and when anyone willing to pretend to be a friend would be invited in. Rasa was not fooled by his promises. She was not deceived by the fact that his soldiers had withdrawn from the streets. They still held the walls and the gates, didn't they?

And even Moozh was tied to her, just as Wetchik and Gaballufix and Nafai and Rashgallivak had been tied. For he had come with her letter, and it was by using her name that he had first gained entry into the city.

Things could not possibly get any worse. And then, this morning, Nafai and Elemak had come into her house— from the forest side, which meant that they had both been creeping through lands that were forbidden to men. And why had they come? To inform her that the Oversoul required her to leave the city and join her husband in the desert, bringing with her whatever women she thought might be appropriate.

"Appropriate for what?" asked Rasa.

"Appropriate for marrying," said Elemak, "and bearing children in a new land far from here."

"I should leave the city of Basilica, taking some poor innocent women with me, and go out to live like a tribe of baboons in the desert?"

"Not like baboons," Nafai had said helpfully. "We still wear clothing, and none of us barks."

"I will not consider it," said Rasa.

"Yes you will, Mother," said Nafai.

"Are you threatening me?" asked Rasa—for she had heard too many men say such words recently.

"Not at all," said Nafai. "I'm predicting. I'll bet that before a half hour goes by, you'll be considering it, because you know the Oversoul wants you to do it."

And he was right. Not ten minutes. She couldn't get the idea out of her mind.

How did he know? Because he understood how the Oversoul worked. What he didn't know was that the Oversoul was already working on her. When Wetchik first left for the desert, he asked her to come with him. There was no talk of other women then, but when she prayed to the Oversoul, she was answered as clearly as if a voice had spoken in her heart. Bring your daughters, said the Oversoul. Bring your nieces, any who will come. To the desert, to be the mothers of my people.

To the desert! To be animals! In all her life, Rasa had tried to follow the teachings of the Oversoul. But now she asked too much. Who was Rasa, outside of Basilica, outside of her own house? She was no one there. Just Wetchik's wife. It would be men who ruled there—feral men, like Wetchik's son Elemak. He was one frightening boy, that Elemak; she couldn't believe that Wetchik couldn't see how dangerous he was. It would be Elemak the hunter that she'd depend on for food. And what influence would she have there? What council would listen to her? The men would hold the councils, and the women would cook and wash and care for the babies. It would be like primitive times, like animal times. She could not leave the city of women, for if she did, she would cease to be the Lady Rasa and would become a beast.

I only exist in this place. I am only human in this place.

And yet as she walked into the council chamber she knew that "this place" had ceased to be the city of women. As she looked at the frightened, solemn, angry faces in the council, she knew that Basilica as it once had been would never exist again. A new Basilica might rise in its place, but never again would a woman like Rasa be able to raise her daughters and nieces in perfect peace and security. Always there would be men trying to own, to control, to *meddle*. The best she could hope for would be a man like Wetchik, whose kindness would temper his instinct for power. But was there another Wetchik to be found in this world? And even his benign interference would be too much. All would be ruined. All would be poisoned and defiled.

Oversoul! You have betrayed your daughters!

But she did not cry out her blasphemy. Instead she took her place at one of the tables in the middle of the chamber, where non-voting counselors and clerks sat during the meetings. She could feel their eyes upon her. Many, she knew, blamed her for everything—and she could hardly disagree with them. Her husbands, her son, her daughters; her house where Rashgallivak lost control of his soldiers; and, above all, her letter in the hands of the Gorayni general when he came into the city.

The meeting began, and for the first time in Rasa's memory, the rituals of the opening were rushed, and some were eliminated entirely. No one complained. For they all knew that the deadline the council had imposed on the Gorayni to leave the city now loomed as a deadline on themselves—for it was clear now to all of them that the Gorayni did not intend to leave.

The argument soon raged. No one disputed the fact that the Gorayni now were masters of the city. The city debate was whether to defy the general—some called him Moozh, but only in ridicule, for he refused to answer to the name Vozmuzhalnoy Vozmozhno, and yet told them no other name to use for him—or give his occupation a legal gloss. They hated the idea of giving in to him, but if they did, there was a hope that he'd let them continue to govern the city in exchange for letting him use Basilica as a military base for his operations against the Cities of the Plain and, no doubt, Potokgavan. Yet by making his occupation legal, as he had requested, they gave him power in the long run to destroy them.

Still, what was the alternative? He had made no threats. In fact, all he had sent them was a very respectful letter: "Because my troops have not yet succeeded in abating the danger in Basilica, we are reluctant to abandon our dear friends to the return of such chaos as we found on our arrival. Therefore if you invite us to stay until such time as order is fully restored, we are willing to become your obedient servants for the indefinite future." On its face, the letter portrayed the Gorayni as being docile as lambs.

But they knew by now that nothing with the Gorayni was what it seemed. Oh, they bowed to every order or request of the city council, promising to obey. But only the orders that suited their purpose were actually carried out. And the city guard, too, was unreliable, for their officers had begun practically to worship the Gorayni general, and now were following his example of swearing obedience and then doing as they liked. Oh, the general was a clever man! He provoked no one, he argued with no one, he agreed with everything that was said . . . and yet he was immovable, doing all that he pleased, while never giving them anything they could attack him for. Everyone in the council chamber must have felt it as keenly as Rasa did, the slipping away of their own power, the centering of the city on the will of this one man, and all without any overt word or deed of his.

How does he do it? Rasa wondered. How does he master people without bluster or bullying? How does he make people fear him or love him, not in spite of his ruthlessness but because of it?

Maybe it is simply that he knows so clearly how he wants things to be, she thought. Maybe the fact that he believes in his vision of the world so intensely makes it impossible for those around him not to believe as well. Maybe we're all so hungry for someone to tell us what is true, what we can count on, that we'll accept even a vision that makes us weak and him strong, just for the sake of having a secure world at all.

"We are only a few minutes from the deadline," said old Kobe. "And in all our discussion this morning we have heard nothing from the Lady Rasa."

A murmur of approval arose, but it was immediately drowned in a growl of anger. "We shouldn't hear from her except at her trial!" cried one woman. "She brought all this on us!"

Rasa calmly turned and looked at the woman who spoke. It was Frotera, of course, the lady of another teaching household, who had long been envious of Rasa. "My Lady Frotera," Rasa said, "I fear you may be right."

That silenced them.

"Do you think I haven't also looked and seen what you all can see? Which of the calamities that has befallen us has not been tied to me? My son is accused of murder, my daughters have betrayed each other, Rashgallivak tried to drag them from my own house, my beloved city has been torn by riot and fire, and the army that squats in the gates of Basilica shows you a letter that I wrote. And I did write it, though I never dreamed that it would be used as he has used it. Sisters, all of this is true, but does it mean I have brought all of this upon us? Or does it mean that it has fallen more heavily on me than on any except those whose loved ones perished in the rioting?"

It made them think; ah, yes, she still had the power to tell them a story and make them see, at least for a moment, through her eyes.

"Sisters, if I believed that I was truly the cause of all the evil that has come to Basilica, I would leave at once. I love Basilica too much to be the cause of its downfall. But I am not the cause. The first cause was the greed of Gaballufix—and he married me as his first attempt to make an inroad against our ancient laws. Was it my husband who brought private soldiers into this city? No. It was a man whom I had *refused* to have as my husband. I repudiated Gaballufix while many of you on this council kept voting to tolerate his abuses! Do not forget that!"

Oh, they didn't forget, as they shrank back in their seats.

"Now the Gorayni have come with my letter. But I wrote that letter to help a young Basilican guard obtain refuge with the Gorayni. I knew he was in danger from Rashgallivak's mercenaries, and he had been kind to my son, so I gave him what small protection I could. Now I see that this was a terrible mistake. My letter alerted them to our weakness, and they came to exploit it. But I didn't create our weakness, and if the Gorayni hadn't come, would we be in *better* condition this morning than we are now? Would we even be holding this meeting, or would we all be victims of rape and plunder by the Palwashantu mercenaries? Would our city be in ashes? So tell me, sisters, which is better, to be in a bad situation, yet with *some* hope, or to be destroyed, powerless, utterly hopeless?"

Again a murmur, but she was carrying them. Only rarely had she spoken at such length or with such force—she had long since learned that she remained more powerful by never openly committing herself to anything, but rather working behind the scenes. Still, she had spoken often enough to know how to bend them, at least a little, to her will. It was a power that would be less effective every time she used it, but this was a time when she must use it or lose everything.

"If we defy him, what will happen then? Even if he keeps his word and leaves, can any of you say that our city guard will be as docile as they once were? And I don't believe that he *will* keep his word. Have you ever heard of General Vozmuzhalnoy Vozmozhno giving up one village, one field, one *pebble* that he has conquered?" A growing murmur. "Yes, it *is* General Moozh—we'd be fools to imagine otherwise for a moment. What other Gorayni general would have the audacity to do what he has done? Don't you see how daring and brilliant his plan has been? He came here with only a thousand men, but for a few crucial hours we believed he had a hundred times that number. He has been subservient and obsequious, and yet he has deployed his soldiers where he wanted them, seduced our city guard, and seized whatever supplies he needed. Always he apologizes and explains. Always he keeps us believing that he means well. But he is a liar with every breath he takes, and nothing that he says to us is true. He means to add Basilica to the Gorayni Empire. He will *never* let us go."

Loud muttering filled the room as she waited. Several of the women wept. "Defy him then!" one of the councilors cried.

"And what good would defiance do?" asked Rasa. "How many of us would die? And to what purpose? A fifth of our city is already in ashes. We have already huddled in terror as drunken men rampaged through our city. What would happen if now the plunderers were sober? If they were the same disciplined killers who nailed the rioters to the walls with their own knives? There'd be no refuge for us then!"

"So . . . what do you propose we do, Lady Rasa?"

"Give him what he has asked for. Permission to stay. Only make provision for his soldiers to be quartered outside the walls of the city. Make them take the same oaths that men are required to take when they become our husbands—to stay out of the forbidden parts of the city, to refrain from attempting to own any real property, and to leave when their term is up."

A murmur of approval.

"Will he accept it, Lady Rasa?"

"I have no idea," she said. "But so far, he has made an effort at least to *seem* to comply with our wishes. Let us make our offer as public as possible, and then hope he'll find it more convenient to adhere to its terms than not."

Rasa's exhortations were too successful by half. Yes, they approved her proposal, almost unanimously. But they also appointed her the ambassador to deliver their "invitation" to General Moozh. It was not an interview she looked forward to, but she had no time even to wonder what she ought to say or how she ought to act. The invitation had to be delivered personally and immediately; it was printed out, signed, and sealed on the spot, and the council watched as she left the chamber with the document in hand, minutes before the deadline that they themselves had set.

It was not Mebbekew's finest morning. He had dutifully trudged through the forbidden slopes of Basilica as Nafai led the way, just as he had followed Elemak all the way from the desert around the city to the northern woods. But when they came within sight of Rasa's house, Mebbekew slipped away. He had no intention of being a pawn in *their* plans. If they were here to do some wife-finding, Mebbekew would pick his own, thank you kindly. He would certainly *not* tag along behind his older brother, taking second choice forever; nor would he swallow the humiliation of going into his little brothers' mother's house and pleading with *her* to give up one of her precious nieces. Elemak had his heart set on that porcelain doll, Eiadh . . . well, that was his privilege. Mebbekew preferred women with blood in their veins, women who grunted and growled when they made love, women of vigor and strength. Women who loved Mebbekew.

Well, he found out about vigor and strength, right enough! The fires had been worst in Dolltown and Dauberville, so few of his old lovers were in the houses where he had known them. The few that he could find were *glad* to see him. They were all over him with tears and kisses, eager to have him stay with them. Stay with them *where?* In a half-burnt house with no running water? And *why* did they want him? So he could do all the brute man-labor required to rebuild, to repair; and so he could be their guardian. What a joke! Mebbekew, standing guard over some poor frightened girl! No doubt they would have rewarded him generously with their bodies if he had played the role they scripted for him, but it wasn't worth it—*no* woman was worth it right now, if her needs were even greater than his own. He wasn't here to be a protector or a provider, he was here to find protection and providence.

So he left them with a kiss and a promise, without even staying long enough to bathe or eat, because he knew that if he once got within their clinging embrace these women-in-need would make of him a husband. He had no intention of husbanding himself to women who had nothing to offer him but work and trouble!

As for suggesting to any of his old lovers that she give up everything in Basilica and come wander with him in the desert until they found a promised land, meanwhile having a passel of babies in order to populate their new home—it never seemed to come up in any of his conversations. Not that some of them wouldn't have done it. As they surveyed the ruin of their once-frivolous lives in Basilica, as they remembered the fear of that awful night of rioting, and then the horror of the dead bodies pinned to the walls by the Gorayni, the idea of striding out into the desert with a *real* man to lead and protect them would appeal to some of them. For the first few days, anyway; then they'd realize that the desert was lonely and no fun at all, and they'd be as eager to return to Basilica, ruined or not, as Mebbekew himself was.

It hardly mattered. He never intended to make such a proposal to any of his womenfriends. Let Elemak and Nafai play along with Father and have their stupid visions if they wanted to. All Mebbekew wanted was some woman to take him in to a nice, clean house and a nice clean bed, and hide him and console him for the loss of his fortune until Elemak and Nafai went away. Why should Mebbekew ever go out in the desert again? Basilica might be half-burnt and terrorized and occupied by Gorayni troops, but the toilets and baths still worked in *most* houses, and the food was fresh and there was plenty of pleasure and fun in the old town yet.

Yet even that limited plan wouldn't have worked for long, he gradually came to realize. During his early-morning wanderings through Dolltown, he realized that he couldn't hide in Basilica for long. For he had entered the city illegally, without being recorded, and somewhere along the line he'd get picked up and taken in. The city guard were quite active in the streets now, more than he'd ever seen, and they were demanding thumbscans and eyescans at checkpoints on several streets. He was bound to be picked up one of these days. Indeed, it wasn't easy getting from Dolltown to Rasa's house on Rain Street.

Yes, Rasa's house. It galled him, but he had tried everything else; so here he was, ready to surrender completely to his brothers and his father and their idiotic plans.

Standing in the street, looking at the front of Rasa's house, ready to give in—and yet not ready. It was unbearable. Humiliating. Knock, knock. Good morning, I'm Rasa's sons' half-brother, and I'm here because all my ex-lovers sent me packing and so I'd be grateful if Rasa and my half-brothers would take me in and give me something to eat and drink, not to mention a long hot shower, before I die.

It was a hideous scene to imagine, and even though he

knew he had to do it, Mebbekew had never acquired much practice in doing unpleasant things just because he knew he had to do them. So instead he did what he *usually* did under such circumstances. He waited, just within reach of his painful goal, and then proceeded to do nothing.

He did nothing—suffering imagined torments all the while—for at least twenty minutes, watching the classes of young girls and boys that were meeting on the porch. Now and then he could even catch a word that was said, and so he tried to guess the subjects being taught and what the particular lesson was. It took his mind off his troubles for a moment or two, at least. The nearer class, he decided, was studying either geometry or organic chemistry or building with blocks.

A young woman left one of the classes, jogged down the steps of the porch, and then strode purposefully toward him. No doubt she had seen him watching the porch and decided he was a would-be child molester or burglar. He thought of turning and leaving before she reached him— which was what she almost certainly expected him to do—but instead he studied her face and realized that he recognized her.

"Good morning," she said icily, as soon as she was close enough to say it without shouting.

Mebbekew wasn't worried about the prospect of an argument. He had never yet met a young and beautiful woman he couldn't warm up quickly enough, if he tried hard enough to find out what she hungered for, and then gave it to her. It was always a pleasure dealing with a woman he had never worked on before. Especially because he recognized her at once—or at least saw a resemblance.

"Didn't you used to be Dolya?" he asked.

Her face turned scarlet, but her expression became colder and angrier. So he was right—she *was* Dol. "Shall I send for the Guard to send you away?"

"I saw you in *Pirates* and *West Wind*. You were brilliant," he said.

Her blush deepened and her expression softened.

"You had the talent," he went on. "It wasn't just looks. It

wasn't just that you were young and sweet. I never understood why they didn't give you adult parts as you got older. I know you could have carried it off. It was damned unfair."

And now her expression wasn't angry at all, but rather bemused. "I have never heard anyone engage in such transparent, cynical flattery," she said.

"Ah, but I meant every word. Dolya—I suppose you go by the adult name, Dol, now?"

"To my friends, I do. Others call me ma'am."

"Ma'am, I hope that someday I can earn the right to be your friend. In the meantime, I was hoping you might tell me if my half-brothers Elemak and Nafai are in Rasa's house."

She eyed him up and down. "I don't see that you look all that much like either of them."

"Ah, but now you flatter *me*," he said.

She laughed a little and stepped toward him, offering her hand. "I'll take you in, if you're really Mebbekew."

He withdrew a pace from her. "Don't touch me! I'm filthy. Two days' traveling in the desert isn't the best perfume, and if my body's stench didn't kill you my breath would."

"I didn't expect you to be a bouquet," she said. "I'll risk taking your hand to lead you in."

"Then you have courage to match your beauty," he said, taking her hand. "By the Oversoul," he whispered, "your hand is cool and soft to touch."

She laughed again—an actress with as much experience as Dol had had, back when she was famous, could never be fooled by flattery. But Mebbekew figured that it had been years now since anyone had bothered to flatter her at all, so the very fact that he thought it was worth trying would be a sort of meta-flattery against which she wouldn't be able to protect herself. And, indeed, it seemed to be working quite well.

"You don't have to say such things," she said. "Aunt Rasa left instructions for you to be admitted as soon as you— how did she say it—as soon as you 'bothered to show up.'"

"If I had known I'd find you here, ma'am, I'd have come

much sooner. And as you say, I don't have to flatter anybody to get into Rasa's house this morning. So what I say to you now isn't flattery. It's my own heart. When I was a boy I fell in love with the image of Dolya on the stage. Now I see you with a man's eyes. I see you as a woman. And I know that your beauty has only increased. I never knew you were one of Rasa's nieces or I would have stayed in school."

"I *was* her niece. I'm a teacher here now. Comportment, that sort of thing. I've been teaching Eiadh in particular. You know, the one your brother Elemak is wooing."

"It's just like Elemak to woo the pale copy, while he ignores the original." Mebbekew deliberately kept his eyes on her face, but not on her eyes—instead he studied her lips, her hair, all her features, knowing that she would see how his eyes moved, how he was drinking her in. "Elemak's only my half-brother, by the way," said Mebbekew. "When I'm all cleaned up you'll see that I'm much better looking."

She laughed, but he knew he had won her interest—he had long since learned that flattery always works, and that even the most outrageously dishonest praise is believed, if you repeat it and elaborate on it enough. In this case, though, he really didn't have to lie. Dol *was* beautiful, though of course nowhere near as lovely as she had been when she was an ethereal child of thirteen. Still, she had grace and poise and a smile that dazzled, and, now that he had been working on her for a few minutes, her eyes were bright and wide whenever she looked at him. It was desire. He had kindled desire in her. It wasn't the desire for passion, of course; rather it was the desire to hear more of his praise for her beauty, more of his verbal petting. Yet he knew from experience that it would be easy enough to get from here to there, if he wasn't too tired after breakfast and a bath.

She showed him to her own bedroom—a good sign— where the servants ran a bath for him. He was still in the water, luxuriating in his cleanliness, when she came back in with a tray of food and a pitcher of water. She had brought it with her own hands, and they were alone. All the time she chattered—not nervously, either, but comfortably. That was Mebbekew's greatest talent, that women so easily became comfortable with him that they talked to him with the kind of candor they usually had only with their girlfriends.

As she talked, he rose up out of the water; when she turned around from setting the tray on her dresser, she saw him toweling himself down, quite naked. She gasped prettily and looked away.

"I'm sorry," he said. "It didn't occur to me that you'd be startled. You must have seen so many men in your days as an actress—I've been on the stage, too, and no one is shy or modest backstage."

"I was young," said Dol. "They always protected me in those days."

"I feel like some kind of beast, then," said Mebbekew. "I didn't mean to shock you."

"No," she said. "No, I'm not shocked."

"The trouble is that I haven't anything to wear. I don't think it would be helpful to put my dirty clothes back on."

"The servants already took your clothes to be washed. I have a robe for you, though."

"One of yours? I doubt it will fit *me*." All this time, of course, he had continued toweling, still making no effort to cover himself. And as they talked, she had turned back around and now was looking at him quite frankly. Since things were going so smoothly and he anticipated making love to this woman very soon, his body had become quite alert. As soon as he caught her looking at his crotch, he pretended to notice for the first time and made a show of putting the towel in front of himself. "I'm sorry," he said. "I've been alone on the desert so long, and you're so beautiful—I meant no insult."

"I'm not insulted," she said. And he could see the desire in *her* eyes, too. She wanted more than pretty words from him now. As he had guessed, she probably didn't get many suitors these days. With her beauty, she'd have had no lack of lovers in Dolltown, but as a teacher in Rasa's house the opportunities would be much more limited. So she was almost certainly as eager as he was.

This was what he had come back to Basilica for. Not those frightened, hungry women in Dolltown, who needed him to be strong and dependable, but *this* woman, who needed him only to be passionate and flattering and fun. Dol felt herself to be safe and comfortable enough in Rasa's house that she could still be what Basilican women were *supposed* to be—self-supporting providers for men, needing nothing more from their lovers than a little pleasure and attention.

She brought him her robe. It probably could have fit well enough, but he made a show of jamming his arm so far in the sleeve that it barely passed his elbow. "Oh, that won't do," she said.

"It hardly matters by now," he said. "I don't exactly have any secrets from you anymore!"

Of course, he had dropped the towel to try on the robe. He bent over to pick it up, even as he was taking the robe off his arm. But when he stood again, she took both the towel and the robe away from him. "You're right," she said. "There's little point in trying for modesty now." She tossed the robe and towel into a corner and then brought him a handful of grapes from the food tray on the dresser. "Here," she said.

She held out the grape, not to his hand, but to his lips. He leaned forward farther than he needed to, and got her fingers into his mouth along with the grape. She let her fingers linger in his mouth as he slowly pulled the grape away. At last he bit down on the grape and felt the juice of it squirt inside his mouth. It was tart and sweet and delicious. He sat on the bed and she fed him another, and then another. But the rest of the grapes ended up on the floor.

Moozh had waited with great anticipation to meet Lady Rasa at last, and she did not disappoint him. He had installed himself in Gaballufix's house—the symbolism was deliberate—and he knew that she would certainly see the true meaning of his residence here. Lady Rasa would not be a *complete* fool, that much he was sure of, from what he had heard about her. All that remained now was to see which of several plans he ought to follow with her. She might be turned into an ally. She might be turned into a dupe. She might, of course, be an implacable enemy. No matter which, he would make use of her.

She did not carry herself with any particular majesty; she made no attempt to entice or intimidate him. But that was just about the only way a woman could impress him anymore. He had been worked on by the finest court women in Gollod, but it was plain that Rasa had no interest in working on him. Rather she spoke with him as with an equal, and he liked it. He liked *her*. It would be a good game.

"Of course I want to accept the invitation of the city council," he said. "We are only too happy help this beautiful city maintain order and security while rebuilding from these unfortunate events of the past weeks. But I have a problem that perhaps you can help me with."

He could see from the look on her face that she had expected more demands from him—and he knew, too, that she had no illusions about the fact that he was in a position to make demands, and make them stick, too.

"You see," he said, "the traditional way for a Gorayni general to reward his men after a great victory is to divide up the conquered territory and give them land and wives."

"But you have not conquered Basilica," said Rasa pointedly.

"Exactly!" he said. "You see my dilemma. My men performed with extraordinary heroism and discipline in this campaign, and their victory over the ruffians and rioters was complete. And yet I lack a means to reward them!"

"Our treasury is deep," said Rasa. "I'm sure the city council can make each of your thousand men as rich as you please."

"Money?" asked Moozh. "Oh, you hurt me deeply. Me and my men alike. We are not mercenaries!"

"You accept land, but not the money with which to buy land?"

"Land is a matter of title and honor. A landed man is a

lord. But *money*—that would be like calling my soldiers *tradesmen*."

She gazed at him for a moment, and then said, "General Vozmuzhalnoy Vozmozhno, does the Imperator know that you call these men *your* soldiers? *Your* men?"

Moozh felt a sudden thrill of fear. It was delicious indeed—it had been a long time since he had sat across a table from someone who knew how to take the initiative away from him. And she had struck immediately at his weakest point. For not only had he defied the Imperator's orders about not making any offensive maneuvers, he had also left behind the corpses of the Imperator's public and private spies to come here. His greatest danger at the moment came from the Imperator, who would surely by now have heard of his venture. Moozh knew the Imperator well enough to know that he would not act rashly—indeed, that was the Imperator's primary fault, that he was terrified of risk—but already a new intercessor would certainly be on his way southward, and not without temple troops to back him up. Either Moozh would be able to put a good face on things and win back the Imperial trust, or he would have to commit himself to open rebellion with only a thousand troops and a hundred kilometers deep in hostile territory. It was not a good moment for him to face an opponent who understood exactly what his weakness was.

"When I call them mine," said Moozh, "of course I recognize that they are mine only as long as the Imperator permits me to be his servant."

"I notice that you don't deny that you *are* Vozmuzhalnoy Vozmozhno."

He shrugged. "I recognize that you are far too clever for me. Why should I try to conceal my identity from *you?*"

She frowned. His flattery and his frank admission had set her back a bit. Now she would no doubt be wondering why he so willingly admitted his true name, and why he was calling her clever. She would assume that because he called her clever, it must mean she had *not* been clever at all. Thus she would no longer trust her belief that the way to get at him was by exploiting differences between him and the

Imperator. He had long since learned that one of the best ways to disarm a genuinely clever opponent was to make him mistrust his own strengths, and it seemed to be working well enough with Rasa.

"Cleverness doesn't enter into it," she said. "Truth is what matters. I don't believe there's a word of truth in what you say. You don't usually reward your soldiers with land, or you'd have no soldiers left. Your officers, perhaps. But this talk of land is just your first bid in an effort to destroy the land law of the city of women. Let me guess how the game goes: I return to the council with your humble request, and they send me back with an offer to settle your men outside the city. You praise our generosity, and then point out that your men could never be content as second-class citizens of a land they had rescued from destruction. How could he explain to Gorayni soldiers that they could never own land inside the city? Then you would propose a compromise— just to allow them and us to both save face. Your compromise would be that Gorayni soldiers who married Basilican women would be allowed to hold half-ownership with them of their land inside the city. The women would, of course, remain completely in control of the land, but your soldiers could keep their self-respect."

"You have a gift of prescience," said Moozh.

"Not so—I'm only improvising," she said. "Half-rights in property would lead within weeks to a series of opportune marriages, and then there'd be pressure for an equal vote—especially since you will have proved that your men are meek and obedient husbands who make no effort to control the property in which they have a titular half-interest. How many steps from there to the day when women have *no* vote, and all the property of Basilica is owned by men?"

"My dear lady, you misjudge me."

"You don't have much time," said Rasa. "Your Imperator will certainly have representatives here within two weeks at the latest."

"All Gorayni armies travel with Imperial representatives."

"Not yours," said Rasa. "Or the city guard would know

it. We've read accounts here of how your army works, and there is no intercessor's tent. Some of your soldiers feel the lack of confession quite keenly."

"I have nothing to fear from the coming of an intercessor."

"Then why did you try to fool me into thinking you had one here already? No, General Vozmuzhalnoy Vozmozhno, I think you have to move swiftly indeed to consolidate your position here before you face the challenge of the Imperator. I think you don't have time to deal with any kind of uprising, either—it has to be settled peacefully and at once."

So she had not been deflected at all by his flattery. The thrill of fear once again pulsed through him. "Ma'am, you are wise indeed. It is possible that the Imperator will misconstrue my actions, even though my motive was purely to serve him. But you're mistaken to think it will take many gradual steps to consolidate my position here."

"You think not?" asked Rasa.

"It won't take many marriages, I think, but only one." He smiled. "Mine."

At last he had succeeded in startling *her*. "Aren't you already married, sir?" she asked.

"As a matter of fact I am not," said Moozh. "I have never been married. Until now it has always been politically preferable."

"And you think that your marriage to a Basilican woman will solve everything for you? Even if they grant you a special exception and let you share in your wife's property, there's no one woman in Basilica who controls so much property that it would make any difference to you."

"I don't intend to marry for property."

"For what, then?"

"For influence," he said. "For prestige."

She studied his face for a moment. "If you think *I* have that kind of influence or prestige, you're a fool."

"You are a striking woman, and I confess that you are of the right age for me—mature and accomplished. To marry you would make life a dangerous and engrossing game, and you and I would both enjoy it. Alas, though, *you* are already married, even if your husband is rumored to be a mad prophet hiding in the desert. I don't believe in breaking up happy families. Besides, you have too many opponents and enemies in this city for you to be a useful consort."

"Imperators have consorts, General Vozmuzhalnoy Vozmozhno; generals have wives."

"Please, call me Moozh," he said. "It's a nickname that I only permit my friends to use."

"I am not your friend."

"The nickname means 'husband,'" he said.

"I know what it means, and neither I nor any woman of Basilica will ever call you that to your face."

"Husband," said Moozh, "and Basilica is my bride. I will wed her, I will bed her, and she will bear me many children, this fair city. And if she doesn't take me willingly as her husband, I will have her anyway, and in the end she *will* be docile."

"In the end this city will have your balls on a plate, General," she retorted. "The last lord of this house discovered that, when he tried to do what you are doing."

"But he was a fool," said Moozh. "I know it, because he lost *you*."

"He didn't lose *me*," said Rasa. "He lost himself."

He smiled at her. "Farewell, ma'am," he said. "Till we meet again."

"I doubt we will," she said.

"Oh, I'm sure we'll converse again."

"After I return and tell them what you really are, there'll be no more emissaries from the city council."

"But my dear lady," said Moozh, "did you think I'd have spoken to you so freely, if I intended to let you speak again to the council?"

Her face blanched. "So you *are* no different from any of the other bullies. Like Gaballufix and Rashgallivak, you love to hear your own bluster. You think it makes you manly."

"Not so," said Moozh. "Their posturing and boasting came to nothing—they did it because they feared their own weakness. I never posture and I never boast, and when I decide what is necessary I do it. You will be escorted from here to your own house, which is already surrounded by Gorayni troops. All the non-resident children in your house have been sent safely home; the others will be kept indoors, since from this point on no one will be allowed to enter or leave your house. We will, of course, deliver food to you, and I believe your water supply is entirely provided by wells and a clever rain collection system."

"Yes," she said. "But the city will never stand for your arresting me."

"You think not?" asked Moozh. "I have already sent one of the Basilican guard to inform the city council that I have arrested you in their name, in order to protect the city from your plotting."

"My *plotting!*" she cried, rising to her feet.

"You came to me and suggested that I abolish the city council and establish one man as king of Basilica. You even had a candidate in mind—your husband, Wetchik, who already had his sons murder his chief rivals and even now is waiting in the desert for me to call for him to come and rule the city as a vassal of the Imperator."

"Monstrous lies! No one will believe you!"

"You know that your statement is false, even as you make it," said Moozh. "You know that there are many on that council who will be only too happy to believe that all your actions have been inspired by private ambition, and that you have been involved in causing all your city's misfortunes from the start."

"You'll see that the women of Basilica are not so easily fooled."

"You have no idea, Lady Rasa, how happy I would be if the women of Basilica proved to be so wise that I could not deceive them. I have longed all my life to find people of such exemplary wisdom. But I think I have not found them here, with the single exception of yourself. And *you* are completely under my control." He laughed merrily. "By the Incarnation himself, ma'am, after conversing with you this morning it terrifies me to know that you are even *alive*. If you were a man with an army I would be afraid to campaign against you. But you are not a man with an army, and so you pose no threat to me—not anymore."

She rose from her chair. "Are you finished?"

"Do your household a favor—don't try to send anyone out with secret messages. I *will* catch anyone you send, and then I'll probably have to do something grisly like delivering the next day's rations to your house sewn up inside your would-be messenger's skin."

"You are exactly the reason why Basilica banned men from the city in the first place," she said coldly.

"And you are exactly the reason why the city of women is an abomination in the sight of God," he answered. But his voice was warm with admiration—even affection—for the truth was that this woman alone had taught him that the city of women was not as weak and effeminate as he had imagined all these years.

"God!" she said. "God means nothing to you. The way you think, the way you live—I daresay that you spend every moment of your life trying to flout the will of the Oversoul and unmake all her works in this world."

"You are close to the mark, dear lady," he said. "Closer than you ever imagined. Now do please bow to the inevitable and make no trouble for my poor soldiers who have the unpleasant duty of taking you home under public arrest through the streets of Basilica."

"What trouble could I make?"

"Well, for one thing, you could try to shout some ridiculous revolutionary message to the people you pass. I would recommend silence."

She nodded gravely. "I will accept your recommendation. You can be sure that I'll despise you in silence all the way home."

It took six of them to walk her home. His lies about her had been so persuasive that crowds gathered in many places to vilify her as a traitor to her city. That was bad enough, to be unjustly loathed by her beloved city, but it didn't gall her half as much as the other shouts—the cheers for General Moozh, the savior of Basilica.

FIVE

HUSBANDS

THE DREAM OF THE HOLY WOMAN

Her name was Torstiga in the language of her homeland, but she had been so long away from *that* place, far in the east, that she didn't even remember the language of her childhood. She had been sold into slavery by her uncle when she was seven years old, was carried west to Seggidugu, and there was sold again. Slavery was not intolerable—her mistress was stict but not unfair, and her master kept his hands to himself. It could have been much worse, she well knew—but it was not freedom.

She prayed constantly for freedom. She prayed to Fackla, the god of her childhood, and nothing happened. She prayed to Kui, the god of Seggidugu, and still she was a slave. Then she heard stories of the Oversoul, the goddess of Basilica, the city of women, a place where no man could own property and every woman was free. She prayed and prayed, and one day when she was twelve, she went mad, caught up in the trance of the Oversoul.

Since many slaves pretended to be god-mad in order to win their freedom, Torstiga was locked up and starved during her frenzy. She did not mind the darkness of the tiny cubicle where they confined her, for she was seeing the visions that the Oversoul put into her mind. Only when the visions ended at last did she notice her own physical discomfort. Or at least, that was how it seemed to her mistress, for she cried out again and again from her cubicle: "Thirsty! Thirsty! Thirsty!"

They did not understand that she was crying out that one word, not because she needed to drink—though indeed she was far along with dehydration—but because it was her name, Torstiga, translated into the language of Basilica. The language of the Oversoul. She called her own name because she had lost herself in the midst of her visions; she hoped that if she called out loud enough and long enough, the girl she used to be might hear her, and answer, and perhaps come back and live in her body once again.

Later she came to understand that her true self had never left her, but in the confusion and ecstacy and terror of her first powerful visions she was transformed and never again would she be the twelve-year-old girl she once had been. When they let her out of her confinement, warning her not to pretend to be god-mad again, she didn't argue with them or protest that she had been sincere. She simply drank what they gave her to drink, and ate until the food they set before her was gone, and then returned to her labor.

But soon they began to realize that for once a slave was *not* pretending. She looked at her master one day and began to weep, and would not be comforted. That afternoon, as he oversaw construction of a fine new house for one of the richest men of the city, he was knocked down by a stone that got away from the crew that was trying to manhandle it into place. Two slaves suffered broken bones in the mishap, but Thirsty's master fell into the street and a passing horse stamped on his head. He lingered for a month, never regaining consciousness, taking small sips that his wife gave him every half hour, but vomiting any food she managed to get down his throat. He starved to death.

"Why did you weep that day?" his widow demanded.

"Because I saw him fallen in the street, trampled by a horse."

"Why didn't you warn him?"

"The Oversoul showed it to me, mistress, but she forbade me to tell it."

"Then I hate the Oversoul!" cried the woman. "And I hate you, for your silence!"

"Please don't punish me, mistress," said Thirsty. "I wanted to tell you, but she wouldn't let me."

"No," said the widow. "No, I won't punish you for doing what the goddess demanded of you."

After the master was buried, his widow sold most of the slaves, for she could no longer maintain a fine household in the city, and would have to return to her father's estate. Thirsty she did not sell. Instead she gave her her freedom.

Her freedom, but nothing else. Thus Thirsty began her time as a wilder, not because she was driven into the desert by the Oversoul, but because she was hungry, and in every town the other beggars drove her away, not because her small appetite would have deprived them of anything, but rather because she was slight and meek and so she was one of the few creatures in the world they had the power to drive away.

Thus she found herself in the desert, eating locusts and lizards and drinking from the rank pools of water that lingered in the shade and in caves after each rainstorm. Now she lived her name indeed, but in time she became a wilder in fact, and not just in appearance and habits of life. For she *was* dirty, and she *was* naked, and she starved in the desert like any proper holy woman—but she raged against the Oversoul in her heart, for she was bitterly angry at the way the Oversoul had answered her prayer. I asked for freedom, she howled at the Oversoul. I never asked you to kill my good master and impoverish my good mistress! I never asked you to drive me out into the desert, where the sun burns my skin except where I've managed to produce enough sweat that the dust will cling to my naked body and protect me. I never asked for visions or prophecies. I asked only to be a free woman, like my mother was. Now I can't even remember her name.

The Oversoul was not done with her, though, and so she

could not yet have peace. When she was only fourteen years old, by her best reckoning, she had a dream of a place that was mountainous and yet so lush with life that even the face of the sheerest cliff was thickly green with foliage. She saw a man in her vision, and the Oversoul told her that this was her true husband. She cared nothing for that news—what she saw was that this man had food in his hand, and a stream of water ran at his feet. So she headed north until she found the green land, and found the stream. She washed herself, and drank and drank and drank. And then one day, clean and satisfied, she saw him leading his horse down to the water.

Almost she ran away. Almost she fled from the will of the Oversoul, for she didn't want a husband now, and there had been berries enough by the riverbank that she hungered for nothing that he might offer.

But he saw her, and gazed at her. She covered her breasts with her hands, knowing vaguely that this was what men desired, for that was what they looked at; she had no experience of men, for the Oversoul had protected her from desert wanderers until now.

"God forbids me to touch you," he said softly. He spoke in the language of Basilica, but with an accent very different from the speech of Seggidugu.

"That is a lie," she said. "The Oversoul has made me your wife."

"I have no wife," he answered. "And if I did, I wouldn't take a puny child like you."

"Good," she said. "Because, *I* don't want *you,* either. Let the Oversoul find you an *old* woman if she wants you to have a wife."

He laughed. "Then we're agreed. You're safe from me."

He took her home, and clothed her, and fed her, and for the first time in her life she was happy. In a month she fell in love with him, and he with her, and he took her the way a man takes a wife, though without a ceremony. Oddly, though, *she* was convinced that marrying him was exactly what the Oversoul required of him, while *he* was convinced that taking her into his bed was pure defiance of the will of

God. "I will defy God every chance I get," he said. "But I would never have taken you against your will, even for the sake of defying my enemy."

"Is God your enemy, too?" she whispered.

For a month they were together. Then the madness came upon her and she fled into the desert.

It happened once again, several years later, only this time there was no month of waiting, and she didn't find him in his homeland, but rather in a cold foreign land with pine trees and a trace of snow on the ground, and this time there was no month of chastity before they were together as man and wife. And again, after a month she became god-mad and fled again into the desert.

Both times she conceived a child. Both times she longed to take her daughter to him, and lay the babe at his feet, and claim her right as his wife. But the Oversoul forbade it, and instead she brought the baby into the city of women, into Basilica, to the house that the Oversoul had shown her in a dream, and both times she gave her child into the arms of a woman that the Oversoul truly loved.

Thirsty envied that woman so much, for when you have the love of the Oversoul, you are given a house, and freedom, and happiness, and you are surrounded by daughters and friends. But Thirsty had only the hatred of the Oversoul, and so she lived alone in the desert.

Until, at last, ten years ago, the madness left her for good—or so she thought. She came down out of the desert then, into the land of Potokgavan, where kind strangers took her in. She was not beautiful or desirable, but she was striking in a strange way, and a good plain farmer with a strong house that stood on thick stilts asked for her to be his wife. She said yes, and together they had seven children.

But she never forgot her days as a holy woman, when the Oversoul hated her, and she never forgot the two daughters she bore to the strange man who was the husband the Oversoul gave her. The elder daughter she had named Hushidh, which was also the name of a desert flower which smelled sweet, but often held the larvae of the poisonous saberfly. The younger daughter she had named Luet, after the lyuty plant, whose leaves were ground up and soaked to make the sacred tea that helped the women who worshipped the Oversoul to enter a trance that sometimes, they said, gave them true visions. She never forgot her daughters, and prayed for them every morning, though she never told her husband or their children about the two she had been compelled to give into the hands of another.

Then one night she dreamed again, a god-mad dream. She saw herself once again walking into the presence of the husband the Oversoul had given her, the father of her first two daughters. Only now he was older, and his face was terrible and sad. In the dream he had his two daughters, the younger one beside him, the elder kneeling before him, and Thirsty saw herself walk to him and take him by the hand and say, "Husband, now that you have claimed your daughters, will I be your wife in the eyes of men, as well as in the eyes of the Oversoul?"

She hated this dream. Hated it deeply, for it denied the husband she had now, and repudiated the children they had together. Why did you set me free to have this life in Potokgavan, O cruel Oversoul, if you meant to tear me away from them? And if you meant me to be with my first two daughters, why couldn't you have let me keep them from the start? You are too cruel to me, Oversoul! I will not obey you!

But every night she dreamed the same dream. Again and again, all night long, until she thought she would go mad with it. Yet still she did not go.

Then, on one morning, at the end of the same relentless vision, there came something new into her dream. A sweet high keening sound. And in her dream she looked around and saw a furred creature flying through the air, and she knew that the sweet high song was this angel's song. The angel came to her in the dream, and landed on her shoulder, and clung to her, wrapping his leathery wings around her and his song was piercing and brilliant in her ear.

"What should I do, sweet angel?" she asked him in the dream.

In answer, the angel threw himself backward onto the

ground before her, and lay there in the dust. And as he lay there, exposed and helpless, his wings useless and vulnerable and slack, there came creatures that at first seemed to be baboons, from their size, but then seemed to be rats, from their teeth and eyes and snout. They came to the angel, and sniffed at him, and when he did not move or fly, they began to gnaw at him. Oh, it was terrible indeed, and all the time his eyes looked at Thirsty, so sadly.

I must save him, thought Thirsty. I must shoo away these terrible enemies. Yet in the dream she could not save him. She could not act at all.

When the fell creatures finally left, the angel was not dead. But his wings had been chewed away, and in their place were left only two spindly, fragile arms, with barely a fringe under them to show where once the wings had been. She knelt by him, then, and cradled him up into her arms, and wept for him. Wept and wept and wept.

"Mother," said her middle son. "Mother, you're weeping from a dream, I think. Wake up."

She woke up.

"What was it?" asked the boy. He was a good boy, and she did not want to leave him.

"I must take a journey," she said.

"Where?"

"To a far place, but I'll come home, if the Oversoul will let me."

"Why must you go?"

"I don't know," she said. "The Oversoul has called me, and I don't know why. Your father is already working in the fields. Don't tell him until he comes home for his noon meal. By then I'll be gone too far for him to pursue me. Tell him that I love him and that I'll return to him. If he wants to punish me when I come back, then I will submit to his punishment gladly. For I would rather be here with him, and with our children, than to be a queen in any other country."

"Mama," said the boy, "I've known for a month that you would go."

"How did you know?" she asked. And for a moment she

feared that he, too, might be cursed with the voice of the Oversoul in his heart.

But it was no god-madness the boy had—instead it was common sense. "You kept looking to the northwest, and Father tells us sometimes that that was where you came from. I thought I saw you wishing to go home."

"No," she said. "Not wishing to go home, because I *am* home, right here. But there's an errand I must tend to, and then I'll come back to you."

"If the Oversoul will let you."

She nodded. Then, taking a small bundle of food and a leather bottle filled with water, she set out on foot.

I had no intention of obeying you, Oversoul, she said. But when I saw that angel, with his wings torn away because I did nothing to help him in his moment of need, I did not know if that angel represented my daughters or the man who gave them to me, or even perhaps yourself—I only knew that I could not stand in my place and let some terrible thing happen, though I don't know what the terrible thing will be, or what I must do to stop it. All I know is that I will go where you lead me, and when I get there I will try to do good. If that ends up serving your purpose, Oversoul, I will do it anyway.

But when it's done, please, oh! Please, let me go home.

IN BASILICA, AND NOT IN A DREAM

It had come now to getting permission from Rasa, and Elemak was by no means certain she would grant it. Word throughout the house was that she had come home from her meeting with the Gorayni general in a foul humor, and no one could miss the fact that there were Gorayni soldiers in the street outside the house. Yet no matter what happened in Basilica, Elemak would not go back into the desert without a wife. And since she was willing, it would be Eiadh, with or without Rasa's permission.

But better *with* her permission. Better if Rasa herself performed the ceremony.

"This is an inauspicious time," said Rasa.

"Don't speak like an old woman, please, Aunt Rasa," said

Eiadh. Her voice was so soft and sweet that Rasa showed no sign of being offended at what could only be regarded as sauciness. "Remember that *young* women are not timid. We marry most readily when our men are about to go to war, or when times are hard."

"You know nothing of desert life."

"But *you* have gone out into the desert with Wetchik, from time to time."

"Twice, and the second time was because I failed to trust my memory of how much I loathed the first time. I can promise you that after a week in the desert you'd be willing to come back to Basilica as a bondservant, just so you could come back."

"My lady Rasa," began Elemak.

"If you speak again, dear Elemak, I will send you from the room," said Rasa, in her gentlest tones. "I'm trying to talk sense to your beloved. But you needn't worry. Eiadh is so besotted with love of—what, your strength? I suspect she has visions of perfect manhood in her heart, and you fulfill all those fantasies."

Eiadh blushed. It was all Elemak could do to keep from smiling. He had hoped this from the start—that Eiadh was not a girl who looked for wealth or position, but rather one who looked for courage and strength. It would be boldness, not ostentation, that would win her heart: So Elemak had determined at the outset of his wooing, and so it had turned out in the end. Rasa herself confirmed it. Elemak had chosen a girl who, instead of loving him as the Wetchik's heir, would love him for those very virtues that were most evident in Elemak out in the desert—his ability to command, to make quick, bold decisions; his physical stamina; his wisdom about desert life.

"Whatever dreams she has in her heart," Elemak said, "I will do my best to make them all come true."

"Be careful what you promise," said Rasa. "Eiadh is quite capable of sucking the life out of a man with her adoration."

"Aunt Rasa!" said Eiadh, genuinely horrified.

"Lady Rasa," said Elemak, "I can't imagine what cruel intent you must have, to say such a thing about this woman."

"Forgive me," said Rasa. She looked genuinely sorry. "I thought my words would be taken as teasing, but I haven't the heart for levity right now, and so it became an insult. I didn't intend it that way."

"Lady Rasa," said Elemak, "all things are forgiven when Wethead soldiers stand watch in the street outside your house."

"Do you think I care about that?" said Rasa. "When I have a raveler and a waterseer in my house? The soldiers are nothing. It's my city that I fear for."

"The soldiers are *not* nothing," said Elemak. "I've been told how Hushidh unbound poor Rashgallivak's soldiers from their loyalty to him, but you must remember that Rashgallivak was a weak man, newly come into my brother's place."

"Your father's place, too," said Rasa.

"Usurping both," said Elemak. "And the soldiers that Shuya unbound were mercenaries. General Moozh is said to be the greatest general in a thousand years, and his soldiers love and trust him beyond understanding. Shuya wouldn't find it easy to unweave *those* bonds."

"Suddenly you're an expert on the Gorayni?"

"I'm an expert on how men love and trust a strong leader," said Elemak. "I know how the men of my caravans felt about me. True, they all knew they would be paid. But they also knew that I wouldn't risk their lives unnecessarily, and that if they followed me in all things they would live to *spend* that money at journey's end. I loved my men, and they loved me, yet from what I hear of General Moozh, his soldiers love him ten times more than that. He has made them the strongest army of the Western Shore."

"And masters of Basilica, without one of them being killed," said Rasa.

"He hasn't mastered Basilica yet," said Elemak. "And with you as his enemy, Lady Rasa, I don't know if he ever will."

Rasa laughed bitterly. "Oh, indeed, he removed *me* as a threat from the start."

"What about our marriage?" asked Eiadh. "That *is* what we're meeting about, isn't it?"

Rasa looked at her with—what, pity? Yes, thought Elemak. She hasn't a very high opinion of this niece of hers. That remark she let slip, that insult, it was no joke. Suck the life out of a man with her adoration—what did that mean? Am I making a mistake? All my thought was to make Eiadh desire me; I never questioned my desire for *her*.

"Yes, my dear," said Rasa. "You may marry this man. You may take him as your first husband."

"Technically," said Elemak, "it wasn't permission we were seeking, since she's of age."

"*And* I will perform the ceremony," said Rasa wearily. "But it will have to be in this house, for obvious reasons, and the guest list will have to consist of all those who find themselves in residence here. We must all pray that Gorayni soldiers do not also choose to attend the ceremony."

"When?" asked Eiadh.

"Tonight," said Rasa. "Tonight will be soon enough, won't it? Or does your clothing itch so much you want it to come off at noon?"

Again, an insult beyond bearing, and yet Rasa plainly did not see that she was being crude. Instead she arose and walked from the room, leaving Eiadh flushed and angry on the bench where she sat.

"No, my Edhya," said Elemak. "Don't be angry. Your Aunt Rasa has lost much today, and she can't help being a little mean about also losing you."

"It sounds as though she'd be *glad* to get rid of me, she must hate me so," said Eiadh. And a tear slipped from Eiadh's eye and dropped, twinkling for a moment in the air, onto her lap.

Elemak took her in his arms then, and held her; she clung to him as if she longed to become a part of him forever. This is love, he thought. This is the kind of love that songs and stories are made of. She will follow me into the desert and with her beside me I will fashion a tribe, a kingdom for her to be the queen. For whatever this General Moozh can do, *I* can do. I am a truer husband than any Wethead could ever be. Eiadh hungers for a man of mastery. I am that man.

Bitanke was not happy with all that had happened in Basilica these past few days. Especially because he could not get free of the feeling that perhaps it was all his fault. Not that he had had much choice in those moments at the gate. His men had fought valiantly, but they were too few, and the mob of Palwashantu mercenaries was bound to win. What hope, then, would he have had, standing against the Gorayni soldiers who came out of nowhere and promised alliance with him?

I could have called to the Palwashantu mercenaries and begged them to make common cause with me against the Gorayni—it might have worked. Yet at the time the Gorayni general had seemed so earnest. And there were all those firelights out on the desert. It looked like an army of a hundred thousand men. How was I to know that their entire army was the men standing at the gate? And even then, we could not have stood against them.

But we could have fought. We could have cost them soldiers and time. We could have alerted all the other guards, and sent the alarm through the city. I could have died there, with a Gorayni arrow through my heart, rather than having to live and see how they have conquered my city, my beloved city, without even one of them suffering a wound serious enough to keep him from marching boldly wherever he pleases.

And yet. And yet even now, as he was called into the presence of General Moozh for still another interview, Bitanke could not help but admire the man for his audacity, his courage, his brilliance. To have marched so far in such a short time, and to essay to take a city with so few men, and then to have his way when even now the guard outnumbered his army significantly. Who could say that Basilica might not be better off with Moozh as its guardian? Better him than that swine Gaballufix would have been, or the contemptible Rashgallivak. Better even than Roptat. And better than the women, who had proven themselves weak and foolish indeed, for the way they now believed Moozh's obvious lies about Lady Rasa.

Couldn't they see how Moozh manipulated them to divide against each other and ignore the one woman who might have led them to effective resistance? No, of course they couldn't see—any more than Bitanke himself could see that first night that, far from helping, the Gorayni stranger was controlling him and making him betray his own city without even realizing it.

We are all fools when one wise man appears.

"My dear friend," said General Moozh.

Bitanke did not take the offered hand.

"Ah, you're angry with me," said Moozh.

"You came here with Lady Rasa's letter, and now you have her under arrest."

"Is she so dear to you?" asked Moozh. "I assure you that her confinement is only temporary, and is entirely for her protection. Terrible lies about her are circulating through the city right now, and who can tell what might happen to her if her house was not cordoned off?"

"Lies invented by you."

"My lips have said nothing about Lady Rasa except my great admiration for her. She is the best of the women of this city, with the wit and courage of a man, and I will never permit a hair of her head to be harmed. If you don't know that about me, Bitanke, my friend, you know nothing about me at all."

Which was almost certainly true, thought Bitanke. I know nothing about you. *No* one knows anything about you.

"Why did you summon me?" asked Bitanke. "Are you going to strip away yet one more power from the Basilican guard? Or do you have some vile work for us to do that will humiliate and demoralize us all the more?"

"So angry," said Moozh. "But think hard, Bitanke. You feel free to say such things to me, and without fear that I'll strike your head off. Does that seem like tyranny to you? Your soldiers all have their arms, and they are the ones keeping the peace in this city now—does that sound as though I'm a treacherous enemy?"

Bitanke said nothing, determined not to let himself be taken in again by Moozh's smooth talking. And yet he felt the stab of doubt in his heart, as he had so many times before. Moozh *had* left the guard intact. He had done no violence against any citizen. Perhaps all he meant to do was use Basilica as a staging area and then move on.

"Bitanke, I need your help. I want to restore this city to its former strength, before Gaballufix's meddling."

Oh, yes, I'm certain that's all you desire—Moozh the altruist, going to all this trouble just so you can help the city of women. Then you'll march your men away, rewarded with a warm glow in your heart because you know you leave so much happiness behind you.

But Bitanke said nothing. Better to listen than to speak, at a time like this.

"I won't pretend to you that I don't intend to turn things here to my own purposes. There is a great struggle ahead between the Gorayni and the miserable puddle swimmers of Potokgavan. We know that they were maneuvering to take control of Basilica—Gaballufix was their man. He was prepared to overthrow the city of women and let his thugs rule. And now here I am, with my soldiers. Have I or my men ever done anything to make you think our intentions are as ruthless or brutal as Gaballufix?

Moozh waited, and at last Bitanke answered, "You have never been so obvious, no."

"I will tell you what I need from Basilica. I need to know, securely, that those who rule her are friends of the Gorayni, that with Basilica at my back I don't have to fear any treachery from this city. Then I can bring supply lines through the desert to this place, completely bypassing Nakavalnu and Izmennik and Seggidugu. *You* know that this is good strategy, my friend. Potokgavan counted on our having to fight our way south to the Cities of the Plain; they counted on having at least a year, perhaps several years, to strengthen their position here—perhaps to bring an army here to try to stand against our chariots. But now we will command the Cities of the Plain—with my army in Basilica, none of them will resist. And then Nakavalnu and Izmennik and Seggidugu will not dare to make any alliance with Potokgavan. Without conquest, without war, we will have secured the entire Western Shore for the Imperator, years before Potokgavan would have imagined possible. That is what I want. That is *all* I want. And to accomplish it, I don't need to break Basilica, I don't need to treat you as a conquered people. All I need is to be certain that Basilica is loyal to me. And that purpose is better accomplished through love than through fear."

"Love!" said Bitanke derisively.

"So far," said Moozh, "I have not had to do anything that was not gratefully received by the people of Basilica. They have more peace and security now than in the past several years. Do you think they don't understand that?"

"And do you think the worse men of Dogtown and Gate Town and the High Road aren't hoping that you'll let them come into the city and rule here? Then you'd have your loyal allies—if you give them what Gaballufix promised, a chance to dominate these women who have barred them from citizenship for all these thousands of centuries."

"Yes," said Moozh. "I could have done that. I could do it still." He leaned forward across the table, to look Bitanke in the eye. "But you *will* help me, won't you, so that I don't have to do such a terrible thing?"

Ah. So this was the choice, after all. Either conspire with Moozh or watch the very fabric of Basilica be destroyed. All that was beautiful and holy in this place would now be hostage to the threat of turning loose the covetous men from outside the walls. Hadn't Bitanke seen how terrible that would be? How could he let it happen again?

"What do you want from me?"

"Advice," said Moozh. "Counsel. The city council is not a reliable instrument of control here. It's fine for passing laws governing local matters, but when it comes to making a firm alliance with the army of the Imperator, who's to say a faction won't arise within a week to strike down that policy? So I need to set up a single individual as . . . what . . .

"Dictator?"

"Not at all. This person would merely be the face that Basilica turns to the outside world. He, she—whoever it is— will be able to promise that Gorayni armies may pass through here, that Gorayni supplies can be stored here, and that Potokgavan will find no friends or allies here."

"The city council can do this."

"You know better."

"They will keep their word."

"You have seen this very day how treacherously and unfairly they dealt with Lady Rasa, who has done nothing but serve them loyally all her life. How then will they deal with the stranger? My men's lives, my Imperator's power, all will depend on the loyalty of Basilica—and this city council has proven itself incapable of being loyal even to their own worthiest sister."

"*You* started those rumors about her," said Bitanke, "and now you use them to show how unworthy the council is?"

"Before God I deny that I started any slander about Lady Rasa—I admire her above any other woman I have met. Yet no matter who started the rumor, Bitanke, what matters is that it was *believed*. By this city council, which you tell me I can trust with the lives of my men. What is to stop Potokgavan from starting rumors of their own? Tell me honestly, Bitanke, if you were in *my* place, with *my* needs, would you trust this city council?"

"I have served this council all my life, sir, and I trust them," said Bitanke.

"That's not what I asked you," said Moozh. "I am here to accomplish the purpose of the Imperator. Traditionally we have done this by slaughtering the ruling class of the lands we conquer, and replacing them with men of some long-disfranchised oppressed people. Because I love this city, I wish to find another way here. I am taking great risks to do so."

"You have only a thousand men," said Bitanke. "You want to subdue Basilica without bloodshed because you can't afford to suffer *any* losses."

"You see half the truth," said Moozh. "I have to *win* here.

If I can do it without bloodshed, then the Cities of the Plain will say that I must have the power of God with me, and they will submit to my orders. But I can also achieve the same end by terror. If their leaders are brought here and find this city desolate, burned to the ground, house and forest, and the lake of women thick with blood, they will also submit to me. But one way or another, Basilica will serve my purpose."

"You are truly a monster," said Bitanke. "You speak of sacrilege and massacre of innocents, and then ask me to trust you."

"I speak of necessity," said Moozh, "and ask you to help me keep from being a monster. You have served a higher purpose—the will of the council. Sometimes, in their name, you have done that which you, of yourself, would not wish to do. Is that not so?"

"That's what it means to be a soldier," said Bitanke.

"I also am a soldier," said Moozh. "I also must accomplish the purpose of my master, the Imperator. And so I will even be a monster if I must, to accomplish it. As you have had to arrest men and women you thought were innocent."

"Arrest is not slaughter."

"Bitanke, my friend, I keep hoping that you will be what I thought you were when first I met you bravely fighting at that gate. I imagined that night that you fought, not for some institution, not for that feeble city council that believes any slander that flies through the city, but rather for something higher. For the city itself. For the *idea* of the city. Wasn't *that* what you were prepared to die for at the gate?"

"Yes," said Bitanke.

"Now I offer you the chance to serve the city again. *You* know that long before there *was* a council, Basilica was a great city. Back when Basilica was ruled by the priestesses, it was still Basilica. Back when Basilica had a queen, it was still Basilica. Back when Basilica put the great general Snaceetel in charge of its army and fought off the Seggid-ugu warriors, and then let him drink of the waters of the lake of women, it was still Basilica."

Against his will Bitanke saw that Moozh was right. The

city of women was not the council. The form of government had changed many times before, and would change again. What mattered was that it remain the holy city of women, the one place on the planet Harmony where women ruled. And if, for a short time, because of great events sweeping through the Western Shore, Basilica had to be subservient to the Gorayni, then what of that—as long as the rule of women was preserved within these walls?

"While you consider," said Moozh, "consider *this*. I could have tried to frighten you. I could have lied to you, pretended to be something other than the calculating general that I am. Instead I have spoken to you as a friend, openly and freely, because what I want is your willing help, not your mere obedience."

"My help to do what?" asked Bitanke. "I will *not* arrest the council, if that's what you hope for."

"Arrest them! Haven't you understood me at all? I need the council to continue—without replacing a single member of it! I need the people of Basilica to see that their internal government is unchanged. But I also need a consul of the people, someone to set in place *above* the council, to handle the foreign affairs of Basilica. To make an alliance with us that will be adhered to. To command the guards at the city gates."

"Your men already perform that office."

"But I *want* it to be *your* men who do it."

"I'm not the commander of the guard."

"You're one of the leading officers," said Moozh. "I wish you *were* commander, because you're a better soldier than any of the men above you. But if I promised you the office of commander, you would think I was trying to bribe you and you would reject me and leave this house as my enemy."

Bitanke felt a great relief inside. Moozh knew, after all, that Bitanke was no traitor. That Bitanke would never act for his own self-interest. That Bitanke would act only for the good of the city.

"The men of the guard will be reluctant," said Bitanke, "to take their orders from anyone but their own commander, appointed by the city council."

"Imagine, though, that the city council has unanimously appointed someone to be consul of the city, and has asked the guard to obey that consul."

"It would mean nothing if they thought for a moment that the consul was a mere puppet of the Gorayni. The guard are not fools, and we are not traitors, either."

"So. You see my dilemma. I must have someone who will understand the necessity of Basilica remaining loyal to the Imperator, and yet this consul will only be effective if the people of Basilica trust her—or him—to be a loyal Basilican, and not a puppet."

Bitanke laughed. "I hope you don't imagine for a moment that *I* would do for that purpose. There are already plenty of people whispering that I must be your puppet for having let you into the city in the first place."

"I know," said Moozh. "You were the first one I thought of, but I realized that you can only serve Basilica—and my purposes, too—by remaining where you are, with *no* obvious advantage coming to you because of my influence in the city."

"Then why am I here?"

"To advise me, as I told you before. I need you to tell me who in this city, if she—or he—were appointed as consul, the guard and the city as a whole would follow and obey."

"There *is* no such creature."

"Say this, and you might as well ask me to pour the blood and ashes of the city into the lake of women."

"Don't threaten me!"

"I'm not threatening you, Bitanke, I'm telling you what I have done before and what I do not want to do again. I beg you, help me to find a way to avoid that dreadful outcome."

"Let me think."

"I ask for nothing more."

"Let me come to you tomorrow."

"I must act today."

"Give me an hour."

"Can you do your thinking here? Can you do it without leaving the house?"

"Am I under arrest, then?"

"This house is watched by a thousand eyes, my friend. If

you are seen leaving and then returning in an hour, it will be said that you make too many visits to General Vozmuzhalnoy Vozmozhno. But if you want to leave, you may."

"I'll stay."

"I'll have you shown to the library, then, and given a computer to write on. It will help my thinking, if you write down the names and your reasons why they might or might not be good for this purpose. In an hour, come to me again with your list of names."

"For Basilica I do this, and not for you." And not for any advantage to myself.

"It's for Basilica that I ask it," said Moozh. "Even though my first loyalty is to the Imperator, I hope to save this city from destruction if I can."

The interview was over. Bitanke left the room, and was immediately joined by a Gorayni soldier who led him to the library. Moozh had said nothing to this soldier, and yet he knew where to take him. Knew to assign him a computer to use. Either this meant that the general let his junior officers listen in to his negotiations, which was almost unthinkable, or it meant that Moozh had given these orders before Bitanke even arrived.

Could it be that Moozh had planned it all, every word that passed between them? Could it be that Moozh was so good at manipulation that he could determine all outcomes in advance? Then in that case Bitanke might just be another dupe, betraying his city because he had been twisted into believing whatever Moozh wanted.

No. No, that was not it at all. Moozh simply counted on being able to persuade me to act intelligently in the best interest of Basilica. And so I will find candidates for him, if it is possible to imagine anyone serving as consul, appointed because of the Gorayni and yet holding the loyalty of the people, the council, and the guard. If it is possible, I will bring the name to the General.

"I need to speak to my children," said Rasa. "*All* of them."

Luet looked at her for a moment, uncertain what to do; this was the sort of thing a lady might say to her servants, giving orders without seeming to. But Luet was not a servant in this house, and never had been, and so she was supposed to ignore such expressions of desire. Yet Rasa seemed not to realize she had spoken as if to a servant, when no servant was present. "Madam," she said, "are you sending me on this errand?"

Rasa looked at her almost in surprise. "I'm sorry, Luet. I forgot who was with me. I'm not at my best. Would you please go find my children and my husband's children for me, and tell them I want to see them now?"

Now it was a request, a favor, and asked directly of her, so of course Luet bowed her head and left in search of servants to help her. Not that Luet wouldn't willingly have done the task herself, but Rasa's house was large, and if there was any urgency in Rasa's request—as there seemed to be—it would be better to have several people searching. Besides, the servants were more likely to know exactly where everyone was.

It was easy enough to find out where Nafai, Elemak, Sevet, and Kokor were, and send servants to summon them. Mebbekew, however, had not been seen for several hours, not since he first came into the house. Finally Izdavat, a youngish maid of more eagerness than sense, reluctantly mentioned that she had brought Mebbekew breakfast in Dol's room. "But that was some time ago, lady."

"I'm only sister, or Luet, please."

"Do you want me to see if he's still there, sister?"

"No, thank you," said Luet. "It would be improper for him still to be there, and so I'll go ask Dolya where he went." She headed off to the stairs in the teachers' wing of the house.

Luet was not surprised that Mebbekew had already managed to attach himself to a woman, even in this house where women were taught to see through shallow men. However, it *did* surprise her that Dolya was giving the boy the time of day. She had been worked over by champion flatterers and sycophants in her theatre days, and shouldn't have noticed Mebbekew except to laugh discreetly at him.

But then, Luet was quite aware that she saw through flatterers more easily than most women, since the flatterers never actually tried to work their seductive magic on *her*. Waterseers had a reputation for seeing through lies— though, truth to tell, Luet could only see what the Oversoul showed her, and the Oversoul was not noted for helping a daughter with her love life. As if I had a love life, thought Luet. As if I needed one. The Oversoul has marked my path for me. And where my path touches others' lives, I will trust the Oversoul to tell them her will. My husband will discover me as his wife when he chooses to. And I will be content.

Content . . . she almost laughed at herself. All my dreams are tied up in the boy, we've been to the edge of death together, and still he pines for Eiadh. Are men's lives nothing but the secretions of overactive glands? Can't they analyze and understand the world about them, as women can? Can't Nafai see that Eiadh's love will be as permanent as rain, ready to evaporate as soon as the storm passes? Edhya *needs* a man like Elemak, who won't tolerate her straying heart. Where Nafai would be heartbroken at her disloyalty, Elemak would be brutally angry, and Eiadh, the poor foolish creature, would fall in love with him all over again.

Not that Luet saw all this herself, of course. It was Hushidh who saw all the connections, all the threads binding people together; it was Hushidh who explained to her that Nafai seemed not to notice Luet because he was so enamored of Eiadh. It was Hushidh who also understood the bond between Elemak and Eiadh, and why they were so right for each other.

And now Mebbekew and Dol. Well, it was another piece of the puzzle, wasn't it? When Luet had seen her vision of women in the woods behind Rasa's house, that night when she returned from warning Wetchik of the threat against his life, it had made no sense to her. Now, though, she knew why she had seen Dolya. She would be with Mebbekew, as Eiadh with Elemak. Shedemei would also be coming out to the desert, or at least would be involved with their journey, gathering seeds and embryos. And Hushidh also would come. And Aunt Rasa. Luet's vision had been of the women called out into the desert.

Poor Dolya. If she had known that taking Mebbekew into her room would take her on a path leading out of Basilica, she would have kicked him and bit him and hit him, if need be, to get him out of her room! As it was, though, Luet fully expected to find them together.

She knocked on Dol's door. As she expected, there was the sound of a flurry of movement inside. And a soft thump.

"Who is it?" asked Dol.

"Luet."

"I'm not conveniently situated at the moment."

"I have no doubt if it," said Luet, "but Lady Rasa sent me with some urgency. May I come in?"

"Yes, of course."

Luet opened the door to find Dolya lying in bed, her sheets up over her shoulders. There was no sign of Mebbekew, of course, but the bed had been well-rumpled, the bath was full of grey water, and a bunch of grapes had been left on the floor—not the way Dolya usually arranged things before taking a midday nap.

"What does Aunt Rasa want of me?" asked Dol.

"Nothing of *you*, Dol," said Luet. "She wants all her children and Wetchik's children to join her at once."

"Then why aren't you knocking at Sevet's or Kokor's door? They aren't here."

"Mebbekew knows why I'm here," said Luet. Remembering the thump she heard, and the brief amount of time before she opened the door, she reached a conclusion about his present whereabouts. "So as soon as I close the door, he can get up off the floor beside your bed, put some kind of clothing on, and come to Lady Rasa's room."

Dol looked stricken. "Forgive me for trying to deceive you, Waterseer," she whispered.

Sometimes it made Luet want to scream, the way everyone assumed that when she showed any spark of wit it must be a revelation from the Oversoul—as if Luet would be incapable of discerning the obvious on her own. And yet it was also useful, Luet had to admit. Useful in that people tended to tell her the truth more readily, because they believed she would catch them in their lies. But the price of this truthfulness was that they did not like her company, and avoided her. Only friends shared such intimacies, and only freely. Forced, or so they thought, to share their secrets with Luet, they withheld their friendship, and Luet was not part of the lives of most of the women around her. They held her in such awe; it made her feel unworthy and filled her with rage, both at once.

It was that anger that led Luet to torment Mebbekew by forcing him to speak. "Did you hear me, Mebbekew?"

A long wait. Then: "Yes."

"I'll tell Lady Rasa," said Luet, "that her message was received."

She started to back out the door and draw it closed behind her, when Dol called out to her. "Wait . . . Luet."

"Yes?"

"His clothes . . . they were being washed . . ."

"I'll send them up."

"Do you think they'll be dry by now?"

"Dry enough," said Luet. "Don't you think so, Mebbekew?"

Mebbekew sat upright, so his head appeared on the other side of the bed. "Yes," he said glumly.

"Damp clothes will cool you off," said Luet. "It's such a hot day, at least in this room." It was a fine joke, she thought, but nobody laughed.

Shedemei strode vigorously along the path to Wetchik's coldhouse, which was nestled in a narrow valley and shaded by tall tress just outside the place where the city wall curved around the Old Orchestra. It was the last and, she feared, the hardest part of her task of assembling the flora and fauna for the mad project of a voyage through space, back to the legendary lost planet Earth. I am going to all this trouble because I had a dream, and took it for interpretation to a dreamer. A journey on camels, and they think it will lead them to Earth.

Yet the dream was still alive within her. The life she carried with her on the cloud.

So she came to the door of Wetchik's coldhouse, not certain whether she really hoped to find one of his servants acting as caretaker.

No one answered when she clapped her hands. But the machines that kept the house cold inside might well mask her loudest clapping. So she went to the door and tried it. Locked.

Of course it was. Wetchik had gone into the desert weeks ago, hadn't he? And Rashgallivak, his steward and, supposedly, the new Wetchik, had been in hiding somewhere ever since. Who would keep the place running, with both of them gone?

Except that the machines here *were* running, weren't they? Which meant *somebody* was still caring for the place. Unless they carelessly left them on, and the plants untended inside.

That was quite possible, of course. The cold air would keep the specialized plants thriving for many days, and the coldhouse, drawing its power from the solar scoops on the poles rising high above the house, could run indefinitely without even drawing on the city's power supply.

And yet Shedemei knew that someone was still taking care of this place, though she could not have said *how* she knew it. And furthermore, she knew that the caretaker was inside the coldhouse right now, and knew she was there, and wanted her to go away. Whoever was in here was hiding.

And who was it who needed to hide?

"Rashgallivak," called Shedemei. "I'm only Shedemei. You know me, and I'm alone, and I will tell no one you are here, but I must talk to you." She waited, no response. "It's nothing about the city, or the things going on in there," she called out loudly. "I simply need to buy a couple of pieces of equipment from you."

She could hear the door unbolting from the inside. Then it swung open on its heavy hinges. Rashgallivak stood there, looking forlorn and wasted. He held no weapon.

"If you've come to betray me, then I welcome it as a relief."

Shedemei declined to point out that betrayal would only be pure justice, after the way Rashgallivak had betrayed the Wetchik's house, allying himself with Gaballufix in order to steal his master's place. She had business to do here; she was not a justicer.

"I care nothing for politics," she said, "and I care nothing for you. I simply need to buy a dozen drycases. The portable ones, used for caravans."

He shook his head. "Wetchik had me sell them all."

Shedemei closed her eyes for a weary moment. He was forcing her to say things she had not wanted to throw in his face. "Oh, Rashgallivak, please don't expect me to believe that you actually sold them, knowing that you intended to take control of the house of Wetchik and would need to continue in the business."

Rashgallivak flushed—in shame, Shedemei hoped. "Nevertheless, I sold them, as I was told to do."

"Then who bought them?" asked Shedemei. "It's the drycases I want, not you."

Rashgallivak didn't answer.

"Ah," said Shedemei. "*You* bought them."

After a moment's pause, he said, "What do you need them for?"

"You're asking *me* to account for myself?" asked Shedemei.

"I ask, because I know you have plenty of drycases at your laboratory. The only conceivable use of the portable ones is for a caravan, and that's a business you know nothing about."

"Then no doubt I will be killed or robbed. But that's no concern of yours. And perhaps I won't be killed or robbed."

"In which case," said Rashgallivak, "you would be selling your plants in far-off countries, in direct competition with me. So why should I sell my competitor the portable drycases she needs?"

Shedemei laughed in his face. "What, do you think that there is any business as usual in this place? I'm not going on a trading journey, you poor foolish man. I'm removing my

entire laboratory, *and* myself, to a place where I can safely pursue my research without being interrupted by armed madmen burning and looting the city."

Again he flushed. "When they were under my command, they never harmed anyone. I was no Gaballufix."

"No, Rash. You are no Gaballufix."

That could be taken two ways, but Rash apparently decided to take it as a confirmation of her belief in his fundamental decency. "You're not my enemy, are you, Shedya."

"I just want drycases."

He hesitated a moment more, then stepped back and beckoned her inside.

The entry of the coldhouse wasn't chilled like the inner rooms, and Rash had turned it into a pathetic sort of apartment for himself. A makeshift bed, a large tub that had once held plants, but which he no doubt used now for bathing and washing his clothes. Very primitive, but resourceful, too. Shedemei had to admire that in the man—he had not despaired, even when everything worked against him.

"I'm alone here," he said. "The Oversoul surely knows I need money more than I need drycases. And the city council has cut me off from all my funds. You can't even pay me, because I haven't an account anymore to receive the money."

"That shouldn't be a problem," said Shedemei. "As you might imagine, a lot of people are pulling their money out of the city accounts. I can pay you in gems—though the price of gold and precious stones has tripled since the recent disturbances."

"Do you think I imagine myself to be in a position to bargain?"

"Stack the drycases outside the door," said Shedemei. "I'll send men to load them and bring them to me inside the city. I'll give you fair payment separately. Tell me where."

"Come alone, afterward," said Rash. "And put them into my hand."

"Don't be absurd," said Shedemei. "I'll never come here

again, and we'll never meet, either. Tell me where to leave the jewels for you."

"In the traveler room of Wetchik's house."

"Is it easy to find?"

"Easy enough."

"Then it will be there as soon as I have received the drycases."

"It hardly seems fair, that I must trust you completely, and you don't have to show any trust in me at all."

Shedemei could think of nothing to say that would not be cruel.

After a while he nodded. "All right," he said. "There are two houses on Wetchik's estate. Put the jewels in the traveler room of the smaller, older house. On top of one of the rafters. I'll find it."

"As soon as the drycases are at my laboratory," said Shedemei.

"Do you think I have some network of loyal men who will ambush you?" asked Rashgallivak, bitterly.

"No," said Shedemei. "But knowing you will soon have the money, there'd be nothing to stop you from hiring them now."

"So you'll decide when to pay me, and how much, and I get no voice in the matter."

"Rash," said Shedemei, "I will treat you far more fairly than you treated Wetchik and his sons."

"I'll have a dozen drycases outside within a half hour."

Shedemei got up and left. She heard him close the door behind her, and imagined him timidly drawing the bolts closed, fearful that someone might discover that the man who had, for a day, ruled the petty empires of Gaballufix and Wetchik both, now cowered inside these heavy shaded walls.

Shedya passed through Music Gate, where the Gorayni guards checked her identity with dispatch and let her through. It still bothered her to see that uniform in the gates of Basilica, but like everyone else she was growing accustomed to the soldier's perfect discipline, and the new orderliness that had come to the chaotic entrances of the city. Everyone waited patiently in line now.

And something else. There were now more people waiting to get into the city than waiting to get out. Confidence was returning. Confidence in the strength of the Gorayni. Who would have imagined how quickly people would come to trust the Wethead enemy?

After walking the long passage along the city wall to Market Gate, Shedemei found the muleteer she had hired. "Go ahead," Shedemei said. "There should be a dozen of them." The muleteer bowed her head and set off at a jog. No doubt that show of speed would stop the moment Shedemei could no longer see her, but Shedemei nevertheless appreciated the attempt at *pretending* to be fast. It showed that the muleteer knew what speed *was*, and thought it worthwhile to give the illusion of it.

Then she found a messenger boy in the queue waiting just inside the Market Gate. She scribbled a note on one of the papers that were kept there at the messenger station. On the back of the note she wrote directions to Wetchik's house, and instructions about where to leave the note. Then she keyed in a payment on the station computer. When the boy saw the bonus she was giving him for quick delivery, he grinned, snatched the note, and took off like an arrow.

Rashgallivak would be angry, of course, to find a draft against one of the Market Gate jewelers, instead of the jewels themselves. But Shedemei had no intention of either carrying or sending an enormous sum of completely liquid funds to some lonely abandoned place. It was Rash who needed the money—let *him* take the risk. At least she had drawn the draft on one of the jewelers who kept a table outside Market Gate, so he wouldn't have to pass any guards to get his payment.

Rasa looked at her son and daughters, and Wetchik's two boys by other wives. Not the world's finest group of human beings, she thought. I'd be a bit more contemptuous of Volemak's failure with his two older boys, if I didn't have my two prize daughters to remind me of my own lack of brilliance as a parent. And, to be fair, all these young people have their gifts and talents. But only Nafai and Issib, the two children Volya and I had together, have shown themselves to have integrity, decency, and love of goodness.

"Why didn't you bring Issib?"

Elemak sighed. Poor boy, thought Rasa. Is the old lady making you explain again? "We didn't want to worry about his chair or his floats on this trip," he said.

"It's just as well we don't have him locked up in here with us," said Nafai.

"I don't think the general will keep us under arrest for long," said Rasa. "Once I'm thoroughly discredited, there'd be no reason to do something as clearly repressive as this. He's trying to create an image of himself as a liberator and protector, and having his soldiers in the streets here isn't helpful."

"And then we leave?" asked Nafai.

"No, we put down roots here," said Mebbekew. "Of course we leave."

"I want to go home," said Kokor. "Even if Obring is a wretched miserable excuse for a husband, I miss him."

Sevet said nothing.

Rasa looked at Elemak, who had a half-smile on his face. "And you, Elemak, are you also eager to leave my house?"

"I'm grateful for your hospitality," he said. "And we'll always remember your home as the last civilized house we lived in for many years."

"Speak for yourself, Elya," said Mebbekew.

"What is he talking about?" said Kokor. "I have a civilized house waiting for me right now."

Sevet gave a strangled laugh.

"I wouldn't boast about how civilized my house is, if I were you," said Rasa. "I see, too, that Elemak is the only one who understands your true situation here."

"I understand it," said Nafai.

Of course Elemak glared at Nafai under hooded eyes. Nafai, you foolish boy, thought Rasa. Must you always say the thing that will most provoke your brothers? Did you think I had forgotten that you have heard the voice of the

Oversoul, that you understand far more than your brothers or sisters do? Couldn't you trust me to remember your worthiness, and so hold silence?

No, he couldn't. Nafai was young, too young to see the consequences of his actions, too young to contain his feelings.

"Nevertheless, it is Elemak who will explain it to us all."

"We can't stay in the city," said Elemak. "The moment the soldiers leave their watch, we have to escape, and quickly."

"Why?" asked Mebbekew. "It's Lady Rasa who's in trouble, not us."

"By the Oversoul, you're stupid," said Elemak.

What a refreshingly direct way of saying it, thought Rasa. No wonder your brothers worship you, Elya.

"As long as Lady Rasa is under arrest, Moozh has to see to it that no harm comes to anyone here. But he's set it up so that Rasa will have plenty of enemies in the city. As soon as his soldiers step out of the way, some very bad things will start to happen."

"All the more reason for us to get out of Mother's house," said Kokor. "Mother can flee if she wants, but they've got nothing against *me.*"

"They've got something against *all* of us," said Elemak. "Meb and Nafai and I are fugitives, and Nafai in particular has been accused of two murders, one of which he actually committed. Kokor can be charged with assault and attempted murder against her own sister. And Sevet is a flagrant adulterer, and since it was with her own sister's husband, the incest laws can be dredged up, too."

"They wouldn't dare," said Kokor. "Prosecute *me!*"

"And why wouldn't they dare?" asked Elemak. "Only the great respect and love people had for Lady Rasa protected you from arrest in the first place. Well, *that's* gone, or at least weakened."

"They'd never convict me," said Kokor.

"And the adultery laws haven't been enforced for centuries," said Meb. "And people are disgusted by incest between in-laws, but as long as they're at the age of consent . . ."

"Is *everyone* here criminally dumb?" asked Elemak. "No, I forget—*Nafai* understands *everything*."

"No," said Nafai. "I know we need to go out to the desert because the Oversoul commanded it, but I don't have any idea what *you're* talking about."

Rasa couldn't stop herself from smiling. Nafai could be foolish sometimes, but his very honesty and directness could also be disarming. Without meaning to, Nafai had pleased Elemak by humbling himself and acknowledging Elya's greater wisdom.

"Then I'll explain," said Elemak. "Lady Rasa is a powerful woman—even now, because the wisest people in Basilica don't believe the rumors about her, not for a moment. It won't be enough for Moozh just to discredit her. He needs her to be either completely under his control, or dead. To accomplish the former, all he needs to do is put one or all of Rasa's children on trial for murder—or Father's sons, too for that matter—and she'll be helpless. Lady Rasa is a brave woman, but I don't think she has the heart to let her children or Father's sons go to prison just so she can play politics. And if she *did* have that degree of ruthlessness, Moozh would simply up the stakes. Which of us would he kill first? Moozh is a deft man—he'd do only enough to communicate his message clearly. He'd kill *you,* I think, Meb, since you're the one who is most worthless and whom Father and Lady Rasa would miss the least."

Meb leaped to his feet. "I've had enough of you, fart-for-breath!"

"Sit down, Mebbekew," said Lady Rasa. "Can't you see he's goading you for sport?"

Elemak grinned at Mebbekew, who wasn't mollified. Mebbekew glowered as he sat back down.

"He'd kill *somebody,*" said Elemak, "just as a warning. Of course, it wouldn't be *his* soldiers. But he'd know that Lady Rasa would see his hand in it. And if holding us as hostages for her good behavior didn't work, Moozh has already laid the groundwork for murdering Lady Rasa herself. It would be easy to find some outraged citizen eager to kill her for her supposed treachery; all Moozh would have to do is set up an opportunity for such an assassin to strike. It would be simple. It's when the soldiers *leave* the streets outside this house that our true danger begins. So we have to prepare to leave immediately, secretly, and permanently."

"Leave Basilica!" cried Kokor. Her genuine dismay meant that she had finally grasped the idea that their situation was serious.

Sevet understood, that was certain. Her face was tilted downward, but Rasa could still see the tears on her cheeks.

"I'm sorry that your close association with me is costing you so much," said Rasa. "But for all these years, my dear daughters, my dear son, my beloved students, you have all benefitted from the prestige of my house, as well as the great honor of the Wetchik. Now that events have turned against us in Basilica, you must share in paying the price, as well. It is inconvenient, but it is not unfair."

"Forever," murmured Kokor.

"Forever it is," said Elemak. "But I, for one, will not go out into the desert without my wife. I hope my brothers have made some provision for themselves. It *is* the reason we came here."

"Obring," said Kokor. "We must bring Obring!"

Sevet lifted her chin and looked into her mother's face. Sevet's eyes were swimming with tears, and there was a frightened question in her face.

"I think that Vas will come with you, if you ask him," said Rasa. "He's a wise and a forgiving man, and he loves you far more than you deserve." The words were cold, but Sevet still took them as comfort.

"But what about *Obring*," insisted Kokor.

"He's such a weak man," said Rasa, "I'm sure you can persuade him to come along."

In the meantime, Mebbekew had turned to Elemak. "Your *wife?*" he asked.

"Lady Rasa is going to perform the ceremony for Eiadh and me tonight," said Elemak.

Mebbekew's face betrayed some powerful emotion— rage, jealousy? Had Mebbekew also wanted Eiadh, the way poor Nafai had?

"You're marrying her *tonight?*" demanded Mebbekew.

"We don't know when Moozh will lift our house arrest, and I want my marriage to be done properly. Once we're out in the desert, I don't want any question about who is married to whom."

"Not that we can't change around as soon as our terms are up," said Kokor.

Everyone looked at her.

"The desert isn't Basilica," said Rasa. "There'll only be a handful of us. Marriages will be permanent. Get used to that idea right now."

"That's absurd," said Kokor. "I'm not going, and you can't make me."

"No, I can't make you," said Rasa. "But if you stay, you'll soon discover how different life is when you're no longer the daughter of Lady Rasa, but merely a young singer who is notorious for having silenced her much more famous sister with a blow from her own hand."

"I can live with that!" said Kokor defiantly.

"Then I'm sure I don't want you with me," said Rasa angrily. "What good would a girl with no conscience be on the terrible journey that lies ahead of us?" Her words were harsh, but Rasa could taste her disappointment in Kokor like a foul poison on her tongue. "I've said all I have to say. You all have work to do and choices to make. Make them and have done."

It was a clear dismissal, and Kokor and Sevet got up and left at once, Kokor sweeping past, her nose in the air in a great show of hauteur.

Mebbekew sidled up to Rasa—couldn't the boy walk naturally, without looking like a sneak or a spy?—and asked his question. "Is Elya's wedding tonight an exclusive affair?"

"Everyone in the house is invited to attend," said Rasa.

"I meant—what if I were to marry someone, too. Would you do the ceremony tonight?"

"Marry *someone*? I assure you, Dolya may have been indiscreet, but I'll be surprised if she takes you on as a husband, Mebbekew."

Meb looked furious. "Luet told you."

"Of course she told me," said Rasa. "Half a dozen servants and Dolya herself would have told me before nightfall. Do you actually imagine anyone can keep a secret like *that* from me in my own house?"

"*If* I can persuade her to accept a piece of unworthy slime like myself," said Meb, his voice dripping with sarcasm, "will you condescend to include us in the ceremony?"

"It would be dangerous to bring you out into the desert without a wife," said Rasa. "Dolya would be more than enough woman for *you,* though she could hardly do worse for herself."

Mebbekew's face was red with fury. "I have done nothing to deserve such scorn from you."

"You have done nothing *but* to earn it," said Rasa. "You seduced my niece under my own roof, and now you contemplate marrying her—and don't think I'm fooled, either. You want to marry her, not to join your father in the desert, but to use her as your license to remain in Basilica. You'll be unfaithful to her the moment we're gone and you have your papers."

"And I swear to you in the eyes of the Oversoul that I will bring Dolya out into the desert, as surely as Elya is bringing Eiadh."

"Be careful when you make the Oversoul the witness of your oath," said Rasa. "She has a way of making you hold to your word."

Mebbekew almost said something else, but then thought better of it and stalked out of Rasa's private receiving room. No doubt off to flatter Dolya into proposing marriage to *him.*

And it will work, thought Rasa bitterly. Because this boy, who has so little else going for him, *is* good with women. Haven't I heard of his exploits from the mothers of so many girls in Dolltown and Dauberville? Poor Dolya. Has life left you so hungry that you'll swallow even the poor imitation of love?

Only Elemak and Nafai remained.

"I don't want to share my ceremony with Mebbekew," said Elemak coldly.

"It's tragic, isn't it, that we don't always get what we want in this world," said Rasa. "Anyone who wants to be married tonight, will be. We don't have time to satisfy your vanity, and you know it. You'd tell me so yourself, if you were giving me impartial counsel."

Elemak studied her face for a few moments. "Yes," he said. "You're very wise." Then he, too, left.

But Rasa understood him, too, better than he imagined. She knew that he had sized her up and decided that, while she might be powerful in Basilica, she would be nothing in the desert. He would bow to her rule tonight, but once they got out into the desert he would delight in subjugating her. Well, I am not afraid to be humiliated, thought Rasa. I can bear much more than you imagine. What will your torments mean to me, when I will feel the agony of my beloved city, and know that in my exile I can do nothing to save it after all?

Only Nafai was with her now.

"Mother," he said, "what about Issib? And Gaballufix's treasurer, Zdorab? They'll need wives. And Elemak saw wives for all of us, in his dream."

"Then the Oversoul must provide wives for them, don't you think?"

"Shedemei will come," he said. "She had a dream, too. The Oversoul is bringing her. And Hushidh. She's part of this, isn't she? The Oversoul will surely bring her. For Issib, or for Zdorab."

"Why don't you ask her?" said Rasa.

"Not *me*," said Nafai.

"You told me that the Oversoul said you would lead your brothers someday. How will that happen, if you haven't the strength inside yourself to face even a sweet and generous girl like Shuya?"

"To you she seems sweet," said Nafai. "But to *me*—and asking her such a thing—"

"She knows you boys came back here for wives, you foolish child. Do you think she hasn't counted heads? She's a raveler—do you think she doesn't already see the connections?"

He was abashed. "No, I didn't think of that. She probably knows more than I do about everything."

"Only about some things," said Rasa. "And you're still hiding from the most important question of all."

"No, I'm not," said Nafai. "I know that Luet is the woman I should marry, and I know that I will ask her. I didn't need your advice about that."

"Then I have nothing to fear for you, my son," said Rasa.

The soldiers brought Rashgallivak into his room and, as Moozh had instructed them beforehand, cast him down brutally onto the floor. When the soldiers had left, Rashgallivak touched his nose. It wasn't broken, but it was bleeding from its impact with the floor, and Moozh offered him nothing to wipe the blood. Since the soldiers had stripped Rashgallivak naked before bringing him here, there was nothing for Rashgallivak to do but let the blood flow into his mouth or down his chin.

"I knew I'd see you sooner or later," said Moozh. "I didn't have to search. I knew there'd come a time when you imagined that you had something I'd want from you, and then you'd come to me and try to bargain for your life. But I can assure you, I need nothing that you have."

"So kill me and have done," said Rashgallivak.

"Very dramatic," said Moozh. "I say I *need* nothing that you have, but I might *want* something, and I might even want it enough not to put your eyes out or castrate you or some other small favor before you are burned to death as a traitor to your city."

"Yes, so deeply you care for Basilica," said Rashgallivak.

"You gave me this city, you poor fool. Your stupidity and brutality gave it to me as a gift. Now it's the brightest jewel in my possession. Yes, I care deeply for Basilica."

"Only if you can keep it," said Rashgallivak.

"Oh, I assure you, I'll keep this jewel. Either by wearing it to adorn me, or by grinding it to powder and swallowing it down."

"So fearless you are, brave General. And yet you've got Lady Rasa under house arrest."

"I still have many paths that I can follow," said Moozh. "I can't think why any of them lead to anything but your immediate death. So you'll have to do better than tell me what I already know."

"Like it or not," said Rashgallivak, "I *am* the legal Wetchik and the head of the Palwashantu clan, and while no one has much love for me right now, if the disfranchised men outside the walls saw that I was in your favor and had some power to bestow, they would rally to me. I could be useful to you."

"I see that you harbor some pathetic dreams of being my rival for power here."

"No, General," said Rashgallivak. "I was a steward all my life, working to build and strengthen the house of Wetchik. Gaballufix talked me into acting on ambitions that I never had until he made me feel them. I've had plenty of time to regret believing him, to scorn myself for strutting around as if I were some great leader, when in fact what I am is a born steward. I was only happy when I served a stronger man than myself. I was proud that I always served the strongest man in Basilica. That happens to be yourself, and if you kept me alive and used me, you would find I am a man of many good gifts."

"Including unquestionable loyalty?"

"You will never trust me, I know that. I betrayed Wetchik, to my shame. But I only did it when Volemak was already exiled and powerless. You will *never* weaken or fail, and so you can trust me implicitly."

Moozh couldn't help laughing. "You're telling me that I can trust you to be loyal, because you're too much of a coward to betray a strong man?"

"I've had plenty of time to know myself, General Vozmuzhalnoy Vozmozhno. I have no desire to deceive either myself or you."

"I can put anyone in charge of the rabble of men who call themselves Palwashantu," said Moozh. "Or I can lead them myself. Why would I need you alive, when I can gain so much more from your public confession and execution?"

"You're a brilliant general and leader of men, but you still don't know Basilica."

"I know it well enough to rule here without losing the life of a single man of mine."

"Then if you're so all-knowing, General Vozmuzhalnoy Vozmozhno, perhaps you'll understand immediately why it is important that Shedemei bought a dozen drycases from me today."

"Don't play games with me, Rashgallivak. You know that I have no notion of who this Shedemei is, or what his buying drycases might mean."

"Shedemei is a woman, sir. A noted scientist. Very clever with genetics—she has developed some popular new plants, among other things."

"If you have a point . . ."

"Shedemei is also a teacher in Rasa's house, and one of her most beloved nieces."

Ah. So Rashgallivak *might* have something worth learning. Moozh waited to hear more.

"Drycases are used to transport seeds and embryos across great distances without refrigeration. She told me that she was moving her entire research laboratory to a faraway city, and that's why she needed drycases."

"And you don't believe her."

"It is unthinkable that Shedemei would move her laboratory *now*. The danger is clearly over, and ordinarily she would simply bury herself in her work. She is a very focused scientist. She barely notices the world around her."

"So her plan to leave comes from Rasa, you think."

"Rasa has been faithfully married to Wetch—to Volemak, the former Wetchik—for many years. He exiled himself from the city several weeks ago, ostensibly in obedience to some vision from the Oversoul. His sons came back to the city and tried to buy the Palwashantu Index from Gaballufix."

Rashgallivak paused, as if waiting for Moozh to make some connection; but of course Rashgallivak would know that Moozh lacked the information necessary to make this connection. It was Rashgallivak's way of trying to assert

Moozh's need for him. But Moozh had no intention of playing this game. "Either tell me or don't," he said. "Then I'll decide whether I want you or not. If you continue to imagine you can manipulate my judgment, you only prove yourself to be worthless."

"It's clear that Volemak still dreams of ruling here in Basilica. Why else would he want the Index? Its only value is as a symbol of authority among the Palwashantu men; it reminds them of that ancient, ancient day when they were not ruled by women. Rasa is his wife and a powerful woman in her own right. Alone she is dangerous to you—in combination with her husband, they would be formidable indeed. Who else could unite the city against you? Shedemei would not be preparing for a journey like this unless Rasa asked her to. Therefore Rasa and Volemak must have some plan that requires drycases."

"And what kind of plan would that be?"

"Shedemei is a brilliant geneticist, as I said. What if she could develop some mold or fungus that would spread like a disease through Basilica? Only Rasa's and Volemak's supporters would have the fungicide to kill it."

"A fungus. And you think this would be a weapon against the soldiers of the Gorayni?"

"No one's ever used such a thing as a weapon, sir," said Rashgallivak. "I could hardly think of it myself. But imagine how well your soldiers would fight if their bodies were covered with an excruciating, unbearable itch."

"An *itch*," echoed Moozh. It sounded absurd, laughable. And yet it might work—soldiers distracted by an itching, ineradicable fungus would not fight well. Nor would the city be easily governed, if people were suffering from such a plague. Governments were never less imposing than when they showed themselves impotent against disease or famine. Moozh had used this fact against the enemies of the Imperator many times. Was it possible that Rasa and Volemak were so clever, so evil-hearted, that they could conceive of such an inconceivable weapon? To use a scientist as a weapon maker—how could God allow such a vile practice to come into the world?

Unless . . .

Unless Rasa and Volemak have, like me, learned to resist God. Why should I be the only one with the strength to ignore God's efforts to turn men stupid when they attempted to walk on the road leading to power?

But then, couldn't Rashgallivak also be a tool God was using to mislead him? It had been many days since God had attempted to block him from any action. Was it possible that God, having failed to dominate Moozh directly, might now be trying to control Moozh by leading him after foolish imagined conspiracies? Many generals had been destroyed by just such fancies as the one Rashgallivak had now brought to him.

"Couldn't the drycases be for something else?" asked Moozh, testing.

"Of course," said Rashgallivak. "I only pointed out the most extreme possibility. Drycases also work very well for transporting supplies through the desert. Volemak and his sons—his oldest boy, Elemak, in particular—are more familiar with the desert than most. It holds no fear for them. They could be planning to build an army. You *do* have only a thousand men here."

"The rest of the army of the Gorayni will be here soon."

"Then perhaps that's why Volemak needed only twelve drycases—he won't need to supply his little army for very long."

"Army," said Moozh scornfully. "Twelve drycases. You were found with a draft for jewels of very high value. How do I know you haven't been bribed to tell me foolish lies and waste my time?"

"I wasn't *found,* sir. I turned myself over to your soldiers deliberately. And I brought the draft instead of the jewels because I wanted you to see that it was Shedemei's own hand that wrote the note. This amount is far more than the drycases are worth. She is clearly trying to buy my silence."

"So. This is where you are now, Rashgallivak. A few days ago you thought you were master of the city. And now you betray your former master once again, in order to ingratiate yourself with a new one. Explain to me why I shouldn't retch at the sight of you."

"Because I can be useful to you."

"Yes, yes, I can imagine, like a vicious but hungry dog. So tell me, Rashgallivak, what bone do you want me to toss you?"

"My life, sir."

"Your life will never be your own again, as long as you live. So again I ask you to tell me what bone you want to gnaw on."

Rashgallivak hesitated.

"If you pretend to have some altruistic desire to serve me or the Imperator or Basilica, I'll have you gutted and burned in the marketplace within the hour."

"We don't burn traitors here. It would make you look monstrous to the Basilicans."

"On the contrary," said Moozh. "It would make them very happy to see such treatment meted out to *you*. No one is so civilized as not to relish vengeance, even if later they're ashamed of how they loved to see their enemy suffer before he died."

"Stop threatening me, General," said Rashgallivak. "I've lived in terror and I've come out of it. Kill me or not, torture me or not, it doesn't matter to me. Just decide what to do."

"Tell me first what you want. Your secret desire. Your dream of the best thing that might come to you from all of this."

Again he hesitated. But this time he found the strength to name his desire. "Lady Rasa," he whispered.

Moozh nodded slightly. "So ambition isn't dead in you," he said. "You still have dreams of living infinitely above your station."

"I told you because you insisted, sir. I know it could never happen."

"Get out of here," said Moozh. "My men will take you to be bathed. And then dressed. You will live at least another night."

"Thank you, sir."

The soldiers came in and took Rashgallivak away—but

this time without dragging him, without any brutality. Not that Moozh had decided to use Rashgallivak. His death was still an attractive possibility—it would be the most decisive way for Moozh to declare himself the master of Basilica, to mete out justice so publicly, so popularly, and so clearly in violation of all Basilican law and custom and decency. The citizens would love it, and in loving it they would cease to be the old Basilica. They would become something new. A new city.

My city.

Rashgallivak married to Rasa. That was a nasty thought, conceived in a nasty little mind. Yet it would certainly humiliate Rasa, and clinch the image of her in many people's minds as a traitor to Basilica. And yet she would still be a leading citizen of Basilica, with an aura of legitimacy. After all, she *was* on Bitanke's list. As was Rashgallivak.

It was a fine list, too. Well thought out, and quite daring. Bitanke was a bright man, very useful. For example, he was wise enough not to underestimate Moozh's powers of persuasion. He didn't leave people off his list just because he fancied that they'd never be willing to serve Moozh by ruling Basilica for him.

So the names that led the list were, unsurprisingly, the very names that Rashgallivak had mentioned as possible rivals: Volemak and Rasa. Rashgallivak's name, too, was there. And Volemak's son and heir, Elemak, because of both his ability and his legitimacy. Volemak's and Rasa's youngest, too—Nafai, because he linked those two great names and because he had killed Gaballufix with his own hands.

Was everyone who might serve Moozh's need linked to Rasa's house? That was no surprise to him—in most cities he'd conquered, there were at most two or three clans that had to be either eliminated or co-opted in order to control the populace. Almost everyone else on Bitanke's list was far too weak to rule well without constant help from Moozh, as Bitanke himself pointed out: They were too closely linked with certain factions, or too isolated from any support at all.

The only two who weren't tied by blood to Volemak or

Rasa were nevertheless nieces in Rasa's house: The water-seer Luet and the raveler Hushidh. They were still only girls, of course, hardly ready to handle the difficult work of governance. But they had enormous prestige among the women of Basilica, especially the waterseer. They would be only figureheads, but with Rashgallivak to actually run things, and Bitanke to watch Rashgallivak and protect the figurehead from being manipulated against Moozh's best interest, the city could run very well while Moozh turned his attention to his real problems—the Cities of the Plain, and the Imperator.

Rashgallivak married to Rasa. It sounded so pleasantly dynastic. No doubt Rash's dreams included supplanting Moozh one day and ruling in his own right. Well, Moozh could hardly begrudge him those dreams. But there would soon be a dynasty that would surpass Rash's poor dreams. Rash might take the Lady Rasa, but how would that compare with the glorious marriage of the waterseer or the raveler with General Moozh himself? That would be a dynasty that could stand for a thousand years. That would be a dynasty that could topple the feeble house of that pathetic little man who dared to call himself the incarnation of God—the Imperator, whose power would be nothing when Moozh decided to move against him.

And, best of all, by marrying and using one of these chosen vessels of the Oversoul, Moozh would have the triumph that pleased him most: The triumph over God. You were never strong enough to control me, O Almighty One. And now I'll take your chosen daughter, filled with your visions, and make her the mother of a dynasty that will defy you and destroy all your plans and works.

Stop me if you can! I am far too strong for you.

Nafai found Luet and Hushidh together, waiting for him in the secret place on the roof. They looked very grave, which did nothing to calm the fear in Nafai's heart. Until now, Nafai had never felt himself to be young; he had always felt himself to be a person, equal to any other. But now his youth pressed in on him. He had not thought to marry now, or even really to *decide* whom to marry. Nor was it the easy, temporary union that he had expected his first marriage to be. His wife would probably be his only wife, and if he did badly in this marriage, he'd have no recourse. Seeing Luet and Hushidh, both looking at him solemnly as he made his way across the brightly sunlit roof, he wondered again if he could do this: If he could marry this girl Luet, who was so perfect and wise in the eyes of the Oversoul. She had come to the Oversoul with love, with devotion, with courage—he had come like a bratty child, taunting and testing his unknown parent. She had years of experience in speaking with the Oversoul; perhaps more important, she had had years in speaking *for* the Oversoul, to the women of Basilica. She knew how to dominate others—hadn't he seen it there on the shores of the lake of women, when she faced them down and saved his life?

Will I be coming to you as a husband or a child? A partner or a student?

"So the family council is over," said Hushidh, when at last he was near enough for easy speech.

He seated himself on the carpet under the awning. The shade gave him little enough respite from the heat. Sweat dripped under his clothing. It made him aware of his own naked body, hidden from view. If he married Luet, he would have to offer that body to her tonight. How often had he dreamed of such an offering? And yet never once had he thought of coming to a girl who filled him with awe and shyness, and yet who was herself utterly without experience; always in his dreams the woman was eager for him, and he was a bold and ready lover. There would be nothing like that tonight.

He had a wrenching thought. What if Luet wasn't ready yet? What if she wasn't even a *woman* yet? He quickly spoke a prayer in his heart to the Oversoul, but couldn't finish it, because he wasn't sure whether he hoped she *was* a woman, or hoped that she was *not*.

"How thickly woven are the bonds already," said Hushidh.

"What are you talking about?" asked Nafai.

"We're tied to the future by so many cords. The Oversoul

has always told dear Luet, here, that she wants human beings to follow her freely. But I think she has caught us in a very tight-woven net, and we have about as much choice as a fish that's been dragged up from the sea."

"We have choices," said Nafai. "We always have choices."

"Do we?"

I don't want to talk to *you*, Hushidh. I came here now to talk to Luet.

"We have the choice to follow the Oversoul or not," said Luet, her voice coming soft and sweet, compared to Hushidh's harsher tone. "And if we choose to follow, then we are not caught in her net, but rather carried in her basket into the future."

Hushidh smiled wanly. "Always so cheerful, aren't you, Lutya."

A lull in the conversation.

If I am to be a man and a husband, I must learn to act boldly, even when I'm afraid. "Luet," he began. Then: "Lutya."

"Yes?" she said.

But he could not ignore Hushidh's eyes boring into him, seeing in him things that he had no desire for her to see.

"Hushidh," he said, "could I speak to Luet alone?"

"I have no secrets from my sister," said Luet.

"And will that be true, even when you have a husband?" asked Nafai.

"I have no husband," said Luet.

"But if you did, I would hope that he would be the one you shared your inmost heart with, and not your sister."

"If I had a husband, I would hope that he would not be so cruel as to require me to abandon my sister, who is my only family in the world."

"If you had a husband," said Nafai, "he should love your sister as if she were his own sister. But still not as much as he loved *you*, and so you should not love your sister as much as you loved *him*."

"Not all marriages are for love," said Luet. "Some are because one has no choice."

The words stung him to the heart. She knew, of

course—if the Oversoul had told *him,* it would certainly have told *her,* as well. And she was telling him that she didn't love him, that she was marrying him only because the Oversoul commanded it.

"True," said Nafai. "But that doesn't mean that the husband and the wife can't treat each other with gentleness and kindness, until they learn trust for each other. It doesn't mean they can't resolve to love each other, even if they didn't choose the marriage freely, for themselves."

"I hope that what you've said is true."

"I promise to make it true, if you'll promise me the same."

Luet looked at him with a chagrined smile on her face. "Oh. Is this how I'm to hear my husband ask me to be his wife?"

So he had done it wrong. He had offended her, perhaps hurt her, certainly disappointed her. How she must loathe the idea of being married to him. Didn't she see that he would never have chosen to force such a thing on her? As the thought formed in his mind, he blurted it out. "The Oversoul chose us for each other, and so yes, I'm asking you to marry me, even though I'm afraid."

"Afraid of *me?*"

"Not that you mean me any harm—you've saved my life, and my father's life before that. I'm afraid—of your disdain for me. I'm afraid that I'll always be humiliated before you and your sister, the two of you, seeing everything weak about me, looking down on me. The way you see me now."

In all his life, Nafai had never spoken with such brutal frankness about his own fear; he had never felt so exposed and vulnerable in front of anyone. He dared not look up at her face—at their faces—for fear of seeing a look of wondrous contempt.

"Oh, Nafai, I'm sorry," whispered Luet.

Her words came as the blow that he had most dreaded. She pitied him. She saw how weak and frightened and uncertain he was, and she felt sorry for him. And yet even in the pain of that moment of disappointment, he felt a small bright fire of joy inside. I can do this, he thought. I have shown my weakness to these strong women, and still I am myself, and alive inside, and not defeated at all.

"Nafai, I only thought of how frightened I was," said Luet. "I never imagined that you might feel that way, too, or I would never have asked Shuya to stay here when you came to me."

"It's no great pleasure to *be* here, I assure you," added Hushidh.

"It was wrong of me to make you say these things in front of Shuya," said Luet. "And it was wrong of me to be afraid of you. I should have known that the Oversoul wouldn't have chosen you if you weren't a good-hearted man."

She was afraid of *him*?

"Won't you look at me, Nafai?" she asked. "I know you never looked at me before, not with hope or longing, anyway, but now that the Oversoul has given us to each other, can't you look at me with—with kindness, anyway?"

How could he lift his face to her now, with his eyes full of tears; and yet, since she asked him, since it would mean disappointment to her if he did not, how could he refuse? He looked at her, and even though his eyes swam with tears—of joy, of relief, of emotions even stronger that he didn't understand—he saw her as if for the first time, as if her soul had been made transparent to him. He saw the purity of her heart. He saw how fully she had given herself to the Oversoul, and to Basilica, and to her sister, and to him. He saw that in her heart she longed only to build something fine and beautiful, and how readily she was willing to try to do that with this boy who sat before her.

"What do you see, when you look at me like that?" asked Luet, her voice timid, yet daring to ask.

"I see what a great and glorious woman you are," he said, "and how little reason I have to fear you, because you'd never harm me or any other soul."

"Is that all you see?" she asked.

"I see that the Oversoul has found in you the most perfect example of what the human race must all become, if we are to be whole, and not destroy ourselves again."

"Nothing more?" she asked.

"What can be more wonderful than the things I've told you that I see?"

By now his eyes had cleared enough to see that *she* was now on the verge of crying—but not for joy.

"Nafai, you poor fool, you blind man," said Hushidh, "don't you know what she's hoping that you see?"

No, I don't know, thought Nafai. I don't know any of the right things to say. I'm not like Mebbekew, I'm not clever or tactful, I give offense to everybody when I speak, and somehow I've done it again, even though everything I said was what I honestly feel.

He looked at her, feeling helpless; what could he do? She looked at him so hungrily, aching for him to give her— what? He had praised her honestly, with the sort of praise that he could have spoken to no other woman in the world, and it was nothing to her, because she wanted something more from him, and he didn't know what it was. He was hurting her with his very silence, stabbing her to the heart, he could see that—and yet was powerless to stop doing it.

She was so frail, so young—even younger than he. He had never realized that before. She had always been so sure of herself, and, because she was the waterseer, he had always been in awe. He had never realized how . . . how *breakable* she was. How thinly her luminous skin covered her, how small her bones were. A tiny stone could bruise her, and now I find her battered with stones that I cast without knowing. Forgive me, Luet, tender child, gentle girl. I was so afraid for myself, but I turned out not to be breakable at all, even when I thought you and Hushidh had scorned me. While you, whom I had thought to be strong . . .

Impulsively he knelt up and gathered her into his arms and held her close, the way he might hold a weeping child. "I'm sorry," he whispered.

"Don't be sorry, please," she said. But her voice was high, the voice of a child who is trying not to be caught crying, and he could feel her tears soaking into his shirt, and her body trembling with silent weeping.

"I'm sorry that it's only me you get as a husband," he said.

"And I'm sorry that it's only me you get as a wife," she said. "Not the waterseer, not the glorious being you imagined that you saw. Only me."

Finally he understood what she had been asking for all along, and couldn't help but laugh, because without knowing it he had just now given it to her. "Did you think that I said those things to the *waterseer?*" he asked. "No, you poor thing, I said those things to *you,* to Luet, to the girl I met in my mother's school, to the girl who sassed me and anybody else when she felt like it, to the girl I'm holding in my arms right now."

She laughed then—or sobbed harder, he wasn't sure. But he knew that whatever she was doing now, it was better. That was all she had needed—was for him to tell her that he didn't expect her to be the waterseer all the time, that he was marrying the fragile, imperfect human being, and not the overpowering image that she inadvertently wore.

He moved his hands across her back, to comfort her; but he also felt the curve of her body, the geometry of ribs and spine, the texture and softness of skin stretched taut over muscles. His hands explored, memorizing her, discovering for the first time how a woman's back felt to a man's hands. She was real and not a dream.

"The Oversoul didn't give you to me," he said softly. "You are giving yourself to me."

"Yes," she said. "That's right."

"And I give myself to you," he said. "Even though I, too, belong to the Oversoul."

He drew back a little, enough to cup the back of her head in his right hand as she looked up at him, enough to touch her cheek with the fingers of his left.

Then, suddenly, as if they both had the same thought at the same moment—which, quite certainly, they did— they looked away from each other, and toward the spot where Hushidh had been sitting through this whole conversation.

But Hushidh wasn't there. They turned back to each

other then, and Luet, dismayed, said, "I shouldn't have made her come with me to—"

She never finished the sentence, because at that moment Nafai began to learn how to kiss a woman, and she, though she had never kissed a man before, became his tutor.

SIX

WEDDINGS

THE DREAM OF THE RAVELER

Hushidh saw nothing joyful about the wedding. Not that anything went wrong. Aunt Rasa had a way with rituals. Her ceremony was simple and sweet, without a hint of the false portentousness that so many other women resorted to in their desperate desire to seem holy or important. Aunt Rasa had never needed to pretend. And yet she still took great care that when the public passages of life—weddings, comings-of-age, graduations, embarkations, divinations, deathwatches, burials—were under her care, they took place with an easy grace, a gentleness that kept people's minds focused on the occasion, and not on the machinery of celebration. There was never a hint of anyone hurrying or bustling; never a hint that everything had to be *just so,* and therefore you'd better watch your step so you don't do anything wrong . . .

No, Rasa's wedding for her son Nafai and his two brothers—or, if you looked at it the other way, Rasa's wedding for her three nieces, Luet, Dol, and Eiadh—was a lovely affair on the portico of her house, bright and aromatic with flowers from her greenhouse and the blossoms that grew on the portico. Eiadh and Dol were astonishingly beautiful, their gowns clinging to them with the elegant illusion of simplicity, their facepaint so artfully applied that they seemed not to be painted at all. Or *would* have seemed so, had it not been for Luet.

Sweet Luet, who had refused to be painted at all, and whose dress really *was* simple. Where Eiadh and Dol had all the elegance of women trying—very successfully—to seem bright and young and gay, Luet really *was* young, her gown artlessly covering a body that was still more the promise than the reality of womanhood, her face bright with a grave and timid sort of joy that made Eiadh and Dol look older and far too experienced. In a way, it was almost cruel to make the older girls have their weddings in the presence of this girl who rebuked them by her very naivete. Eiadh had actually noticed, before the ceremony began—Hushidh overheard her urging Aunt Rasa to "send somebody up with Luet to help her choose a dress and to do something with her face and hair" but Aunt Rasa had only laughed and said, "No art will help that child." Eiadh took that, of course, to mean that Aunt Rasa thought Luet to be too plain to be helped by costume and makeup; but Hushidh caught Aunt Rasa's eye the moment afterward, and Aunt Rasa winked at her and rolled her eyes to let her know that *they* both understood that poor Eiadh hadn't a clue about what would happen at the wedding.

And it did happen, though fortunately Eiadh and Dol had no idea that when the watching servants and students and teachers whispered, "Ah, she is so lovely"; "Ah, so sweet"; "Look, who knew she was so beautiful," they were all speaking of Luet, only of Luet. When Nafai, as the youngest man, came forward to be claimed by his bride, the sighs were like a song from the congregation, an improvised hymn to the Oversoul, for having brought this boy of fourteen, who had the stature and strength of a man and the bright fire of the Oversoul in his eyes, to marry the Oversoul's chosen daughter, the waterseer, whose pure beauty grew from the soul outward. He was the bright gold ring in which this jewel of a girl would glow with unreflected luster.

Hushidh saw better than anyone how the people belonged to Luet in their hearts. She saw the threads between them, sparkling like the dew-covered strands of a spider's web in the first sunlight of morning; how they love the waterseer! But most of all Hushidh saw the firming bonds between the husbands and wives as the ceremony progressed. Unconsciously she took note of each gesture, each glance, each facial expression, and in her mind she was able to understand the connection.

Between Elemak and Eiadh, it would be a strange sort of unequal partnership, in which the less Eiadh loved Elemak, the more he would desire her; and the more he treated her gently and lovingly, the more she would despise him. It would be a painful thing to watch, this marriage, in which the agony of coming apart was the very thing that would hold them together. But she could say nothing of this—neither one would understand this about themselves, and would only be furious if she tried to explain it.

As for poor Dolya and her precious new lover, Mebbekew, it was an ill-considered marriage indeed—and yet there was no reason to suppose it would be less viable than Elemak's and Eiadh's. At the moment, flushed with the glory of being, as they supposed, the center of attention, they were happy with the new bonds between them. But soon enough the reality would settle in. If they stayed in the city, they would hate each other within weeks—Dol because of Mebbekew's betrayals and unfaithfulness, Mebbekew because of Dol's clinging, possessive need for him. Hushidh imagined their domestic life. Dol would be forever throwing her arms around him in wonderfully enthusiastic hugs, thinking she was showing her love when really she was asserting her ownership; and Meb, shuddering under her profuse embraces, slipping away at every opportunity to find new bodies to possess, new hearts to ravish. But in the desert, it would be very different. Meb would find no woman who desired him except Dolya, and so his own lusts would throw him back into her arms again and again; and the very fact that he *could* not betray her would ease Dol's lonely fears, and she would not oppress him so much with her need for him. In the desert, they could make a marriage of it, though Mebbekew would never be happy with the boredom of making love with the same woman, night after night, week after week, year after year.

Hushidh imagined, with a pleasure she wasn't proud of, what Elemak would do the first time Meb made some flirting advance toward Eiadh. It would be discreet, so as to avoid weakening Elemak's public position by hinting that he feared being cuckolded. But Meb would never so much as look at Eiadh again afterward . . .

The bonds between Elemak and Eiadh, between Dol and Mebbekew, they were the sort of links that Hushidh saw every day in the city. These were Basilican marriages, made more poignant—and perhaps more viable—by the fact that soon the Oversoul would bring them out into the desert where they would need each other more and have fewer alternatives than in the city.

The marriage between Luet and Nafai, however, was not Basilican. For one thing, they were too young. Luet was only thirteen. It was almost barbaric, really—like the forest tribes of the Northern Shore, where a girl was bought as a bride before her first blood had stopped trickling. Only Hushidh's sure knowledge that the Oversoul had brought them together kept her from recoiling from the ceremony. Even at that, she felt a deep anger that she did not fully understand as she watched them join hands, make their vows, kiss so sweetly with Aunt Rasa's hands on their shoulders. Why do I hate this marriage so much, she wondered. For she could see that Luet was full of hope and joy, that Nafai was in awe of her and eager to please her—what more could Hushidh have hoped for, for her dear sister, her only kin in this world?

Yet when the wedding ended, when the newly married couples made their laughing, flower-strewn procession back into the house and up the stairways to their balcony rooms, Hushidh could not contain herself long enough even to watch her sister out of sight. She fled into a servants' corridor, and ran, not to her room, but to the rooftop where she and Luet had so often retreated together.

Even here, though, it was as if she could still see, in the

gathering dark of evening, the shadow of Luet's and Nafai's first embrace, their first kiss. It filled her with rage, and she threw herself down onto the rug, beating on the thick fabric with her fists, weeping bitterly and sobbing, "No, no, no, no."

To what was she saying no? She didn't understand it herself. There she lay and there she wept until, weary with knowing too much and understanding not enough, she fell asleep in the cooling air of a Basilican night. Late in spring the breezes blew moist and cool from the sea, dry and warm from the desert, and met to do their turbulent dance in the streets and on the rooftops of the city. Hushidh's hair was caught in these breezes, and swirled and played as if it had a life of its own, and longed for freedom. But she did not wake.

Instead she dreamed, and in her dreams her unconscious mind brought forth the questions of fear and rage that she could not voice when she was awake. She dreamed of her own wedding. On a desert pinnacle, herself standing on the very tip of a high spire of rock, with no room for anyone else; yet there was her husband, floating in the air beside her: Issib, the cripple, blithely flying as she had seen him fly through the halls of Rasa's house during all his student years. In her dream she screamed the question that she had not dared to voice aloud: Why am I the one who must marry the cripple! How did you come up with my name for that life, Oversoul! How have I offended you, that I will never stand as Luet stood, sweet and young and blossoming with love, with a man beside me who is strong and holy, capable and good?

In her dream, she saw Issib float farther away from her, still smiling, but *she* knew that his smile was merely his own kind of courage, that her cries had broken his heart. As she watched, his smile faded; he crumpled, he fell like a bird taken out of the sky by a cruel miraculous arrow. Only then did she realize in the dream that he had been flying only by the power of his love for her, his need for her, and when she recoiled from him he had lost his power of flight. She tried to reach for him, tried to catch him, but all that happened then was that she herself lost her footing on the spire of rock and tumbled after him, downward to the ground.

She woke, panting, trembling in the cold. She gathered the free end of the carpet and pulled it over her and huddled under it, her cheeks cold from the tears drying there, her eyes puffy and sore from crying. Oversoul! she cried out silently with all her heart. O Mother of the Lake, tell me that you don't hate me so! Tell me that this is not your plan for me, that it was only accident that left me so bereft of hope on my sister's wedding night!

And then, with the perfect illogic of grief and self-pity, she prayed aloud, "Oversoul, tell me why you planned this life for me. I have to understand it if I'm going to live it. Tell me that it means something. Tell me why I am alive, tell me if some plan of yours brought me into this life as I am. Tell me why this power of understanding you gave me is a blessing, and not a curse. Tell me if I'll ever be as happy as Luet is tonight!" And then, ashamed of having put her jealousy and longing in such naked words, Hushidh wept again and drifted back into sleep.

Under the carpet she grew warm, for the night was not so cold yet, when she was covered. Her tears were replaced by sweat, drips of it tickling across her body like tiny hands. And again she dreamed.

She saw herself in the doorway of a desert tent. She had never seen a pitched tent before, except in holograms, yet this was not a tent she had seen in any picture. There she stood, holding a baby in her arms, as four other children, like stepstairs in height, rushed forth from the tent, and in the dream she thought it was as though the tent had just given birth to them, as though they were just now explod-ing into the world. If I had to, I would bear them all over again, and bring them here just to see them living so, brown and laughing in the desert sunlight. Around and around the children ran, chasing each other in some childish game while Hushidh watched. And then in her dream she heard the baby in her arms begin to fuss, and so she bared a breast and let the baby suckle; she could feel the milk flowing gratefully out of her nipple, could feel the sweet tingling of the baby's lips, kissing and sucking and smacking for life, warm life, wet life, a mingling of milk and saliva making a froth of tiny bubbles at the corners of the baby's mouth.

Then, through the door of the tent, there floated a chair, and in the chair a man. Issib, she knew at once. But there was no anger in her heart when she saw him, no sense that she had been cheated out of some good thing in life. Instead she could see herself bound to him, heart to heart, by great ropes of glowing silk; she took the baby from her breast and laid it in Issib's lap, and he talked to the baby, and made her laugh as Hushidh lazily dried her breast and covered it again. All of them bound together, mother, father, children . . . she saw that this was what mattered, not some imagined ideal of what a husband ought to be. The children ran to their father and circled his chair, and he spoke to them, and they listened raptly, laughed when he laughed, sang with him when he sang. This Issib-of-dreams was not a burden for her to bear, he was as true a friend and husband as any she had ever seen.

Oversoul, she prayed in her dream, how did you bring me here? Why did you love me so much that you brought me to this time, to this place, to this man, to these children?

At once the answer came, with threads of gold and silver. The children connected to Hushidh and Issib, and then threads reaching out from them, backward, to other people. A rush, a haze of people, a billion, a trillion people, she saw them milling around, marching forward on some unknowable quest, or perhaps a migration. It was a fearful vision, so many people all at once, as though Hushidh were being shown every man and woman who had ever lived on Harmony. And among them, here and there, those same silver and golden threads.

All at once she understood: These are the ones in whom the connection with the Oversoul bred true. These are the ones who are best able to hear the voice of the Oversoul, in whom the genetic alteration of Harmony's founding has been doubled, redoubled, so that instead of receiving only vague feelings, a stupor of thought when they venture onto some forbidden avenue of invention or action, these special ones, these gold and silver ones can receive clear ideas, images, even words.

At first the gold and silver threads were short and thin, only glimpses here and there—mutations, chance connections, random variations in the genetic molecules. But here and there they found each other, these people, and married; and when they mated, gold to gold or silver to silver, some of their children were also linked to the Oversoul. Two different strains, two different kinds of genetic link, Hushidh understood; when gold mated with silver, the children were almost never gifted this way. Over the centuries, over the uncountable multitudes, she could see that now the Oversoul was nudging gifted people, trying to bring them together, and after millions of years the gold and silver were no longer threads, they were strong cords, passing from generation to generation with much more regularity.

Until at last there came a time when one parent alone could pass the gold thread on to all his children; and then, many generations later, a time when the silver thread, too, became a dominant trait, that one parent could pass on regardless of whether the other parent was gifted or not.

Now the Oversoul grew more eager, and nudges became intricate plots as people were drawn together over thousands of kilometers, improbable marriages and matings. She saw a woman rise naked out of a stream to couple with a man she had come a thousand kilometers to find, the woman never knowing that this was the Oversoul's purpose. The man had in him both the gold and silver, strong and true, and so did the woman, and their daughter was born with cords of the brightest metal, shining as if with its own light.

In her dream Hushidh saw the mother take her baby and lay it in the arms of Rasa, who was herself linked to generations past with strands of gold and silver. And then the same woman, the same mother, laying yet another daughter, brighter still, in Rasa's arms. Before her eyes the second baby grew and became Luet, and now Hushidh saw what she had seen this very night, Luet and Nafai being bound together, but now she could see that, more than the cords of love and loyalty, of need and passion that Hushidh always saw, there were also these gold and silver cords, brighter in Luet and Nafai than in any others in the room. No wonder their eyes shone with such grace and beauty, thought Hushidh. They were created by the Oversoul, as surely as if she had come and smelted them out of perfect ore and touched them with the magic of life from her own hand.

Then Hushidh rose up as if she were flying over the portico, and she could see that all the couples being married there had these threads in them. Not as bright and strong as in Luet and Nafai, but they had them. Mebbekew and Elemak both had silver and gold in them; Dol had the silver only, and Eiadh the gold, with just a trace of silver.

Who else? How many others have you brought together, Oversoul?

Higher and higher she rose over the city, but because this was a dream she could still clearly see the people on the streets and in their houses. There were many bright traces of gold and silver here, far more than in any other place in all the world. Here in this city of women, many traders had come and brought, not just their goods, but their seed; many women had come on pilgrimage and stayed, at least long enough to bear a child; many families had sent their daughters and their sons to be educated; and now there was hardly a person in Basilica who was not touched with the gift to feel the influence of the Oversoul, to one degree or another. And those who were so touched could feel, not only the Oversoul, but also each other, though they never realized how much they understood. No wonder this is a holy city, thought Hushidh in her dream. No wonder it is known throughout the world for beauty and for truth.

Beauty and truth, but also darker things. The connection with the Oversoul did not mean that a person would be kinder or more generous. And unconscious knowledge of another person's heart could easily be turned to exploitation, manipulation, cruelty, or domination. Hushidh saw Gaballufix and realized that the threads in him were almost as bright as in Rasa or Wetchik. No wonder he knew so well how to lead the men of the Palwashantu, how to intimidate the women of Basilica, how to dominate those close to him.

Then Gaballufix as she saw in her dream stepped forth from his house, flailing about himself with his charged-wire blade as if a thousand invisible enemies attacked him. Hushidh understood that this was his own madness, and the Oversoul grieved at what he was doing. So she made Gaballufix stumble. He fell to the ground and lay there, still bright with gold and silver, but helpless and harmless for the moment.

As he lay there, another came: Nafai, she knew. She was being shown Luet's husband in his most terrible moment, for she could see how he stood over the body and pleaded with the Oversoul not to require him to do what he was being asked to do. Yet when he sliced off Gaballufix's head, he was not being controlled by the Oversoul. He had freely chosen to follow the Oversoul's path. Gaballufix was extinguished, and Nafai stood alone in the street, shining and ashamed.

Hushidh fairly flew over the city, catching glimpses of the brightest ones. Shedemei, alone in her laboratory, filling portable drycases with seeds and embryos. A man walking with Nafai toward the city gate, carrying a globe wrapped in a cloth—it had to be Zdorab, the one Nafai had told them about—and Zdorab was also bright with gold and silver. Sevet's husband, Vas. Kokor's husband, Obring. Both almost as bright as Rasa's and Gaballufix's daughters themselves. All these people brought together in this city, at this moment, and all the best of them were coming out into the desert to join Wetchik. The Oversoul had bred them for this, and now was calling them forth out of the world to take them to another place.

What will our children be? And our grandchildren?

Again she rose up over the city, rejoicing now to understand the Oversoul's plan, when she caught a glimpse of yet another gold and silver cord, as bright as any she had seen. She wanted to look, and because it was a dream she immediately swooped down and saw that the light came from Gaballufix's house, but the man was not Gaballufix. Instead he wore a strange uniform, and his hair was oiled and hung in wet-looking ringlets.

General Vozmuzhalnoy Vozmozhno, she realized. Moozh. He, too, has been brought here! He, too, is one that the Oversoul desires!

But as she watched, she saw Moozh stand up and draw his metal sword. Was he like Gaballufix, then? Would he flail about himself in a frenzy of killing?

No. He turned and saw the gold and silver cords that bound him to the Oversoul, and hacked at them with the blade. He cut them off, and then fled from them. Yet in a moment the cords grew back again, and once again he chopped them away and ran from where the cords had once led him. Again and again it happened, and Hushidh knew that he hated his connection with the Oversoul.

Yet he was here. However it had happened, the Oversoul had brought him here. And then she understood: The Oversoul, knowing how he hated her, how Moozh rebelled against her, had simply pushed him *not* to do whatever she actually wanted him to do. So easily he had been fooled! So easily he had been guided. And in her sleep she laughed.

Laughed and began to waken; she could feel the sleep falling away from her, could feel her body now, the real one, wrapped in a carpet, sweating even though the air was chill around her.

In that moment, as wakefulness drove away the dream, there came a sudden flash of vision that seemed different from all that had come before. She saw the image from her earlier dream, the one where she stood on the spire of rock and Issib floated in the air beside her, and he tumbled and fell and she also fell after him; it passed through her mind in a single flash, and then she saw something new: Winged creatures, hairy as animals and yet able to soar and fly; they swooped out of the sky and caught Issib and Hushidh by the arms and legs as they tumbled toward the ground, and with a great beating and pounding of their wings, they kept them from striking the rocks below, and instead carried them upward into the sky.

It terrified her, this sudden unexpected dream, for Hushidh knew that she was not really asleep, and no dream should have come at all, especially not one as clear and frightening as this. Hadn't the Oversoul already shown her everything she asked for? Why now did she bring her back to this old image?

And again, she flashed on a former moment in this night's dreams: She stood with Issib in the doorway of the tent, with the baby in Issib's lap and the children gathered around his floating chair. No sooner had she recognized the scene than it changed; they were no longer in the desert, but instead in lush forest, in the doorway of a wooden house in a clearing, and all at once giant rats rose up out of holes in the ground and dropped from the limbs of trees and rushed at them, and Hushidh knew they meant to steal their children, to carry them off and eat them, and she screamed in terror. Yet before the sound could even reach her lips, there came those flying creatures again, tumbling out of the sky to catch her children and lift them up out of the jaws and hands of the huge ravenous rats. Seeing what was happening, she snatched her own baby from Issib's lap and held it high above her head, and one of the flying creatures swooped down and snatched it from her hands and carried it away. And she stood there and wept, because she did not know if she had simply given her children from one predator to another . . . and yet she *did* know. She had made her choice, and when they came again she took Issib's arms and held them upward for the flying creatures to take him, to carry him away. Only before they could come, the rats were on them, tumbling them down, and a hundred tiny savage hands fumbled and seized at her, tugged at her—

She awoke with the sound of her own scream in her ears, and an unsoothable fear clawing at her heart. She was drenched in sweat, and the night was dark around her, the breeze chilling her, but her trembling was not from cold. She threw off the carpet that covered her and ran, stumbling, still half-blind from the sleep in her eyes and awkward from the stiffness of uncomfortable rest, to the gap in the gable that led her into an attic of the house.

By the time she got to her own room, she could see well enough, and walked smoothly and quietly, but she was still weak and terrified, and she could not bear the thought of being alone. For there was Luet's bed—Luet, who should be there to soothe her now—but it was empty, because Luet had gone to another bed, and held someone who needed her far less than Hushidh did tonight. Hushidh huddled on her own bed, alternating between silent trembling and great, gasping sobs, until she feared that someone in another room might hear her.

They'll think I'm jealous of Luet, if they hear me weeping. They'll think I hate her for marrying before me, and that isn't so . . . not now, anyway, not since the Oversoul showed me the meaning of it all. She tried to bring that dream back into her memory—of herself and her children and her husband at the door of the tent—but the moment she did, it transformed again and she was possessed by the terror of the rats coming out of their holes, out of the trees, and her only hope the desperate strangeness of the flying beasts—

And she found herself in the corridor outside her room, running away from a fear that she carried with her as she ran. Ran and ran until she hurled open the door to the room where she knew that Luet would be, for she couldn't bear this, she had to have help, and it could only be Luet, only Luet could help her . . .

"What is it?" The fear in Luet's voice was an echo of the terror in Hushidh's own. Hushidh saw her sister, sitting bolt upright on the bed, holding a sheet up to her throat as if it were a shield. And then Nafai, awakened more by her voice than by the door, sleepily rising from the bed, standing on the floor, coming toward Hushidh, not yet understanding who it was but knowing that if an intruder came it was his job to block the way . . .

"Shuya," said Luet.

"Oh, Luet, forgive me," Hushidh sobbed. "Help me. Hold me!"

Before Luet could reach her, Nafai was there, helping her, leading her into the room from the doorway. Then Luet was with her and brought her to sit on the rumpled bed, and now Hushidh could let out her sobs as her sister held her. She was vaguely aware of Nafai moving through the room; he closed the door, then found clothing enough for himself and Luet that they didn't need to be embarrassed when Hushidh stopped crying and came to herself.

"I'm sorry, I'm so sorry," Hushidh said again and again as she wept.

"No, please, it's all right," said Luet.

"Your wedding night, I never would have . . . but I dreamed, it was so terrible—"

"It's all right, Shuya," said Nafai. "Only I wish you could cry a little softer, because if anybody hears you they're going to think it's Luet sobbing her heart out on her wedding night and then who knows what they'll think of me." He paused. "Of course, come to think of it, maybe you should cry a little louder."

There was laughter and calm in Nafai's voice, and Luet also laughed a little at his jest. It was what Hushidh needed, to take away her terror: She could think of Luet and Nafai instead of her dream.

"No one has ever done anything as wretched as this," said Hushidh, miserable and ashamed and yet so deeply relieved. "Bursting in on my own sister's wedding night."

"It's not as if you interrupted anything," said Nafai, and then he and Luet both burst into laughter—no, *giggling* was what it was. Like little children with a ridiculous secret.

"I'm sorry to laugh when you're so unhappy," said Luet, "but you have to understand. We were both so bad at it." They both burst into giggles again.

"It's an acquired skill," said Nafai. "Which we haven't acquired."

Hushidh felt herself enfolded by their laughter, included in the calm that they created between them. It was unthinkable, that a young husband and his bride, interrupted in their first night together, should so willingly include and comfort an intruding sister; yet that was who they were,

Lutya and her Nyef. She felt herself filled with love and gratitude for them, and it spilled out in tears, but glad ones, not the desperate tears born of loneliness and terror in the night.

"I wasn't weeping for myself," she said—for now she could speak. "I *was* jealous and lonely, I admit it, but the Oversoul sent me a kind dream, a good one, and it showed me and . . . my husband, and our children . . ." Then she had a thought that had not occurred to her before. "Nafai, I know that I am meant for Issib. But I have to ask—he *is* . . . capable, isn't he?"

"Shuya, he could hardly be *less* capable than I was tonight."

Luet playfully slapped at Nafai's hand. "She's asking a real question, Nafai."

"He's as much a virgin as I am," said Nafai, "and away from the city he has scant use of his hands. But he isn't paralyzed, and his . . . involuntary responses, well, *respond.*"

"Then the dream *was* true," said Hushidh. "Or it can be, anyway. I dreamed of my children. With Issib. That could be true, couldn't it?"

"If you want it to be," said Nafai. "If you're willing to accept him. He's the best of us, Shuya, I promise you that. The smartest and the kindest and the wisest."

"You didn't tell me that," said Luet. "You told me *you* were the best."

Nafai only grinned at her with stupid joy.

Hushidh felt better now, and also knew that it wasn't right for her to remain between them like this; she had received all that she could hope for from her sister, and now she could return to her room and sleep alone. The shadow of the evil dream had passed from her. "Thank you both," she whispered. "I will never forget how kind you were to me tonight." And she arose from the edge of the bed and started for the door.

"Don't go," said Nafai.

"I must sleep now," said Hushidh.

"Not until you tell us your dream," he said. "We need to

hear it. Not the sweet dream, but the one that made you so afraid."

"He's right," said Luet. "It may be our wedding night, but the whole world is dark around us and we must know everything the Oversoul says to any of us."

"In the morning," said Hushidh.

"Do you think that we can sleep, wondering what terrible dream could strike so hard at our sister?" said Nafai.

Even though Hushidh knew how carefully he had chosen his words, she was grateful for the good and loving impulse behind them. In his heart he might very well fear or resent her close connection with his new wife, but instead of trying to resist that closeness or drive them apart, Nafai was deliberately working to include himself in their sisterhood, and include Hushidh in the closeness of their marriage. It was a generous thing to do, on this night of all nights, when it must have seemed to him that his worst fears about Hushidh were true, what with her plunging into their bridal chamber sobbing her eyes out in the middle of the night! If he was willing to try so hard, could she do any less than accept the relationship he wanted to create? She was a raveler, after all. She knew about binding people together, and was glad to help him tie this knot.

So she came back and they sat together on the bed, making a triangle with their crossed legs, knee to knee, as she told her dreams, from beginning to end. She spared herself nothing, confessing her own resentments at the beginning so that they could understand how glad she was for the Oversoul's assurances.

Twice they interrupted her with their astonishment. The first time was when she told of seeing Moozh, and how the Oversoul was ruling him through his very rejection of her. Nafai laughed in wonderment. "Moozh himself—the bloody-handed general of the Gorayni, running away from the Oversoul into the very path the Oversoul laid out for him. Who could have guessed it!"

The second time was when Hushidh told of the winged beasts that caught her and Issib as they fell. "Angels!" cried Luet.

At once Hushidh remembered the dream that Luet had told her days before. "Of course," Hushidh said. "That's why they came into my dream—because I remembered your telling me about those angels and the giant rats."

"Don't reach conclusions now," said Luet. "Tell us the rest of the dream."

So she did, and when it was done, they sat in silence, thinking for a while.

"The first dream, of you and Issib, I think that was from yourself," said Luet at last.

"I think so, too," said Hushidh, "and now that I remember your telling me that dream of hairy angels . . ."

"Quiet," said Luet. "Don't get ahead of the dream. After that first vision that came from your fears about marrying Issib, you begged the Oversoul to tell you her purpose, and she showed you that wonderful dream of the gold and silver cords binding people together—"

"Breeding us like cattle," said Nafai.

"Don't be irreverent," said Luet.

"Don't be too reverent," said Nafai. "I sincerely doubt that the Oversoul's original programming told it to start a breeding program among the humans of Harmony."

"I know that you're right," said Luet, "that the Oversoul is a computer established at the dawn of our world to watch over human beings and keep us from destroying ourselves, but still in my heart I feel the Oversoul as a woman, as the Mother of the Lake."

"Woman or machine, it's developed purposes of its own, and I'm not comfortable with this one," said Nafai. "Bringing us together to make a journey to Earth, I accept that, I'm glad of it—it's a glorious undertaking. But this breeding thing. My mother and father, coupling like a ewe and a ram brought together to keep the bloodlines pure . . ."

"They still love each other," said Luet.

He reached out a hand to her and cupped her fingers gently in his. "Lutya, they *do,* as we will love each other. But what we've done, we've done willingly, knowing the Oversoul's purpose and consenting to it, or so we thought. What other plots and plans does the Oversoul have in mind for us, which we'll only discover later?"

"The Oversoul told me this because I asked," said Hushidh. "If she *is* a computer, as you say—and I believe you, I really do—then perhaps she simply can't tell us what we haven't yet asked to know."

"Then we must ask. We must know *exactly* what she— what *he*—what *it* is planning," said Nafai.

Luet smiled at his confusion but did not laugh. Hushidh was not his loyal wife; she could not suppress a small hoot.

"However we think of the Oversoul," Nafai said patiently, "we have to ask. What it means for Moozh to be here, for instance. Are we supposed to try to bring him out into the desert, too? Is that why the Oversoul brought him here? And these strange creatures, these angels and rats— what do they mean? The Oversoul has to tell us."

"I still think the rats and angels came because Lutya dreamed them and told me about them and there they were, ready to give a face to my fears," said Hushidh.

"But why did they come into Lutya's dream?" asked Nafai. "*She* didn't fear them."

"And the rats weren't terrible or dangerous in my dream," said Luet. "They were just—themselves. Living their lives. They had nothing to do with human beings in my dream."

"Let's stop guessing," said Nafai, "and ask the Oversoul."

They had never done this before. Men and women did not pray together in the rituals of Basilica—the men prayed with blood and water in their temple, or in their private places, and the women prayed in water at the lake, or in *their* private places. So they were shy and uncertain. Nafai impulsively reached out his hands to Hushidh and Luet, and they took his hands and joined to each other as well.

"I speak to the Oversoul silently," said Nafai. "In my mind."

"I, too," said Luet, "but sometimes aloud, don't *you?*"

"The same with me," said Hushidh. "Luet, speak for us all."

Luet shook her head. "It was you who saw the dream

tonight, Hushidh. It was you the Oversoul was speaking to."

Hushidh shuddered in spite of herself. "What if the bad dream comes back to me?"

"What does it matter which of us speaks?" said Nafai, "as long as we ask the same questions in our hearts? Father and Issib and I speak to the Oversoul easily, when we have the Index with us, asking questions and getting answers as if we spoke with the computer at school. We'll do the same here."

"We don't have the Index," Luet pointed out.

"No, but we are bound to the Oversoul with threads of gold and silver," said Nafai, glancing at Hushidh. "That should be enough, shouldn't it?"

"Speak for us then, Luet," said Hushidh.

So Luet spoke their questions, and then spoke aloud her own worries, and those Nafai had expressed, and the terror Hushidh had experienced. It was to that question that the first answer came.

I don't know, said the Oversoul.

Luet fell silent, startled.

"Did you hear what I heard?" asked Nafai.

Since no one knew what Nafai had heard, no one could answer. Until Hushidh dared to say the thing *she* had heard inside her mind. "She doesn't know," whispered Hushidh.

Nafai gripped their hands tighter, and spoke to the Oversoul, his voice now and not Luet's speaking for them all. "What don't you know?"

I sent the dream of the gold and silver threads, said the Oversoul. I sent the dream of Issib and the children at the door of the tent. But I never meant you to see the general. I never showed you the general."

"And the . . . the rats?" asked Hushidh.

"And the angels?" asked Luet.

I don't know where they came from or what they mean.

"So," said Hushidh. "It was just a strange chance dream in your mind, Luet. And then because you told your dream it became a memory in *my* mind, and that's it."

No!

It was as if the Oversoul had shouted into her mind, and Hushidh shuddered under the force of it.

"What, then!" cried Hushidh. "If you don't know where it came from, how do you know that it isn't just an ordinary frightening dream?"

Because the general had it too.

They looked at each other in amazement.

"General *Moozh?*"

To Hushidh's mind there came a fleeting image of a man with a flying creature on his shoulder, and a giant rat clinging to his leg, and many people—humans, rats, and angels—approaching, touching the three of them, worshipping. As quickly as it came, the image receded.

"The general saw this dream?" asked Hushidh.

He saw it. Weeks ago. Before any of you dreamed of these creatures.

"Three of us then," said Luet. "Three of us, and we have never met the general, and he has never met us, and yet we all dreamed of these creatures. He saw worship, and I saw art, and you saw war, Hushidh, war and salvation."

"If it didn't come from you, Oversoul," said Nafai, urgently pressing the question, holding tightly to their hands. "If it didn't come from you, then where could such a dream have come from?"

I don't know.

"Is there some other computer?" asked Hushidh.

Not here. Not in Harmony.

"Maybe you just didn't know about it," suggested Nafai.

I would have known.

"Then why are we having these dreams?" demanded Nafai.

They waited, and there was no answer. And then there *was* an answer, but one that they did not wish for.

I'm afraid, said the Oversoul.

Hushidh felt the fear return to her own heart, and she gripped her sister's hand more tightly, and Nafai's hand as well. "I hate this," said Hushidh. "I hate it. I didn't want to know it."

I'm afraid, said the Oversoul, as clear as speech in

Hushidh's mind—and, she hoped, in the minds of the other two as well. I'm afraid, for fear is the name I have for uncertainty, for impossibility that is nevertheless real. Yet I also have a hope, for that is another name for the impossible that might be real. I have a hope that what you have been given is from the Keeper of Earth. That across these many lightyears the Keeper of Earth is reaching out to us.

"Who is the Keeper of Earth?" asked Hushidh.

"The Oversoul has mentioned it before," said Nafai. "It's never been clear, but I think it's a computer that was set up as guardian of Earth when our ancestors left forty million years ago."

Not a computer, said the Oversoul.

"What is it then?" asked Nafai.

Not a machine.

"What, then?"

Alive.

"What could possibly be alive after all these years?"

The Keeper of Earth. Calling to us. Calling to you. Maybe my desire to bring you back to Earth is also a dream from the Keeper. I have also been confused, and did not know what I should do, and then ideas came into my mind. I thought they were the result of the randomizer routines. I thought they were from my programming. But if you and Moozh can dream strange dreams of creatures never known in this world, can't I also be given thoughts that were never programmed into me, that do not come from anything in this world?

They had no answer for the Oversoul's question.

"I don't know about you," said Hushidh, "but I was definitely counting on the Oversoul to be in charge of everything, and I really don't like the idea of her not knowing what's going on."

"Earth is calling to us," said Nafai. "Don't you see? Earth is calling to us. Calling the Oversoul, but not *just* the Oversoul. *Us.* Or you two, anyway, and Moozh. Calling you to come home to Earth."

Not Moozh, said the Oversoul.

"How do you know, not Moozh?" asked Hushidh. "If

you don't know why or how or even *whether* the Keeper of Earth gave us these dreams, then how do you know that Moozh is not supposed to come out onto the desert with us?"

Not Moozh, said the Oversoul. Leave Moozh alone.

"If you didn't mean Moozh to join us, then why did you bring him here?" asked Nafai.

I brought him here, but not for you.

"He has the same gold and silver threads as we do," said Luet. "And the Keeper of Earth has spoken to him."

I brought him here to destroy Basilica.

"That tears it," said Nafai. "That really tears it. The Oversoul has one idea. The Keeper of Earth has another. And what are *we* supposed to do?"

Leave Moozh alone. Don't touch him. He's on his own path.

"Right," said Nafai. "A minute ago you tell us that you don't know what's going on, and now we're supposed to take your word for it that Moozh isn't part of what we're doing! We're not puppets, Oversoul! Do you understand me? If you don't know what's going on, then why should we follow your orders in this? How do you know you're right, and we're wrong?"

I *don't* know.

"Then how do you know I shouldn't go to him and ask him to come with us?"

Because he's dangerous and terrible and he might use you and destroy you and I can't stop him if he decides to do it.

"Don't go," said Luet.

"He's one of *us,*" said Nafai. "If our purpose is a good one in the first place, then it's a good one *because* there's something right about *us,* the people that the Oversoul has bred, going back to Earth. If it's good it's good because the Keeper of Earth is calling us."

"Whatever sent me that terrible dream," said Hushidh, "I don't know if it's good or not."

"Maybe the dream was a warning," said Nafai. "Maybe there's some danger we'll face, and the dream was warning you."

"Or maybe the dream was a warning for you to stay away from Moozh," said Luet.

"How in the world could the dream possibly mean *that?*" he asked. He was shucking off the odd clothing he had thrown on in a hurry a short while before, and dressing seriously now, dressing to go out into the city.

"Because that's what I want it to mean," said Luet, and suddenly she was crying. "You've only been my husband for half a night, and suddenly you want to go to a man that the Oversoul says is dangerous and terrible, and for what? To invite him to come out into the desert? To invite him to give up his armies and his kingdoms and his blood and violence and travel with us in the desert on a journey that will somehow end with us on Earth? He'll kill you, Nafai! Or imprison you and keep you from coming with us. I'll *lose you.*"

"You won't," said Nafai. "The Oversoul will protect me."

"The Oversoul warned you not to go. If you disobey . . ."

"The Oversoul won't punish me because the Oversoul doesn't even know that I'm not right. The Oversoul will bring me back to you because the Oversoul wants me with you almost as much as *I* want me with you."

I don't know if I can protect you.

"Yes, well, there's an awful lot that you don't know," said Nafai. "I think you've made that clear to us tonight. You're a very powerful computer and you have the best intentions in the world, but you don't know what's right any more than *I* do. You don't know whether all your plans for Moozh might have been influenced by the Keeper of Earth, do you—you don't know whether the *Keeper's* plan is for me to do exactly what I'm doing, and let your plot to destroy Basilica go hang. To *destroy Basilica,* of all things! It's your chosen city, isn't it? You've brought together all the people who are closest to you in this one place, and you want to destroy it?"

I brought them together to create *you,* foolish children. Now I'll destroy it to spread my people out again throughout the world. So that whatever influence I have left in this world will reach into every land and nation. What is the city of Basilica, compared to the world?

"The last time you talked that way, I killed a man," said Nafai.

"Please," said Luet. "Stay with me."

"Or let me come with you," said Hushidh.

"Not a chance," said Nafai. "And Lutya, I *will* come back to you. Because the Oversoul *will* protect me."

I don't know if I can.

"Then do your best," said Nafai. With that he was out the door and gone.

"They'll arrest him the minute he tries to go anywhere in the street," said Hushidh.

"I know," said Luet. "And I understand why he's doing it, and it's a brave thing to do, and I even think it's the right thing to do, and I *don't want him to do it!*"

Luet wept, and now it was Hushidh's turn to hold and comfort *her*. What a dance this has been tonight, she thought. What a wedding night for you, what a night of dreams for me. And now, what morning will it be? You could be left a widow without even his child inside you. Or—why not?—the great general Moozh might come with Nafai, renounce his army, and disappear with us into the desert. Anything could happen. Anything at all.

IN GABALLUFIX'S HOUSE, AND NOT IN A DREAM

Moozh spread out his map of the Western Shore on Gaballufix's table, and let his mind explore the shape of things. The Cities of the Plain and Seggidugu were spread out before him like a banquet. It was hard to guess which way to move. By now they all must have heard that a Gorayni army held the gates of Basilica. No doubt the hotheads in Seggidugu were urging a quick and brutal response, but they would not prevail—the northern border of Seggidugu was too close to the main Gorayni armies in Khlam and Ulye. It would take so many soldiers to take Basilica, even if they knew there were only a thousand Gorayni to defend it, that it would leave Seggidugu vulnerable to counterstrike.

Indeed, many faint hearts in Seggidugu would already be wondering if it might not be best to come before the Imperator now, as supplicants, begging him to take their nation under his beneficent protection. But Moozh was sure that these would have no more luck than the hotheads. Instead the coolest minds, the most careful men would prevail. They would wait and see. And that was what Moozh was counting on.

In the Cities of the Plain, there was no doubt already a movement afoot to revive the old Defense League, which had driven off the Seggidugu invaders nine times. But that was more than a thousand years ago, when the Seggidugu had first stormed over the mountains from the desert; it was unlikely that more than a few of the cities would unite, and even in supposed unity they would be quarreling and stealing from each other and weakening each other more than if each stood alone.

What was in Moozh's power to make happen? At this moment, if he sent a delegation with a sternly worded demand for the surrender of the nearest cities, they would no doubt receive quick compliance. But the refugees would gout out of those cities like blood from a heart-wound, and the other Cities of the Plain *would* unite then. They might even ask Seggidugu to lead them, and in that case Seggidugu might well act.

Instead he might demand Seggidugu's surrender. If they complied, then the Cities of the Plain would all roll over and play dead. But it was too big a gamble, if he could find a better way. He really *could* force the surrender of any one or even two of the Cities of the Plain, but he had far too few men—and far too tenuous a link with the main Gorayni armies—to make his ultimatum stick if Seggidugu decided to defy him. Great wars had been avoided, great empires had been created by just such dangerous bluffs, and Moozh was not afraid to take the chance if there was no better way.

And if there *was* a better way, he would have to find it soon. By now the Imperator himself would know that both Plod and the intercessor assigned to Moozh's army had been killed—by a Basilican assassin, of course, but no one had been able to question him because Moozh had killed the man with his own hands. Then Moozh took off with a thousand men and no one knew where he was. That bit of news would strike terror into the heart of the Imperator, for he knew quite well how fragile the power of a ruler is, when his best generals become too popular. The Imperator would be wondering how many of his own men would flock to Moozh if he raised a flag of rebellion in the mountains; and how many others, too loyal to defect, would nevertheless be terrified to fight against the greatest general of the Gorayni. All these fears would prompt the Imperator to put his armies in motion, and to have them moving south and west, toward Khlam and Ulye.

All well and good . . . that would frighten the Seggidugu even more, and increase the chance that bluffing them into submission might work. And these army movements would *not* get far before the next news reached the Imperator—that Moozh's bold movement had succeeded brilliantly, that the fabled city of Basilica was now in Gorayni hands.

Moozh smiled in pleasure at the thought of how that news would strike terror in the hearts of all the courtiers who had been whispering to the Imperator that Moozh was a traitor. A traitor? A man who has the wit and courage to take a city with a thousand men? To march past two powerful enemy kingdoms and take a mountain fortress perched in their rear? What kind of traitor is this? the Imperator would ask.

But still, he would be afraid, for boldness in his generals always terrified him. Especially boldness in Vozmuzhalnoy Vozmozhno. So the Imperator would send him a legate or two—certainly an intercessor, probably a new friend, and also a couple of close and trusted family members. They would not have the authority to overrule Moozh—the Gorayni would never have conquered so many kingdoms if the imperators had allowed their underlings to countermand the orders of generals in the field. But they *would* have the ability to interfere, to question, to protest, to demand explanations, and to send word back to the Imperator of anything they didn't like.

When would these legates arrive? They would have to take the same desert route that Moozh had taken with his men. But now that road would be closely watched by Seggidugu and Izmennik, so there would have to be a ponderous bodyguard, and supply wagons, and many scouts and tents and all sorts of livestock. Thus the legates would have neither the desire nor the ability to move even half as quickly as Moozh's army had moved. So it would be at least a week before they arrived, probably longer. But when they came, they would have many soldiers—perhaps as many as Moozh had already brought—and these soldiers would almost certainly not be men who had fought under Moozh, men he had trained, men he could count on.

A week. Moozh had at least a week in which to set in motion the course he was going to follow. He could try his bluff against Seggidugu now, and risk deep humiliation if he was defied—the Cities of the Plain would certainly unite against him then, and he'd soon be defending Basilica from a siege. This would not lead to his ouster as general, but it would take the luster off his name, and it would put him back under the thumb of the Imperator. These last few days had been so delicious, not to have to play the games of deception and subterfuge that consumed half his life when he had to deal with a friend appointed by the Imperator, not to mention some career-advancing, meddlesome intercessor. Moozh had killed relatively few people with his own hands, but he certainly relished the memory of those deaths—the surprise on their faces, the exquisite relief that Moozh felt then. Even the necessity of killing that good soldier of Basilica, Smelost, even *that* did not take away the sheer joy of his new freedom.

Am I ready?

Am I ready to make the move of my life, to strike in vengeance against the Imperator in the name of Pravo Gollossa? To risk all on my ability to unite Basilica, Seggidugu, and the Cities of the Plain, along with every

Gorayni soldier who will follow me and whatever support we can eke out from Potokgavan?

And if I am not ready for that, am I ready to set my neck back into the collar that the Imperator forces all his generals to wear? Am I ready to bow to the will of God's incarnation here on Harmony? Am I ready to wait years, decades for an opportunity that may never be closer than it is right now?

He knew the answer even as he asked the question. Somehow he must turn this week, this day, this hour into his opportunity, his chance to bring down the Gorayni and replace their cruel and brutal empire with a generous and democratic one, led by the Sotchitsiya, whose vengeance was long delayed but not one whit less sure for all that. Here Moozh stood with an army—a small one, but *his*—in the city that symbolized all that was weak and effete and cringing in the world. I longed to destroy you, Basilica, but what if instead I make you strong? What if I make you the center of the world—but a world ruled by men of power, not these weak and cringing women, these politicians and gossips and actors and singers. What if the greatest story told about Basilica was not that it was the city of women, but that it was the city of the Sotchitsiya ascendancy?

Basilica, you city of women, your husband is here for you, to master you and teach you the domestic arts that you have so long forgotten.

Moozh looked again at Bitanke's list of names. If he was looking for someone to rule Basilica in the name of the Imperator, then he would have to choose a man as consul: One of Wetchik's sons, if they could be found, or perhaps Rashgallivak himself, or some weaker man who might be propped up by Bitanke.

But if Moozh wanted to unite Basilica and the Cities of the Plain and Seggidugu as well against the Imperator, then what he needed was to become a citizen of Basilica by marriage, and to gain a place for himself at the head of the city; he needed, not a consul, but a bride.

So the names that intrigued him most were the two girls, the waterseer and the raveler. They were young—young enough that it would offend many if he married either of them, especially the waterseer—thirteen! And yet these two had the right kind of prestige, the kind that could include him in its aura if he married one or the other of them. Moozh, the great general of the Gorayni, marrying one of the most holy women of Basilica—humbling himself to enter the city as a mere husband instead of as a conqueror. It would win their hearts, not just those who were already grateful to him for the peace he had imposed, but all of them, for they would see that he desired, not to conquer them, but to lead them to greatness.

With the raveler or the waterseer as his wife, Moozh would not longer merely *hold* Basilica. He would *be* Basilica, and instead of issuing ultimata to the southern kingdoms and cities of the Western Shore, he would issue a battlecry. He would arrest the spies of Potokgavan and send them home to their lazy waterlogged empire with presents and promises. And the word would sweep like wildfire through the north: Vozmuzhalnoy Vozmozhno has declared himself the new incarnation, the true Imperator. He calls upon all loyal soldiers of God to come south to him, or to rise up against the usurper where they are! In the meantime the word would be whispered in Pravo Gollossa: The Sotchitsiya will rule. Rise up and take what has belonged to you for all these years!

In the chaos that would result in the northlands, Moozh would march northward, gathering allies with him as he went. The Gorayni armies would retreat before him; the natives of the conquered nations would welcome him as their liberator. He would march until the Gorayni were thrown back into their own lands, and there he would stop—for one long winter in Pravo Gollossa, where he would train his motley army and weld it into a worthy fighting force. Then in the spring of next year he would move into the hillfast land of the Gorayni and utterly destroy their capacity to rule. Every man of fighting age would have his thumbs cut off, so he could never wield either sword or bow, and with every thumb that was sheared off, the Gorayni would understand again the pain of the tongueless Sotchitsiya.

Let God try to stop him now!

But he knew that God would not. In these last few days, ever since he defied God and came south to seize Basilica, God had not tried to move against him, had not tried to block him in any way. He had half expected that God would make him forget these plans that he was laying out. But God must know now that it wouldn't matter if he did, for the plans were so true and obvious that Moozh would simply think of them again—and again and again, if it were necessary.

For me will be the overthrow of the Gorayni and the uniting of the Western Shore. For my son will be the conquest of Potokgavan, the civilizing of the northern forest tribes, the subduing of the northshore pirates. My son, and the son of my wife.

Which of you will it be? The waterseer was the more powerful of the two, the one with more prestige; but she was younger, too young, really. There would be a danger of people pitying her for such a marriage, unless Moozh could truly persuade her to come of her own free will.

The other one, though, the raveler, even though her prestige was less, would still do, and she was sixteen. Sixteen, a good age for a political marriage, for she had no former husbands and, if Bitanke was right, not even any lovers that anyone had heard about. And some of the prestige of the waterseer would still come to the marriage, because the raveler was her sister, and Moozh would see to it that the waterseer was well treated—and closely tied to the new dynastic house that Moozh would soon establish.

It was a very attractive plan. All that remained now was for Moozh to be sure—sure enough to act. Sure enough to go to Rasa's house and maneuver for the hand of one of these girls in marriage.

A single knock on the door. Moozh rapped once on the table. The door opened.

"Sir," said the soldier. "We have made an interesting arrest on the street in front of Lady Rasa's house."

Moozh looked up from the map on the table and waited for the rest of the message.

"Lady Rasa's youngest son. The one who killed Gaballufix."

"He escaped into the desert," said Moozh. "Are you sure it's not an impostor?"

"Quite possible," said the soldier. "But he did walk out of Rasa's house and straight up to the sergeant in charge and announce who he was and that he needed to speak to you at once about matters that would determine your future and the future of Basilica."

"Ah," said Moozh.

"So he's either the boy with balls of brass who cut off Gaballufix's head and wore his clothes out of the city, or he's a madman with a deathwish."

"Or both," said Moozh. "Bring him to me, and be prepared with an escort of four soldiers to take him directly back to Lady Rasa's house afterward. If I slap his face when you open the door to take him back, then you will kill him on Lady Rasa's front porch. If I smile at him, then you will treat him with courtesy and honor. Otherwise, he is under arrest and will not be permitted to leave the house again."

The soldier left the door open behind him. Moozh sat back in his chair and waited. Interesting, he thought, that I don't have to search for the key players in this city's bloody games. They all come to me, one by one. Nafai was supposed to be safely in the desert, beyond my reach—but he was in Lady Rasa's house all the time. What other surprises have we pent up in her house? The other sons? How had Bitanke summed them up . . . Elemak, the sharp and dangerous caravanner; Mebbekew, the walking penis; Issib, the brilliant cripple. Or why not Wetchik, the visionary plantseller himself? They might all be waiting within Lady Rasa's walls for Moozh to decide how to use them.

Was it possible—barely possible—that God really *had* decided to favor Moozh's cause? That instead of opposing him, God might now be aiding Moozh, bringing into his hands every tool he needed to accomplish his purpose?

I am certainly not the incarnation of anything but myself, thought Moozh; I have no desire to play at holiness, the way the Imperator does. But if God is willing at long last to let me have some help in my cause, I will not refuse it. Perhaps in God's heart the hour of the Sotchitsiya has arrived.

Nafai was afraid, but also he was not afraid. It was the strangest feeling. As if there was a terrified animal inside him, aghast that he was walking into a place where death was only a word away, and yet Nafai himself, that part of him that *was* himself and not the animal, was simply fascinated to find out what he might say, and whether he would meet Moozh, and what would happen next. It was not that he was unaware of the perpetual immanence of death among the Gorayni; rather he had simply decided, at some deep level of his mind, that personal survival was an irrelevant issue.

The soldiers had seemed, if anything, more perplexed than alarmed at his accosting them on the street with the words, "Take me to the general. I'm Wetchik's son Nafai, and I killed Gaballufix." With those words he put his very life into this conversation, since Moozh now had witnesses of his confession of a crime that could lead to his execution; Moozh wouldn't even have to fabricate a pretext to have him killed if he wanted to.

Gaballufix's house had not changed, and yet it was entirely changed. None of the wall hangings, none of the furniture had been altered. All the lazy opulence was still intact, the plushness, the overdecoration in detail, the bold colors. And yet instead of being overpowering, the effect of all this ostentation was rather pathetic, for the simple discipline and brisk, unhesitating obedience of the Gorayni soldiers had the effect of diminishing everything around them. Gaballufix had chosen these furnishings to intimidate his visitors, to overawe them; now they looked weak, effete, as if the person who bought them had been frightened that people might see how weak his soul was, and so he had to hide it behind this barricade of bright colors and gold trim.

Real power, Nafai realized, does not demonstrate itself in anything that can be purchased for mere money. Money only buys the illusion of power. Real power is in the force of will—will strong enough that others bend to it for its own sake, and follow it willingly. Power that is won through deception will evaporate under the hot light of truth, as Rashgallivak had found; but real power grows stronger the more closely you look at it, even when it resides only in a single person, without armies, without servants, without friends, but with an indomitable will.

Such a man waited for him, sitting at a table behind an open door. Nafai knew this room. It was here that he and his brothers had faced Gaballufix, here that Nafai had blurted out some word or other that destroyed Elemak's delicate negotiations for the Index. Not that Gaballufix ever intended anything but to cheat them. The fact remained that Nafai had spoken carelessly, not realizing that Elemak, the sharp businessman, was holding back key information.

For a moment Nafai resolved inside himself to be more careful now, to hold back information as Elemak would have done, to be canny in this conversation.

Then General Moozh looked up and Nafai looked into his eyes and saw a deep well of rage and suffering and pride and, at the bottom of that well, a fierce intelligence that would see through all sham.

Is this what Moozh really is? Have I seen him true?

And in his heart, the Oversoul whispered, I have shown him to you as he truly is.

Then I can't lie to this man, thought Nafai. Which is just as well, because I'm not good at lying. I don't have the skill for it. I can't maintain the deep self-deception that successful lying requires. The truth keeps rising to the surface in my mind, and so I confess myself in every word and glance and gesture.

Besides, I didn't come here to play some game, to try my wits in some contest with General Vozmuzhalnoy Vozmozhno. I came here to give him the chance to join with us in our journey back to Earth. How could he do that if I tell him anything less than the truth?

"Nafai," said Moozh. "Please sit down."

Nafai sat down. He noticed that a map was spread out on

the table before the general. The Western Shore. Somewhere on that map, deep in the southwest corner, was the
stream where Father and Issib and Zdorab waited in their
tents, listening to a troop of baboons hooting and barking
at each other. Is the Oversoul showing Father what I'm
doing now? Does Issib have the Index, and is he asking
where I am?

"I assume that you didn't turn yourself in because your
conscience overwhelmed you and you wanted to be put on
trial for the murder of Gaballufix in order to expunge your
guilt."

"No sir," said Nafai. "I was married last night. I have no
desire to be imprisoned or tried or killed."

"Married last night? And out on the street confessing
felonies before dawn? My boy, I fear you have not married
well, if your wife can't hold you for even one night."

"I came because of a dream," said Nafai.

"Ah—*your* dream, or your bride's?"

"*Your* dream, sir."

Moozh waited, expressionless.

"I believe you dreamed once of a man with a hairy flying
creature on his shoulder, and a giant rat clinging to his leg,
and men and rats and angels came and worshipped them, all
three of them, touching them with . . ."

But Nafai did not go on, for Moozh had risen to his feet
and was boring into him with those dangerous, agonizing
eyes. "I told this to Plod, and he reported it to the
intercessor, and so it was known," said Moozh. "And the
fact that you know it tells me that you have been in contact
with someone from the Imperator's court. So stop this
pretense and tell me the truth!"

"Sir, I don't know who Plod or the intercessor might be,
and your dream wasn't told to me by anyone from the
Imperator's court. I heard it from the Oversoul. Do you
think the Oversoul doesn't know your dreams?"

Moozh sat back down, but his whole manner had
changed. The certainty, the easy confidence was gone.

"Are you the form that God has taken now? Are you the
incarnation?"

"Me?" asked Nafai. "You see what I am—I'm a fourteen-year-old boy. Maybe a little big for my age."

"A little young to be married."

"But not too young to have spoken to the Oversoul."

"Many in this city make a career of speaking to the Oversoul. You, however, God apparently answers."

"There's nothing mystical about it, sir. The Oversoul is a computer—a powerful one, a self-renewing one. Our ancestors set it in place forty million years ago, when they first reached the planet Harmony as refugees from the destruction of Earth. They genetically altered themselves and all their children—to us, all these generations later—to be responsive, at the deepest levels in the brain, to impulses from the Oversoul. Then they programmed the computer to block us from any train of thought, any plan of action that would lead to high technology or rapid communications or fast transportation, so that the world would remain a vast and unknowable place to us, and wars would remain a local affair."

"Until me," said Moozh.

"Your conquests have indeed ranged far beyond the area that the Oversoul would normally allow."

"Because I am not a slave to God," said Moozh. "Whatever power God—or, if you're right, this computer—whatever power it might have over other men is weaker in me, and I have withstood it and overwhelmed it. I am here today because I am too strong for God."

"Yes, he told us that you thought so," said Nafai. "But actually the influence of the Oversoul is even stronger in you than in most people. Probably about as strong as it is in me. If it was appropriate, if you opened yourself to its voice, the Oversoul could talk to you and you wouldn't need me to tell you what I'm here to tell you about."

"If the Oversoul told you that it is *stronger* in me than in most people, then your computer is a liar," said Moozh.

"You have to understand—the Oversoul isn't really concerned with individual people's lives, except insofar as it's been running some kind of breeding program to try to create people like me—and you, of course. I didn't like it when I learned about it, but it's the reason I'm alive, or at least the reason my parents were brought together. The Oversoul manipulates people. That's its job. It has manipulated you almost constantly."

"I'm aware that it has tried. I called it God, you call it the Oversoul, but it has not controlled me."

"As soon as it became aware that you intended to resist it, it simply turned things backward," said Nafai. "Whatever it wanted you to do, it forbade you to do. Then it made sure you remembered to do it and you obeyed almost perfectly."

"A lie," whispered Moozh.

It made Nafai afraid, to see how emotions were seizing this man. The general clearly was not accustomed to feelings he could not control; Nafai wondered if perhaps he ought to let him calm down before proceeding. "Are you all right?" Nafai asked.

"Go on," said Moozh acidly. "I can hear anything that dead men say."

That was such a weak thing to say that Nafai was disgusted. "Oh, am I supposed to change my story because you threaten me with death?" he asked. "If I was afraid to die, do you think I would have come here?"

Nafai could see a change come over Moozh. As if he visibly reined himself in. "I apologize," said Moozh. "For a moment I behaved like the kind of man I most despise. Blustering a threat in order to change the message of a messenger who believes, at least, that he is telling me the truth. But I can assure you, whatever I might feel, if you die today it will not be because of any words you might say. Please go on."

"You must understand," said Nafai, "if the Oversoul really wants you to forget something, you *will* forget it. My brother Issib and I thought we were very clever, forcing our way through its barriers. But we didn't really force it. We simply became more trouble than it was worth to resist us. The Oversoul would rather have us go along with its plans knowingly than to have to control us and manipulate us. That's why I'm here. Because my wife's sister saw in a dream how strong your link with the Oversoul is, and how you waste yourself in a vain effort to resist. I came to tell you that the only way to break free of its control is to embrace its plan."

"The way to win is to surrender?" Moozh asked wryly.

"The way to be *free* is to stop resisting and start talking," said Nafai. "The Oversoul is the servant of humanity, not its master. It can be persuaded. It will listen. Sometimes it needs our help. General, *we* need you, if you'll only come with us."

"Come with you?"

"My father was called out to the desert as the first step in a great journey."

"Your father was driven out onto the desert by the machinations of Gaballufix. I have spoken with Rashgalli-vak, and I can't be deceived."

"Do you honestly believe that speaking with Rashgallivak is a way to ensure that you *won't* be deceived?"

"I would know if he lied to me."

"But what if he believed what he told you, and yet it still wasn't true?"

Moozh waited, unspeaking.

"I tell you that, regardless of the immediate impetus that caused our departure at a certain hour of a certain day, it was the Oversoul's purpose to get Father and me and my brothers out into the desert, as the first step to a journey."

"And yet here you are in the city."

"I told you," said Nafai. "I was married last night. So were my brothers."

"Elemak and Mebbekew and Issib."

Nafai was surprised and a little frightened that Moozh knew so much about them. But he had set out to tell the truth, and tell it he would. "Issib is with Father. He wanted to come. I wanted him to come. But Elemak wouldn't have it, and Father went along. We came for wives. And for Father's wife. When we arrived, Mother laughed and said that she would never go out onto the desert, no matter what mad project Wetchik had in mind. But then you put her under arrest and spread those rumors about her. In effect, you cut her off from Basilica, and now she understands that there's nothing for her here and so she, too, will go with us into the desert."

"You're saying that what I did was all part of the Oversoul's plan to get your mother to join her husband in a tent?"

"I'm saying that your purposes were bent to serve the Oversoul's plans. They always will be, General. They always have been."

"But what if I refuse to allow your mother to leave her house? What if I keep you and your brothers and your wives under arrest there? What if I send soldiers to stop Shedemei from gathering up seeds and embryos for your journey?"

Nafai was stunned. He knew about Shedemei? Impossible—she would never have told anyone. What was this Moozh capable of, if he could come into a strange city and be so aware of things so quickly that he could realize that Shedemei's gathering of seeds had something to do with Wetchik's exile?

"You see," said Moozh. "The Oversoul does not have power where *I* rule."

"You can keep us under arrest," said Nafai. "But when the Oversoul determines that it's time for us to go, you will find that you have a compelling reason to let us go, and so you'll let us go."

"If the Oversoul wants you to go, my boy, you may be sure that you will *not* go."

"You don't understand. I haven't told you the most important part. Whatever this war is that you think you're having with whatever version of the Oversoul it is that you call God, what matters is that dream you had. Of the flying beasts, and the giant rats."

Moozh waited, but again Nafai could see that he was deeply disturbed.

"The Oversoul didn't send that dream. The Oversoul didn't understand it."

"So. Then it was a meaningless dream, a common sleeping dream."

"Not at all. Because my wife also dreamed of those same

creatures, and so did her sister. All three of you, and these were not common dreams. They felt important to all of you. You knew that they had a meaning. Yet they didn't come from the Oversoul."

Again Moozh waited.

"It has been forty million years since human beings abandoned the Earth they had almost completely destroyed," said Nafai. "There has been time enough for Earth to heal itself. For there to be life there again. For there to be a place for humankind. Many species were lost—that's why Shedemei is gathering seeds and embryos for our journey. We are the ones that have the gift of speaking easily with the Oversoul. We are the ones who have been gathered together, here in Basilica, this day, this hour, so that we can go forth on a journey that will lead us back to Earth."

"Apart from the fact that Earth, if it exists, is a planet orbiting a faraway star, to which even birds can't fly," said Moozh, "you have still said nothing about what this journey might have to do with my dream."

"We don't *know* this," said Nafai. "We only guess it, but the Oversoul also thinks it might be true. Somehow the Keeper of Earth is calling us. Across all the lightyears between us and Earth, it has reached out to us and it's calling us back. For all we know, it even altered the programming of the Oversoul itself, telling it to gather us together. The Oversoul thought it knew why it was doing this, but it only recently learned the real reason. Just as you are only now learning the real reason for everything you've done in your life."

"A message in a dream, and it comes from someone thousands of lightyears away from here? Then the dream must have been sent thirty generations before I was born. Don't make me laugh, Nafai. You're far too bright to believe this. Doesn't it occur to you that maybe the Oversoul is manipulating *you?*"

Nafai considered this. "The Oversoul doesn't lie to me," he said.

"Yet you say that it has lied to me all along. So we can't

pretend that the Oversoul is rigidly committed to truthfulness, can we?"

"But it doesn't lie to *me*."

"How do you know?" asked Moozh.

"Because what it tells me . . . *feels* right."

"If it can make *me* forget things—and it can, it's happened so many times that . . ." His voice petered out as
Moozh apparently decided not to delve into those memories. "If it can do *that*, why can't it also make *you*, as you say,
'feel right'?"

Nafai had no ready answer. He had not questioned his
own certainty, and so he didn't know why Moozh's reasoning was false. "It's not just me," said Nafai, struggling to
find a reason. "My wife also trusts the Oversoul. And her
sister, too. They've had dreams and visions all their lives,
and the Oversoul has never lied to them."

"Dreams and visions all their lives?" Moozh leaned
forward on the table. "Whom, exactly, did you marry?"

"I thought I told you," said Nafai. "Luet. She's one of my
mother's nieces in her teaching house."

"The waterseer," said Moozh.

"I'm not surprised that you've heard of her."

"She's thirteen years old," said Moozh.

"Too young, I know. But she was willing to do what the
Oversoul asked of her, as was I."

"You think you're going to be able to take the waterseer
away from Basilica on some insane journey into the desert
in order to find an ancient legendary planet?" asked Moozh.
"Even if *I* did nothing to stop you, do you think the people
of this city would stand for it?"

"They will if the Oversoul helps us, and the Oversoul *will*
help us."

"And your wife's sister, which of your brothers did *she*
marry? Elemak?"

"She's going to marry Issib. He's waiting for us at my
father's tent."

Moozh leaned back in his chair and chuckled merrily. "It's
hard to see who has been controlling whom," he said.
"According to *you*, the Oversoul has a whole set of plans

that I'm a small part of. But the way it looks to me, God is setting things up so that everything plays into my hands. I thought before you came in here that it looked as though God had finally stopped being my enemy."

"The Oversoul was never your enemy," said Nafai. "It was *your* decision to make a contest of it."

Moozh got up from the table, walked around it, sat down beside Nafai, and took him by the hand. "My boy, this has been the most remarkable conversation of my life."

Mine, too, thought Nafai, but he was too astonished to say anything.

"I'm sure you're very earnest about your desire to make this journey, but I can assure you that you've been seriously misled. You're not leaving this city, and neither is your wife or her sister, and neither are any of the other people you plan to take along. You'll realize that sooner or later. If you realize it sooner—if you realize it *now*—then I have another plan for you that I think you'll like a little better than puttering around among the rocks and scorpions and sleeping in a tent."

Again, Nafai wanted to be able to explain to him why he *wanted* to follow the Oversoul. Why he knew that he was freely following the Oversoul, and perhaps the Keeper of Earth as well. Why he knew that the Oversoul wasn't lying to him or manipulating him or controlling him. But because he couldn't find the words or even the reasons, he remained silent.

"Your wife and her sister are the keys to everything. I'm not here to conquer Basilica, I'm here to win Basilica's loyalty. I've watched you now for an hour, I've listened to your voice, and I'll tell you, lad, you're a remarkable boy. So earnest. So *honest*. And eager, and you mean well, it's plain to anyone with half an eye that you mean no harm to anyone. And yet you're the one who killed Gaballufix, and so freed the city from a man who *would* have been tyrant, if he had lived another day or two. And it happens that you've just married the most prestigious figure in Basilica, the girl who commands the most universal love and respect and loyalty and hope in this city."

"I married her to serve the Oversoul."

"Please, keep saying that, I want everyone to believe that, and when you say it it's amazingly truthful-sounding. It will be a simple matter for me to spread this story about how the Oversoul commanded you to kill Gaballufix in order to save the city. And you can even bruit it about that the Oversoul brought, *me* here, too, to save the city from the chaos that came after your wife's sister, the raveler, destroyed Rashgallivak's power. It's all such a neat little package, don't you see? You and Luet and Hushidh and me, sent by the Oversoul to save the city, to lead Basilica to greatness. We all have a mission from the Oversoul . . . it's a story that will make the Imperator's nonsense about being God incarnate look pathetic."

"Why would you do this?" asked Nafai. It made no sense to him, for Moozh to propose making Nafai look like a hero instead of a killer, for Moozh to want to link himself with three people he was keeping prisoner in Rasa's house. Unless . . .

"What do you think?" asked Moozh.

"I think you imagine you can set *me* up as tyrant of Basilica instead of Gaballufix."

"Not tyrant," said Moozh. "Consul. The city council would still be there, quarreling and arguing and doing nothing important as usual. You'd just handle the city guard and the foreign relations; you'd just control the gates and make sure that Basilica remained loyal to me."

"Do you think they wouldn't see through this and realize I was a puppet?"

"They would if I didn't become a citizen of Basilica myself, and your good friend and close kin. But if I become one of them, a *part* of them, if I become the general of the Basilican army and do all that I do in your name, then they won't care who is puppet to whom."

"Rebellion," said Nafai. "Against the Gorayni."

"Against the most cruel and corrupt monsters who ever walked on Harmony's poor face," said Moozh. "Avenging their monstrous betrayal and enslavement of my people, the Sotchitsiya."

"So this is how Basilica will be destroyed," said Nafai. "Not *by* you, but because of your rebellion."

"I assure you, Nafai, I *know* the Gorayni. They're weak in the core, and their soldiers love me better than they love their pathetic Imperator."

"Oh, I have no doubt of it."

"If Basilica is my capital, the Gorayni won't destroy it. Nothing will destroy it, because I will be victorious."

"Basilica is nothing to you," said Nafai. "A tool of the moment. I can imagine you in the north, with a vast army, poised to destroy the army defending Gollod, the city of the Imperator, and at that moment you hear that Potokgavan has taken this opportunity to land an army on the Western Shore. Come back and defend Basilica, your people will beg. *I* will beg you. Luet will beg you. But you'll decide that there's plenty of time to deal with Potokgavan later, after you've defeated the Gorayni. And so you'll stay and finish your work, and the next year you'll sweep south and punish Potokgavan for their atrocities, and you'll stand in the ashes of Basilica and weep for the city of women. Your tears may even be sincere."

Moozh was trembling. Nafai could feel it in the hands that held his.

"Decide," said Moozh. "Whatever happens, either you will rule Basilica for me or you will die in Basilica—also for me. One thing is certain: You will never again *leave* Basilica."

"My life is in the hands of the Oversoul."

"Answer me," said Moozh. "Decide."

"If the Oversoul wanted me to help you subjugate this city, then I would be consul here," said Nafai. "But the Oversoul wants me to journey back to Earth, and so I will not be consul."

"Then the Oversoul has fooled you again, and this time you may well die for it," said Moozh.

"The Oversoul has never fooled me," said Nafai. "Those who follow the Oversoul willingly are never lied to."

"You never catch the Oversoul in his lies, is what you mean," said Moozh.

"No!" cried Nafai. "No. The Oversoul doesn't lie to me because . . . because everything that it has promised me has come true. All of it has been true."

"Or it has made you forget the ones that *didn't* come true."

"If I wanted to doubt, then I could doubt endlessly," said Nafai. "But at some point a person has to stop questioning and *act,* and at that point you have to trust something to be true. You have to act as if something is true, and so you choose the thing you have the most reason to believe in, you have to live in the world that you have the most hope in. I follow the Oversoul, I *believe* the Oversoul, because I want to live in the world that the Oversoul has shown me."

"Yes, Earth," said Moozh scornfully.

"I don't mean a planet, I mean—I want to live in the *reality* that the Oversoul has shown me. In which lives have meaning and purpose. In which there's a plan worth following. In which death and suffering are not in vain because some good will come from them."

"All you're saying is that you want to deceive yourself."

"I'm saying that the story the Oversoul tells me fits all the facts that I see. *Your* story, in which I'm endlessly deceived, can also explain all those facts. I have no way of knowing that your story is not true—but you have no way of knowing that *my* story isn't true. So I will choose the one that I love. I'll choose the one that, if it's true, makes this reality one worth living in. I'll act as if the life I hope for is real life, and the life that disgusts me—*your* life, your *view* of life—is the lie. And it *is* a lie. You don't even believe in it yourself."

"Don't you see, boy, that you've told me exactly the same story I told you? That the Oversoul has been fooling me all along? All I did was turn back on you the mad little tale you turned on me. The truth is that the Oversoul has played us both for fools, so all we can do is make the best life for ourselves that we can in this world. If you think that the best life for you and your new wife is to rule Basilica for me, to be part of the creation of the greatest empire that

Harmony has ever known, then I'm offering it to you, and I will be as loyal to you as you are to me. Decide now."

"I've decided," said Nafai. "There will be no great empire. The Oversoul won't allow it. And even if there were such an empire, it would mean nothing to me. The Keeper of Earth is calling us. The Keeper of Earth is calling *you*. And I ask you again, General Vozmuzhalnoy Vozmozhno, forget all this meaningless pursuit of empire or vengeance or whatever it is that you've been chasing all these yeas. Come with us to the world where humanity was born. Turn your greatness into a cause that's worthy of you. Come with us."

"Come with you?" said Moozh. "You're going nowhere." Moozh arose and walked to the door and opened it. "Take this boy back to his mother."

Two soldiers appeared, as if they had been waiting by the door. Nafai got up from his chair and walked to where Moozh stood, half-blocking the door. They looked into each other's eyes. Nafai saw rage there still, unslaked by anything that had transpired here this morning. But also he saw fear, which had not been in his eyes before.

Moozh raised his hand as if to strike Nafai across the face; Nafai did not wince or shrink from the blow. Moozh hesitated, and the blow, when it came, was upon Nafai's shoulder, and then Moozh smiled at him. In his mind Nafai heard the voice that he knew as that of the Oversoul: A slap on the face was the soldiers' signal to murder you. I have this much power in the mind of this rebellious man: I have turned Moozh's slap into a smile. But in his heart, he wants you dead.

"We are not enemies, boy," said Moozh. "Tell no one what I've said to you today."

"Sir," said Nafai, "I will tell my wife and my sisters and my mother and my brothers anything that I know. There are no secrets there. And even if I didn't tell them, the Oversoul would; my secrecy would accomplish nothing but my loss of their trust."

At the moment he refused to agree to secrecy, Nafai saw that the soldiers stiffened, ready to strike out at him. But whatever the signal was that they waited for, it didn't come.

Instead Moozh smiled again. "A weak man would have promised not to tell, and then told. A fearful man would have promised not to tell, and then would not have told. But you are neither weak nor fearful."

"The general praises me too highly," said Nafai.

"It will be such a shame if I have to kill you," said Moozh.

"It would be such a shame to die." Nafai could hardly believe it when he heard himself answer so flippantly.

"You truly believe that the Oversoul will protect you," said Moozh.

"The Oversoul has already saved my life today," said Nafai.

Then he turned and left, one soldier ahead of him, and one behind.

"Wait," said Moozh.

Nafai stopped, turned. Moozh strode down the hall. "I'll come with you," said Moozh.

Nafai could feel it in the way the soldiers nervously shifted their weight, though they didn't so much as glance at each other: This was not expected. This was not part of the plan.

So, thought Nafai. I may not have accomplished what I hoped for. I may not have convinced Moozh to come with us to Earth. But *something* has changed. Somehow things are different because I came.

I hope that means they're better.

The Oversoul answered in his mind: I hope so, too.

SEVEN

DAUGHTERS

THE DREAM OF THE LADY

Rasa slept badly after the weddings. She had, as a Basilican teacher should, kept her misgivings to herself, but it was emotionally grueling to give her dear weak Dolya to a young man that Rasa disliked as much as Wetchik's son Mebbekew. Oh, the boy was handsome and charming—Rasa wasn't blind, she knew exactly how attractive he could be—and she wouldn't have minded him as Dolya's first husband under ordinary circumstances, for Dolya was no fool and would certainly decide not to renew Meb after a single year. But there would be no question of renewals once they got into the desert. Wherever this journey would take them—Nafai's unlikely theory of Earth or some more possible place on Harmony—there would be no casual Basilican attitude toward marriage there, and even though she had warned them more than once, she knew that Meb and Dolya, at least, did not give her warnings even the slightest heed.

For, of course, Rasa was sure that Meb did not intend to leave Basilica. Married to Dol, he was now entitled to stay—he had his citizenship, and so he intended to laugh at any attempt by anyone to get him out of the city. If there weren't Gorayni soldiers outside the house, Meb would have taken Dolya and left tonight, never to show his face again until the rest of them had given up on him and left the city. So it was only the fact that Rasa was under house arrest that kept Meb in line. Well, so be it. The Oversoul would order things as she saw fit, and Mebbekew was hardly the one to thwart her.

Meb and Dolya, Elya and Edhya. . . . Well, she had seen nieces of hers marry miserably before. Hadn't she watched her own daughters marry badly? Well, actually, it was Kokor who married badly—Obring was a more moral man than Mebbekew only because he was too weak and timid and stupid to deceive and exploit women on Mebbekew's scale. Sevet, for her part, had actually married rather well, and Vas's behavior during the past few days had quite impressed Rasa. He was a good man, and maybe now that her voice had been taken from her Sevet would finally let pain turn her into a good woman. Stranger things had happened.

Yet when Rasa went to bed after the weddings, and could not sleep, it was the marriage between her son Nafai and her dearest niece, Luet, that troubled her and kept her awake. Luet was too young, and so was Nafai. How could they be thrust so early into manhood and womanhood, when their childhood was far from complete? Something precious had been stolen from both of them. And their very sweetness about the whole thing, the way they were trying so hard to fall in love with each other, only served to break Rasa's heart all the more.

Oversoul, you have so much to answer for. Is it worth all this sacrifice? My son Nafai is only fourteen, but for your sake he has a man's blood on his hands, and now both he and Luet share a marriage bed when at their age they should still be glancing at each other shyly, wondering if someday the other might fall in love with them.

She tossed and turned in her bed. The night was hot and dark—the stars were out, but there was little moonlight, and the streetlights shone dimly in the curfewed city. She could see almost nothing in her room, and yet did not want to turn on a light; a servant would see it, and think she might need something, and discreetly enter and inquire. I must be alone, she thought, and so she lay in darkness.

What are you plotting, Oversoul? I'm under arrest, no one can come or go from my house. Moozh has cut me off so that I can't begin to guess whom I might or might not be able to trust in Basilica, and so I must wait here for his plots and yours to unfold. Which will triumph here, Moozh's malevolent scheming or your own, Oversoul?

What do you want from my family? What will you *do* to my family, to my dearest ones? Some of it I consent to, however reluctantly: I consent to the marriage of Nyef and Lutya. As for Issib and Hushidh, when that times comes, if Shuya is willing then I am content, for I always dreamed of Issib finding some sweet woman who would see past his frailty and discover the man he is, the husband he might be—and who better than my precious raveler, my quiet, wise Shuya?

But this journey in the wilderness—we aren't prepared for it, and can't very well *get* prepared here in this house. What are you doing about *that,* in all your scheming? Aren't you perhaps a little over your head in all that's going on? Have you really planned ahead? Expeditions like this take a little planning. Wetchik and his boys could go out into the desert on a moment's notice because they had all the equipment they needed and they had some experience with camels and tents. I hope you don't expect me or my girls to be able to do that!

Then, a little bit ashamed of herself for having told the Oversoul off so roundly, Rasa uttered a much more humble prayer. Let me sleep, she prayed, dipping her fingers into the prayer basin beside the bed. Let me have rest tonight, and if it wouldn't be too much bother, show me some vision of what it is you plan for us. Then she kissed the prayer water off her fingers.

As she did so, more words passed through her mind, like a flippant addendum to her prayer. While you're telling me your plans, dear Oversoul, don't be afraid to ask for some advice. I've had some experience in this city and I love and understand these people more than you do, and you haven't been doing all that well up to now, or so it seems to me.

Oh, forgive me! she cried silently, abashed.

And then: Oh, forget it. And she rolled over and went to sleep, letting her fingers dry in the faint drafts coming in at the windows of her chamber.

She slept at last; she dreamed.

In her dream she sat in a boat on the lake of women, and opposite her—at the helm—sat the Oversoul. Not that Rasa had ever seen the Oversoul before, but after all, this was a dream, and so she recognized her at once. The Oversoul looked rather like Wetchik's mother had looked—a stern woman, but not unkind.

"Keep rowing," said the Oversoul.

Rasa looked down and saw that she was at the oars. "But I don't have the strength for this."

"You'd be surprised."

"I'd rather not be," said Rasa. "I'd rather be doing *your* job. You're the deity here, *you're* the one with infinite power. *You* row. *I'll* steer."

"I'm just a computer," said the Oversoul. "I don't have arms and legs. You have to do the rowing."

"I can see your arms and legs, and they're a great deal stronger than mine. Furthermore, I don't know where you're taking us. I can't see where we're going because I'm sitting here facing backward."

"I know," said the Oversoul. "That's how you've spent your whole life, facing backward. Trying to reconstruct some glorious past."

"So, if you disapprove of that, have the cleverness if not the decency to trade places with me. Let me look into the future while you do the rowing for a change."

"You all push me around so," said the Oversoul. "I'm beginning to regret breeding you all. When you get too familiar with me, you lose your respect."

"That's hardly *our* fault," said Rasa. "Here, we can't pass side by side, the boat's too narrow and we'll tip over. You crawl between my legs, and that way the boat won't spill."

The Oversoul grumbled as she crawled. "See? No respect."

"I *do* respect you," said Rasa. "I just don't have any illusions that you're always right. Nafai and Issib say that you're a computer. A program, in fact, that lives in a computer. And so you're no wiser than those who programmed you."

"Maybe they programmed me to learn wisdom. After forty million years, I may even have picked up a few good ideas."

"Oh, I'm sure you have. Someday you must show me one of them—you certainly haven't done so well till now."

"Maybe you just don't *know* all that I've done."

Rasa settled herself in the stern of the boat, her hand on the prow, and she saw to her satisfaction that the Oversoul had a good grip on the oars and was able to give a good strong pull.

However, the boat merely lurched forward and then stopped dead. Rasa looked around to see why, and she realized that they weren't on water at all, they were in the middle of a waste of wind-rippled sand.

"Well, *this* is a miserable turn of events," said Rasa.

"I'm not terribly impressed with your helmsmanship," said the Oversoul. "I hope you don't expect me to do any serious rowing in *this*."

"*My* helmsmanship," said Rasa. "It's *you* that got us out into the desert."

"And you could have done better?"

"I should hope so. For instance, where are the camels? We need camels. And tents! Enough for—oh, how many of us are there? Elemak and Eiadh, Mebbekew and Dol, Nafai and Luet—and Hushidh, of course. That's seven. And me. And then we'd better take Sevet and Kokor, and their husbands if they'll come—that's twelve. Am I forgetting something? Oh, of course—Shedemei and all her seeds and embryos—how many drycases? I can't remember—at least six camels for her project alone. And our supplies? I'm not even sure how to estimate this. Thirteen of us, and that's a lot of us to feed and shelter along the way."

"Well, why are you telling *me?*" asked the Oversoul. "Do you think I keep some sort of binary camels and tents in my memory?"

"So, just as I thought. You haven't even prepared a thing for the journey. Don't you know that these things can't be done suddenly? If you can't help me, take me to somebody who can."

The Oversoul began to lead her toward a distant hill. "You're so bossy," said the Oversoul. "*I'm* the one who's supposed to be the guardian of humanity, if you'll be so good as to remember that."

"That's fine, you keep doing that job, while I look out for the people I love. Who's going to take care of my household after I'm gone? Did you ever think of that? So many children and teachers who depend on me."

"They'll all go home. They'll find other teachers or other jobs. You're not indispensable."

They had reached the crest of the hill—as with all dreams, they were able to move very quickly sometimes, and sometimes very slowly. Now, at the top of the hill, Rasa saw that she was in the street in front of her own house. She had never known there was a way right down the hill to the desert from her own street. She looked around to see which way the Oversoul had brought her, only to find herself face-to-face with a soldier. Not a Gorayni, to her relief. Instead he was one of the officers of the Basilican guard.

"Lady Rasa," he said, in awe.

"I have work for you to do," she said. "The Oversoul would have told you all this already, only she's decided to leave this particular job up to me. I hope you don't mind helping."

"All I want to do is serve the Oversoul," he said.

"Well, then, I hope you'll be very resourceful and do all these jobs properly, because I'm not an expert and I'll have to leave a good many things to your judgment. To start with, there'll be thirteen of us."

"Thirteen of you to do *what?*"

"A journey in the desert."

"General Moozh has you under house arrest."

"Oh, the Oversoul will take care of that. I can't do *everything*."

"All right, then," said the officer. "A journey into the desert. Thirteen of you."

"We'll need camels to ride on and tents to sleep in."

"Large tents or small ones?"

"How large is large, and how small is small?"

"Large can be up to a dozen men, but those are very hard to pitch. Small can be for two men."

"Small," said Rasa. "Everybody will sleep in couples, except one tent for three, for me and Hushidh and Shedemei."

"Hushidh the raveler? Leaving?"

"Never mind the roster, that's none of your business," said Rasa.

"I don't think Moozh will want Hushidh to leave."

"He doesn't want *me* to leave, either—*yet*," said Rasa. "I hope you're taking notes."

"I'll remember."

"Fine. Camels for us to ride, and tents for us to sleep in, and then camels to carry the tents, and also camels to carry supplies enough for us to travel—oh, how far? I can't remember—ten days should be enough."

"That's a lot of camels."

"I can't help that. You're an officer, I'm sure you know where the camels are and how to get them."

"I do."

"And something else. An extra half-dozen camels to carry Shedemei's drycases. She might already have arranged for those herself—you'll have to check with her."

"When will you need all this?"

"Right away," said Rasa. "I have no idea when this journey will begin—we're under house arrest right now, you might have heard—"

"I heard."

"But we must be ready to leave within an hour, whenever the time comes."

"Lady Rasa, I can't do these things without Moozh's

authority. He rules the city now, and I'm not even the commander of the guard."

"All right," said Rasa. "I hereby give you Moozh's authority."

"You can't give that to me," said the officer.

"Oversoul?" said Rasa. "Isn't it about time you stepped in and did something?"

Immediately Moozh himself appeared beside the officer. "You've been talking to Lady Rasa," he said sternly.

"She's the one who came to *me*," said the officer.

"That's fine. I hope you paid attention to everything she said."

"So you authorize me to proceed?"

"I can't right at the moment," said Moozh. "Not officially, because at the moment I don't actually know that I'm going to want you to do this. So you have to do it very quietly, so that even I don't find out about it. Do you understand?"

"I hope I won't be in too much trouble if you find out."

"No, not at all. I *won't* find out, as long as you don't go out of your way to tell me."

"That's a relief."

"When the time comes for me to want this journey to begin, I'll order you to make preparations. All you have to say is, Yes sir, it can be done right away. Please *don't* embarrass me by pointing out that you've had it ready since noon, or anything like that to make it look as though my orders aren't spur-of-the-moment. Understand?"

"Very good, sir."

"I don't want to have to kill you, so please don't embarrass me, all right? I may need you later."

"As you wish, sir."

"You may leave," said Moozh.

Immediately the officer of the guard disappeared.

Moozh immediately turned into Rasa's dream image of the Oversoul. "I think that about takes care of it, Rasa," she said.

"Yes, I think so," said Rasa.

"Fine," said the Oversoul. "You can wake up now. The real Moozh will soon be at your door, and you want to be ready for him."

"Oh, thanks so very much," said Rasa, more than a little put out. "I've hardly had any sleep at all, and you're making me wake up already?"

"I wasn't responsible for the timing," said the Oversoul. "If Nafai hadn't run off half-cocked in the wee hours of the morning, demanding an interview with Moozh before the sun came up, you could have slept in to a reasonable hour."

"What time *is* it?"

"I told you, wake up and look at the clock."

With that the Oversoul disappeared and Rasa was awake, looking at the clock. The sky was barely greying with dawn outside, and she couldn't see what time it was without getting out of bed and looking closely. Wearily she groaned and turned on a light. Too, too early to get up. But the dream, strange as it was, had been this much true: Someone was ringing the bell.

At this hour, the servants knew they had no consent to open the door until Rasa herself had been alerted, but they were surprised to see her come into the foyer so quickly.

"Who?" she asked.

"Your son, Lady Rasa. And General Vozmoozh . . . the General."

"Open the door and you may retire," said Rasa.

The night bell was not so loud that the whole house heard it, so the foyer was nearly empty anyway. When the door opened, Nafai and Moozh entered together. No one else. No soldiers—though no doubt they waited on the street. Still, Rasa could not help remembering two earlier visits by men who thought to rule the city of Basilica. Gaballufix and Rashgallivak had both brought soldiers, holographically masked, in an attempt not so much to terrify *her* as to bolster their own confidence. It was significant that Moozh felt no need for accompaniment.

"I didn't know my son was out wandering the streets at this hour," said Rasa. "So I certainly appreciate your kindness in bringing him home to me."

"Surely now that he's married," said Moozh, "you won't be watching his comings and goings so carefully, will you?"

Rasa showed her impatience to Nafai. What was he

doing, blurting out the fact that he had just married the waterseer last night? Had he no discretion at all? No, of course not, or he wouldn't even have been outside to be picked up by Moozh's soldiers. What, had he been trying to escape?

But no, hadn't there been something . . . in the dream, yes, the Oversoul had said something about Nafai going off half-cocked, demanding an interview with Moozh. "I hope he hasn't been any trouble to you," said Rasa.

"A little, I will confess," said Moozh. "I had hoped he might help me bring to Basilica the greatness that this city deserves, but he declined the honor."

"Forgive me for my ignorance, but I fail to see how anything my son could do might bring greatness to a city that is already a legend through all the world. Is there any city still standing that is older or holier than Basilica? Is there any other that has been a city of peace for so long?"

"A solitary city, madam," said Moozh. "A lonely city. A city for pilgrims. But soon, I hope, a city for ambassadors from all the great kingdoms of the world."

"Who will no doubt sail here on a sea of blood."

"Not if things work well. Not if I have significant cooperation."

"From whom?" asked Rasa. "From me? From my son?"

"I would like to meet, though I know the honor is inconvenient, with two nieces of yours. One of them happens to be Nafai's young bride. The other is her unmarried sister."

"I do not wish you to meet with them."

"But they will wish to meet with me. Don't you think? Since Hushidh is sixteen, and free to receive visitors under the law, and Luet is also married, and thus also free to receive visitors, then I hope you will respect both law and courtesy and inform them that I wish to meet with them."

Rasa could not help but admire him even as she feared him—for, at a moment when Gabya or Rash would have blustered or threatened, Moozh simply insisted on courtesy. He did not bother reminding her of his thousand soldiers, of his power in the world. He simply relied on her good manners, and she was helpless before him, for right was not yet clearly on her side.

"I dismissed the servants. I will wait with you here, while Nafai goes for them."

When Moozh nodded, Nafai left, walking briskly toward the wing of the house where the bridal couples had spent the night. Rasa vaguely wondered at what hour Elemak and Eiadh, Mebbekew and Dol would rise, and what they would think of the fact that Nafai had gone to General Moozh. They ought perhaps to admire the boy's courage, but Elemak would no doubt resent him for his very intrusiveness, meddling always in affairs that shouldn't concern him. Whereas Rasa didn't resent Nafai's failure to remember that he was only a boy. Rather she feared for him because of it.

"The foyer is not a comfortable place," said Moozh. "Perhaps there might be some private room, where early risers will not interrupt us."

"But why would we have need of a private room, when we don't yet know whether my nieces will receive you?"

"Your niece and your daughter-in-law," said Moozh.

"A new relationship; it could hardly bring us closer than we already were."

"You love the girls dearly," said Moozh.

"I would lay down my life for them."

"And yet cannot spare a private room for their meeting with a foreign visitor?"

Rasa glowered at him and led him out to her private portico—the screened-off area, where there was no view of the Rift Valley. But Moozh made no pretense of sitting in the place on the bench that she patted. Instead he made for the balustrade beyond the screens. It was forbidden for men to stand there, to see that view; and yet Rasa knew that it would weaken her to attempt to forbid him. It would be . . . pathetic.

So instead she arose and stood beside him, looking out over the valley.

"You see what few men have seen," said Rasa.

"But your son has seen it," said Moozh. "He has floated naked on the waters of the lake of women."

"It wasn't my idea," said Rasa.

"The Oversoul, I know," said Moozh. "He takes us down so many twisted paths. Mine perhaps the most twisted one of all."

"And which bend will you take now?"

"The bend towards greatness and glory. Justice and freedom."

"For whom?"

"For Basilica, if the city will accept it."

"We *have* greatness and glory. We *have* justice and freedom. How can you imagine that any exertion of yours will add one whit to what we have?"

"Perhaps you're right," said Moozh. "Perhaps I'm only using Basilica to add luster to my *own* name, at the beginning, when I need it. Is Basilican glory so rare and dear that we can't find a bit of it to share with me?"

"Moozh, I like you so much that I almost regret the terror that fills my heart whenever I think of you."

"Why? I mean no harm to you, or to anyone you love."

"The terror is not for that. It's for what you mean to my city. To the world at large. You are the thing that the Oversoul was set in place to prevent. You are the machineries of war, the love of power, the lust for enlargement."

"You could *not* have made me prouder than to praise me thus."

There were footsteps behind them. Rasa turned to find Luet and Hushidh approaching. Nafai hung back.

"Come with your wife and sister-in-law, Nafai," said Rasa. "General Moozh has decreed our ancient custom to be abrogated, at least for this morning, with the sun preparing to rise behind the mountains."

Nafai walked more briskly then, and they took their places. Moozh easily and artfully arranged them, simply by taking his place leaning against the balustrade, so that as they sat on the arc of benches, their focus, their center was Moozh.

"I have come here this morning to congratulate the waterseer directly on her wedding last night."

Luet nodded gravely, though Rasa was reasonably sure that Luet knew Moozh had no such purpose. In fact, Rasa rather hoped that Nafai had some idea of what he had in mind, and had briefed the girls before they got here.

"It was an astonishing thing, for one so young," said Moozh. "And yet, having met young Nafai here, I can see that you have married well. A fitting consort for the waterseer, for Nafai is a brave and noble young man. So noble, in fact, that I begged him to let me place his name in nomination for the consulship of Basilica."

"There is no such office," said Rasa.

"There will be," said Moozh, "as there was before. An office little called for in times of peace, but needful enough in times of war."

"Of which we would have none, if you would only go away."

"It hardly matters, for your son declined the honor. In a way, it's almost fortunate. Not that he wouldn't have made a splendid consul. The people would have accepted him, for not only is he the bridegroom of the waterseer, but also he hears the voice of the Oversoul himself. A prophet and a prophetess, together in the highest chamber of the city. And for those who feared he might be a weakling, a puppet of the Gorayni overmaster, we need only point out the fact that long before old General Moozh arrived, Nafai himself, under the orders of the Oversoul, boldly ended a great menace to the freedom of Basilica and carried out a just execution of the penalty of death already owed by one Gaballufix, for ordering the murder of Roptat. Oh, the people would have accepted Nafai readily, and he would have been a wise and capable ruler. Especially with Lady Rasa to advise him."

"But he declined," said Rasa.

"He did."

"So what point is there in flattering us further?"

"Because there is more than one way for me to achieve the same end," said Moozh. "For instance, I could de-

nounce Nafai for the cowardly murder of Gaballufix, and bring forth Rashgallivak as the man who heroically tried to hold the city through a time of turmoil. Had it not been for the vicious interference of a raveler named Hushidh, he might have succeeded—for everyone knew that Rashgallivak's hands were not stained with any man's blood. Instead he was the capable steward, struggling to hold together the households of both Wetchik and Gaballufix. While Nafai and Hushidh go on trial for their crimes, Rashgallivak is made consul of the city. And, of course, he quite properly takes Gaballufix's daughters under his protection, as he will also do with Nafai's widow after his execution, and the raveler after she is pardoned for her crime. The city council would not want these poor women under the influence of the dangerous, self-serving Lady Rasa for another day."

"So you *do* make threats, after all," said Rasa.

"Lady Rasa, I am describing serious possibilities—choices that I can make, which will lead me to the end that, one way or another, I *will* achieve. I *will* have Basilica freely allied with me. It will be *my* city before I go on to challenge the tyrannical rule of the Gorayni Imperator."

"There is another way?" asked Hushidh quietly.

"There is, and it is perhaps the best of all," said Moozh. "It is the reason why Nafai brought me home with him—so I could stand before the raveler and ask for her to marry me."

Rasa was aghast. "Marry *you!*"

"Despite my nickname, I have no wife," said Moozh. "It isn't good for a man to be alone too long. I'm thirty years old—I hope not too old for you to accept me as your husband, Hushidh."

"She is intended for my son," said Rasa.

Moozh turned on her, and for the first time his sweet manners were replaced by a biting, dangerous anger. "A cripple who is hiding in the desert, a manlet whom this lovely girl has never desired as a husband and does not desire now!"

"You're mistaken," said Hushidh. "I *do* desire him."

"But you have not married him," said Moozh.

"I have not."

"There is no legal barrier to your marrying me," said Moozh.

"There is none."

"Enter this house and slay us all," said Rasa, "but I will not let you take this girl by force."

"Don't make a drama of this," said Moozh. "I have no intention of forcing anything. As I said, I have several paths open to me. At any point Nafai can say, 'I'll be the consul,' whereupon Hushidh will find the onerous burden of my marriage proposal less pressing—though not withdrawn, if she would like to share my future with me. For I assure you, Hushidh, that come what may, my life will be glorious, and the name of my wife will be sung with mine in all the tales of it forever."

"The answer is no," said Rasa.

"The question is not asked of you," said Moozh.

Hushidh looked from one to another of them, but not asking them anything. Indeed, Rasa was quite sure that Hushidh was seeing, not their features, but rather the threads of love and loyalty that bound them together.

"Aunt Rasa," said Hushidh at last, "I hope you will forgive me for disappointing your son."

"Don't let him bully you," said Rasa fiercely. "The Oversoul would never let him have Nafai executed—it's all bluster."

"The Oversoul is a computer," said Hushidh. "She is not omnipotent."

"Hushidh, there are visions tying you to Issib. The Oversoul has chosen you for each other!"

"Aunt Rasa," said Hushidh, "I can only beg you to keep your silence and respect my decision. For I have seen threads that I never guessed were there, connecting me to this man. I did not think, when I heard his name was Moozh, that I would be the one woman with the *right* to use that name for him."

"Hushidh," said Moozh, "I decided to propose to you for political reasons, having never seen you. But I heard that you were wise, and I saw at once that you are lovely. Now

I have seen the way you think and heard the way you speak, and I know that I can bring you, not just power and glory, but also the tender gifts of a true husband."

"And I will bring you the devotion of a true wife," said Hushidh, rising to her feet and walking to him. He reached for her, and she accepted his gentle embrace and his kiss upon her cheek.

Rasa, devastated, could say nothing.

"Can my Aunt Rasa perform the ceremony?" asked Hushidh. "I assume that for . . . political reasons . . . you'll want the wedding to be soon."

"Soon, but it can't be Lady Rasa," said Moozh. "Her reputation is none too good right now, though I'm sure that situation can be clarified soon after the wedding."

"Can I have a last day with my sister?"

"It's your wedding, not your funeral that you're going to," said Moozh. "You'll have many days with your sister. But the wedding will be today. At noon. In the Orchestra, with all the city as witnesses. And your sister Luet will perform the ceremony."

It was too terrible. Moozh understood too well how to turn this all to his advantage. If Luet performed the marriage, then her prestige would be on it. Moozh would be fully accepted as a noble citizen of Basilica, and he would have no need of any stand-in to be his puppet consul. Rather he would easily be named consul himself, and Hushidh would be his consort, the first lady of Basilica. She would be glorious in her role, worthy of it in every way—except that the role should not be played by anyone, and Moozh would destroy Basilica with his ambition.

Destroy Basilica . . .

"Oversoul!" cried Rasa from her heart. "Is that what you planned from the beginning?"

"Of course it is," said Moozh. "As Nafai himself told me, I was maneuvered here by God himself. For what other purpose, than to find a wife?" He turned again to Hushidh, who still looked up to him, still touched him, her hand on his arm. "My dear lady," said Moozh, "will you come with me now? While your sister prepares to perform the ceremony, we have many things to talk about, and you should be with me when we announce our wedding to the city council this morning."

Luet stood and strode forward. "I haven't agreed to play any part in this abominable farce!"

"Lutya," said Nafai.

"You can't force her!" cried Rasa triumphantly.

But it was Hushidh, not Moozh, who answered. "Sister, if you love me, if you have ever loved me, then I beg you, come to the Orchestra prepared to perform this wedding." Hushidh looked at them all. "Aunt Rasa, you must come. And bring your daughters and their husbands, and Nafai, bring your brothers and their wives. Bring all the teachers and the students of this house, even those who live away. Will you bring them to see me take a husband? Will you give me that one courtesy, in memory of all my happy years in this good house?"

The formality of her speech, the distance of her manner broke Rasa's heart, and she wept even as she agreed. Luet, too, promised to perform the ceremony.

"You will release them from this house for the wedding, won't you?" Hushidh asked Moozh.

He smiled tenderly at her. "They will be escorted to the Orchestra," he said, "and then escorted home."

"That's all I ask," said Hushidh. And then she left the portico on Moozh's arm.

When they were gone, Rasa sank to the bench and wept bitterly. "Why have we served her all these years?" Rasa demanded. "We are nothing to her. Nothing!"

"Hushidh loves us," said Luet.

"She's not talking about Hushidh," said Nafai.

"The Oversoul!" cried Rasa. Then she shouted the word, as if she were crowing it to the rising sun. "Oversoul!"

"If you've lost faith in the Oversoul," said Nafai, "at least have faith in Hushidh. She still has hope of turning this the way we want it to go, don't you realize? She took Moozh's offer because she saw some plan in it. Perhaps the Oversoul even *told* her to say yes, did you think of that?"

"I thought of it," said Luet, "but I can hardly believe it. The Oversoul has hinted nothing of this to us."

"Then instead of talking to each other," said Nafai, "and instead of getting resentful about it, perhaps we should listen. Perhaps the Oversoul is only waiting for us to spare it some scrap of our attention to tell us what's going on."

"I'll wait then," said Rasa. "But this better be a good plan."

They waited, all three with their own questions in their hearts.

From the look on Nafai's and Luet's faces, they received their answer first. And as Rasa waited, longer and longer, she realized that she would get no answer at all.

"Did you hear?" asked Nafai.

"Nothing," said Rasa. "Nothing at all."

"Perhaps you're too angry with the Oversoul to hear anything from her," said Luet.

"Or perhaps she's punishing me," said Rasa. "Spiteful machine! What did she have to say?"

Nafai and Luet glanced at each other. So the news wasn't good.

"The Oversoul isn't exactly in control of this," said Luet finally.

"It's my fault," said Nafai. "My going to the general put things at least a day ahead of schedule. He was already planning to marry one of them, but he would have studied it for another day at least."

"A day! Would that have made so much difference?"

"The Oversoul isn't sure that she can bring off her best plan, so quickly," said Luet. "But we can't blame Nafai for it, either. Moozh is impetuous and brilliant and he might have done it this quickly without Nafai's . . ."

"Stupidity," offered Nafai.

"Boldness," said Luet.

"So we're condemned to stay here as Moozh's tools?" asked Rasa. "Well, he could hardly misuse us more carelessly than the Oversoul has."

"Mother," said Nafai, and his tone was rather sharp. "The Oversoul has not misused us. Whether Hushidh marries

Moozh or not, we will still take our journey. If she does end up as Moozh's wife, then she'll use her influence to set us free—he'll have no need for us once his position in the city is secured."

"*Us?*" asked Rasa. "Set *us* free?"

"All of us that we already planned for the journey, even Shedemei."

"And what about Hushidh?" asked Rasa.

"That's what the Oversoul can't do," said Luet. "If she can't prevent the wedding, then Hushidh will stay."

"I will hate the Oversoul forever," said Rasa. "If she does this to sweet Hushidh, then I'll never serve the Oversoul again. Do you hear me?"

"Calm yourself, Mother," said Nafai. "If Hushidh had refused him, then I would have agreed to be consul, and it would have been Luet and I who stayed behind. One way or another, it was going to happen."

"Is that supposed to comfort me?" Rasa asked bitterly.

"Comfort *you?*" asked Luet. "Comfort *you,* Lady Rasa? Hushidh is my sister, my only kin—you'll have all the children you ever bore with you, *and* your husband. What are you losing, compared with what I'm going to lose? Yet do you see me weeping?"

"You *should* be weeping," said Rasa.

"All the way through the desert I'll do my weeping," said Luet. "But for now we have very few hours to prepare."

"Oh, am I supposed to teach you the ceremony?"

"That will take five minutes," said Luet, "and the priest-esses will help me anyway. The time we have must be spent in packing for the journey."

"The *journey,*" said Rasa bitterly.

"We must have everything ready so it can be loaded onto camels in five minutes," said Luet. "Isn't that so, Nafai?"

"There's still a chance that all will work well," said Nafai. "Mother, now is not the time for you to give up. All my life, you've held firm no matter what the provocation. Are you collapsing now, when we need you most to bring the others into line?"

"Do you expect *us* to get Sevet and Vas, Kokor and Obring to pack up for a desert journey?" asked Luet.

"Do you think Elemak and Mebbekew will take these instructions from *me?*" asked Nafai.

Rasa dried her eyes. "You ask too much of me," said Rasa. "I'm not as young as you. I'm not as resilient."

"You can bend as much as you need to," said Luet. "Now please, tell us what to do."

So Rasa swallowed, for now, her grief, and stepped back into her old familiar role. Within minutes the whole house was set in motion, the servants packing and preparing, the clerks drafting letters of recommendation for every teacher who would be left behind, and reports on the progress of every pupil, so that they could all find new schools easily after Rasa left and the school was closed.

Then Rasa walked the long corridor to Elemak's bridal chamber, to begin the grueling process of informing the reluctant travelers that they *would* attend the wedding, since soldiers would be marching them there, and they *would* prepare for a desert journey, since for some reason the Oversoul had decided that they would not have suffered enough until they were out among the scorpions.

AT THE ORCHESTRA, AND NOT IN A DREAM

This was hardly the way Elemak would have wanted to spend the morning after his wedding. It was supposed to be a leisurely time of dozing and lovemaking, talking and teasing. Instead it had been a flurry of preparations— hopelessly inadequate preparations, too, since they were supposedly preparing for a desert journey and yet had neither camels nor tents nor supplies. And it was disturbing how badly Eiadh had adjusted to the situation. Where Mebbekew's Dol was immediately cooperative—more so than Meb himself, the slug—Eiadh kept wasting Elemak's time with protests and arguments. Couldn't we stay behind and join them later? Why do *we* have to leave just because Aunt Rasa is under arrest?

Finally Elemak had sent Eiadh to Luet and Nafai to get her questions answered while he supervised the packing, to eliminate needless clothing—which meant bitter arguments with Rasa's daughter Kokor, who could not understand why her light and provocative little frocks were not going to be particularly useful out on the desert. Finally he had blown up, in front of her sister Sevet and both their husbands, and said, "Listen, Kokor, the only man you're going to be able to have out there is your husband, and when you want to seduce *him*, you can take your clothes *off*." With that he picked up her favorite dress and tore it down the middle. Of course she screamed and wept—but he saw her later, magnanimously giving away all her favorite gowns—or perhaps trading them for more practical clothing, since it was likely that Kokor had owned nothing serviceable at all.

If the ordeal of packing had not been enough, there was the mortifying passage through the city. True, the soldiers had done a fair job of being discreet—no solid phalanx of brutish men marching in step. But they were still Gorayni soldiers, and so passersby—most of them also heading for the Orchestra—cleared a space around them and then gawked at them as they passed. "They look at us like we're criminals," Eiadh said. But Elemak reassured her that most bystanders probably assumed they were guests of honor with a military escort, which made Eiadh preen. It bothered Elemak just a little, in the back of his mind, that Eiadh was so childish. Hadn't Father warned him that young wives, while they had sleeker, lighter bodies, also had lighter minds? Eiadh was simply young; Elemak could hardly expect her to take serious matters seriously, or even to understand what was serious in the first place.

Now they sat in places of honor, not up among the benches on the upward slopes of the amphitheatre, but down on the Orchestra itself, to the righthand side of the low platform that had been erected in the center for the ceremony itself. They were the bride's party; on the other side, the groom's party consisted of many members of the city council, along with officers of the Basilican guard and a few—only a handful—of Gorayni officers. There was no sign of Gorayni domination here. Not that there needed to be. Elemak knew that there were plenty of Gorayni soldiers and Basilican guards discreetly out of sight, but close enough to intervene if something unexpected should happen. If, for instance, some assassin or other curiosity-seeker should attempt to cross the open space between the benches and the wedding parties around the platform, he would find himself sporting a new arrow somewhere in his body, from one of the archers in the prompters' and musicians' boxes.

How quickly things change, thought Elemak. Only a few weeks ago I came home from a successful caravan, imagining that I was ready to take my place as a man in the affairs of Basilica. Gaballufix seemed to be the most powerful man in the world to me then, and my future as the Wetchik's heir and Gabya's brother seemed bright indeed. Since then nothing had stayed the same for two days at a time. A week ago, dehydrating mind and body on the desert, would he have believed he might be married to Eiadh in Rasa's house not a week thence? And even last night, when he and Eiadh had been the central figures in the wedding ceremony, could he have imagined that at noon the next day, instead of Nafai and Luet being the childish, pathetic hangers-on at Elemak's wedding, they would now sit on the platform itself, where Luet would perform the ceremony and Nafai would stand as General Moozh's sponsor?

Nafai! A fourteen-year-old boy! And General Moozh had asked *him* to stand as his sponsor for citizenship in Basilica, offering him to Hushidh as if Nafai were some important figure in the city. Well, he *was* an important figure—but only as the husband of the waterseer. Nobody could possibly think that he deserved any such honor in and of himself.

Waterseer, raveler . . . Elemak had never paid much heed to such things. It was all priestcraft, a profitable business but one he didn't have much patience with. Like the foolish dream that Elemak had had out on the desert—it was such an easy matter to turn a meaningless dream into a plan of action, because of the gullible fools who believed that the Oversoul was some noble being instead of a mere computer program responsible for pressing data and documents from city to city by satellite. Even Nafai himself was saying that the Oversoul was just a computer, and yet he and Luet and Hushidh and Rasa were all full of tales about how the Oversoul was trying to arrange things so the marriage wouldn't take place and they would all end up out on the desert, ready for the journey, before the day was over. What, could a computer program make camels appear out of nothing? Make tents rise up out of the dust? Turn rocks and sand into cheeses and grain?

"Doesn't he look brave and fine?" asked Eiadh.

Elemak turned to her. "Who? Is General Moozh here?"

"I mean your brother, silly. Look."

Elemak looked toward the platform and did not think Nafai looked particularly brave or fine. In fact, he looked silly, all dressed up like a boy pretending to be a man.

"I can hardly believe he would walk right up to one of the Gorayni soldiers," said Eiadh. "And go speak to General Vozmuzhalnoy Vozmozhno himself—while everyone was still asleep!"

"What was brave about that? It was dangerous and foolish, and look what it led to—Hushidh having to marry the man."

Eiadh looked at him in bafflement. "Elya, she's marrying the most powerful man in the world! And Nafai will stand as his sponsor."

"Only because he's married to the waterseer."

Eiadh sighed. "She *is* such a plain little thing. But those dreams—I've tried to have dreams myself, but no one takes them seriously. I had the strangest dream last night, in fact. A hairy flying monkey with ugly teeth was throwing doo-doo on me, and a giant rat with a bow and arrow shot him out of the sky—can you believe anything so silly? Why can't *I* have dreams from the Oversoul, can you tell me that?"

Elemak was hardly listening. Instead he was thinking of how Eiadh had clearly been envious because Hushidh was marrying the most powerful man in the world. And how she had admired Nafai for his damnable cheek, in going out and accosting General Moozh in the middle of the night. What could he possibly have accomplished, except to infuriate the man? Pure stupid luck that it had ended up with Nafai on that platform. But it galled Elemak all the same, that it was Nafai who was sitting there, with all the eyes of Basilica upon him. Nafai who was being whispered about, Nafai who would be seen as the husband of the waterseer, the brother-in-law of the raveler. And as Moozh installed himself as king—oh, yes, the official word for it would be *consul,* but it would *mean* the same—Nafai would be the brother-in-law of majesty and the husband of greatness and Elemak would be a desert trader. Oh, of course they would restore Father to his place as Wetchik, once Father realized that the Oversoul wasn't going to be able to get anybody out of Basilica after all. And Elemak would again be his heir, but what would *that* title mean anymore? Worst of all would be the fact that he would receive his rank and his future back as a gift from *Nafai.* It made him seethe inside.

"Nafai is so *impetuous,*" said Eiadh. "Aren't you proud of him?"

Couldn't she stop talking about him? Until this morning, Elemak had known that Eiadh was the finest marriage a man could make for himself in this city. But now he realized that in the back of his mind he had really been thinking that she was the finest *first* marriage a *young* man could make. Someday he would need a real wife, a consort, and there was no reason to think that Eiadh would grow up into such a one. She would probably always be shallow and frivolous, the very thing that he had found so endearing. Last night when she had sung to him, her throaty voice full of rehearsed passion, he had thought he could listen to her sing forever. Now he looked at the platform and realized that it was Nafai, after all, who had made a marriage that would be worth having thirty years from now.

Well, fine, thought Elemak. Since we *won't* get away from Basilica, I'll keep Eiadh for a couple of years and then gently ease her away. Who knows? Luet may not stay with Nafai. When she gets older she may begin to wish for a *strong* man beside her. We can look back on these first marriages as childish phases we went through in our youth. Then *I* will be the brother-in-law of the consul.

As for Eiadh, well, with luck she'll bear me a son before we're through. But would that truly be luck? Should my eldest son, my heir, be a boy with such a shallow woman for his mother? In all likelihood, it will be the sons of my later marriages, my mature marriages, who will be the worthiest to take my place.

Then, like a sudden attack of indigestion, there came the realization that Father, too, might feel that way. After all, Lady Rasa was *his* marriage of maturity, and Issib and Nafai the sons of that marriage. Wasn't Mebbekew walking, talking proof of the unfortunate results of early marriages?

But not me, thought Elemak. I was not the son of some frivolous early marriage. I was a son he couldn't have dared to ask for—his Auntie's son, Hosni's son, born only because she so admired the boy Volemak as she introduced him to the pleasures of the bed. Hosni was a woman of substance, and Father trusts and admires me above his other children. Or *did*, anyway, until he started having visions from the Oversoul and Nafai was able to parlay that into an advantage by pretending to have visions, too.

Elemak was filled with rage—old, deep-burning rage and hot new jealousy because of Eiadh's admiration for Nafai. Yet what burned hottest and deepest was his fear that Nafai was not pretending, that for some unknowable reason the Oversoul had chosen Father's youngest instead of his eldest to be his true heir. When Issib's chair was taken over by the Oversoul and stopped Elemak from beating Nafai in that ravine outside the city, hadn't the Oversoul as much as said so? That Nafai would one day lead his brothers, or something to that effect?

Well, dear Oversoul, not if Nafai is dead. Ever think of that? If you can speak to *him* then you can speak to me, and it's about time you started.

I gave you the dream of wives.

The sentence came into Elemak's mind as clearly as speech. Elemak laughed.

"What are you laughing at, Elya, dear?" asked Eiadh.

"At how easily a person can deceive himself," said Elemak.

"People always talk about how a person can lie to himself, but I've never understood that," said Eiadh. "If you tell yourself a lie, then you know you're lying, don't you?"

"Yes," said Elemak. "You know you're lying, and you know what the truth is. But some people fall in love with the lie and let go of the truth completely."

As you're doing now, said the voice in his head. You prefer to believe the lie that I cannot speak to you or anyone else, and so you will deny me.

"Kiss me," said Elemak.

"We're in the middle of the Orchestra, Elya!" she said, but he knew she wanted to.

"All the better," he said. "We were married last night—people expect us to be oblivious to everything but each other."

So she kissed him, and he let himself fall into the kiss, blanking his mind to everything but desire. When at last the kiss ended, there was a smattering of applause—they had been noticed, and Eiadh was delighted.

Of course, Mebbekew immediately proposed an identical kiss to Dol, who had the good sense to decline. Still, Mebbekew persisted, until Elemak leaned across Eiadh and said, "Meb. Anticlimax is always bad theatre—didn't you tell me that yourself?"

Meb glowered and dropped the idea.

I am still in control of things, Elemak thought. And I am *not* about to start believing voices that pop into my mind just because I wish for them. I'm not like Father and Nafai and Issib, determined to believe in a fantasy because it feels so warm and cuddly to think that some superior being is in charge of things. I can deal with the cold hard truth. That's always enough for a *real* man.

The horns began. From all the minarets around the amphitheatre, the horners began their wailing cries. These were ancient instruments, not the finely-tuned horns of theatre or concert, and there was no attempt to create harmony between them. Each horn produced one note at a time, held long and loud, then fading as the horner lost breath. The notes overlaid each other, sometimes with winsome dissonance, sometimes with astonishing harmonies; always it was a haunting, beautiful sound.

It silenced the citizens gathered in the benches, and it filled Elemak with a trembling anticipation, as he knew it did with every other person in the Orchestra. The wedding was about to begin.

Thirsty stood at the gate of Basilica and wondered why the Oversoul had failed her now. Hadn't she been helped every step of the way from Potokgavan? She had come upon a canal boat and asked them to let her ride, and they had taken her aboard without question, though she could give them no fare. At the great port, she had boldly told the captain of the corsair that the Oversoul required her to have the fastest passage to Redcoast ever achieved, and he had laughed and boasted that as long as he took no cargo, he could make it in a day, with such a fair wind. In Redcoast a fine lady had dismounted from her horse and offered it to Thirsty on the street.

It was on that horse that Thirsty arrived at the Low Gate, expecting to be admitted easily, as all women always were, citizens or not. Instead she found the gate tended by Gorayni soldiers, and they were turning everyone away.

"There's a great wedding going on inside," a soldier explained to her. "General Moozh is marrying some Basilican lady."

Without knowing how, Thirsty knew at once that this wedding was the reason she had come.

"Then you must let me in," she said, "because I am an invited guest."

"Only the citizens of Basilica are invited to attend, and only those who were already inside the walls. Our orders allow no exceptions, not even for nursing mothers whose babes are inside the walls, not even for physicians whose dying patients are within."

"I am invited by the Oversoul," said Thirsty, "and by that

authority I revoke any orders you were given by a mortal man."

The soldier laughed, but only a little, for her voice had carried, and the crowd at the gate was watching, listening. They had also been turned away, and were liable to turn surly at the slightest provocation.

"Let her in," said one of the soldiers, "if only to keep the crowd from turning."

"Don't be a fool," said another. "If we let her in we'll have to let them all in."

"They all want me to enter," said Thirsty.

The crowd murmured their assent. Thirsty wondered at this—that the crowd of Basilicans should heed the Oversoul so readily, while the Gorayni soldiers were deaf to her influence. Perhaps this was why the Gorayni were such an evil race, as she had heard in Potokgavan: because they could not hear the voice of the Oversoul.

"My husband is waiting for me inside," said Thirsty, though not until she heard herself say the words did she realize it was true.

"Your husband will have to wait," said a soldier.

"Or take a lover," said another, and they laughed.

"Or satisfy himself," said the first, and they hooted.

"We should let her in," said one of the soldiers. "What if God has chosen her?"

Immediately one of the other soldiers drew his lefthand knife and put it to the throat of the one who had spoken. "You know the warning we were given—that it's the very one that we *want* to allow inside who must be prevented!"

"But she needs to be there," said the soldier who was sensitive to the Oversoul.

"Say another word and I'll kill you."

"No!" cried Thirsty. "I'll go. This is not the gate for me."

Inside her she felt the urgency to enter the city increase; but she would not have this man be killed when it would not get her through the gate in any case. Instead she wheeled the horse and made her way back through the crowd, which parted for her. Quickly she made her way up the steep trail that led to the Caravan Road, but she did not bother trying the Market Gate; she made her way along the High Road, but she did not try to enter at High Gate or Funnel Gate, either. She hurried her mount along the Dark Path, which wound among deep ravines sloping upward into the forested hills north of the city until she reached the Forest Road—but she did not follow it down to Back Gate, either.

Instead she dismounted and plunged into the dense underbrush of Trackless Wood, heading for the private gate that only women knew of, that only women used. It had taken an hour for her to go around the city, and she had gone the long way, too—but there was no horsepath around the east wall, which dropped straight down to crags and precipices, and to clamber that route on foot would have taken far longer. Now the wood itself seemed to snag at her, to hold her back, though she knew that the Oversoul was guiding every step she took, to find the quickest path to the private gate. Even when she entered there, however, it would take time to make her way up into the city, and already she could hear the horns beginning their plaintive serenade. The ceremony would begin in moments, and Thirsty would not be there.

Luet moved and spoke as slowly as she could, but as she stepped and spoke her way through the ceremony, she did not have the option of doing what she desired in her heart—to stop the wedding and denounce Moozh to the gathered citizens. At best she would merely be hustled from the platform before she could say a word, as a more responsible priestess took over; at worst, she might actually speak, might be stopped by an arrow, and then riot and bloodshed would ensue and Basilica could easily be destroyed before another morning came. What would that accomplish?

So she walked through the ceremony—with deliberation, with long pauses, but never stopping altogether, never ignoring the whispered promptings of the priestesses who were with her at every turning, at every speech.

For all the turmoil inside of Luet, though, she could not

see that Hushidh felt anything but perfect calm. Was it possible that Hushidh actually welcomed this marriage, as a way of avoiding life as a cripple's wife? No—Shuya had been sincere when she said that the Oversoul had reconciled her to that future. Her calm must come from utter trust in the Oversoul.

"She is right to trust," said a voice—a whisper, really. For a moment she thought it was the Oversoul, but instead she realized that it was Nafai, who had spoken as she passed near him during the processional of flowers. How had he known what words he needed to say just then, to answer so perfectly her very thoughts? Was it the Oversoul, forging an ever-closer link between them? Or was it Nafai himself, seeing so deeply into her heart that he knew what she needed him to say?

Let it be true, that Shuya is right to trust the Oversoul. Let it be true that we will not have to leave her here when we make our journey to the desert, to another star. For I could not bear it to lose her, to leave her. Perhaps I would know joy again; perhaps my new husband could be a companion to me as Hushidh has been my dear companion. But there would always be an ache, an empty place, a grief that would never die, for my sister, my only kin in the world, my raveler who when I was an infant tied the knot that will bind us to each other forever.

And then, at last, the moment came, the taking of the oaths, Luet's hands on their shoulders—reaching up to Moozh's shoulder, so hard and large and strange, and to Hushidh's shoulder, so familiar, so frail by comparison to Moozh's. "The Oversoul makes one soul from the woman and the man," said Luet. A breath. An endless pause. And then the words she could not bear to say, yet had to say, and so said. "It is done."

The people of Basilica rose from their seats as if they were one, and cheered and clapped and called out their names: Hushidh! Raveler! Moozh! General! Vozmuzhalnoy! Vozmozhno!

Moozh kissed Hushidh as a husband kisses a wife—but gently, Luet saw, kindly. Then he turned and led Hushidh down to the front of the platform. A hundred, a thousand flowers filled the air, flying forward; those thrown from the back of the amphitheatre were picked up and tossed again, until the flowers filled the space between the platform and the first row of benches.

Amid the tumult, Luet became aware that Moozh himself was shouting. She could not hear the words he said, but only the fact that he was saying something, for his back was toward her. Gradually the people on the front row realized what he was saying, and took up his words as a chant. Only then did Luet understand how he was turning his own wedding now to clear political advantage. For what he said was a single word, repeated over and over again, spreading through the crowd until they all shouted with the same impossibly loud voice.

"Basilica! Basilica! Basilica!"

It went on forever, forever.

Luet wept, for she knew now that the Oversoul had failed, that Hushidh was married to a man who would never love *her*, but only the city that he had taken as her dowry.

At last Moozh raised his hands—his left hand higher, palm out to silence them, his right still holding Hushidh's hand. He had no intention of breaking his link to *her*, for this was his link to the city. Slowly the chanting died down, and at last a curtain of silence fell on the Orchestra.

His speech was simple but eloquent. A protestation of his love for this city, his gratitude at having been privileged to restore it to peace and safety, and now his joy at being welcomed as a citizen, the husband of the sweet and simple beauty of a true daughter of the Oversoul. He mentioned Luet, too, and Nafai, how honored he felt to be kinsmen of the best and bravest of Basilica's children.

Luet knew what came next. Already the delegation of councilors had risen from their seats, ready to come forward and ask that the city accept Moozh as consul, to lead Basilica's military and foreign relations. It was a foregone conclusion that the vast majority of the people, overwhelmed with the ecstasy and majesty of the moment, would acclaim the choice. Only later would they realize what they had done, and even then most would think it was a wise and good change.

Moozh's speech was winding toward its end—and it would be a glorious end, well received by the people despite his northern accent, which in other times would have been ridiculed and despised.

He hesitated. In an unexpected place in his speech. An inappropriate place. The hesitation became a pause, and Luet could see that he was looking at something or someone that *she* could not see. So she stepped forward, and Nafai was instantly beside her; together they took the few steps necessary for both of them to be on Moozh's left, behind him still but able now to see whom he was looking at.

A woman. A woman dressed in the simple garb of a farmer of Potokgavan—a strange costume indeed for this time and place. She was standing at the foot of the central flight of steps leading up into the amphitheatre; she made no move to come forward, so neither the Gorayni archers nor the two Basilican guards had made any move to stop her till now.

Because the general said nothing, the soldiers did not know what to do—should they seize the woman and hustle her away?

"You," said Moozh. So he knew her.

"What are you doing?" she asked. Her voice was not loud, and yet Luet heard it clearly. How could she hear so clearly?

Because I am speaking her words again in the mind of every person here, said the Oversoul.

"I am marrying," said Moozh.

"There has been no marriage," she said—again softly, again heard perfectly by all.

Moozh gestured at the assembled multitude. "All these have seen it."

"I don't know what they have seen," said the woman. "But what *I* see is a man holding his daughter by the hand."

A murmur arose in the congregation.

"God, what have you done," whispered Moozh. But now the Oversoul also carried *his* softest voice into their ears.

Now the woman stepped forward, and the soldiers made no effort to stop her, for they saw that what was happening was far larger than a mere assassination.

"The Oversoul brought me to you," she said. "Twice she brought me, and both times I conceived and bore daughters. But I was not your wife. Rather I was the body that the Oversoul chose to use, to bear *her* daughters. I took the daughters of the Oversoul to the Lady Rasa, whom the Oversoul had chosen to raise them and teach them, until the day when she chose to name them as her own."

The woman turned to Rasa, pointed at her. "Lady Rasa, do you know me? When I came to you I was naked and filthy. Do you know me now?"

Aunt Rasa shakily rose to her feet. "You are the one who brought them to me. Hushidh first, and then Luet. You told me to raise them as if they were my daughters, and I did."

"They were not your daughters. They were not my daughters. They are the daughters of the Oversoul, and this man—the one called Vozmuzhalnoy Vozmozhno by the Gorayni—he is the man that the Oversoul chose to be her Moozh."

Moozh. Moozh. The whisper ran through the crowd.

"The marriage you saw today was not between this man and this girl. She only stood as proxy for the Mother. He has become the husband of the Oversoul! And insofar as this is the city of the Mother, he has become the husband of Basilica! I say it because the Oversoul has put the words into my mouth! Now *you* must say it! All of Basilica must say it! Husband! Husband!"

They took up the chant. Husband! Husband! Husband! And then, gradually, it changed, to another word with the same meaning. Moozh! Moozh! Moozh!

As they chanted, the woman came forward to the front of the low platform. Hushidh let go of Moozh's hand and came forward, knelt before the woman; Luet followed her, too stunned to weep, too filled with joy at what the

Oversoul had done to save Hushidh from this marriage, too filled with grief at having never known this woman who was her mother, too filled with wonder at discovering that her father had been this northern stranger, this terrifying general all along.

"Mother," Hushidh was saying—and *she* could weep, spilling her tears on the woman's hand.

"I bore you, yes," said the woman. "But I am not your mother. The woman who raised you, *she* is your mother. And the Oversoul who caused you to be born, *she* is your mother. I'm just a farmer's wife in the wetlands of Potokgavan. That is where the children live who call *me* mother, and I must return to them."

"No," whispered Luet. "Can we only see you once?"

"I will remember you forever," said the woman. "And you will remember me. The Oversoul will keep these memories fresh in our hearts." She reached out one hand and touched Hushidh's cheek, and another to touch Luet, to stroke her hair. "So lovely. So worthy. How she loves you. How your mother loves you now."

Then she turned from them and left—walked from the platform, walked down into the ramp leading to the dressing rooms under the amphitheatre, and she was gone. No one saw her leave the city, though stories of strange miracles and odd visions quickly sprang up, of things she supposedly did but could not possibly have done on her way out of Basilica that day.

Moozh watched her turn and leave, and with her she took all his hopes and plans and dreams; with her she took his life. He remembered so clearly the time he had spent with her—she was the reason he had never married, for what woman could make him feel what he had felt for her. At the time he had been sure that he loved her in defiance of God's will, for hadn't he felt that strong forbidding? When she was with him, hadn't he woken again and again with no memory of her, and yet he had overcome God's barriers in his mind, and kept her, and loved her? It was as Nafai said—even his rebellion was orchestrated by the Oversoul.

I am God's fool, God's tool, like everyone else, and when I thought to have my own dreams, to make my own destiny, God exposed my weakness and broke me to pieces before the people of the city. *This* city of all cities—Basilica. Basilica.

Hushidh and Luet arose from their knees at the front of the stage; Nafai joined them as they came to face Moozh. They had to come very close to him to be heard above the chanting of the crowd.

"Father," said Hushidh.

"Our father," echoed Luet.

"I never knew that I had children," said Moozh. "I should have known. I should have seen my own face when I looked at you." And it was true—now that the truth was known, the resemblance was obvious. Their faces had not followed the normal pattern of Basilican beauty because their Father was of the Sotchitsiya, and only God could guess where their mother might be from. Yet they *were* beautiful, in a strange exotic way. They were beautiful and wise, and strong women as well. He could be proud of them. In the ruins of his career, he could be proud of them. As he fled from the Imperator, who would certainly know what he had meant to attempt with this aborted marriage, he could be proud of them. For they were the only thing he had created that would last.

"We must go into the desert," said Nafai.

"I won't resist it now."

"We need your help," said Nafai. "We must go at once."

Moozh cast his eyes across the party he had assembled on his side of the platform. Bitanke. It was Bitanke who must help him now. He beckoned, and Bitanke arose and bounded onto the platform.

"Bitanke," said Moozh, "I need you to prepare for a desert journey." He turned to Nafai. "How many of you will there be?"

"Thirteen," said Nafai, "unless you decide to come with us."

"Come with us, Father," said Hushidh.

"He can't come with us," said Luet. "His place is here."

"She's right," said Moozh. "I could never go on a journey for God."

"Anyway," said Luet, "he'll be with us because his seed is part of us." She touched Nafai's arm. "He will be the grandfather of all our children, and of Hushidh's children, too."

Moozh turned back to Bitanke. "Thirteen of them. Camels and tents, for a desert journey."

"I will have it ready," said Bitanke. But Moozh understood, in the tone of his voice, in the confident way he held himself, and from the fact that he asked no questions, that Bitanke was not surprised or worried by this assignment.

"You already knew," said Moozh. He looked around at the others. "You all planned this from the start."

"No sir," said Nafai. "We knew only that the Oversoul was going to try to stop the marriage."

"Do you think that we would have been silent," asked Luet, "if we had known we were your daughters?"

"Sir," said Bitanke, "you must remember that you and Lady Rasa told me to prepare the camels and the tents and the supplies."

"When did I tell you such a thing?"

"In my dream last night," Bitanke said.

It was the crowning blow. God had destroyed him, and even went so far as to impersonate him in another man's prophetic dream. He felt his defeat like a heavy burden thrown over his shoulders; it bent him down.

"Sir," said Nafai, "why do you imagine that you've been destroyed? Don't you hear what they're chanting?"

Moozh listened.

Moozh, they said. Moozh. Moozh. Moozh.

"Don't you see that even as you let us go, you're stronger than you were before? The city is yours. The Oversoul has given it to you. Didn't you hear what their mother said? You are the husband of the Oversoul, and of Basilica."

Moozh had heard her, yes, but for the first time in his life—no, for the first time since he had loved her so many years before—he had not immediately thought of what advantage or disadvantage her words might bring to him.

He had only thought: My one love was manipulated by God; my future has been destroyed by God; he has owned me and ruined me, past and future.

Now he realized that Nafai was right. Hadn't Moozh felt for the past few days that perhaps God had changed his mind and was now working *for* him? That feeling had been right. God meant to take his newfound daughters out into the desert on his impossible errand, but apart from that Moozh's plans were still intact. Basilica was his.

Moozh raised his hands, and the crowd—whose chanting had already been fading, from weariness if nothing else— fell silent.

"How great is the Oversoul!" Moozh shouted.

They cheered.

"My city!" he shouted. "Ah, my bride!"

They cheered again.

He turned to the girls and said, softly, "Any idea how I can get you out of the city without it looking like I'm exiling my own daughters, or that you're running away from me?"

Hushidh looked at Luet. "The waterseer can do it."

"Oh, thanks," said Luet. "Suddenly it's up to me?"

"Pretty much, yes," said Nafai. "You can do it."

Luet set her shoulders, turned, and walked to the front of the platform. The crowd was silent again, waiting. She was still hooked up to the amplification system of the Orchestra, but it hardly mattered—the crowd was so united, so attuned to the Oversoul that whatever she wanted them to hear, they would hear.

"My sister and I are as astonished as any of you have been. We never guessed our parentage, for even as the Oversoul has spoken to us all our lives, she never told us we were hers, not in this way, not as you have seen today. Now we hear her voice, calling us into the wilderness. We must go to her, and serve her. In our place she leaves her husband, our father. Be a true bride to him, Basilica!"

There was no cheering, only a loud hum of murmuring. She looked back over her shoulder, clearly afraid that she was handling it badly. But that was only because she was unaccustomed to manipulating crowds—Moozh knew that she was doing well. So he nodded, indicated with a gesture that she must go on.

"The city council was prepared to ask our father to be consul of Basilica. If it was wise before, it is doubly wise now. For when the deeds of the Oversoul are known, all nations of the world will be jealous of Basilica, and it will be good to have such a man as this to be our voice before the world, and our protector from the wolves that will come against us!"

Now the cheering came, but it faded quickly.

"Basilica, in the name of the Oversoul, will you have Vozmuzhalnoy Vozmozhno to be your consul?"

That was it, Moozh knew. She had finally given them a clear moment to answer her, and the answer came as he knew it would, a loud shout of approbation from a hundred thousand throats. Far better than to have a councilor propose it, it was the waterseer who asked them to accept his rule, and in the name of God. Who could oppose him now?

"Father," she said, when the shouting died away. "Father, will you accept a blessing from your daughters' hands?"

What was this? What was she doing now? Moozh was confused for a moment. Until he realized that she wasn't doing this for the crowd now. She wasn't doing this to manipulate and control events. She was speaking from her heart; she had gained a father today, and would lose him today, and so she wanted to give him some parting gift. So he took Hushidh by the hand and they stepped forward; he knelt between them, and they laid their hands upon his head.

"Vozmuzhalnoy Vozmozhno," she began. And then: "Our father, our dear father, the Oversoul has brought you here to lead this city to its destiny. The women of Basilica have their husbands year to year, but the city of women has stayed unmarried all this time. Now the Oversoul has chosen, Basilica has found a worthy man at last, and you will be her only husband as long as these walls stand. But through all the great events that you will see, through all the people who will love and follow you through years to come, you will remember us. We bless you that you will remember us, and in the hour of your death you will see our faces in your memory, and you will feel your daughters' love for you within your heart. It is done."

They passed through Funnel Gate, and Moozh stood beside Bitanke and Rashgallivak to salute them as they left. Moozh had already decided to make Bitanke commander of the city guard, and Rash would be the city's governor when Moozh was away with his army. They passed in single file before him, before the waving, weeping, cheering crowd that gathered there—three dozen camels in their caravan, loaded with tents and supplies, passengers and drycases.

The cheering died away in the distance. The hot desert air stung them as they descended onto the rocky plain where the black chars of Moozh's deceiving fires were still visible like pockmarks of some dread disease. Still they all kept their silence, for Moozh's armed escort rode beside them, to protect them on their way—and to be certain that none of the reluctant travelers turned back.

So they rode until near nightfall, when Elemak determined where they would pitch the tents. The soldiers did the labor for them, though at Elemak's command they carefully showed those who had never pitched a tent how the job was done. Obring and Vas and the women looked terrified at the thought of having to do such a labor themselves, but Elemak encouraged them, and all went smoothly.

Yet when the soldiers left, it was not Elemak that they saluted, but rather Lady Rasa, and Luet the waterseer, and Hushidh the raveler—and, for reasons Elemak could not begin to understand, Nafai.

As soon as the soldiers had ridden off, the quarreling began.

"May beetles crawl into your nose and ears and eat your brain out!" Mebbekew screamed at Nafai, at Rasa, at everyone within earshot. "Why did you have to include *me* in this suicidal caravan?"

Shedemei was no less angry, merely quieter. "I never agreed to come along. I was only going to *teach* you how to revive the embryos. You had no *right* to force me to come."

Kokor and Sevet wept, and Obring added his grumbling to Mebbekew's screams of rage. Nothing that Rasa, Hushidh, or Luet could say would calm them, and as for Nafai, when he tried to open his mouth to speak, Mebbekew threw sand in his face and left him gasping and spitting—and silent.

Elemak watched it all and then, when he figured the rage had about spent itself, he stepped into the middle of the group and said, "No matter what else we do, my beloved company, the sun is down and the desert will soon be cold. Into the tents, and be silent, so you don't draw robbers to us in the night."

Of course there was no danger of robbers here, so close to Basilica and with so large a company. Besides, Elemak suspected that the Gorayni soldiers were camped only a little way off, ready to come at a moment's notice to protect them, if the need arose. And to prevent anyone from returning to Basilica, no doubt.

But they weren't desert men, as Elemak was. If I decide to return to Basilica, he said silently to the unseen Gorayni soldiers, then I will go to Basilica, and even *you,* the greatest soldiers in the world, won't stop me, won't even know that I have passed you by.

Then Elemak went to his tent, where Eiadh waited for him, weeping softly. Soon enough she forgot her tears. But Elemak did not forget his anger. He had not screamed like Mebbekew, had not howled or whined or grumbled or argued. But that did not mean he was any less angry than the others. Only that when he acted, it would be to some effect.

Moozh might not have been able to stand against the plots and plans of the Oversoul, but that doesn't mean that *I* can't, thought Elemak. And then he slept.

Overhead a satellite was slowly passing, reflecting a pinpoint of sunlight from over the horizon. One of the eyes of the Oversoul, seeing all that happened, receiving all the thoughts that passed through the minds of the people under its cone of influence. As one by one they fell asleep, the Oversoul began to watch their dreams, waiting, hoping, eager, for some arcane message from the Keeper of Earth. But there were no visions of hairy angels tonight, no giant rats, no dreams but the random firings of thirteen human brains asleep, made into meaningless stories that they would forget as soon as they awoke.

EPILOGUE

General Moozh succeeded as he had hoped. He united the Cities of the Plain and Seggidugu, and thousands of Gorayni soldiers deserted and joined with him. The Imperator's troops melted away, and before the summer was out, the Sotchitsiya lands were free. That winter the Imperator huddled in the snows of Gollod, while his spies and ambassadors worked to persuade Potokgavan to put an army like a dagger in Moozh's back.

But Moozh had foreseen this, and when the Potoku fleet arrived, it was met by General Bitanke and ten thousand soldiers, men and women of a militia he had trained himself. The Potoku soldiers died in the water, most of them, their ships burning, their blood leaving red foam with every wave that broke upon the beach. And in the spring, Gollod fell and the Imperator died by his own hand, before Moozh could reach him. Moozh stood in the Imperator's summer palace and declared that there *was* no incarnation of God on Harmony, and never had been—except for one unknown woman who came to him as the body of the Oversoul, and bore two daughters for the husband of the Oversoul.

Moozh died the next year, poisoned by a Potoku dart

as he besieged the floodbound capital of Potokgavan. Three Sotchitsiya kinsmen, a half-dozen Gorayni officers, and Rashgallivak of Basilica all claimed to be his successor. In the course of the civil wars that followed, three armies converged on Basilica and the inhabitants fled. Despite Bitanke's brave defense, the city fell. The walls and buildings all were broken down, and the teams of war captives cast the stones into the lake of women until all were gone, and the lake was wide and shallow.

The next summer there was nothing but old roads to show that once there had been a city in that place. And even though some few priestesses returned, and built a little temple beside the lake of women, the hot and cold waters now mixed far below the new surface of the lake, and so the thick fogs no longer rose and the place was not so holy anymore. Few pilgrims came.

The former citizens of Basilica spread far and wide throughout the world, but many of them remembered who they were, and passed the stories on, generation after generation. We were of Basilica, they told their children, and so the Oversoul is still alive within our hearts.